SPECIAL MESSAGE TO READERS

THE ULVERSCROFT FOUNDATION
(registered UK charity number 264873)
was established in 1972 to provide funds for
research, diagnosis and treatment of eye diseases.
Examples of major projects funded by
the Ulverscroft Foundation are:-

- The Children's Eye Unit at Moorfields Eye Hospital, London
- The Ulverscroft Children's Eye Unit at Great Ormond Street Hospital for Sick Children
- Funding research into eye diseases and treatment at the Department of Ophthalmology, University of Leicester
- The Ulverscroft Vision Research Group, Institute of Child Health
- Twin operating theatres at the Western Ophthalmic Hospital, London
- The Chair of Ophthalmology at the Royal Australian College of Ophthalmologists

You can help further the work of the Foundation
by making a donation or leaving a legacy.
Every contribution is gratefully received. If you
would like to help support the Foundation or
require further information, please contact:

THE ULVERSCROFT FOUNDATION
The Green, Bradgate Road, Anstey
Leicester LE7 7FU, England
Tel: (0116) 236 4325

website: www.foundation.ulverscroft.com

Barbara Delinsky was born in Boston in 1945. She led a fairly normal childhood until her mother died when she was eight. This was the defining moment of her early life, and would influence her charitable actions later in life. She earned a B.A. in Psychology at Tufts University, and an M.A. in Sociology at Boston College. Following this, she worked as a researcher for the Massachusetts Society for the Prevention of Cruelty to Children. After reading a newspaper article profiling three female writers, she became intrigued and started writing her own book. She has continued to write ever since, and donates some of the money made from sales to her breast cancer research foundation.

ESCAPE

One Friday morning, Emily realises that, somewhere in life, she has chosen the wrong path. She's stifled by her job as a New York lawyer, she barely sees her husband, James, and their attempts to start a family have proved unsuccessful. So Emily escapes. She walks out of the office, turns her phone off, packs a bag and leaves New York. She doesn't even tell James she's leaving . . . But when a new path leads back to her past, and an old lover, new problems arise. As Emily begins to carve out a new life, where does that leave everything and everyone she left behind?

Books by Barbara Delinsky
Published by The House of Ulverscroft:

A WOMAN'S PLACE
COAST ROAD
LAKE NEWS
THE WOMAN NEXT DOOR
AN ACCIDENTAL WOMAN
FLIRTING WITH PETE
THE SUMMER I DARED
THE FAMILY TREE
THE SECRET BETWEEN US
WHILE MY SISTER SLEEPS
NOT MY DAUGHTER

BARBARA DELINSKY

ESCAPE

Complete and Unabridged

CHARNWOOD
Leicester

First published in Great Britain in 2012 by
Canvas
an imprint of
Constable & Robinson Ltd.
London

First Charnwood Edition
published 2014
by arrangement with
Constable & Robinson Ltd.
London

A catalogue record for this book is available
from the British Library.

ISBN 978–1–4448–1875–8

Published by
F. A. Thorpe (Publishing)
Anstey, Leicestershire

Set by Words & Graphics Ltd.
Anstey, Leicestershire
Printed and bound in Great Britain by
T. J. International Ltd., Padstow, Cornwall

This book is printed on acid-free paper

To Max, with endless Xs and Os

1

Have you ever woken up in a cold sweat, thinking that you've taken a wrong turn and are stuck in a life you don't want? Did you ever consider hitting the brakes, backing up, and heading elsewhere?

How about disappearing — leaving family, friends, even a spouse — ditching everything you've known and starting over again. Reinventing yourself. Rediscovering yourself. Maybe, just maybe, returning to an old lover. Have you ever dreamed about this?

No. Me, neither. No dream, no plan.

It was just another Friday. I awoke at 6:10 to the blare of the radio, and hit the button to silence it. I didn't need talk of politics to knot up my stomach, when the thought of going to work did that all on its own. It didn't help that my husband, already long gone, texted me at 6:15, knowing I'd have my BlackBerry with me in the bathroom.

Can't make dinner tonight. Sorry.

I was stunned. The dinner in question, which had been on our calendar for weeks, involved senior partners at my firm. It was important that James be there with me.

OMG, I typed. *Why not?*

I received his reply seconds before stepping into the shower. *Gotta work late,* he said, and how could I argue? We were both lawyers, seven

1

years out of law school. We had talked about working our tails off now to pay our dues, and I had been in total agreement at first. Lately, though, we had seen little of each other, and it was getting worse. When I pointed this out to James, he got a helpless look in his eyes, like, *What can I do?*

I tried to relax under the hot spray, but I kept arguing aloud that there were things we could do if we wanted to be together — that love should trump work — that we had to make changes before we had kids, or what was the point — that my coyote dreams had begun when I started getting letters from Jude Bell, and though I stuffed those letters under the bed and out of sight, a tiny part of me knew they were there.

I had barely left the shower when my BlackBerry dinged again. No surprise. My boss, Walter Burbridge, always emailed at 6:30.

Client wants an update, he wrote. *Can you do it by ten?*

Here's a little background. I used to be an idealist. Starting law school, I had dreamed of defending innocent people against corporate wrongdoing, and by graduation was itching to be involved in an honest-to-goodness class action lawsuit. Now I am. Only I'm the bad guy. The case on which I work involves a company that produces bottled water that was tainted enough to cause irreparable harm to a frightening number of people. The company has agreed to compensate the victims. My job is to determine how many, how sick, and how little we can get away with doling out, and I don't work alone. We

2

are fifty lawyers, each with a cubicle, computer, and headset. I'm one of five supervisors, any of whom could have compiled an update, but because Walter likes women, he comes to me.

I'm thirty-two, stand five-six, weigh one-twenty. I spin sometimes, but mostly power walk and do yoga, so I'm in shape. My hair is auburn and long, my eyes brown, my skin clear.

We gave them an update Monday, I typed with my thumbs.

Get it to me by ten, he shot back.

Could I refuse? Of course not. I was grateful to have a job at a time when many of my law school friends were wandering the streets looking for work. I was looking, too, but there was nothing to be had, which meant that arguing with the partner-in-charge of a job I *did* have was not a wise thing to do.

Besides, I mused as I slipped on my watch, if I was to put together an update by ten, I had to make tracks.

My BlackBerry didn't cooperate. I was hurrying to finish my makeup when it began making a noise. The wife of one of James's partners wanted the name of a pet sitter. I didn't have a pet, but could certainly ask a friend who did. Thinking that I would have had a dog or cat in a minute if our lifestyle allowed it, I was zipping on a pair of black slacks when another email arrived. *Why won't sharks attack lawyers?* said the subject line, and I instantly clicked DELETE. Lynn Fallon had been in my study group our first year in law school. She now worked with a small firm in Kansas, surely having a kinder, gentler experience than those of us in New York, and she loves lawyer jokes. I do not. I was feeling bad enough about what I do. Besides, when Lynn sent a joke, it went to dozens of people, and I don't do group email.

Nor do I do anything but blue blouses, I realized in dismay as I stood at the closet. Blue blouses were professional, my lawyer side argued, but I was bored looking at them. Closing my eyes, I chose a blouse — any blouse — and was doing buttons when the BB dinged again.

Okay, Emily, wrote my sister. *You booked the restaurant, but you haven't done music, photography, or flowers. Why are you dragging your heels?*

Kelly, it is 7 am, I wrote back and tossed the BlackBerry on the bed. I turned on the radio, heard the word 'terrorism', and turned it off. I was brushing my hair back into a wide barrette when my sister's reply arrived.

Right, and in two minutes I have to get the kids dressed and fed, then do the same for me so I can get to work, which is why I'm counting on you for this. What's the problem?

This party is over the top, I typed back.

We agreed. You do the work, I pay.

Mom doesn't want this, I argued, but my sister was relentless.

Mom will love it. She only turns 60 once. I need help with this, Emily. I can't hear myself think when I get home from work. If you had kids you'd know.

It was a low blow. Kelly knew we were trying. She knew we had undergone tests and were

4

doing the intensive-sex-at-ovulation routine. She didn't know that I'd gotten my period again this month, but I couldn't bear to write the words, and then — *ding, ding, ding* — my in-box began filling. It was 7:10. I had to get to work. Burying the BlackBerry in the depths of my purse so that I wouldn't hear the noise, I grabbed my coat and took off.

We lived in Gramercy Park in a condo we could barely afford, and though we didn't have a key to the park itself, we had passed Julia Roberts on the street a time or two. I saw nothing today — no Julia, no pretty brown-stones, no promising June day — as I hurried to Fifth Avenue, sprinting the last half block to catch the bus as it pulled up at the curb.

I was at my desk at 7:45, and I wasn't the first. A low drone of voices already hovered over the cubicles. I awoke my computer and logged in, then logged in twice more at different levels of database security. Waiting for the final one, I checked my BlackBerry.

Are you going to yoga? asked the paralegal who worked two floors below me and hated going to yoga alone. I would be happy going alone, since it meant less chatter and more relaxation, which was the whole point of yoga. But if I had to go home to change before the firm dinner, yoga was out. *Not tonight*, I typed.

Colly wants Vegas, wrote a book group friend. Colleen Parker was getting married in September, and though I had only known her for the two years I'd been in the group, she had asked me to be a bridesmaid. I would be one of a

5

dozen, paying three hundred dollars each to wear matching dresses. And now a bachelorette party in Vegas? I was thinking the whole thing was tacky, when I spotted the next note.

Hey, Emily, wrote Ryan Mcfee. Ryan worked one cubicle down, two over. *Won't be in today. Have the flu. Don't want to spread it around.*

This should have been important. It meant one man-day of lost work. But what was one more or less in a huge cubicle room?

Logged in now, I set to gathering Walter's information. It was 7:50. By 8:25 I had a tally of the calls we'd received from last weekend's newspaper ads — and I could understand why our client was worried. The number of claimants was mounting fast. Each had been rated on a ten-point scale by the lawyer taking the call, with tens being the most severely affected and ones being the least. There were also zeros; these were the easiest to handle. When callers tried to cash in on a settlement with proof neither of harm nor of having ever purchased the product, they stood out.

The others were the ones over which I agonized.

But statistics were impersonal and, in that, relatively painless. I updated the figures on how many follow-ups we had done since Monday, with a numerical breakdown and brief summaries of the claims. At 8:55 I emailed the spreadsheet to Walter, logged in the time I'd spent making it, shot a look at my watch, and dashed downstairs for breakfast. Though I passed colleagues in the elevator, being competitors in the game of billable hours, we did little more than nod.

Going from the thirty-fifth floor to the ground and up again took time, so it wasn't until 9:10 that I was back at my desk with a doughnut and coffee. By then the cubicles were filled, the tap of computer keys louder, and the drone of voices more dense. I had barely washed down a bite of doughnut when the phone began to blink. Hooking the earpiece over my head, I logged in on my time sheet, pulled up a clear screen on my computer, and clicked into the call.

'Lane Lavash,' I answered, as was protocol with calls coming in on the toll-free lines listed in our ads. 'May I help you?'

There was silence, then a timid 'I don't know. I got this number from the paper.'

Frauds were confident. This woman sounded young and unsure. 'Which paper?' I asked gently.

'The, uh, the *Telegram*. In Portland. Maine.'

'Do you live in Portland?' I readied my fingers to enter this information.

'No. I was there with my brother last weekend and saw the ad. I live in Massachusetts.'

I dropped my hands. Massachusetts was prime Eagle River distribution area. We'd received calls from as far away as Oregon, from people who had been vacationing in New England during the time the tainted water was on sale. Strict documentation of travel was required for these claims, well before we looked at documentation of physical harm.

I cupped my hands in my lap. 'Do you have cause for a claim against Eagle River?'

Her voice remained hesitant. 'My husband says no. He says that these things just happen.'

'What things?'

'Miscarriages.'

I hung my head. This was not what I wanted to hear, but the din of voices around me said that if not this woman, someone else would be getting pieces of the Eagle River settlement. Miscarriage was definitely one of the 'harms' on our list.

'Have you had one?' I asked.

'Two.'

I entered that in the form on my screen, and when the words didn't appear, retyped them, but the form remained blank. Knowing that I wouldn't forget this, and not wanting to lose the momentum of the call, I asked, 'Recently?'

'The first one was a year and a half ago.'

My heart sank. 'Had you been drinking Eagle River water?' Of course she had.

'Yes.'

'Can you document that?' I asked in a kind voice, though I felt cold and mean.

'Y'mean, like, do I have a receipt? See, that's one of the reasons my husband didn't want me to call. I pay cash, and I don't *have* receipts. My husband says I should've made a connection between the water and the miscarriage back then, but, like, bottled water is always safe, right? Besides, we were just married and there was other stuff going on, and I figured I was miscarrying because it wasn't the right time for me to be pregnant.' Her voice shrank. 'Now it is, only they say there's something wrong with the baby.'

My mind filled with static. I tried to remember

the company line. 'The Eagle River recall was eighteen months ago. The water has been clean since then. It wouldn't harm your baby.'

I heard a meek half-cry. 'The thing is, we try to buy in bulk because it's cheaper that way. So we had a couple of twenty-fours in the basement and kind of forgot about them. Then I got pregnant, and my husband lost his job, and money was really tight, so I saw the water and thought I was doing good by using what we had instead of buying fresh. I didn't know about the recall.'

'It was in all the newspapers.'

I don't read newspapers, the ensuing silence said. 'Newspapers cost money.'

'So does bottled water.'

'But the water from the tap tastes so *bad*. We thought of putting a filter on, but that costs more than the bottled water, and it's not like we own this place.'

'Maybe your tap water is tainted,' I said, playing to script. 'Have you asked your landlord to test it?'

'No, because my husband drinks it, and he's healthy. I'm the only one with the problem, and I only drink bottled water. I noticed your newspaper ad because I always drink Eagle River.' Her voice was a whispered wail. 'They say the baby won't be right, and my husband wants to get rid of it, and I have to make a decision, and I don't know what to do. This *sucks*.'

It did suck. *All* of it.

'I don't know what to do,' she repeated, and I realized she wanted my advice, but how could I give that? I was the enemy, an agent for the company whose product had caused a deformity in her child. She should have been yelling at me, calling me the most cold-hearted person in the world. Some of them did. There had been the man whose seamstress wife had developed tremors in her hands and was permanently disabled. Or the woman whose husband had died — and yes, he had a pre-existing medical condition, but he would have lived longer if he hadn't drunk tainted water.

The names they called me weren't pretty, and though I told myself not to take it personally, I did. Thinking that this job *definitely* sucked, I swivelled sideways and lowered my eyes. 'I'm Emily. What's your name?'

'Layla,' she said.

I didn't try to enter it on my form. Nor did I ask for a last name. This had become a personal discussion. 'Have you talked with your doctor about options?'

'There are only two,' she said, sounding frightened. I guessed her to be in her early twenties. 'My mother says I shouldn't kill my baby. She says God chose me to protect an imperfect child, but she isn't the one who'll be paying medical bills or maybe losing a husband because of it.' *Losing a husband* . . . Not on the formal list of 'harms' but a plausible side effect, one that had to resonate with any married woman in this room.

Or maybe not. We didn't talk about this — didn't talk about much of anything, because we were being paid by the hour to do our work, and time sheets would only allow for a lapse or two. What I was doing now was against the rules. I was supposed to stick to business and limit the time of each call. But Layla was talking quickly, going on about the bills that were piling up, and I couldn't cut her off. Somewhere in the middle of it, she said, 'You're a good person, I can tell by your voice, so my husband was wrong when he said I'd be talking to a robot. He also said we'd have to sign away our lives if we got money for this. Would we?'

I was stuck on *good person*, echoing so loudly through my fraudulent soul that I had to consciously refocus at the end. 'No, Layla. You'd have to sign a release saying that you won't further sue Eagle River, its parent company, or distributors, but that's it.'

She was silent for a beat. 'Are you married?'

'Yes.'

'With kids?'

'Someday.' I was on the clock, but I couldn't return to the claim form.

'I'm desperate for them,' Layla said in her very young voice. 'I mean, you work for a law firm. I work in a hardware store. Kids would give my life meaning, y'know?'

'Absolutely,' I replied just as a sharp voice broke in.

'What's happening here, Emily?' Walter asked. 'No one's working.'

I swivelled towards him, then rose from my chair enough to see over the cubicle tops. Sure enough, our team stood in scattered clusters, most looking now at Walter and me.

11

'Computers are down,' called one. 'Forms are frozen.'

Walter eyed me. 'Did you report this?'

I pushed my mouthpiece away. 'I hadn't realized there was a problem. I'm working with a claimant.' Adjusting the mouthpiece, I returned to Layla. 'There's a technical glitch here. Can I call you back in a few?'

'You won't,' she said defeatedly. 'And anyway, I don't know if I should do this.'

'You should,' I advised, confident that Walter wouldn't know what I was saying.

She gave me her number. I wrote it on a Post-it and ended the call.

'He should what?' Walter asked.

'Wait half an hour before going out, so that I can call her back.' I buzzed our technology department.

'Are you *encouraging* people to file claims?' Walter asked.

'No. I'm listening. She's in pain. She needs someone to hear what she's saying.'

'Your job is to document everyone who calls and tell them what medical forms we'll need if they want a piece of the pie. That's it, Emily. You're not being paid to be a shrink.'

'I'm trying to sort through claims so that we know which are legit and which aren't. This is one way to do it.' When I heard a familiar voice in my headset, I said, 'Hey, Todd, it's Emily. We're having trouble up here.'

'Already on it.' He clicked off.

I relayed the message to Walter, who wasn't mollified. 'How long 'til we're running again?'

12

It was 9:40. I figured we'd lost twenty minutes, thirty max. 'Todd is fast.'

Walter leaned closer. A natty dresser, he never looked ruffled. The only things that ever gave him away were his grey eyes and his voice. Those eyes were rocky now, the voice low and taut. 'I'm under pressure, Emily. We were named to manage this settlement only after I personally assured the judge that we could do it quickly and economically. I can't afford to have my lawyers wasting time holding hands. I'm counting on you to set an example; this is important for your career. Get the facts. That's it.' With a warning look, he left.

I should have felt chastised, but all I could think was that if anyone was wasting time, it was the people who called us hoping for help. They wouldn't get what they deserved; the system was designed to minimize reward. Besides, how did you price out a damaged baby, a ruined life?

I was telling myself not to be discouraged — to keep avoiding wine and caffeine and always wash my prenatal vitamins down with *good* water — when a crescendoing hum came, spreading from cubicle to cubicle as the computers returned to life. I should have been relieved, but to my horror, my eyes filled with tears. Needing a distraction, even something as frivolous as Vegas talk from Colly's friends, I turned when my BlackBerry dinged. It was James. Maybe coming tonight? I wondered with a quick burst of hope.

Just got a brilliant idea, he wrote, and for a final minute, still, I believed. *The dinner Sunday night?* That was *his* firm's dinner. *I want you to do it up big — new dress, hair, nails, the works. I have to work tomorrow anyway.* That would be Saturday, the one day we usually managed a few hours together. *A couple of favours? Pick up my navy suit and my shirts. And my prescription. And get cash for the week. Thanks, babe. You're the best.*

I scrolled on, thinking there had to be more, because if that was all, I would be livid.

But that was it. *Thanks, babe. You're the best.*

Keyboards clicked, voices hummed, electronics dinged, jangled, and chimed, and still, as I stared at the words, I heard James's voice. *I want you to do it up big — new dress, hair, nails, the works.* Like I needed his permission for this?

Suddenly it all backed up in my throat like too much bad food — bad marriage, bad work, bad family, friends, feelings — and I couldn't swallow. Needing air, I grabbed my purse and, as an afterthought, the Post-it with Layla's name and number.

Tessa Reid was as close as I came to having a friend in the firm, which was as sad a statement as any. We never socialized outside of work. I did know that she had two kids and two school loans, and that she shared my revulsion for what we did. I saw it in her eyes when she arrived at work, the same look of dread reflected in my own mirror each day.

She lived three cubicles to the right of mine. Ducking in there now, I touched her shoulder. Her earpiece was active, her hands typing. One look at my face and she put her caller on hold.

14

'Do me a huge favour, Tessa?' I whispered, not for privacy, because, Lord knew, my voice wouldn't carry over the background din, but because that was all the air I could find. I pressed the Post-it to her desk. 'Call this claimant for me? We were talking when the system went down. She's valid.' I was banking on that, perhaps with a last gasp of idealism. For sure, though, Tessa was the only one in the room whom I could trust to find out.

She was studying me with concern. 'What's wrong?'

'I need air. Do this for me?'

'Of course. Where are you going?'

'Out,' I whispered, and left.

A gaggle of clicks, dings, and murmurs followed me, lingering like smog even when the elevator closed. I made the descent in a back corner, eyes downcast, arms hugging my waist. Given the noise in my head, if anyone had spoken, I mightn't have heard, which was just as well. What could I have said if, say, Walter Burbridge had stepped in? *Where are you going?* I don't know. *When'll you be back?* I don't know. *What's wrong with you?* I don't know.

The last would have been a lie, but how to explain what I was feeling when the tentacles were all tangled up? I might have said that it went beyond work, that it covered my entire life, that it had been building for months and had nothing to do with impulse. Only it did. Survival was an impulse. I had repressed it for so long that it was weak, but it must have been beating somewhere in me, because when the elevator

15

opened, I walked out.

Even at 9:57, Fifth Avenue buzzed. Though I had never minded before, now the sound grated. I turned right for the bus and stood for an excruciating minute in traffic exhaust, before giving up and fleeing on foot, but pedestrian traffic was heavy, too. I walked quickly, dodging others, dashing to make it over the cross street before a light changed. When I accidentally jostled a woman, I turned with an apology, but she had continued on without looking back.

I had loved the crowds when I first came here. They made me feel part of something big and important. Now I felt part of nothing. If I wasn't at work, others would be. If I bumped into people, they walked on.

So that's what I did myself, just walked on, block after block. I passed a hot dog stand but smelled only exhaust fumes from a bus. My watch read 10:21, then 10:34, then 10:50. If my legs grew tired, I didn't notice. The choking feeling had passed, but I felt little relief. My thoughts were in turmoil, barely touched by the blare of a horn or the rattle of the tailgate of a truck at the curb.

Nearing our neighbourhood, I stopped for my husband's suit and shirts, and picked up his prescription, then entered the tiny branch office of our bank. The teller knew me. But this was New York. If she wondered why I withdrew more money than usual, she didn't ask.

The bank clock stood at 11:02 when I hit the air again. Three minutes later I turned down the street where we lived and, for a hysterical

16

second, wondered which brownstone was ours. Through my disenchanted eyes, they all looked the same. But no; one had a brown door, another a grey one, and there was my window box, in which primrose and sweet pea were struggling to survive.

Running up the steps, I let myself in, emptied my arms just inside, and dashed straight up the next flight and into the bedroom. I pulled my bag from the closet floor, but paused only when I set it on the bed. What to bring? That depended on where I was going, and I didn't have a clue.

2

Where I was going depended on what I wanted, and that part was easy. I wanted to have fun.

Picturing the beach, I pulled out a bathing suit. And a sundress.

But I also liked antiquing. I used to tag along with a high school friend and her mom, and though I knew little about antiques, I remembered the smell of history and the quiet. Both appealed to me now. So I pulled out a peasant blouse and shorts, jeans and T-shirts and sandals.

But I also liked hiking. At least, I had liked it that one college summer. Jude had known the forests — every tree, every stream, every creature — and had taught me well. Mountaintops were cold. I added a sweater and a fleece to the pile. Having tossed out my hiking boots long ago, I added sneakers. And heavy socks. And underwear, nightshirt, and hairbrush.

Did I want my laptop? Kindle? iPod? No. I didn't even want my BlackBerry, but it was my phone, which, in an emergency, was a good thing to have.

Makeup? I didn't want it, but didn't have the courage to leave it at home. That said, I didn't need purple eye shadow, navy liner, or two spare blushers. Leaving these on the bathroom counter, I put the makeup case on top of the pile.

It was a big pile. No way would everything fit

in my bag. I thought of taking a second one, but vetoed the idea. A second bag meant clutter. If I was running away from a tangled life, simplicity was key.

I changed my blue shirt and black slacks for one of those T-shirts and jeans, switched diamond studs for gold ones, and glanced at my watch. It was 11:23.

I turned away, then back. This was no digital watch. Yet I knew it was 11:23 — now 11:24 — because in this life that I'd made for myself, every minute had to be accounted for.

Defiant, I removed the watch and left it with the earrings, then packed what I could and returned the excess to a drawer. Only when I lifted the closed bag did I notice the unmade bed beneath — beige sheets rumpled on a black platform bed, all sleek and minimalistic, like the rest of the place.

The bed went unmade often, a concession to the rush of our lives, but I made it now as a small gesture to James. Quickly done, I ran down a flight to our beige-and-black front hall, dropped my bag there, ran down another flight to our beige-and-black kitchen. Grabbing granola bars (colourfully wrapped) and bottled water (not Eagle River), I ran back up to the front door.

The mail had just arrived and was strewn under the slot in a way that previewed its contents. Resigned, I singled out my credit card bill. The company had notified me that I was maxed out, and I knew the offending charge wasn't mine. Seeing it on the bill, though, rubbed salt on the wound.

I was returning it to the fanned-out mail, feeling discouraged, when another letter caught my eye. It was from Jude.

I didn't have time to read it. I had to leave.

But I couldn't *not* read it.

Like its predecessors, it was postmarked Alaska. Jude was fishing for crab on the Bering Sea, and he wrote remarkably well for a man who had thumbed his nose at every teacher he'd ever had in school. His lengthy descriptions of his boat, the sea, the nets spilling their jumble of bodies and legs on the deck, even the other men aboard, were riveting.

This letter was a single sheet.

Hey, Em, life does funny things. I'm forty and have been away from Bell Valley for ten years, fishing crab for six of those. But a good buddy of mine just died. Swept overboard, just like that. Death never bothered me before. But I'm thinking big-picture thoughts now, and I see a load of unfinished business at home.

So I'm going back to Bell Valley. I haven't told anyone. They'll make plans, and I hate plans. But I should get there at the end of the month. Who knows. I may not last the summer. I always felt strangled in Bell Valley.

I don't know why I'm telling you this. You never answered any of my letters. Maybe you tear them up and toss them without reading them, in which case you won't read this. But I still think of you as my conscience. I want to think you'll be pleased. JBB

Pleased? Jude had nearly killed me once. *Pleased?*

I was in the middle of my own personal crisis. I couldn't process this now.

Tucking the letter in my back pocket, I called the garage where we kept our car. I would be there in five minutes, I said, and yes, I would like the tank filled with gas, put the charge on our tab, please. That was poetic.

Another poetic thought? If I had kids, I wouldn't have been able to do this. No way could I leave kids. But then, if I was a mom, I wouldn't want to leave. So maybe it was good I hadn't conceived. Maybe there was a reason.

Shouldering the bag, I was halfway out the door when I had a last thought. James would hardly miss me; he was too busy. But he was my husband.

Returning to the hall console, I pulled paper and pen from the drawer. *I'm fine*, I wrote. *Need a break. Will be in touch.*

Leaving the note in clear view on top of the bills, I grabbed the car keys and was through the door without a backwards glance. The rising humidity worsened my mood, making my need to escape stronger than ever.

Escape. The word was perfect. I didn't want to arrange a party that my mother would hate. Didn't want to be a bridesmaid at the wedding of a woman I barely knew. Didn't want to tell a client that her deformed fetus was worth $21,530. Didn't want to smile through one minute of my firm dinner, with my husband or without.

21

An ambulance sped through the intersection ahead, its siren just one more everyday ho-hum. Crossing the street, I hurried to the end of the next block, where the nose of my car edged out. As getaway cars went, it was high-end — and largely responsible for my maxed-out credit card — but James loved this car. Me, I wanted reliability, so his high-end car would do.

Stowing my bag in the trunk, I slipped behind the wheel, blasted the AC, and headed for FDR Drive, but crosstown traffic was thick. A single truck, stopped for a delivery, was enough to slow everything down. As I watched the light ahead turn green, then red, then green again, I tried to relax, but I was out of practice. When I consciously slackened my limbs, it worked. As soon as my mind wandered, though, my muscles tightened right up.

Tension was my body's default, and it did follow, in a sense. A trial lawyer had to be alert to hear every nuance of every argument, so that on a second's notice she could argue in defence of her client's rights.

Only I wasn't in a courtroom. I hadn't been in one since being a summer associate at Lane Lavash, when I'd been wined and dined and shown what it would be like if I joined the firm. No one had mentioned a cubicle. The tension in a cubicle was bad, but for different reasons.

Relax, Emily. Do not think about this.

What to think about then? Handsome, irrepressible, unattainable Jude?

Not a good idea. This was my escape — from *everything*.

22

On the Bruckner now, I turned the radio on, then off. I needed silence, but I also needed food, since I was starting to shake. The console said it was 1:08. What had breakfast been? A doughnut. Had I eaten it? I couldn't recall.

Driving one-handed, I scarfed down a granola bar and crumpled the empty wrapper. Then I uncrumpled it and held it up beside the wheel. Chocolate peanut butter. That sounded good. Had it tasted good? I had no idea. I had eaten it too quickly to know.

At least I was making progress. Hitting the Hutchinson heading north, I followed the signs for New England. The route was familiar; I had driven it dozens of times to visit my mother in Maine.

Thinking of Mom, I reached for my BlackBerry, then thought twice. Turning it on meant hearing the *ding* of messages that were waiting, but I didn't want to talk, didn't want to text. Besides, no one would worry. Walter Burbridge would be annoyed when I wasn't at the firm dinner, but James and I were maybe two of eighty. My sister would be annoyed when I didn't call her back with a party update, but I was used to her scolding. No one would miss me at yoga, what with different classes at different times. And book group wasn't meeting for another two weeks.

My mother would be fine. She was the most undemanding of people in my world. We had talked on Thursday. If she didn't hear from me over the weekend, she would wait.

My father might not. Once, when I was in

college and he couldn't reach me, he had called a cop friend, who had called the campus police, who had personally tracked me down at a weekend retreat for my sorority. Talk about embarrassing? But Mom knew how to handle him now. She had wised up after the divorce, coming into her own enough to tell him when she thought he was wrong. They actually had a great relationship. I've often thought they should remarry, but Mom insists that the key to their friendship is distance.

And my husband? Would James worry when he got my note? Probably. I had never before been even remotely flighty. But he would be busy at work, surrounded by associates with whom he spent far more time than he did with me. One of those associates was a new hire I had met at James's last firm dinner. She was single and strikingly attractive, and she had been cool and disinterested in me to the point of rudeness. When I told James that she had her eye on him, he had given me a quick hug and laughed.

I didn't find it funny. Jude had cheated on me, so I knew what it felt like to have the bottom drop out of your world. I didn't think I could bear it with James. But we rarely saw each other. Rarely talked the way we used to. Rarely shared dreams as we had once.

Feeling the impact of something tragic, I cracked open the window and let the fresh air brush my face. If this trip was my escape, I had to relax.

Thankfully, the farther I got from New York, the easier it was. Out of sight, out of mind?

24

Partly. The rest was pure denial. Had I not been so good at it, I might have left the Big Apple months ago. Was that ironic or what? Denial had kept me in a bad place. Now it would help me escape.

Once I passed the haze of Bridgeport, my shoulders began to unknot. With fewer trucks after New Haven, I grew light-headed. Approaching Providence, I actually felt wisps of euphoria. I was free! No work, no family, no demands. I was on my own, and I was headed for the beach.

Unfortunately, so was everyone else, to judge from the traffic in Massachusetts. As I shot toward Cape Cod, there were slowdowns with no cause other than the sheer volume of cars. As I inched over the Sagamore Bridge, I looked at my watch. The bare spot on my wrist was a reminder that I was in no rush.

I headed for Chatham because I had heard it was charming, and once I reached trees, shingled houses weathered by sea salt, and June gardens, it was. I found a vacancy at a modest motel not far from the beach, two levels of rooms shaped in a U around a pool. Leaving my bag, I walked into town. The air off the Atlantic was salty and cool, and moving felt good. In time, growing hungry, I sat on the outside deck of a restaurant and ordered a cod salad. It looked amazing, I was famished, and it was gone in minutes.

Determining to work on actually tasting my food, I glanced at the watch that wasn't there, then at the low-slung sun. Guessing it was eight, I bought several magazines and, back at the motel, stretched out by the pool with *Women's*

Health. I was just getting into an article on vitamin D when a couple arrived with two cranky toddlers. They were followed by a pair of families with eight kids between them, splashing and shrieking as they played in the pool.

No reading here. Closing the magazine, I went back to my room and undressed. And there was Jude's letter, stuffed in my back pocket.

Coming home? What was I supposed to do with *that*?

I tried to read and failed. I dozed off, only to bolt up moments later, disoriented. The bedside clock read 11:04. It was another minute before I got my bearings.

Wondering if James had come home and seen my note yet, I watched the clock until I couldn't bear the suspense a minute longer. I turned on my BlackBerry. It was midnight.

What do you mean, you need a break? he had texted. *Where are you?* He had left an identical voice message, then a second text. *This isn't funny, Emily. Where the hell are you?* All three had come in the last half hour, which meant he had worked pretty late.

He hadn't said he was worried. What I heard, in my vulnerable frame of mind, was *Cut it out, Em, I don't have time for this*.

Disappointed, I turned off the BlackBerry.

Only then, knowing that James knew I was gone, did I feel the shock of what I'd done. But not regret. His response clinched it. I needed a break.

The sounds outside now were adult — drunken whoops and hollers, the shudder of a diving

26

board, the explosion of water. For a split second, I wished I'd brought my iPod. But covering one noise with another wasn't the answer.

Wondering what was, I drifted into a fitful sleep, but I was up before dawn, waiting for the sun. Dressing warmly then, I walked into town for a newspaper and breakfast. The newspaper was a mistake — not much happy news — but by the time I realized that, my eggs and toast had disappeared, inhaled like so much else of what I ate.

Vowing *again* to work on that, I returned to the motel to change and, a short time later, hit the beach. The ocean air gradually warmed, but along with the strengthening sun came families, boom boxes, and volleyball. Seeking peace, I walked far enough off to be able to hear the gulls and the tide, but when sand gave way to rocks, I had to turn. I stretched out on my towel again and ate a hot dog at the beach bar for lunch, but by mid-afternoon I was antsy.

This wasn't fun. It wasn't where I wanted to be. I had traded one noise for another — city sounds for pounding waves, shrieking kids, blaring boom boxes.

Returning to the motel, I packed and checked out. Then I sat in my car trying to decide where to go. I thought of continuing to Provincetown, which was the practical choice, since I was already on the Cape.

Rejecting practical, I considered heading up to Ogunquit. My mother lived an hour from there, making it the safe choice.

The safest choice, of course, would be to head

south to New York. If I did it now, I could be back with no one but James the wiser. Much longer, and the consequences would grow.

Oh yeah, New York was definitely the safest choice, but safe choices were what had done me in. Right now I was a rebel, and this was still my escape.

Aiming west, I breezed back over the Sagamore Bridge towards the Mass Pike. Traffic was light; weekenders were already where they wanted to be. The farther I went, the more the land opened, the meadows greened, the woods thickened. Daring the radio, I found a classical station that soothed, and set the volume only high enough to feel the effect.

By the time I reached the Berkshires, the shadows were long. Wanting quiet, I avoided Stockbridge and Lenox, instead following signs to a lesser town whose name I knew. There was only one place to stay, an inn that would likely cost a lot, but for this night, that was fine. There was no sign indicating a vacancy, and the parking lot was full, but I was here, and it was worth a shot. Finding a sliver of space at the back, I eased the car in and shouldered my bag.

The inn was a rambling affair whose main attraction was a wraparound porch with rocking chairs, but the people in those chairs and the ones walking inside for dinner looked to be young professionals like James and me. Most had kids.

Letting a party of six pass, I followed them in. The clerk at the front desk was older, more starched than the guests, and reluctantly

— *Well, we do usually have a two-night minimum* — gave me a room. It was over the kitchen, but the noise of pots and pans was mild, and the smell of sizzling tenderloin so tempting that I ordered it for dinner. I ate at the bar, which was quiet and dark. No one bothered me, and I actually tasted the beef.

My senses were returning, which was nice. Along with it, though, came my conscience. I was starting to feel guilty. And sad. This was the first Saturday night I'd been without James.

I figured it had to be ten. I wondered if I should call just to say I was okay.

But what if he was working? He often did on Saturday nights. If he didn't answer his phone, I might worry that he was with *her* — and if he did pick up, he would want to know where I was and when I'd be back. But I couldn't go back yet. I had barely begun to relax.

Bent on doing that, I settled on the porch and rocked for a while, then borrowed a book from the little library in the living room and headed upstairs. But I couldn't concentrate. I kept thinking of James. Wondering if he was thinking of me, I turned on my BlackBerry.

You took my car! Where ARE you? Please call, he had typed earlier that afternoon, and barely an hour later, *Why did you take so much money?*

You maxed out my credit card, I typed, *so I'm using cash.*

That's a lot of cash for the weekend, he replied. *My firm dinner is tomorrow night. You'll be back by then, won't you?*

He was worried. I considered giving in. I truly

29

might have, if he had asked how I was or what was wrong. I surely *would* have, if he'd said that he loved me or missed me. But I saw none of those words on the screen.

I'll let you know, I replied and, feeling a profound sadness, turned off the BlackBerry before James could text back. I might hate electronic wizardry, but it was my ally now. I could use it or not, could respond to James or not, and with my calls simply showing 'New York' on his caller ID, he had no idea where I was.

That knowledge didn't help me sleep. I kept waking to the strangeness of what I'd done and a disconcerting sense that I was treading water. And then came the coyote dream, which had to have some sort of message, I knew, though I couldn't figure out what it was. I brooded for most of the night.

Respite came with the sun in the form of the smell of fresh-baked bread, wafting up through the old oak floorboards from the kitchen below. I hadn't smelled fresh-baked bread in months — and bread was only the start. By the time I reached the dining room, the cook was adding breakfast meats and waffles. I filled my plate with eggs, a scoop of hash, thick slices of bacon and banana bread, and ate slowly, chewing deliberately between sips of joe. The coffee was dark and rich, its mug warm in my hands.

Other families had drifted in by now, leaving tennis rackets and golf gloves by their chairs as they went to the buffet. There was no talk between tables, but I was used to this. People weren't unfriendly, simply minding their own business, which was what we urbanites generally did, and these folks were from the city, no doubt about that. They might have been my neighbours, attending a week of tennis or golf camp now that their kids had finished school for the year.

Wondering why I was sitting in a room with the same people I wanted to escape, I swallowed the last of my coffee and, skirting Mountain Buggies on the porch, went off to see the town. For a sophisticated place, it was little more than a crossroads, a modest mix of small Colonials and cottages, private homes and shops. I did my antiquing, browsed through a closet-size art gallery, even stood at the window of a yarn store and watched the women inside. A latecomer invited me to join them as she opened the cranberry door, and though I envied them their friendship, I didn't knit.

Consoling myself with the quiet, I walked on. I was free, but I couldn't feel the rush of it. I sat for a while on a bench where the road forked. But euphoria didn't come.

Discouraged, I returned to the inn, took newspaper and pen from the front desk, and sank into an overstuffed chair in the library. Crossword puzzles were a distraction, though I had never been terribly good at them. After an hour, I gave up and went out to the gazebo to think about freedom. But thinking about freedom made me think about Jude, and I didn't want to do that.

So I followed the other guests when they headed in for lunch. After waiting in line, I fixed a sandwich from the make-your-own at the buffet table, and settled in a rocker on the front porch, but the families around me made me think of my own. Taking the BlackBerry from my pocket, I checked for messages from my parents. There were none. My sister made up for it. She had sent multiple notes and wanted to know why I wasn't answering.

Fearing she would make trouble if I didn't act, I shot her a quick reply. *No time now. I'll write later in the week.*

Walter Burbridge had sent a slew of emails. I didn't read Friday's batch but, rather, allowing him time to cool off, read the one he had sent late yesterday. *Tessa said you were sick, but it isn't like you not to respond. What's going on?* And then, earlier this morning, *Are you all right? Let me know if I can help.*

He actually sounded concerned, but I wasn't fooled. Working weekends at Lane Lavash was optional, but there was nothing optional about Mondays. If I didn't head back soon, I wouldn't be at my desk in the morning. Walter would be pissed. Word would spread. My job would be at risk.

First, though, came James. There were lots of missed calls from him, with no messages left, and his texts were brief.

This dinner is important, babe.

Then, *Please answer me. I know you're seeing this.*

Then, *If you're having a nervous breakdown we can deal but you have to call. I'm starting to worry.*

Then, *WHERE ARE YOU?*

He sounded frantic, and I almost did call. But I knew how persuasive he could be. What was it they said about the difference between a lawyer and a bucket of crap being the bucket? James was a brilliant negotiator and, though barely thirty-five, had already made a name for himself.

I didn't trust myself to talk with him. He would have me back there in two minutes flat. But when I pictured driving south, everything inside me backed up again.

I pulled in a slow, painful breath that must have opened a window of thought, because, sitting on that porch with the remains of a half-eaten sandwich and a once-promising life, I realized that this wasn't about James. It wasn't about work or Manhattan or my sister, Kelly, and it wasn't about having fun. It wasn't even about Jude. It was about me. Where I was headed. Who I wanted to be.

But I did owe James, and texting wouldn't do. So I steeled myself and called his cell.

He answered with a worried 'Where are you?'

'I won't be back in time, James. I'm sorry. Just tell them I'm sick.'

'Where *are* you?'

'It doesn't matter. I need to think, and I can't do it there.'

'Think about what? You're my wife.'

'I need time.'

'For *what*? You're giving me a heart attack here, Emily. What happened? You were fine Thursday night.'

'Was I?' I asked, thinking of all the times I'd

floated the idea that I wasn't fine at all. 'I'll call once I know where I'm at. I'm sorry about tonight, James, I really am.' I disconnected before he could say anything else, and turned off the BlackBerry with a sense of relief. I was glad I'd called. With all the wrong things I'd done, this was right.

Returning to my room, I re-stowed the few things I'd taken from my bag. The Berkshires were an improvement over the Cape, but both were way stations. If the point was to figure out who I was, I had to go back to the place that had set me on this course. That place wasn't New York.

I started the car. With each mile, the consequences loomed, but they were in my rear-view mirror. I was headed north.

3

By the time I left I-91 for the back roads of New Hampshire, the hills were higher and the woods more dense. Gradually, those hills became mountains that blocked the sun, dimming the route. But I didn't need bright sun. My memory held a vivid picture of these roads — and of the small town where I was headed. Nestled in a valley in the centre of the state, Bell Valley was quintessentially New England, with a covered bridge on the approach, a town green ringed by historic houses, and a church spire sticking up through the trees like an eager finger saying, *Me, see me, here I am!* There were neither motels nor hotels, just a single bed-and-breakfast. If it was full, I would camp out in the gardener's shed at the back. Lord knew, I had done that before.

Dusk had fallen by the time I passed under that covered bridge, and the arms of the town opened. Bell Valley was a place of benches, luring takers to the green, the fringe of stores, the church. At this evening hour, it was also a place of soft light spilling from windows, brightest at The Grill, where dinner was in high gear. Cars were parked diagonally there, though the only movement came from a handful of walkers on the sidewalk that circled the green.

Ten years later, this was still familiar to me. And that brought pain. My last memories of this place were of breaking up with Jude. He had

35

been my first love, different from any man I've known to this day. As I pictured him as he was then, so blond and wild, my eyes filled with tears, and for a split second I wondered if I was crazy to have come.

You didn't come here for Jude ten years ago, I reminded myself as I brushed at the tears, *and you're not here for him now. You're here for you.*

Back then, my burnout had been from finals, senior theses, even graduation parties. The cause was different now, but Bell Valley's arms were still open.

The town was a haven, from its protected spot between mountains to its spirit. Settled by the eponymous Jethro Bell in the late 1700s, it had been conceived of as a sanctuary for non-fishermen, and though agricultural interests had never fully caught on, its identity as a shelter had. The Bell Valley Refuge was known worldwide for taking in puppies from puppy mills, injured and abused cats, unwanted horses and donkeys, as well as pets that had been victimized by earthquake, tsunami, and war.

I hadn't been victimized as those animals had. But I did need rescue. My tears told me that. I was wiping with both hands but couldn't stop them, and it was terrifying, this loss of control. For the past two days, I'd been in check. For the past ten years, I'd been in check. Suddenly not.

Then came a sign. I had barely started around the town green, eyes welling still, when my car — that high-end marvel of foreign engineering — stalled. Coasting to the side where spaces in front of the General Store were empty for the night, I turned the key and tried to restart it once, twice, three times.

Nothing.

I might have laughed through my tears, if I hadn't been so upset. I could call the service station just north of town, but if it was still there, it would be closed for the night. I could call James and crow, *Reliability? Hah!* But I didn't want to talk with James, especially not when I was holding it together by a thread.

The last thing I wanted was to draw attention to my return, yet here I sat, stalled in an expensive piece of automotive bling in a town of trusty pickups. Ah, the irony of that.

But I was where I needed to be. My car must have known that.

Besides, the bed-and-breakfast was right across the green, and though my composure was gone, my feet still worked.

I was pulling my bag from the trunk, fighting the memory that came with the smell of pine sap in the air, when a couple approached. I didn't recognize them, which was good. Some of those I did know in town wouldn't be pleased to see me back.

'Problems?' the man asked.

'Seems it,' I said, pressing the back of my hand to my nose as I shot a despairing look at the car. 'It can wait 'til morning, though. I'm only going to the Red Fox.'

'Do you need a hand with the bag?'

Whether it was his kindness or the fact that he reminded me of my father, the offer choked me up more. Mortified, I forced a smile, shook my head, shouldered the bag, and set off.

Only to the Red Fox, I thought, only that far, but my heart beat faster as I crossed the grass. I had burned bridges since leaving here, the worst being the one linking me to my college roommate, Vicki Bell.

Except she wasn't Vicki Bell anymore. She was Vicki Bell Beaudry, owner of the Red Fox with her husband, Rob, whose family was nearly as rooted in Bell Valley as the Bell family was, hence a questionable welcome there, too.

But I couldn't retreat. My car had ensured that. And the Red Fox beckoned. A bona fide farmhouse, it had been moved here from the outskirts of town in the early 1900s, over time gaining wings and inching close to the woods. Like the town, where carpenters and painters commonly exchanged services for goods, the Red Fox, I guessed, had provided many a blueberry scone in exchange for the fresh yellow paint I saw now, the smart white trim, and the hand-etched sign at the head of the walk that sported a new logo in crimson and gold. A wide cobblestone path led to the porch, which was partially hidden behind a stand of rhododendron whose buds were ready to pop.

I had raised a foot to the bottom-most step, when I was suddenly hit by fatigue. It was as if I'd been driving not for three days but for ten years of hours, and now that I was here, just about to let down my guard, the exhaustion beat me to it.

If Vicki wasn't home, I didn't know what I'd do.

Likewise, if she didn't want me here.

Taking the steps slowly, I crossed the porch, but it was a minute before I could muster the wherewithal to open the screen. When I did, a soft bell tinkled somewhere inside.

The front hall was empty. From the threshold, it looked familiar — same furniture, same floor plan — yet different. No longer shabby, the stuffed armchairs were now a dozen shades of green. No longer old and dim, the oils on the wall were vibrant. And not only had the antique writing table been refurbished, but between a tall lamp and a vase of yellow roses, albeit discreet, stood a computer screen.

Vicki Bell had left her mark.

Heart pounding, I stepped inside, at which point the emotion was too much. Unable to move, even to drop my bag, I stood with my hands steepled at my mouth and my eyes awash with the greens of sea, grass, and forest, until an image intruded. Tears couldn't hide its identity. Though Vicki was blonde, we were so alike in other regards — same height, shape, New England roots — that people took us for sisters, which we might well have ended up being, had Jude not messed up.

'Emily?' she asked, sounding shocked.

Brokenly, because the single word said nothing of my welcome, I wailed a soft 'I need you to be home.'

After staring for another disbelieving second, she threw her arms around me. 'I should absolutely not know who you are. You haven't been here since that day with Jude, and okay, you were at my wedding, but only because it wasn't in Bell Valley, and even then only because *he* wasn't there. After that you stopped answering emails or returning phone calls, just drifted away like a stranger.' She drew back, scowling. 'It's like you dropped off the face of the earth — more like I dropped off the face of *your* earth — and I don't want to hear about how busy you are down there in New York, because I'm busy, too, my husband's busy, my friends are busy, we're *all* busy, but that is not the way you treat people you love. After a while, friends think that you just don't care — that we're *annoying* you — so we give up — and suddenly you show up here without a word of warning? *That's* some nerve.' She scowled more darkly. 'What are you smiling at?'

'You.' I couldn't help it. She was so familiar, so dear. 'How much you talk. How *New Hampshire* you talk.' *Suddenly you show up hea without a weud of wauning.*

'That isn't funny.'

'It is.' It was warm and real, enough to stop my tears. 'You wear your heart on your sleeve, so people know where you stand. Do you know how refreshing that is?'

She made a disparaging sound. 'Everyone here talks like that. You used to talk like me, too, until something happened to your speech right along with your loyalty to friends.' Feature by feature, she searched my face. 'You look awful. What's wrong?'

Where to begin? My eyes filled again, but all I could think of to say was 'My car died.'

40

'Your car?'

'In front of the General Store.' Of course, I wasn't crying over the car. Vicki Bell knew me well enough for that. She knew me as well as anyone did, which wasn't saying a whole lot right now, but she was the last really good friend I'd had.

She glanced warily at the door. 'Where's James?'

'In New York. I ran away.'

'You wouldn't do that. You're too responsible.'

'I did it.'

Her brown eyes grew larger '*Left* him?' Her eyes shot to my left hand, but my wedding band was still there. It hadn't occurred to me to take it off. Hadn't *occurred* to me.

'Not left him, like maritally. I needed a break from work, the city, my life.'

'If you're here for Jude — '

'I'm not.'

'Good. We don't know where he is. He's never been back — and I'm not blaming you for that, he was the one who cheated — '

'And broke up, Vicki. He didn't want to be tied down.' I just then heard what she'd said. 'You don't know where he is?'

'No. He cut every tie. No cards, no calls. Hasn't been back in ten years.'

He will be, I thought, and wanted to say it aloud, but that would require sensitivity, picking words that would go easiest on Vicki Bell, and I just didn't have the strength.

Vicki studied me a minute longer. If she had questions — which, going back a ways with Vicki

41

Bell, who was curious to the extreme, I knew she did — she was wise enough not to ask. Instead, in a gentle tone, she said, 'We were just having dinner, Rob and me. Are you hungry?'

'More tired than hungry. I need a place to sleep.'

'When did you sleep last?'

'Last night. For maybe an hour.' I sputtered out a half sob. 'Pretty pathetic, huh? I was fine on the road, but it's like now that I'm here, I can't *move*.'

Taking the bag from my shoulder, she guided me up the stairs. We passed the second flight and went to the third, where there was only one room. It had dormers front and back and skylights above, the latter the first thing Vicki had added when turning the attic into a guestroom. She called this room a little piece of heaven, and yes, when she lit a small lamp, I was vaguely aware of billowing sky and clouds, everything blue and white, but I was too weak to see more. She put my bag on a bench at the foot of the bed, pulled back a voluminous comforter, and opened the sheets.

I sat tentatively in the space she'd made. 'This could be awkward for you.'

'Yes.'

'You're still angry.'

Her frown was begrudging now. 'Wouldn't you be? You were my very best friend. I know Jude hurt you, but he hurt us, too, just vanishing. Okay, so you couldn't talk about it — '

'I still can't,' I cut in by way of warning, then, softening, pleaded, 'Maybe later?'

She stared at me, sighed, and hitched her chin toward the bed. Sliding out of my flip-flops, I pulled my legs up and lay down. Once there, I didn't move.

★ ★ ★

Vicki must have left, because the next thing I knew, she was putting a small tray beside the bed. It held a glass of orange juice, pastries that I was sure were home-made, and a pitcher of well water.

'Will Rob know the car?' she whispered when I cracked open an eye.

'Oh yeah,' I whispered back. 'Black BMW. Can't miss it.'

She touched my head. 'Sleep.'

4

I slept. If there were sounds from other guests, I heard none. Nor did I dream. I was too tired for that. When I awoke, the window above was a wash of azure sky and Norway maple red. The sheets smelled of sunshine, and the billows of clouds and sky I had glimpsed the night before went beyond the voluminous comforter to a blue ceiling and walls, a white dresser and chair, and plaid floor pillows stacked in the corner under the eaves. The tray by the bed now held an aromatic blend of scones and tea.

Heaven? Absolutely.

Vicki sat in a ladder-back chair by the bed. 'Much longer, and I'd have called the EMTs,' she remarked.

I turned onto my side to fully take her in: Vicki Bell — not just Vicki, but Vicki Bell — both names affectionately spoken as one through our college years. Medicinal to me now, she wore a sweater and jeans, and had her hair tacked back, ends sticking out at odd places, as they always had. Her skin was scrubbed clean, another down-to-earth Vicki trait. But her cheeks were pink and her features soft.

'You look amazing,' I said.

'Amazing good, or amazing familiar?'

'Both. What time is it?'

'Eleven.'

Eleven. I bolted up and, with a moan, fell right

44

back. Vicki was alarmed. 'Easy does it. How do you feel?'

Thick. Sluggish. 'Hungover.'

'*Drinking?*'

'Crying. Maybe sleeping too much.' I shut my eyes tight, but they popped back open. 'Eleven Monday morning? Oh boy.'

'What?'

'Work.' The old tension returned. 'I was there one minute and gone the next. A friend covered for me Friday, but the partner-in-charge has been emailing all weekend. I didn't read any of it.'

'Nothing new there,' Vicki remarked dryly as she poured me some tea.

'No, I do read everything you send,' I insisted. 'But you're a good friend, and I can't send short answers. So I save it all up until I have time to call on the phone, and then I never . . . never find the time.'

'After Jude, you moved on.' She handed me the tea.

It was an offering of warmth, literally, figuratively. I wasn't ready to talk about Jude yet, but it might be the price I'd have to pay for this room. Pushing my pillows higher, I took the tea. 'You won't let that go.'

'I can't. Seeing you brings it back. You went in such a different direction after that summer, like you were repudiating him, me, Bell Valley.'

'Not repudiating,' I said quickly, then thought back on my life at that time. Painful as it was, this was why I had come — to find out what had happened to me after I'd left. 'He took himself out of my life. I had to make another one.'

45

'The opposite of what you had here.'

'Yes. Reminders hurt.'

'Do tell,' she drawled.

'I'm sorry. I tried other places before coming back here, only they didn't work. They were too much like what I was trying to escape.'

'Which is?'

I told her what my Friday morning had been like, ending with, 'Noise, lots of noise. And machines. And traffic. This is the quietest place I know. I mean, listen.' I stopped talking. The silence spoke for itself.

Her voice was gentle. 'There are lots of other quiet places, Emmie.'

None with a coyote waiting on the edge of a clearing, I might have said if I had wanted to talk about dreams. 'None where I know people. That's part of the problem, too. There are times in New York when I don't feel like I *know* anyone. I need human contact. I knew I could get it here.'

She stared at me for a minute, then broke off a corner of a scone and pressed it into my mouth. 'The blueberries are from New Jersey. Ours won't ripen for another month.'

I chewed the scone, tasting every crumb, and washed the last down with tea. 'See?' I said when my insides were soothed. 'You made my point. You're the best friend I've ever had. If I wanted to escape, where better to go? Where would *you* go?'

'A hotel.' When I gave her a puzzled look, she smiled. 'Have you seen *Date Night*?' I shook my head. 'Steve Carell plays Tina Fey's husband,

and they've designated a weekly date night to stir up a little excitement between them. So they're at a restaurant, and he asks if she's ever wanted to have an affair. She quickly says no, then grows sheepish and confesses to having times, like really bad days, when work stinks and the kids are acting up, when she'd give anything to check into a hotel and be alone. I'm there, too. You may think my life is quiet, certainly compared to yours, but chatter is not always audible. I have days when the oven malfunctions so the muffins won't crust, when guests have a gazillion requests that take time to fill, and Rob wonders why I haven't put out fresh flowers, and Charlotte just cling cling clings — '

'Charlotte,' I broke in, appalled. 'I haven't asked.'

'No.' Vicki's eyes scolded. 'You haven't. She's three now, and she's great — sweet and adorable and slow to talk because we always know what she wants, so she doesn't have to ask. Rob and I waited to have kids, and I think because of that, we appreciate her more. Being a mom is the best thing in the world. I know you probably don't want to hear that. You always used to say you wanted a baby, and it obviously hasn't happened yet.'

'We're trying.'

'Oh. Good.'

'No, I mean, we've been trying for a while. Lots of women put it off while they build their careers. Me, I wanted a baby three years ago. We've had tests. The doctors don't know why it hasn't happened.'

47

Vicki stared at me. 'I'm no doctor, but if you think you'll get pregnant in the condition you are in right now, think again.'

'I'm pathetic.'

She squeezed my hand. 'You are not pathetic, just misguided. Your priorities are messed up. They didn't used to be, before Jude.'

'I can't blame Jude for the last ten years. He wasn't telling me what to do.'

'And here you are. The problem, Emmie, is that if you stay even one more night, you'll see Charlotte. And my mom. She's here all the time, going back and forth with Charlotte.'

That brought a curious smile. 'Amelia? Babysitting?'

Vicki bobbed her eyes, a little shrug of the lids that I'd always appreciated. 'Weird, isn't it? It's actually nice. She's a very involved grandmother — far better with Charlotte than she ever was with us.'

The last time I saw Amelia was at Vicki's wedding. To say that she hadn't welcomed me was putting it mildly. 'Does she still blame me for Jude leaving?' I asked. Vicki's silence said yes. 'But I was not the offender. And he would have left here anyway. A part of him hated this town. I told him I'd have gone anywhere with him.'

'Which likely scared him shitless, but Mom can't accept that. She believes that you asked more of him than he could give and that he felt like a failure, so he left.'

My jaw dropped. 'I asked more of him than he could give? Is fidelity asking too much?'

'No,' Vicki drawled, 'but moms aren't always

rational.' She grew apologetic. 'I used to think she was crazy, but now that I'm a mom myself, I understand the concept of needing to blame someone for losing a child. It doesn't have to make sense. But if anything happened to Charlotte, I'd need someone — *anyone* — to go after.'

'Jude isn't lost,' I said, because I really did need to tell Vicki Bell what I knew.

'Well, not dead, not yet, but he asks for it all the time. Think Iraq. After Saddam fell and chaos broke out, he raced there to rescue injured pets and was caught in the crossfire. He went places he should never have gone.'

'He was on a humanitarian mission.'

'Yes, but there are right and wrong ways to go about it. Our military had to use valuable resources protecting him, and they weren't happy. Jude took chances he didn't need to take. He was too cocky for his own good.'

'Not cocky,' I reasoned, because that wasn't how I saw Jude. 'Self-assured. He was committed to ideals.'

'Emily, he was a rebel.'

'An adventurer,' I insisted.

'Well, that's the nice word. You always picked those when it came to Jude. He wasn't rude, he was honest. He wasn't rash, he was spirited. Don't get me wrong. I love my brother. But I saw his faults. You? You were blinded by first love.'

'But he was so much fun,' I argued. 'Rash, spirited — call him what you will, but there was an irreverent streak in him that was totally creative. He was the muscle behind the Refuge's outreach program, and look at how much good it's done. Okay. He was impulsive. But maybe,' I added in a troubled tone, 'that's better than overthinking every last decision.'

Vicki got it. I could tell by the way she studied me. 'Is that what you've done?'

'I don't know. I really don't. I wasn't aware of it, because it came easily, like law school led to James, who led to New York, which led to my firm. But it was all so *cerebral*.'

'Do you love James?'

'Yes,' I said quickly, then paused. 'I think so.'

'What does that mean?'

A door closed somewhere downstairs, the gentleness of it a reminder of where I was and, in that, encouragement. I couldn't talk with anyone in New York about James. It would have felt like a betrayal. But this was Bell Valley, and I had roomed with Vicki Bell through four years of college, which made her part of my life well before James.

'I was bowled over when I met him,' I told her. 'I mean, there he was — blue eyes, dark hair, six-two, and toned. He was a runner.' Jude had been a climber and, by contrast, stood six-four, had gold eyes and a tumble of blond hair. 'James was smart and hardworking. He was driven, but so was I. It was like I'd found a twin. We wanted to make law review, and we did. We wanted to graduate *summa cum laude*, and we did. When it came to law, James had a plan for success. We set out to accomplish it.' I recalled the conclusion I'd reached sitting alone on that porch in the Berkshires.

50

'And now?' Vicki prompted.

'I'm not sure the plan's right for me. It is for James. He's going full-speed ahead. I'm the problem.' Saying it aloud made it more real. But today was Monday, which made my escape itself more real — terrifying, actually. 'I feel like I'm skipping school.'

'You never skipped school.'

'Right. I never hated school like I hate work. This case, another case, would it matter? It's the culture of the firm, the race to rack up billable hours, the lack of warmth among partners even at the top levels. Walter Burbridge is probably furious at me right now, but when I think of being back there, my head fills with static. It is *deafening*.'

'Have you told James all this?'

'I've tried, but he doesn't want to hear. Besides, if we're not working, we're sleeping, unless the chart says I'm ovulating, in which case we're making love, which is not terribly romantic when it's scheduled like that. In any case, we're too tired to have a substantive discussion.'

'Have you talked with him since you left?'

'Briefly. He thinks I'm having a nervous breakdown. Is that what this is?'

Vicki snickered. 'Seems to me like you're living a fantasy. Just putting a stop to the things you hate in your life and taking time off. Any chance he'll follow you here?'

'He can't. He doesn't know where I am.'

She looked startled by that. 'Shouldn't you tell him? He's your husband. Don't you owe it to him?'

'More than I owe myself time away to think?' the newly assertive me asked.

'But won't he worry?'

'Yes. But he's busy with work.'

'Okay, then there's this. You met him right after you left here. Won't he put two and two together and guess that you're here?'

'No. I never talked about this place much to him.'

'Does he know about Jude?'

'No.'

'You're kidding.'

'No.'

'Emily,' she protested. 'Jude was your *life* that summer. How could you not talk about him?'

'Have you told Rob about every guy you ever dated?'

'He was the only guy I ever dated.'

I rolled my eyes. 'Okay. Big picture, here. Does a husband need to know everything about his wife's past? If it's over and done, *no*. I'm sure James dated in college, but I don't know the girls. He worked for three years before law school. Of course he dated, but I don't want to know the details. When it came to Jude, well, when I left here, I closed that door. It was a clean break. That was the only way I could handle it.'

'And you never talked about it later?'

I shook my head. 'James and I talk about present and future. He knows nothing about Bell Valley.'

'Wow,' Vicki breathed, but I was distracted by a movement behind her, a small face at the crack of the door. It was instantly familiar, like that of her mom. When a warmth spread in my chest, I caught in a breath and whispered, 'Oh my.'

Vicki turned. 'Oh my, is right,' she gently scolded. 'How many guest rooms did you peek into before you found me here, Charlotte Bell?' But she wasn't angry. I knew it. So did Charlotte Bell.

The little girl looked from her mother to me, remaining at the door until Vicki waved her in. She walked slowly, cautious eyes on me the whole way. Small and perfectly formed, she had her father's grey eyes, her mother's blond hair, and curls nearly as long as Jude's. She wore a jersey dress that was purple and pink, with leggings in the reverse pattern. When she was within reach, Vicki scooped her up and settled her on her lap.

If I was enthralled by the child, Vicki was that much more so. The love in her eyes was something to behold. 'This is Emily,' she said against a small ear. 'I knew Emily at school, just like you know Clara at school. We used to have overnights, like you sometimes have with Nana Amelia. Remember, you had pizza?' Eyes still on mine, the child gave a tiny nod. 'Charlotte loves pizza,' Vicki told me. 'And hot chocolate. Emmie and I used to have hot chocolate,' she told Charlotte. 'With marshmallows. And whipped cream.'

'At two in the morning,' I put in.

'But only during exams.'

'Hah. We gave meaning to the Freshman Fifteen.'

Vicki squeezed her daughter and said into that little ear again, 'Remember I told you I went to school for a while in England, where everyone talks like Alec, the little boy in your class? Emmie was with me. We travelled all around Europe.'

I doubted the child knew what Europe was, but I jumped aboard the memory. 'If I had to choose the highlight of my college experience, it'd be our semester in Bath. I still have the scarf I bought at the bridge. Remember that?'

'How could I forget?' Vicki crowed. 'It was neon pink and *awful*. You wore it constantly.'

'And that gorgeous Italian guy — '

'Dante.'

'That was not his real name,' I insisted.

'He said it was, but he was bad. He never studied. I swear, his goal was to corrupt *us*. Remember that one night — '

'At the Roman baths.' Embarrassed, I covered my face. 'Omigod. Beer. *Guinness*.'

Vicki grew wistful. 'I haven't thought about that in a long time. It was another life.'

A sobering thought there. A better life? A freer life? It had sure been fun.

Vicki was on the same wavelength. 'We should have gone for the whole year, not just the fall. Coming back was a drag.'

'I wear the scarf sometimes. It spices up my uniform. Not that it gets past the coatroom. I haven't been bold at Lane Lavash.' Not until now. Of course, the question remained as to whether what I was doing was bold or just plain irresponsible. I thought of Layla and the other

54

innocent people suffering from drinking water that they thought was safe. Someone did have to help them, but that wouldn't be me today. Maybe not tomorrow or Wednesday either.

'Big frown,' Vicki observed.

'Big worry.' But for later. Determinedly, I returned to the present, to Vicki and her precious little girl. 'So you go to school?' I asked Charlotte.

The little girl nodded.

'Every day?'

'Three mornings a week,' Vicki said. 'It's been an adjustment, but we wanted her to be with other children. Come fall, it'll be five mornings a week. The timing's good.'

Something about her tone and a certain look in her eye made me catch my breath a second time. Another baby on the way?

'Early December,' she confirmed with a look of terrified anticipation that was almost comical.

'Oh, Vicki Bell, I am so happy for you.'

'Are you really? You're not just saying that?'

I knew what she meant. 'Absolutely not. I'm thrilled. You're obviously a great mom. You could have *five* kids and not be fazed. Children fit in your life. Maybe they don't fit in mine.'

Charlotte had settled snugly into her mother, who said, 'Is that what you're running from?'

'Maybe. I'm discouraged, but if what we're doing now doesn't work, we do have options. It's the rest that . . . that just clogs me up.'

'There have to be some good things.'

'There are. I have a job, a husband, and a great place to live. And I'm healthy.'

'But unhappy. So why are you in Bell Valley? It made you miserable ten years ago.'

'*Jude* made me miserable,' I said, 'but I loved Bell Valley even before that summer. The weekends I visited with you were vacations, even when we had studying to do. I relax here. I can think. That's what I need to do now.'

I thought of Jude. His brief letter had changed things. But maybe not. I figured I had maybe two weeks before he arrived.

I needed to tell Vicki about that.

But she was stuck on what I'd last said. 'Think about where you want to go from here?'

'First, think about why I went where I did after I left here. Maybe you're right. Maybe I was on the rebound from Jude and took it too far. Coming back here is like starting over.'

'How long will you stay?'

I felt a stab of hysteria. 'My car may have a say in that.'

'No. It's an electronics problem. Nestor says they'll have it back by the end of the day. It'd be even sooner, if his boy wasn't so enthralled. The kid's sixteen and a total geek. It isn't often he gets to play with a car like yours.'

'If he messes it up, James will never forgive me,' I warned.

'He won't mess it up. Technology is his thing. He runs a repair shop out of the garage. Computers, cell phones, small appliances — we wouldn't take them anywhere else.'

'Runs a repair shop? At sixteen? What about school?'

'He says he's found his life's work, and given

how good he is, I believe him.'

I considered it. 'Well, that says something. He's a high school dropout and has a job he loves. I have three degrees and a job I hate.'

'Get another one,' Vicki said.

'I'm trying, but it isn't easy. I don't want to go from bad to worse, and it's not like I can look for a clerkship in Oregon, if I'm married to someone who's dead set on New York.' I returned to her earlier question. 'I don't know how long I'll stay here, and that is totally unsettling.' I'd always been a directed sort of woman. 'Have I ever winged anything before?'

'Your summer here. You came not knowing what you'd be doing.'

'Right. And I had the wildest, most spontaneous and passionate summer of my life. So is that who I really am? Or was it an aberration? I have to find out.' I glanced at my watch, which, of course, wasn't there. No clock on the nightstand, or on the dresser, either.

'Our guests like to chill,' Vicki explained.

'I need to learn how.' I made a helpless little sound. 'Old habits die hard. And now it's Monday. If I don't make a call within the next day or two, I won't have a job to return to. Help me with this, Vicki. You were always so good at getting to the heart of the matter. What should I do?'

Charlotte whispered something to Vicki that I didn't catch. I had assumed that our conversation would be over her head, and was wondering if I was wrong, when Vicki said, 'O-kay. Potty time.' She rose, at which point Charlotte became

57

a little monkey, four limbs clinging to her mom, which was good. Otherwise, she'd have fallen when Vicki bent forwards and wrapped an arm around my neck.

'I want you here,' she whispered fiercely, and, straightening, held Charlotte with both arms and backed up. I was thinking that I needed to tell her about Jude, but she was saying, 'Make yourself at home. Books and puzzles are in the parlour, bikes are out back. If you want to drive somewhere, the keys to the van are on the board by the door. The kitchen's yours. If you happen on a short, dark-haired woman there, that's my baker, Lee. She has an interesting story.'

I was still obsessed with my own. 'What about my boss? And what about James?'

Vicki paused at the door. 'That depends on what you want, and you're the only one who knows.'

But I didn't know, which was why I was here. I didn't even know how to go about finding out.

I did know that what had started as an act of impulse — rebellion, perhaps — was growing more grave by the minute. Much longer, and there'd be no going back.

Frightened, I slipped lower on the pillow and pulled the comforter to my ears, hoping to bury reality under the billowy down. But the smell of flower-fresh Vicki and her powder-soft child lingered in my psyche, making me feel grubby. Getting out of bed, I showered, put on jeans and a sweater to look as much like Vicki as possible — inconspicuousness being the goal — and pulled my damp hair through the back of my hat.

I finished my tea as I stood at the window, looking out over the backyard. There were benches there, and Adirondack chairs scattered in pairs. Beyond lay the woods.

I knew these woods. They held pine and hemlock, fir, spruce, and birch, and their foliage varied greatly. With the sun blindingly bright in the foreground, the colours behind bled into the deepest, darkest forest green.

In my dreams, that green was nearly black. My dreams took place at night.

I needed to visit those woods. But not yet. At a time when I was feeling weak, that took more courage than I had.

5

Sunglasses in hand, I tiptoed from my room, but the caution was unnecessary. I made it to the first floor without seeing a soul. Loath to trust my luck, I went straight to the kitchen, which was empty as well, and slipped quietly through the screen door and down the back steps.

As Vicki had promised, there were bikes. I spotted one that was my size and imagined myself pedalling hard through the Bell Valley roads, because pedalling hard was like spinning at my gym in New York. But the thought of it now made my legs hurt — surely emotions at play, because I had never been afraid of a workout.

But I did need to learn how to chill.

So I walked down the parking lot to the street. There were a few cars in front of the stores and one parked at the end of the green. Crossing the grass, I sank down beside a bench. The sun soothed. Sounds wafted about — the burr of a mower on the church lawn, the murmur of a couple emerging now from the Red Fox, the su-*weet* of a goldfinch on a nearby oak. I took one slow breath, then a second deeper one, aware of the novelty as my lungs filled and stretched. It struck me that other than during yoga class, I'd been breathing shallowly — running everywhere, stressing about everything, always connected to machines — for ten years.

60

Just thinking about it quickened my breath.

Drawing in another lungful, I was thinking how peaceful Bell Valley was in contrast to Lane Lavash, where by rights I should be at this moment with my cubicle, computer, and headset, when I saw Vicki striding over from the Red Fox.

'Going incognito today?' she asked, coming down to the grass beside me. I had done right dressing like her. Jeans, sweater, sunglasses — we looked like sisters, which made me feel like I belonged.

I smiled and made a sound of assent. No more was needed with Vicki Bell.

'Did you meet my baker?' she asked.

'No. She wasn't in the kitchen.'

'Later then.' Removing the sunglasses, she studied my face. 'What're you thinking?'

I felt a catch in my throat. 'That I've missed you. Seeing you makes me realize how much. Call me disloyal to Kelly, but you were always the sister I would have chosen to have. Even the question you just asked. You always cared what I thought.' In case she was still even the tiniest bit annoyed with me, I added, 'We have a history together. That counts for something.'

'Uh-huh. Getting older.' She grew speculative. 'Do birthdays bother you?'

Dropping my sunglasses to the grass, I turned my face to the sun. The warmth felt wonderful, cleaner than New York's, friendlier than Chatham's. Eyes closed, I considered. 'Thirty was something. James thought we should celebrate, only we never had time.' I righted my head. My eyes sought hers. 'Is that what this is about? Am I

61

having an early-life crisis?'

Vicki smiled crookedly. 'I did. Kind of.'

'You? No way.' Vicki was the most stable person I knew.

'Way. Rob and I grew up together, and I adore him. But I've never known anything else. Four years away at college was all. Then it was back here, same guy, same town.'

'Not really,' I reminded her. 'You got married. That was big. Then Rob's parents retired, and you guys took over the inn. The place looks great, Vicki Bell.'

She sputtered a laugh. 'Anything would, by comparison. His parents had let things go. And yeah, it's nice to spruce things up, but that's not the same as doing something completely, entirely, way-out-there different.' She was pensive for a minute, then resigned. 'Each birthday that passes makes me realize it ain't gonna happen. I went into a blue funk for a little while.'

'Hence, the new baby?'

'Oh no. I didn't even try to conceive until I was sure I was okay with my life here. Which isn't to say I don't sometimes wonder what might have been.'

'It's the Jude gene,' I remarked, to which she snorted her disagreement.

'Jude was about rebellion.'

'Adventure,' I insisted.

'Emmie, he was a *bad boy*,' she argued, impatient with me now. 'Do you honestly think he would have married you? Yes, I know he asked you to, but he had asked three women before you, the last of whom was Jenna Frye, who took it really

62

hard when he dumped her for you, and then he dumped you for *her*. Jude was all about the chase. Commitment terrified him. If you hadn't come along, he'd have found another way to break up with Jenna, and if she hadn't loved him enough to forgive him, he'd have found another way to break up with *you*.'

I wanted to argue. But Vicki had known Jude a lot longer than I had. What she said did make sense.

'He's coming back,' I said quietly.

She frowned, sceptical. 'Jude? Here? How do you know?'

'I got a letter from him Friday. He'll be here at the end of the month.'

Suddenly, she was barely breathing. 'Here? *Seriously?*'

'He's been crab fishing in the Bering Sea.'

'And he just . . . just wrote to you out of the blue?'

'He does it sometimes,' I said, feeling more than a little guilt.

'And you didn't *tell* us?'

'I assumed you knew where he was. The letter Friday said he hadn't told anyone else he was coming back, which is why I'm telling you now. For what it's worth, I've never answered his letters.'

But Vicki was pressing a hand to her chest. 'Omigod. What do we do? Who do we tell? No one,' she decided, erasing the news with both hands. 'We can't tell anyone. Jude is the most irresponsible, unpredictable person I know. He may say he's coming and then chicken out and go somewhere more exciting. Mom is used to the idea of his being gone. If I tell her he's coming back and he doesn't show, she'll be destroyed.'

I couldn't imagine Amelia being destroyed by much, and might have asked more, if Vicki hadn't narrowed her eyes.

'*That's* why you're here? Not to see me, but because *he's* coming back?'

'No. *No.* I'm here because I need you and I need the peace of this town. Maybe I'm even here because I needed to give you this news, but I am not here for Jude. I'm here for me. Call me selfish. I am.'

'You're not,' she muttered grudgingly. 'If you were, your life wouldn't be in this mess. You'd have stood up for yourself and your needs before this.' She slouched against my side. 'Why is he coming back? He won't stay. He'll just stir things up and leave. His idea of hell is being stuck here.'

'Maybe he's grown up — you know, seen other kinds of hell.'

But Vicki was shaking her head, seeming more sad now than annoyed. 'He's a Bell. Bells have lived here for generations. He may fight the pull, but it's strong. *That's* what's in our genes.' She reached for my hand. 'I could never have walked away from my life, certainly not the way you've done. But you doing it doesn't surprise me. You were always the bolder of us. Like the semester abroad. I wouldn't have done it if it hadn't been for you. Wouldn't have had the courage to go so far for so long. You were my more spirited half.'

64

I couldn't remember the last time I'd held a friend's hand, but with Vicki Bell, it was the most natural thing in the world — the great connector, not to mention a ticket to confession. 'And you my saner half.' I had a qualifying thought. 'Except for Jude. You didn't stop me there.'

'How could I? He was my brother. I was hoping you'd be a good influence on him. Besides, there was no stopping what you two had. It was like wildfire — *poof*, hot as hell in an instant, pure animal magnetism.'

I might have argued that there had been far more than that, only she had given me the opening, and if my dreams were to be believed, the subject had a grip on at least a small part of my mind. 'Speaking of animals, there were coyotes that summer. Are they still here?'

'No. Not since Jude left. He was the only one who saw them, or said he did.'

'I saw them.' I could vouch for Jude on this. 'There was actually just one, up by his cabin. We watched it — and it us — for hours. Jude used to whisper to it, like they had this awesome connection. He was sure it had a mate in the woods, but we never saw the pair together. So, you haven't heard them?'

She shook her head.

Not since Jude left. That gave me a little chill. It was only in recent months that my dreams had begun. I wondered what the significance of that was.

'He always drew creatures that way,' Vicki mused. 'Like I said, animal magnetism.' Her eyes found mine. 'He's coming back after all this time? Did he say what he wanted to do here or how long he'd stay?'

'He mentioned unfinished business, but he didn't elaborate, and he knew he might have trouble staying here long.'

'That is Jude. I wonder what he looks like.'

So did I. One look at him that summer, and I'd been lost.

Vicki read my mind. With a little squeeze, she dropped my hand. 'Is it good with James?'

'Sex?' Only with Vicki could I have this conversation. 'It used to be fabulous,' I said, folding my legs. 'Trying to get pregnant makes it less fun.'

'Does James agree?'

'Not in as many words. He would never tell me it isn't good.'

'Would he ever have an affair?'

I didn't immediately answer, as if saying the words aloud would make them real. But they were real. At least, my worry was real. 'He may be.'

'Having one now?'

'I don't know for sure. There's one woman. They work together all the time. Breakfast, lunch, everything in between. When they work late, it's take-in dinner in the conference room.'

'Aren't other people there?'

'Sometimes.'

'Have you asked him about it?'

'Indirectly, like a joke.' Unable to meet her eye, I pulled at the grass between my legs. 'He laughs it off.' I straightened. 'I really don't think he is. He is not that kind of person.' I wanted to believe, oh, I did. 'And I'm hypersensitive about it because of Jude.'

'I'll never forgive him for that.'

'It's done.'

'So now you worry about James. Would you ever cheat on him?'

'Never. Of course, he'd probably say I'm cheating on him now.'

'By being here?'

'By not telling him I'm here.'

Vicki was silent. She would agree with James on that one.

'Maybe it's a power thing,' I suggested. 'I've felt so *without* power for so long.'

'He is your husband.'

'But I don't want him coming after me.' I shot a look at the guy in the car at the end of the green. For all I knew, he was a detective. James couldn't have sent him so fast, but my father might have. More likely, he was the husband of a woman having her hair done in the shop behind the General Store.

I sighed. 'And that's all I know, that I want time without James. Pathetic, isn't it? I mean, I'm sitting here trying not to think. But if I don't think, I won't figure out my life. And what do I do in the meanwhile?'

Vicki's smile was warm. 'Whatever your heart desires. Isn't that what Bell Valley's about?'

This time, it was me taking her hand. 'You are such a good friend. I don't have friends in New York. Well, I do, but it's different.'

'Different, how?'

'Less personal. Less face-to-face. Mostly we text, and when we're together, one of us is either typing or talking to someone else entirely. We're all on all the time, so any one relationship is diluted by the others. It's sad. I'm supposed to be a bridesmaid at Colleen Parker's wedding, but we're not even close. We met through a book group, and since we're both lawyers, we figured there ought to be a connection, but I wouldn't call it strong. Book group meets once a month, and we relate the books to our own lives because we're so hungry to talk about feelings. But there are ten of us in the group, so it isn't intimate, and we only meet for an hour because that's all we have. Colly and I used to meet for lunch, but even that stopped. No time.' I was working myself into a snit. 'Maybe Colly defines friendship this way, but I don't. I don't know where she comes from, don't know where she's headed or what she dreams. I don't know her family or her friends, and I don't want to be in her wedding.'

'Why did you tell her yes?'

I had asked myself that dozens of times, kicking myself then and now for not having gently refused when she first asked. Explaining it to Vicki, I squirmed a little. 'Because I want close friends, and this is what close friends do, and for whatever reason, Colly was desperate for it. Her specialty is patents, which I don't understand, so it's not like we even talk about work. Once the wedding's over, we'll probably only see each other at book group. We don't have much in common' — I grabbed a breath — 'which, in a nutshell, describes the friends I've made.'

'Then you haven't found the right ones.'

'You're right. But I've been in the city seven years. What's the problem?'

Vicki's eyes spoke for her.

'Okay. It's me. I neglect friends, like I neglected you, so relationships never have a chance to develop, which would be fine if I didn't want them, but I do.' I rubbed my forehead, pushing the dilemma around.

'Do not do that,' Vicki ordered. 'You're here to relax.'

'I'm here to decide what to *do* with my life,' I said, mildly hysterical.

'Shh. One step at a time. Right now, what are your choices?'

There were three. 'Stay here. Go back to New York. Go somewhere else.'

'Forget somewhere else. Short run, it's here or New York. Start with New York. If you went back, what would change?'

'Nothing. That's the problem. If I go back, I have to accept that that's my life, but I don't know if I can. The alternative — staying here — creates other problems.'

'Like Jude?'

'No. Jude is not a factor in my being here. I told you that.'

'Okay.' She indulged me. 'Then James. If he knew you were here, you could buy time with less guilt.'

'What about Lane Lavash?'

'Tell them you're sick,' she said as she stood.

'That'd work if I planned to be back by the

end of the week, but maybe I won't.' I eyed her cautiously.

I'd said it before, but it bore repeating: when it came to me, Vicki Bell got it.

'The room is yours as long as you want it. I don't hate you anymore — not even for telling me about Jude, because I'd rather know than not.' She studied me for another minute, before reaching down with a hug. 'I don't live in the city, and I do have lots of friends, but you were always the best of the bunch.'

★ ★ ★

The feeling was mutual. I thought about that as Vicki walked back to the Red Fox. What made a friend a best friend? Did it have to be someone who knew your people, who shared your life outlook or your views on religion or politics? Could it just be someone who could talk and listen and commiserate?

Vicki and I were strangers until we were eighteen. It was move-in day freshman year. Assigned to different roommates down the hall from each other, we met for the first time in the communal bathroom. I was brushing my hair, she was brushing her teeth, both of us needing to escape the scary newness of our lives by doing the mundane.

She was from New Hampshire, I was from Maine, she wanted Art, I wanted English, but we started to talk and didn't stop until my worried mother came looking for me. I found myself looking for Vicki wherever I went, and she did the same. When her roommate dropped out after a week, my moving into her room was a no-brainer.

Chemistry. Vicki and I had that. Right from the start.

But wasn't a best friend also someone you could trust not to hurt you? I had hurt Vicki, yet here she was, opening her home and heart to me again. So maybe being a best friend entailed the ability to forgive.

Gradually, the sun moved, casting me in the dappled shade of the goldfinch's oak. Thinking about friendship, then marriage, then dreams, I sat on the grass as the life of Bell Valley flowed by. It was a leisurely life, but it had purpose. There was Carl Younger, owner of the hardware store, carrying a bag of trash out the side door and pausing to check a birdfeeder before disappearing around back. And Sara Carney, adjusting the big OPEN flag in front of The Fiber Store, which had been The Sewing Store when I was here last but had expanded into yarn, to judge from the colourful window display. Likewise, the telephone store was now The Gadget Store.

Simple and straightforward. That's Bell Valley. What you see is what you get.

Take The Bookstore. A hot new release was advertised in the window, along with displays of other books, but I also saw puzzles, games, and gift wrap. Vickie Longosz — the Book V, we called her — had branched out, which made total sense, given the economic reality. I wondered if she would think me a traitor for owning a Kindle.

I was thinking that I ought to drop in and buy

a few books with the cash that my husband was worried about, when I saw the car that had been parked at the end of the green move closer. It was a small charcoal SUV. I smiled, wondering if the hair shop was still doing the same tight perms, when I heard another car, this one *mine*, coasting around the green. Slowing, it turned into the parking lot of the Red Fox. A second car followed and waited while the gangly boy who'd been driving mine went inside. This would be his ride back to the garage.

The responsible thing would have been to act. Nestor's son should be thanked, and he would need to be paid. But I remained in the shadow of the bench, watching as the door of the second car opened and a chocolate lab hopped out. It trotted across the street and onto the green, pausing to pee before making for me. Its nose was cold, but its eyes were beseeching, and when I scratched its ears, its whole rear end wagged. Its tongue followed, licking me into a laugh.

I loved dogs. We'd always had one when I was growing up, first Morgan, then Dane. I cried for weeks when Morgan died, and leaving Dane when I went to college was harder than leaving my mom. At least Mom and I could talk on the phone. She used to put the handset to Dane's ear, and she told me that my voice made him grin, but did he understand where I was, why I was there, and that I loved him even though I'd left?

Did James?

At the sound of a whistle, the dog loped back to the car. I wanted to think he watched me out the window as, with Nestor's son inside, they drove off. I wanted to think we had connected and that he would seek me out whenever I was within sniffing distance. I wanted to think it had been love at first sight.

My car dying had been a sign telling me I was right to have come to Bell Valley. I wanted to think meeting this dog was a sign I should stay.

Foolish me. It was a sign, all right — a sign that I was hungry for love. Thought of that choked me up, and since I was tired of crying, I closed my eyes, put my head back against the side of the bench, and changed the subject.

With one sense closed off, the others sharpened. The Grill might be the only restaurant for miles around, but the lack of competition hadn't hurt it any. The food had always been good. From the smell of it now, nothing had changed. My mind's eye pictured a bacon cheeseburger, a BLT, even a Cobb salad with warm goodies crumbled all over the top.

I was definitely hungry. But having lunch at The Grill would mean Exposure with a capital 'E.' So I returned to the Red Fox and entered the kitchen through the back door, then stopped short when I spotted Rob. Brown-haired and lanky, he was standing at the counter forking down lunch. I might have backed away, postponing the moment of reckoning, if he hadn't looked up.

'Hey,' I said with a sheepish smile. I had always liked Rob. He was quiet, perhaps a tad boring, but kind-hearted. Taking off my hat, which somehow felt wrong in such a personal

73

place, I kissed his cheek. 'Good to see you, Rob.'

'And you,' he replied, and though I heard caution, his voice felt like home. 'Vicki's putting Charlotte in for a nap.' *Chahlette*. Definitely like home.

'That's good.' I leaned against the counter. 'She's precious, Rob. And a new baby on the way?' I clucked in admiration. 'That's great.'

He was studying me, waiting.

I sighed. 'I've been a bad friend, Rob. I'm sorry. It wasn't intentional.'

'Vicki was hurt.'

'I know.'

'Don't do it again.'

I smiled. With Vicki the talker, Rob never said much. Like her, though, he let you know where he stood.

'I'm serious,' he said, but I could see he was softening.

'Hey, in shutting her out, I hurt me, too. I need to mend that for both our sakes.'

Looking down, he studied his fork as it moved macaroni and cheese around the plate. When he looked back at me, there were furrows on a brow that was normally smooth. 'It isn't just Vicki and me or even Charlotte. It's the rest of Bell Valley. You left abruptly.'

'So did Jude.'

'Jude's one of ours. You're not.'

'But if Bell Valley is a refuge, shouldn't everyone be welcomed?'

Maybe it was my words, maybe the sound of my need. Looking chastened, he set down his fork and pulled me close. 'Just a warning, kiddo.

I know how Bell Valley thinks. Once burned, twice shy.' The phone rang. The arm that had held me let go to stretch past for the handset. 'You've reached the Red Fox. May I help you? Oh. Good God. No, we need decaf, too. That was s'posed to have been an automatic delivery. We're almost out.'

Leaving him to business, I opened the fridge. It was stuffed in ways my own had never, ever been. For James and me, eating in was about bare essentials. I might blame that for my being a lousy cook, but I had been a lousy cook well before James and New York. My mother was a great cook. There had been no need for me to learn. I didn't have to serve breakfast to upwards of twenty people a day, like Vicki did. Nor did I serve tea, and though I guessed that cookies and cakes would be baked fresh that afternoon, the plastic bins in the fridge said that the fruit tray would be huge.

I didn't want fruit now. I *lived* on fruit — no, that was wrong. I lived on *salad*. Which meant I didn't want salad now, either. Studying my options, I realized that I craved good, old-fashioned comfort food, which made Rob's mac and cheese too tempting to ignore. Removing the container, I heated a small dish. Rob was still on the phone. Catching his eye with a tiny wave, I pointed to the backyard.

With other guests likely gone to the Refuge for the day, I had my choice of seats. Not wanting to be too close to the woods, I headed for the Adirondack chair that sat at the trunk of the Norway maple I had seen from my room. Setting

75

the dish on one of its wide arms, I sank into it, but had barely tucked up my legs when I saw a small, dark-haired figure scurry from the parking lot to the back steps. This would be Vicki's baker, here to make those cookies and cakes. Head down, she looked like she didn't want to be seen any more than I did.

She disappeared inside, leaving me alone with the woods.

The sun had shifted, shedding light on the face of the trees. I saw the broad, tri-tipped leaves of the sugar maple, the single, soft-green ones of the beech, and the paper birch, standing out not for its leaves but for its peeling white bark. At their feet were a bed of last fall's leaves, as packed down as the winter snows had been heavy. There were spruce here, conically shaped, and more evergreens behind. I picked out the graceful arms of the hemlock, the blue-green needles of the balsam fir, and, towering above, the white pine. All would be rising from beds of moss, which I couldn't see from here. Nor could I see the boulders that were strewn about in the forest, whether standing alone or guiding the brook.

These woods were dense. Level for a short stretch before starting to climb, they grew increasingly rugged the higher they went, eventually giving way to a bald granite peak that was easily fifteen degrees colder than the air where I sat.

And no, these woods weren't for wimps. They held black bears with ferocious claws and fisher cats with ferocious screams. They held owls and the occasional eagle. And coyotes. Yes, there were those. They might not have been here lately, but I had seen one myself, first in the flesh, then in my dream.

Lest I've built it up into something it's not, let me say here that the dream isn't earthshaking. There's no action, simply two creatures staring at each other, one human, one not. I see gold eyes that shimmer, though reflecting what in the pitch black of night, I don't know. It's always the same. We watch. We wait.

In time I wake up. And that's when the heart of the dream takes hold. In those woods, I feel haunted. I awake to a stark loneliness, and I feel a yearning.

The feeling always fades, forgotten in the rush of my life until the dream recurs — and I do yearn for something. I don't think it's Jude. I love James. But Jude is wild and unchained, like the coyote. How not to envy that, when my life is the opposite? Particularly now. I had a decision to make. It wouldn't wait much longer.

I needed another sign. A sign would tell me which way to go without my having to make the decision myself.

So I waited, keeping to myself as I vegged the afternoon away. Was I bored? Surprisingly not. Into my third day of escape, my limbs were starting to relax on their own. I sat, I walked, I read a magazine. I worked on the communal jigsaw puzzle in the living room, and when Charlotte wandered in, I coaxed her onto my lap and guided her hand to fit in a piece.

This was what people did with leisure time. I

wasn't entirely comfortable with it, partly because it lacked direction, partly because, much as I pushed it to the back of my mind, the weight of decision was there. Stay or go? It wasn't a simple choice. There would be consequences either way.

As the afternoon stretched on, the air grew warmer. A dog barked, a robin hopped across the lawn. I watched guests return for tea. Not a one held a cell phone to his ear.

By the time Charlotte was in bed, the backyard was alive with a chorus of crickets. Charmed, I ate dinner on the back porch with Vicki while Rob mingled in the parlour with guests. She wanted to talk about Jude, grilling me about his letter until I finally brought it down from my room and let her read it herself. We talked about sobering experiences in life — Vicki's dad's death when she was sixteen, my grandmother's when I was twelve, Jude's friend's when he was forty. We talked about Jude's conscience having to be newly dreamed up, since he hadn't had much of a conscience at all when he was here. But if I was hoping for a personal ah-hah moment in which she said something that would shed new light on my dilemma, it didn't come.

I went to bed in my room in the clouds, no closer to a decision. Then came the dream. It was late and very dark when it began.

Have you ever heard a coyote howl? It's an eerie sound that undulates from high to low in pitch. The sound is often broken by barks or yips, but the howling is what makes you shiver.

In some instances, multiple voices join in. Though coyotes mate for life, they often travel with others that help rear their pups. I had used the word 'pack' when Jude had first told me this, but he quickly objected. Wolves ran in packs, he explained, and though coyotes were descendants of wolves, they banded more for domesticity than power.

In the darkness this night, I heard only one. Its howl wasn't prolonged, but since my dream didn't usually have a soundtrack, it was enough to jolt me awake.

I was lying in bed wide-eyed when the sound came again.

Incredulous, I held my breath. When a third howl pierced the night, I flew to the window and pushed it as high as it would go.

Vicki swore there had been no coyotes here since Jude, but either she was wrong or one had suddenly returned. More than one? I couldn't tell. I heard a few yips and another howl, then nothing but the bark of a dog from a house on the green, and the resumption of cricket chirps in the woods.

I sat back on my heels. Maybe I was grasping at straws, but the coincidence was too great. There had to be some meaning to the fact that the coyotes had returned to Bell Valley just when I had. Could I leave until I knew what that meaning was?

Here was my sign.

Now came the tough part.

6

I had to tell James what I'd decided. But a basic premise of trial work is that you don't plea-bargain until you know the strength of your case. So I called Walter first.

I knew that losing my job was a distinct possibility. Associates were sometimes asked to leave Lane Lavash, usually for lack of productivity but occasionally for crimes as simple as sending an email to another associate criticizing an equity partner. The firing was done nicely, with the associate simply told that he had 'no future with the firm' and ought to look elsewhere, but the end result was the same.

What's the difference between a dead dog in the road and a dead lawyer in the road? There are skid marks in front of the dog.

Unfortunately, one dead lawyer in the road meant twenty live ones panting for his job. And my finding a job I liked better would be harder with this on my record. Lane Lavash would have little good to say about me.

Still, I was ready to take the risk. That was how strongly I felt about this all-wrong life I had built. I had to take it apart and rebuild. I had to salvage what was good.

James was good. At least I thought he was, assuming he wasn't having an affair, which I desperately wanted to believe. He didn't have the commitment problem Jude did. And though he and I had barely seen each other in recent months, I did miss him. Tall and solid, he had a way of looking at me that made my toes curl, a middle-of-the-night way of pulling me into his body to spoon that made me feel protected. And the intellectual connection? When it was good, it was *good*.

Was Walter good? I resented his impatience and his nose-to-the-grindstone mind-set, but he did have one good feature — predictability. Since he always emailed me at 6:30 AM, I knew I could reach him then. Lacking a clock, I turned my BlackBerry on and off three times Tuesday morning before the time on it was right. Walter picked up after a single ring.

'Yeah,' he said distractedly.

I cleared my throat. 'Walter?'

After only the seconds it took for him to recognize my voice, he erupted in barely restrained anger. 'Well, thank you very much for returning my calls, Mrs Aulenbach. Would you care to tell me what you're doing? Better still, would you like to tell me when you'll be back, because there's a shit-load of work here, and you've left me one man short. I have a computer that's going to waste. If you don't value this job, there are plenty of others who do.'

Contritely, I said, 'I value it. But I've been struggling with some personal issues.'

'Serious enough for you to walk out in the middle of a work day without a word to anyone?' he went on, and I didn't interrupt. If I were to look at it from his point of view, he had a right to be annoyed. 'That was Friday morning, Emily.

I've been calling you ever since. Did you even check your messages?'

'No.' I had made a point to ignore all those dings on the few occasions when I'd turned on my BlackBerry. It was actually easy to do in the sky and clouds of this attic room, where the intrusion *really* grated.

'*No?* Well, I guess that tells me where I am on your totem pole.'

'It isn't just you, Walter. It's everyone. I've had my BlackBerry off.'

'Why?' he asked, as if I'd lost my mind.

It would have been easy to say that a family member was sick, but I couldn't. I might be irresponsible, but I wasn't dishonest. Besides, sitting on the edge of the bed in nothing but my nightshirt, I felt exposed. 'I'm trying to figure out who I am and what I want.'

'Aren't we all? That doesn't mean we bail out on people who depend on us. I'm fifty-eight, and I'm *still* trying to figure out what I want, but I come to work every morning, and I do what I'm being paid to do.'

Maybe it was his personal work ethic, or his having three kids in college. Maybe it was just *different* for men.

'I see burnout all the time,' he lectured. 'I've felt it myself. You can't just quit. You have to work through it.'

I'd heard that one from the guy who taught my spinning class. 'This isn't a charley horse.'

'Okay,' he said shortly. 'When will you be back?'

I cleared my throat. 'That's what I need to talk with you about. I have to be away from New York for a little while, and I fully understand the position this puts you in. I also understand that you may need to hire someone in my place.'

'But you're one of my best workers,' he whined, and gentled a bit. 'What if I gave you the week off? Can you be back next Monday?'

'No. I need more time.'

'How much?' he asked, but I knew how he worked. I had seen him bargain up the fee a client would pay. He knew the art of negotiation. I had learned from the best.

'Three months,' I said, knowing that I would never get that much but that if I started higher, I would lack credibility. Four months would have been beyond the pale in Lane Lavash time. Three months was an opening bid.

He was silent for a beat. 'Are you seeing a shrink?'

'No.'

'Then who says three months?'

'Me.'

'I can give you two weeks. You have that coming.'

Uh-huh. Two weeks of unpaid leave. They called it personal time, and it covered vacation days, sick days, and family days. I would have had more than two weeks if personal time could build from one year to the next. I rarely used my two weeks; a day off was a day with no billable hours at all.

'I need more than two weeks,' I said. Four minimum, I thought.

'Three, then.'

'Nine,' I countered.

'Bring me verification from two independent doctors that you need nine weeks, and I'll give you that.'

I was silent, trying to choose my next move, when he said on a surprisingly compassionate note, 'Four. That's my best offer. We never do this, Emily. The only reason I'm even considering it is that I like you, and that I trust that you can work through this and return to be one of the firm's leaders. You know how to handle people. You could be our managing partner someday, and that makes what you and I decide right now crucial. We'll call it an administrative leave, but four is the best I can do. I'll hold your job that long.'

Four wasn't enough, but it was better than none. 'I'll take four. Thank you, Walter. You've been incredibly generous.'

'Will you keep in touch?' he asked with what sounded like actual concern. And funny, if I had ever heard that before in my dealings with Lane Lavash, I might have felt better about the culture of the place. Honestly? The idea of my being managing partner one day was pushing it a little — actually, pushing it a lot. Still, I appreciated his accommodation. Four weeks wasn't anywhere near what I'd need, but at least I'd have a job at the end.

If I wanted it. Which I might not. But burning every bridge made no sense.

So I promised to keep in touch and ended the call feeling a brief satisfaction. Now came James.

Bracing myself on pillows against the headboard, I tucked my knees up and dug my cold feet into the comforter. Holding the BlackBerry close, I put through the call.

His phone rang once, twice, a third time. I was trying to decide whether to leave a message, when he finally clicked in, but he didn't say a word.

'Are you there?' I asked timidly.

There was another silence before he said, 'I'm here.'

'Are you okay?' His voice didn't sound right. It wasn't familiar.

'What the fuck kind of question is that?' he shot back, but he sounded tired, like we'd been arguing for hours. 'My wife picks up and leaves without a word, and — and she wants to know if I'm okay? How would you be if I did that to you?'

'Devastated.'

'I am. And — and confused. If you want to leave me, the least you can do is to tell me why. Did I offend you? Is this about my ditching your firm dinner Friday night?'

I was silent. James knew me better than to think I'd done something so big for such a petty reason.

'Emily?' he asked cautiously, apparently afraid I'd hung up.

'I'm here. I just don't know what to say. That isn't why I left.'

'You were fine Thursday night.'

'You said that last time we talked, and maybe I was fine on the surface. But is what's on the surface all that counts?'

'If it's all I know, it is. Talk — talk to me, babe,' he begged.

85

'I've been talking for *months* about how much I hate my job and about how little time we have together.'

'Come on, Em.' He did sound familiar now, even the repeating of words that he did when he was too tired to be crisp. 'We all — all say those things. It's the nature of the beast.'

'What if I don't like that beast?'

'Don't like me?'

'Don't like our *lives*,' I corrected. 'It isn't just one thing — it's *everything*. I feel like a robot, clocking in, clocking out, rushing to yoga, rushing to book club, rushing to the dry cleaners before they close for the night. I can't breathe. That's what happened Friday morning. I was at work and I absolutely couldn't breathe.'

'Where are you?'

I ignored the question. 'We lead a life dominated by machines. Our careers were supposed to be about helping people, but we've become mid-level bureaucrats. We have no time for friends or for each other. I have never been so *lonely*. Don't you feel it?'

'I'm too busy to feel it.'

'But aren't you *hungry* to connect with another human being on a personal level?' I asked pleadingly, because I wasn't getting through, and that hurt. The James I'd known in law school would have understood. That James would have felt the loneliness. So either he had changed, or I had misjudged him from the start.

'Speaking of friends,' he said, 'Colleen Parker keeps calling here. You accuse *me* of not connecting, while you — you blow *her* off?'

'Colly's a perfect example of what I'm saying. I have no business being in her wedding. We're barely friends. And that's supposed to be okay? It's like the whole concept of friendship has been redefined. It's shallow. I am *lonely*.'

There was silence, then a quiet 'Is that your way of telling me you're seeing someone else?'

I thought of Jude. I wasn't seeing him, but I would if I stayed. Did I want that? No. Could I resist? No more than I'd been able to resist rushing to the window to hear the coyote last night. The two were related. On some level in me, there remained a fascination with both.

No way would James understand that, though, and he had given me the perfect opening. 'Are you?' I asked back.

'Agh. Is this about Naida again? Emily, I am not having an affair, not with Naida or anyone else.' He was so straightforward, so *blunt*, with no words repeated, that I actually believed him. 'I'm married to you, though it doesn't feel it right now. You left me. Do you want a divorce?'

'I did not leave you. I left the life that was consuming us, and *no*, I don't want a divorce. I want to work things out.'

'How can we, if we can't talk face-to-face? Where are you? You're not with your mom. I already called her.'

I pressed my fingertips to my brow. 'Oh, James.'

'She said walking out would be the last thing you'd do unless you were desperate. So if she believes you were desperate — and she claims not to know where you are — why isn't she worried?'

87

'Because she has faith in me,' I said. 'She's always believed I have common sense.'

'I used to, too, but — but this is insane.'

'Okay.' I tried a different tack, because this one clearly wasn't working. 'Suppose you're on the road, driving somewhere. What do you do when you take a wrong turn?'

'Ahh, hell,' he brayed. 'Here we go. Men are from Mars, yada yada. I keep going, you ask directions.'

'But I kept going, too, because I didn't realize I'd taken a wrong turn — because I didn't *want* to realize it until it got so bad I couldn't ignore it anymore. Last Friday was horrendous from the minute I woke up, but it was only more of what our lives have been for months, for *years*. What do you do when you take a wrong turn?' I asked rhetorically this time. 'Stop. Turn around. Go back.'

'You forgot the asking for directions part.'

'Who do I ask? I've been dropping hints to you for months, only you're too busy to hear. I want a marriage, James. I want there to be a you and me, but we don't have time. I want to be a lawyer, but the work I do isn't practising law. I want to have friends, but they're running like zombies themselves. I thought having a baby would help.'

'*Help?*'

'Force a change in my life. Get me off the treadmill. I want to hold something small and warm,' I pleaded, 'something that needs *me* and not just any woman, and I want to watch it grow without clocking in. I left my watch at

88

home, did you see? I want to make time stop — well, not stop, but slow down.'

'And that'll solve the baby problem? I hate to tell you this, but you can't get pregnant unless we have sex, and if you're there, and I'm here, we can't have sex. Where the hell are you?'

I sighed. 'It doesn't matter.'

'It sure does. My life is here, Emily. If you're not coming back, we have a problem.' He sounded worried. 'Is that what you're thinking?'

'I haven't thought that far.'

'What about your job? You can't just walk away from Lane Lavash and — and think they'll hold it while you decide whether or not you want it.'

'Walter's giving me four weeks. I talked with him a few minutes ago — and don't get in a huff about that,' I hurried to add, so that I didn't further bruise my husband's ego. 'I haven't been in touch with him since I saw him at work Friday morning, and I only called him now so that I'd know where I stood before I called you. He doesn't know anything, except that I have to be away.'

James was quiet.

'For what it's worth,' I added, 'he was very decent at the end.'

'How was he at the start?'

'Angry. Like you.'

'A major difference being that I'm your husband,' he said, but he was subdued.

I was thinking about these two men in my life. 'That's one of the problems, James. The way our lives work, I have more face time with Walter than with you. You have more face time with Naida than with me. We spend more time at work than anywhere else, including our home. Why are we carrying that huge mortgage, if we use the place only to sleep?'

'It's an investment. That's what all of it is, Em, an investment in our future. We discussed this. We knew what we were getting into when we took these jobs. We knew we'd be eaten alive in the short run.'

'For two years, maybe four, but it's been seven, and it's only getting worse. I don't see a light at the end of the tunnel, I'm sorry, but I don't.'

Neither of us spoke for a while.

Finally, sounding defeated, James said, 'Where does that leave us?'

'I need time.'

'Time to decide if you want me?'

'Time to decide what happened to our dreams.'

He didn't answer.

'Do you remember those dreams?' I asked. 'We dreamed of being good lawyers and really helping people. Instead, I spend my days in a cubicle, wearing a headset, typing complaints into a form, and you spend yours plea-bargaining. I know it takes time to build a practice, but the kinds of cases we're working on won't get us where we want to be. They may bring in big fees, but is that what it's all about? There has to be more. We were going to be the golden couple — outstanding at work, outstanding at home. Remember?'

'Maybe we were naïve.'

'Or took a wrong turn. Look at the whole

picture — work, friends, food, weekends. Even when you factor in the reality of paying our dues, we're not living out even a *shadow* of those dreams. Are *you* happy with the way we live?'

He seemed to consider that. 'No. But I can bear it until it improves.'

'That's all I'm asking now, James. Bear with me until I figure things out.'

'But what do I do in the meanwhile?'

I knew what he was about. James was goal-oriented, which was one of the things I had first loved. We had shared a goal in law school, shared a goal in taking the jobs that we had. Sitting idle would drive him crazy, not that there were many choices.

There was one, though. Vicki had cited a movie. I tweaked the concept. 'We could talk on the phone — like, set aside a time, make a date.'

He said nothing at first. Then, 'What kind of marriage is that?'

'A better one than we've had.' The idea was growing on me. 'We could talk, maybe argue, possibly find common ground.'

'On the *phone?* Who was complaining that her life was dominated by machines?'

He'd been listening. That was good. 'This is different,' I pushed. 'We'd be the ones in charge. I'm not averse to machines, James. I just think they've gotten the upper hand. We could reverse that.'

He grunted. 'Wouldn't it be a whole lot easier if you came back here so we could talk? Why won't you tell me where you are? What's the big secret?'

'No big secret. I just need to be alone.'

'I'm your *husband*,' he reasoned, setting off such silent fury in me — *my husband, where've you been, why do we never see each other, why the concern now?* — that I was mute. He must have felt the fury, though, because he said, 'Okay, we could meet halfway between there and here.'

'James,' I replied seriously, 'you could sell a GPS to a carrier pigeon. I can't do face-to-face yet. In two seconds flat, you'd convince me that my life isn't so bad.'

'It isn't.'

'For me it is.' It was as simple as that.

After a bit, he said quietly, 'Okay. I hear you. But I don't know. Phone sex?'

'Not sex.'

'Just kidding.'

'I'm not. I'm dead serious about this, James. I will not meet you in person until I get a grip on myself. The phone works for me. If you're talking with me, I know you're focused on me and not work. And I do like hearing your voice,' I added quietly, because even through his frustration, the familiar was there. James's voice is very male. Husky, it has depth and authority. And yes, sex appeal. All three would serve him well before a jury, *if* he ever got to court.

'I don't know,' that deep voice said, but I could tell he was wavering. 'It's embarrassing that we can't meet in person.'

'We will. Just not yet.'

'Nnnn, I don't like it.'

I held my breath. This was the moment when he might say that if I didn't return to New York, he would file for divorce. Like with the possibility of losing my job at Lane Lavash, I had thought this through, too. I didn't want a divorce, but I wasn't ready to return to New York. Call me stubborn. Or selfish. But I could still feel the panic of being unable to breathe, and until I was past that, I needed space. This was non-negotiable.

James must have heard it in my silence, because he said a conciliatory 'Will you leave your BlackBerry on so I can text in between?'

'If you were the only one texting, I could do that, but there's all this other stuff that makes me gag. I'll just turn it on for the phone. Today's Tuesday. How about Friday night? Say, seven o'clock?'

'Come on, babe,' he complained. 'Neither one of us is home by seven.'

'Maybe that needs to change.'

'Maybe I don't want it to change.'

A stalemate? Possibly. Alternately, he might be simply wanting to save face. I could compromise. In the end, I might have to. But not yet.

'Then I guess you have as much to think about as I do,' I said quietly. 'I'll call Friday at seven. Bye, James.' I ended the call before the awkwardness of saying *I love you* could creep in, though, truth be told, we hadn't said those words in months. I'm not saying we didn't feel them, just that we didn't say them.

But I wanted to say them. And I wanted to hear them.

So, with barely a breath, I made a final call.

7

'Mom?'

She gave a cry. 'Thank goodness, Emily! I've been thinking of you nonstop since James called! Are you all right?'

The sound of her voice brought a lump to my throat. As brightly as I could, I said, 'I'm fine. He said you weren't worried.'

'Well, of course he said that, because he doesn't know me. Did he think I would fall apart? Did he think I wouldn't have a clue where this had come from? Did he not realize I would *know* what you're feeling?'

Her words startled me. 'Actually, no,' I said slowly. 'He wouldn't realize it. I never told him what you did. I wasn't thinking about it myself. Wow. That's amazing.'

'Like mother like daughter, your father said.'

'You told Dad about me?' I felt a flicker of fear, which was sad. I was a grown woman, married, a lawyer. I had nothing to fear from my father.

Except his disappointment.

Which was no small thing.

'I had to,' my mother reasoned. 'You call him every Sunday. When you didn't this week, he called me, and then he called three times yesterday asking if I'd heard from you. As soon as James called me, I knew what you'd done.'

'And Dad blamed you? I'm sorry, Mom.'

'Don't be! I'm not. I am no longer married to the man, and as far as I'm concerned, *he* was the one who set the bad example, always talking about getting a better job, moving up, leaving a mark on the world. I am ten times happier not having that monkey on my back. And I am leaving my mark on the world, just not in a way that your father would put on a couple's résumé.'

Claire Scott currently sold underwear at Macy's, where there was no chance of upward mobility, only the satisfaction of fitting bras properly. As jobs went, it wasn't on his approved list, which, I had always suspected, was part of its appeal for Mom. She worked only enough hours to pay the bills, not a minute more, since her real love was holding babies. To satisfy that, she volunteered at a local NICU, and to see her work there, which I'd done, you would think she had a nursing degree.

What she did have, after raising two children, was the equivalent of a PhD in mothering and my undying respect. She had infinite patience with babies, an instinctive feel for how to hold this one or feed that one, a calm that children fed off, and a built-in alarm that told her when something was amiss. Mothering was all she had ever wanted to do.

My father had never accepted that. As soon as we were in school, he wanted her working outside the home, and it wasn't about money, it was the principle of it, he said. He claimed her intelligence was going to waste.

As a woman who wanted a baby and considered it a *luxury* to be a stay-at-home mom, I found that offensive.

On the flip side, despite his myopia, Dad has his strengths. I am a lawyer because of the example he had set practising law now for thirty-five years. Forever a public servant, Roger Scott never earned much, but he was scrupulously honest — and idealistic. He believed that even the most heinous criminal had civil rights. When it came to a rapist or serial killer, I had my doubts. But Dad insists that a civilized society has to maintain its civility by rising above.

When I chose law, he had been proud, and when I chose James, even more so. He believed that we would do as a couple what he and Mom had not.

He would not be happy with me now. I felt a pang thinking about that.

'Don't worry about your father,' Mom said now. 'I can handle him.'

'What about Kelly?' I asked cautiously. 'Is she driving you nuts?'

'Well, yes, there've been lots of calls from her, too.'

'Mom, about this party — '

'I don't want it, Emmie. You know that. I'd have gone along if you girls were both dead set on it, but big parties aren't my style. I'd far rather cook dinner for my family.'

'Not on your own birthday.'

'Yes, on my own birthday. Cooking's my thing. I'm having twelve for dinner tonight.'

That sounded like hell to me. Cooking brought out the worst of my insecurities. 'Who are they?'

96

'Just friends, but life is about people, and people need food to survive, and I do love to cook. I'm good at it. Even your father admits that. Given my druthers, I'd have you all over — children, grandchildren, even your father.' Her tone changed. 'Tell me about you.'

'You first,' I insisted. 'What were you feeling when you ran away?' I had never asked at the time, not wanting to know the details of my parents' divorce. And Mom usually avoided badmouthing Dad. But she must have known I needed honesty now, because she was blunt.

'I felt inadequate. In your dad's eyes, I was always that. This particular day, he made a snide remark when he was leaving for work, and I snapped — not at him, but inside me. You kids were all in college, and I suddenly saw that I was stuck alone with a man who, all those years later, was still wanting me to be someone I wasn't.'

Suddenly saw. That was what had happened to me Friday morning. I could also relate to *wanting me to be someone I wasn't*, though James couldn't be faulted for that. It had been all my doing. The question was whether James would love me if I was someone else.

'Were you thinking of divorce when you walked out?' I asked my mother.

'I'd been thinking about it for years.' She paused, guarded. 'Are you?'

'No,' I replied. Fingering my wedding band, I was suddenly weepy. 'I love the James I married. It's our life that I hate.' I began to cry, to sob actually, but this was different from my crying with Vicki. That was from exhaustion. With Mom

97

I was a child, small and confused.

Offering the occasional soothing murmur, she waited me out. When my tears finally slowed, I gave her a sniffly account of my flight from New York. I ended with Walter's offer.

'Four weeks is something,' she mused. 'I only took a week, but my choice was simpler. Stay with your father or not.'

'Where did you go?' Incredible that I had never asked before, but it was another of those details I hadn't wanted to know, and once she was back, it hadn't mattered.

'Cape Elizabeth.'

Whoa. 'That's only twenty minutes from the house.'

She chuckled. 'If you want to disappear, Emily, you can do it almost anywhere. Truth was, I didn't have the courage to go farther. I've always loved Cape Elizabeth. I felt at home by the sea. How could your father not have guessed?'

'Maybe it was too obvious.'

'Maybe he just didn't know me well enough.'

I might have said the same about James, only I was the guilty party in this, too. I was the one who had been less than forthright about certain parts of my past.

'Was it important to you that Dad not know?' I asked, because James was most bothered by that. I had never thought him to be controlling, certainly not of me, but he had repeatedly asked where I was.

'Roger's not knowing made me feel safe,' my mother said. 'He was always so quick to judge me. I knew that if I talked with him, he would convince me I was stupid to leave. But I couldn't think straight at home. Home was so cluttered with memories that I couldn't see the forest through the trees.'

At mention of the forest, I left the bed and went barefoot to the window. Clouds were drifting, turning the woods darker, but I knew what was there. A coyote had spoken to me last night. It might be hidden away now, asleep — or looking straight at me. I searched beside tree trunks and through ferns for a pair of golden eyes or large, pointy ears. Jude's coyote had been russet, with a bushy tail long enough to leave a trail in the snow, he said, and I half imagined he had run with it a time or two. Not that I'd seen it in winter myself.

Nor did I see it now. But that didn't mean it wasn't there. Coyotes knew how to be invisible.

'I didn't want him dragging me back until I'd made my decision,' Mom was saying.

My eyes continued to search the forest. 'How did you finally make it?'

'The hurricane. There was a bad one that year, do you remember?' I actually did. 'The phones were out. I couldn't reach Dad.'

'Mmm. The surf was ferocious. Three people died on the Maine coast, but a lot more might have, had they not evacuated and moved inland. I helped with cooking at one of the shelters.' A smile warmed her words. 'People kept thanking me, like I was worth something. It was food for my hungry soul — which isn't to say I wasn't looking over my shoulder half the time, afraid

99

your dad would have one of his investigators track me down.'

I froze, remembering the charcoal SUV that had been parked by the green. If it was waiting for someone, that someone had been remarkably slow. 'Would he do that to me? Ask him not to, Mom. Please? I'm in a totally safe place, a place where *I* feel at home. If he sends someone after me, I swear I will never talk to him again. Tell him that. Tell him I'm *fine*.'

'Are you, honey? I knew this was coming.'

That stopped me. 'How?'

'Your lifestyle. There's a sharp edge to it. James eggs you on.'

My head snapped back. Mom had never said anything negative about James before. Maybe I was being oversensitive, but I couldn't let the statement stand. 'He doesn't. We don't compete.'

'No?'

'No,' I argued, feeling betrayed. 'He and I have been a team from the start. It's always been us against them. James is my life,' I insisted.

'What about Jude?' Mom asked.

I barely breathed. 'What about him?'

'What part does he play in all this?'

'I haven't seen Jude in ten years,' I said with perhaps too much force, but she had taken me by surprise. She hadn't mentioned Jude once since my marriage to James.

'And you're not with him now?'

'Absolutely not!' I cried.

'Oh dear. I hit a nerve.'

'Mom,' I warned.

She paused, then let Jude go, but not the rest.

'Do you know, Emily, this is the longest conversation we've had in months?'

I calmed a little. 'That's not true. I was at the house with you in March.'

'With your laptop and your phone. You were never not plugged in.'

'Wrong. Wireless.'

'Emily. You know what I'm saying. We were never not interrupted.'

She might have been right, but this wasn't what I wanted to hear. 'You think James is bad for me.'

'I didn't say that, Emily. I said he eggs you on, and you buy into it. You create an intensity together.'

'But don't you see,' I said, desperate to explain it, 'the power thing is personal with you. It's everything Dad wanted and you didn't. But maybe I do.'

'Do you?'

Yes, I wanted to say but couldn't. 'I don't know,' I cried. 'That's what I have to decide.' *Tell me what to do*, I nearly added, wondering if this was what I needed most from her. But she couldn't tell me what to do. Her priorities weren't mine.

Not that I knew what mine were. That was a problem.

We let the argument cool. Finally, she sighed and said a quiet 'I love you, sweetheart.'

'I love you, too, Mom, which is why I need your support. James is my husband. Are you okay with that?'

'I want what you want.'

'Will you love me if I choose to go back to New York?'

'I want what you want,' she insisted. 'I worry, is all. Will you call again?'

I waited, hoping that in my silence she would actually answer what I'd asked. As the silence dragged on, though, the questions receded.

'Yes,' I finally said, 'I'll call.'

'Do you promise?'

'Yes,' I repeated, and only after we'd clicked off realized she hadn't asked where I was. I kind of figured that she knew, since she'd asked about Jude. Either that, or she didn't *want* to know, giving her one less thing to hide from my dad.

I moved my thumb to power off the BlackBerry, then paused. Powering off wasn't enough. I had talked with the three people who truly needed to hear my voice. The rest was trash.

Pulling up my in-box, I erased everything there. Had I erased something important? Possibly. Did I care? No. Looking at that little blank screen, I felt liberated.

In the same clean-slate spirit, I showered and, for the first time since leaving New York, blew my hair dry so that I could wear it down, and put on enough make-up so that I wouldn't look sick. I did this for me — not for James or for anyone at work — just for me.

When I reached the first floor, breakfast was being served in the dining room, where the large table was set and several guests were already seated. The Red Fox buffet might have been more modest than the one in the Berkshires, but it was no less appealing. I helped myself to a poached egg and bacon, and put a slice of thick cinnamon bread in the toaster, then poured a glass of fresh grapefruit juice and took coffee from the urn. When the toast was done, I joined the group at the table.

I got smiles from the five people there, the nearest being a woman close to my age, also alone. 'Morning,' she said as I settled into a chair. 'Are you here for the Refuge?'

'I am.' In the broadest sense of the word. 'You?'

She nodded. 'This is my vacation, third year in a row. I've been at the Refuge every day. I can't have a dog, no room, so I hang with them here. They're so needy, they just love you to bits, these dogs do. It's the best feeling.'

It was. The summer I was here, I had set out to work with dogs, but Kitty City had been two caretakers short. Some things happen for a reason; once I had cat fur on my jeans, I couldn't leave. Cats are about subtlety and reserve. Since their trust is harder to win, it is that much more precious when it comes.

In the years since that Bell Valley summer, a simple rub by a cat at the home of a friend had me aching to adopt. Though James wasn't a pet person, he certainly wasn't allergic.

But to bring a cat into a home where it would be alone for endless hours each day was cruel. Cats might be independent and self-sufficient if given a litter box and a bowl of food, but they remain social creatures. Kitty City proves that. It isn't that you're mobbed when you open the

103

door, but spend a week in Kitty City, and you'll be greeted, in one form or another, by every cat in the place.

Having finished eating, the woman put her dishes on a small tray by the kitchen door, waved at me, and left.

By the time I finished my protein, my toast had gone cold. Back home, I would have eaten it anyway. But I wasn't back home, and I had time to eat something else, and, yes, toast was the healthier choice, but the pecan muffin tops on the buffet looked too good.

Indulging myself, I took one and returned to the table. I was eating slowly, enjoying the act of enjoying the taste of something rich and robust, when I sensed I was being watched. Guilt, I thought, and, sitting straighter, sucked in my stomach. But the sensation remained. I glanced up, found no one, glanced farther up — and caught my breath. Jethro Bell was staring at me. He stood at the centre of a large, ornately framed painting, and though he was surrounded by family, the oils gave light to his eyes alone.

The last time I saw this painting it was hanging in Vicki Bell's family home. Jude had commented on the power of those piercing gold eyes, which was actually quite funny, since he had the same ones. Jethro had died long before Jude was born, but it was Jude's eyes I saw now, as fiercely independent as ever.

That stopped me short. Fiercely independent, but warm? Would I describe Jude as a warm human being? Passionate, yes. Totally, sexually hot. But did he genuinely care for people?

Studying that painting, I saw passion in those gold eyes but not warmth. I didn't see it in any of the family members portrayed here.

With one last look, I returned to my breakfast. Better Jude watching me than a goon of my dad's, I thought, but moments later, felt the eyes again. This time they belonged to Vicki, who stood at the kitchen door, clearly pleased to see me in public. She held my gaze for a minute before approaching the table to chit-chat with her guests. I listened as I ate, marvelling at how good she was at small talk. Baseball, butterflies, the weather — what might have been considered shallow in another setting was human interest here. Vicki made her guests feel at home. I suspected that Bell Valley repeaters came as much for the Red Fox as the Refuge.

After directing several new arrivals to the buffet, she hunkered down by my chair and said a private 'You look better. Sleep well?'

Actually, I had not. But I didn't want to talk about that, or about the calls I had made. Seeing Vicki now, there was only one thing to say. 'I heard it,' I whispered. 'Last night. A coyote.'

She looked doubtful. 'You must have been dreaming.'

'I thought I was, then I woke up and heard it twice more. You didn't hear it?' She shook her head. 'I didn't imagine it, Vicki. It was talking to me.'

'Emmie.' This, sympathetically.

'I swear it,' I insisted, because I knew what I'd heard. 'There's a coyote in the woods. I heard dogs barking in response. Ask your neighbours.'

'I will, but I know you, Emmie, you're thinking that this is poetic. Do. Not. Go chasing it. What there *are* in those woods are bears.'

I wasn't rushing into the woods, but that didn't mean my thoughts didn't. 'What happened to Jude's cottage?'

'It's still there.'

'Is it occupied?'

'Not by any human I know,' she warned, 'so if you're thinking you want to spend a few days there communing with nature, I'd think again.' Her voice returned to a whisper. 'Have you heard anything more?'

From Jude. I shook my head.

'I'm feeling guilty not warning Mom, but I can't get her hopes up. He said he'd be here at the end of the month. So, does that mean the twenty-eighth? Twenty-ninth? Thirtieth? Typical Jude not to be specific. He'll do what suits him.'

'Did your mom keep up the cottage for him?'

'Are you kidding? She *hated* that place. It stood for everything Jude rejected in us. Besides, it's bad luck. Jude was the first one to live there in fifty years, and the man before him was a hermit who froze to death in the snow. So Jude lived there and disappeared.'

'He didn't disappear in the woods.'

'You know what I mean. Please, Emmie. If you want to camp near the woods, take the gardener's shed.'

The gardener's shed was safe, with its awning shutters and door bolts. It housed no bears, fisher cats, or foxes, just spiders crawling over vintage lawn mowers, hoes, and hoses. There was, though, plenty of room on the dirt floor for sleeping bags. I knew this for a fact.

But ten years later, I wanted a bed. 'Thanks, but I'll stay where I am. My room has charm.'

Vicki smiled. 'So does the shed. We put guests there sometimes.'

'You do not.'

'We do.'

'Then you've renovated that, too,' I guessed, and looked up at the painting. 'Jude would be disappointed.'

'He is not in that painting,' Vicki whispered.

'His eyes are.'

'I try not to look.' She rose, leaving a hand on my shoulder. 'So we've established that you're not going into the woods? Good. What'll you do today instead?'

The painting held me. There were fifteen Bells in it — eight adults and seven children — and though the family resemblance was marked, looks seemed to be the only thing tying the fifteen together. There were no laced fingers, no linked arms. I saw one hand on one shoulder, but it wasn't warm and natural, like Vicki's. It was formal and cold.

Cold. That described it. Gold eyes notwith-standing, this group was cold — which was so totally the opposite of what I needed in my life.

Unconditional love. In that instant, I felt a sharp craving for it, and there was one place I knew I would find it in spades.

8

The charcoal SUV was there again when I left the Red Fox, but it didn't follow me. I would have known if it had. Only one road went to the Bell Valley Refuge, a two-laner that hugged the hills, but I saw nothing in my rearview mirror during the ten-minute drive.

There was plenty to see ahead, though. With the hills on my left, on my right were June fields that held the beginnings of corn stalks, neat green rows of lettuce, and the first of the strawberry harvest. Beyond were rows of carefully cropped trees that would yield a dozen varieties of apples in September and, even farther, the spiked tops of Christmas-trees-to-be.

I eased up on the gas as I drove, everything around me saying, *Slow down, there's no rush.* Traffic was non-existent. The only vehicles I passed were pickups heading into town with lawn mowers, electrical supplies, cartons of dawn-picked strawberries destined for the General Store.

The sign marking the Refuge entrance was discreet, though the wide driveway flanked by stone columns couldn't be missed. The nearby maples had grown taller and wider in the years since I had been here last, but otherwise it was exactly the same. I parked in the lot adjacent to a Colonial that had been built in the style of the houses in town. It held the administrative offices of the Refuge, as well as the visitors centre.

I had barely opened the car door when I smelled horse and hay, bringing warm memories to chase away the last of the Bell portrait chill. Amazing, really, that this shelter, which exuded heart, could have been created by a cold man. Of course, I'm jumping to conclusions. I hadn't known Jethro Bell. I'm not even sure why I had such a negative reaction to him now. A painting was only as honest as the artist, and I knew nothing about this one.

But I did know the Refuge. And it knew me, I realized with a start. I had been here nearly every day for three months, and not with Jude. He liked his animals wild — as in dangerously feral, which was why he lived deep in the woods — and though he guided major benefactors through the Refuge, it was more for the sake of money than interest. His charisma got them every time, and, of course, if there was a woman in the group, he poured it on. Though Amelia considered this to be productive management, for Jude it was pure ego. Given a choice, he would be in Amelia's office lobbying for policy issues that appealed to him, like how large a team to send to the latest global disaster.

No, that summer I had come out here alone. I was guessing the personnel hadn't changed much, which meant I might be recognized, and I wasn't eager for that.

But this was where I needed to be. So I put on my hat, pulled my hair through the back, and, dragging in that familiar horse-and-hay scent to ease my unease, left the car.

The receptionist did look familiar. But she was in her early twenties, too young for me to have worked with back then, and she looked like Vicki, a Bell cousin, hence the familiarity.

I signed in as Em Aulenbach, not the Emily Scott I had been ten years before. There was a form to fill out, with boxes to check and signatures releasing the Refuge from responsibility should I be bitten by an animal. This was new and good, I supposed. Fear of litigation was a fact of modern life.

The girl was working her iPhone and didn't look up when I set off. The lawyer in me — perhaps the part of me that felt protective of this place — wanted to remind her of another fact of modern life. Bad guys. For all she knew, I was a crazy woman wanting to run from cage to cage setting animals free.

But Bell Valley was a trusting place. I had locked my car here out of habit; you didn't leave things unlocked in New York. But this young woman was used to people who cared. She was spoiled. Complacent, perhaps — like me, building the life I was running from now.

Actually, that was wrong. I had never been complacent. I was driven.

But it was forgotten the minute I went out the back door and entered the heart of the Refuge. Like the smell of horse and hay, there was nothing stressful here. The only sounds were leisurely — barks, clucks, the occasional whinny or bray. The humans I saw were walking alone or in twos, without pressure or rush.

The Refuge was a warren of bungalows, each

built of wood from local trees. The history of the place could be told by the weathering of that wood, with the lighter, newer structures proof of the Refuge's expanding mission. I passed the weather vane of lopsided signs pointing every which way for barn, pasture, dogs, rabbits, or cats. But here, at least, I knew where I was going.

Kitty City had grown since I'd been here last, with several new wings and a screened-in playground at the back. With the roof screened as well, cats could bask in the sun yet be safe from predators — yes, like coyotes, which do go for small pets, though strictly for survival, Jude always said. They generally avoided civilization as long as there was prey enough in the woods.

Entering Kitty City now, I felt a wave of nostalgia. The reception area was small, with one cat curled on the desk chair, another in the wire in-box, another atop the filing cabinet, sitting straight, staring at me. That one was missing a front leg. I guessed that the two others had disabilities as well. That they looked healthy and content was a tribute to the care they received.

'Hi, there,' said a stocky woman, coming in from a side room.

'I hope you're here to work. We're in need.'

'So am I,' I said. 'Where first?'

She gestured me through another door. 'To the end of the hall, then right. That's the Rescue Centre. They blame the economy for making people drive miles from home to abandon pets on the roadside, but these cats can't survive on their own. They're brought in here maimed and malnourished. A few of the ones that are here

111

now were rescued from a house where authorities found twenty-two dead cats. Can you imagine? The ones that survived need patience and love. I'm Katherine, by the way. I used to be Kat, but that didn't . . . ' *work here for obvious reasons*, I finished silently as she spoke the words. It was her stock line, used ten years ago, too. Some things never changed. That was actually refreshing.

'You look familiar,' she said, studying my face.

'I was here a while back,' I remarked offhandedly.

She nodded, seeming satisfied, as we reached the end of the hall. 'You remember the drill.'

'I do.'

'Are you okay here by yourself?'

'I am.' I preferred it, actually. I hadn't come here for people.

Opening the door only enough to slip through, I closed it before any cats could escape. As it happened, the precaution was unnecessary. There was no rushing to greet me; these cats had seen the worst of humanity, and I was not to be trusted. Cats were discriminatory that way. They didn't go to just anyone.

I felt eyes studying me, but there was no mystery to it here. Cats were everywhere — on walkways, under chairs, inside boxes deliberately left for those needing to hide. Large pet crates sat in a clump, their doors open, fleece beds and old blankets holding cats at every tier. I saw a small tiger with a scab on its shoulder, above it a dun tabby with vulnerable eyes, and, below, a furry grey creature that was badly in need of a brushing.

Instinctively soothing, I cooed, 'Hello, you're so sweet, ooooh look at you, pretty thing, come say hi, I won't hurt,' and still there was no movement. I heard the occasional soft meow, though couldn't figure out which had spoken. Cats of all sizes and shapes were statue-still, watching me with a wariness that broke my heart. I had my work cut out for me.

Energized, I took supplies from the closet. Talking softly all the while, I cleaned litter boxes, refilled food bowls, freshened water. I mopped the floor, careful not to sweep the yarn mop too close to any cat, and, even then, a few scattered from its reach. By the time I was done, though, others had begun to approach. Holding a handful of treats, I sat on the floor in the middle of the room. One cat approached guardedly, sniffed, jerked back. Apparently liking what it sniffed, it came forward again and cautiously, cautiously, took the treat from my hand with the faintest whisper of a tiny wet nose. A second cat followed, then a third. Gradually the meows grew more confident.

I'm not sure how long I sat, but I greeted each cat in the same soft breath. Some had bald spots where an infection was being treated, others had scars or scabbed ears or crooked limbs. When a tiny calico, likely full-grown but malnourished, rubbed its sweet little apricot-and-white head against my arm, my heart melted.

'Hello, angel,' I murmured, feeling victorious when it let me scratch it between the ears. I told another curious comer, 'Aren't *you* a handsome boy,' and a third, this one with a bright red scar where an ear had once been, 'You are a *total* love.'

They were. Each one of them. They needed love, and little by little, despite their scars, bruises, and maimings, they were loving me back, each one telling me how right I was to come here. Even scut work felt good. There were no hums, whirs, or dings; the smell of cat food was preferable to that of the sub a colleague at Lane Lavash ate in his cubicle daily, and as for caring, cats had it over the firm management any day.

I had a focus here and refused to look past the moment. This wasn't my future. But it was the very last place where I had been unequivocally happy, which made it a good place to start.

★   ★   ★

I spent all of Tuesday in the Rescue Centre. *Hiding out with the cats,* Vicki accused that night, but I wasn't deterred. Absent a clock, time passed in the most natural of ways, the quiet broken only by soft mews and my own coos.

I made headway with all but the most emotionally bruised of the cats, but it was during a short stint in Rehab on Wednesday morning that I fell in love. She was three months old, a nondescript grey kitten that could have curled up on my Kindle with no overhang at all. Smaller than the others there, most of whom had fresh scars and missing limbs, she was watching from the wall nearly a dozen feet from where I sat on the floor, and showed no outward sign of disability until she moved. Though her stance was wide enough to give her balance, her movements were jerky. She was sidling against the wall, clearly using it for support, but her eyes never left mine.

'Oh my,' I whispered, and leaned back on an elbow to be closer. 'Hi, there. How are you?'

Determined, I thought in response. Despite tremors and a near spill, she continued toward me, leaving the wall only when she was close enough to shift her negligible weight to my arm. 'Oooh, pretty,' I crooned, letting her rub me, and still her eyes held mine. They were green and, like her ears, disproportionately large. *Don't leave*, those big eyes said, piercingly plaintive. *I'm trying, really I am.*

With exquisite care, I lifted her and, stroking her quivering body, settled her into my lap.

The woman who headed the Rehab Centre knelt beside me.

'She has cerebellar hypoplasia. Her brain didn't develop properly. The cerebellum is too small.'

'What causes that?'

'A number of things can. We're guessing she was exposed to feline distemper at a crucial gestational stage. Kittens like this look normal until they start to move around. Then, well, you just saw it.'

'Tremors?'

'Tremors, poor coordination, lack of balance. She falls in the litter box. She falls trying to eat and drink. They found her cowering beside a shelf in the supermarket. She must have been left there by someone who didn't want her but couldn't completely throw her away.'

Throw her away. My heart broke. I leaned closer to the kitten. She had the same faint barn smell as the Refuge, but her little body was comfortingly warm. 'How long can she last?'

'Oh, very long. We can't do anything about the underlying condition, but with certain adjustments, she can live well. She needs a litter box with a low entry point and high sides. She needs her water and food in raised bowls. Walkways are a danger — she'd easily fall from a high place, which is one of the reasons she's in this room. Here, she's in a safe environment so that she can move around. The more she moves, the better she'll adapt to her condition.'

I stroked her tiny head, fragile beneath my fingers. Her fur was of medium length and stood on end, giving her a wild look, though she was totally docile in my lap. Eyes half shut, she was tucked in the crook of my leg with one little paw against my knee.

'She is precious,' I said. 'Does she have a name?'

'We've been calling her Baby because she's so small, but I like what you just said. Precious. Her birth family had low expectations of her, but she's apt to surprise us all.'

'Precious,' I whispered, and imagined that her ears perked up, but her eyes had closed, and she slept.

★   ★   ★

116

Other volunteers came and went. They called me Em and had no knowledge of my history with the Bells. At times, I even forgot it myself. This was part of my therapy, supplanting old memories with new ones, and I was successful at it until Wednesday afternoon, when I was leaving the Refuge and felt I was being watched. I half expected to see the charcoal SUV parked nearby, but it was not. Instead, glancing back at the Administration Building from my car, I saw Amelia Bretton Bell on the front porch. She was leaning against the railing holding a tall glass, and might have been leisurely enjoying a cold drink at the end of the day, had it not been for the intensity of her stare.

My heart fell. My link to Amelia should have been Vicki, but it was the spectre of Jude that stood between us.

I smiled, waved. When she returned neither, I thought of simply climbing into my car and driving off. I had been hoping to make tea at the inn. After a long day of work, I was tired.

But it was a good tired. I felt mellow. And she was Vicki's mother, the matriarch of the family, the Grand Dame of the Refuge. Out of respect alone, I slipped the keys back in my pocket and crossed the parking lot.

Halfway to the Colonial, I called, 'How are you, Amelia?'

'Surprised,' she replied in the bold alto I remembered so well. An attractive woman with salty hair and eyes whose gold was a mere dusting on fawn, she didn't look surprised. She looked *annoyed*. 'I hadn't thought you'd come

117

back here. How did the big city spare you? Isn't scooping cat litter a tad beneath lawyering in New York?'

'Litter is the least of it,' I said, humouring her as I climbed the porch steps. 'Working with cats is emotional. It's refreshing.' And exactly what I had missed. There was nothing intellectually taxing here, just plenty of heart and soul. 'Besides,' I added, making light of her dig, 'I shovel my share of waste in New York.'

'But you're used to excitement. I hate to tell you this, honey,' she said, cutting to the chase, 'but Jude is gone.'

Not for long, I thought as I had when Vicki had made a similar remark. But Vicki didn't want to tell Amelia, and I respected her reasons.

'I didn't come here for Jude,' I replied now.

'Of course not. You have a husband. It didn't take you long to find one after you dumped my son.'

The charge startled me. 'I didn't dump him, Amelia. He dumped me.'

'And you ran.' I was searching for a response while she drank from her glass, but she was quick. 'You could have fought for him. But you never planned to stay here. All along, you had your eye on something bigger.'

I sputtered a facetious laugh. 'Bigger than Jude? Jude Bell was bigger than life.'

'The expression is '*larger* than life',' Amelia corrected, and frowned at her glass. 'He was my son. He was the light of my life.'

When he was younger, certainly. When he faced a life of promise. Jude the Adult had been

118

an everyday thorn in her side, though Amelia wouldn't be thinking of that. She spoke as though he were dead, and her pain was very real. Vicki Bell might be right. If he didn't show, it would kill her again.

Thinking that he was a selfish bastard, I said, 'I'm sorry, Amelia.'

Her eyes flew to mine. 'Excuse me?' she asked with feigned politeness. 'Is that an apology? For what? Running away? Not fighting to keep him here?' Her face held the same coldness I had seen in the Bell family portrait. 'You were selfish. It was all about Emily. You hung around only as long as it suited you, then you ran. I always wondered why your parents never came here. If you were so in love with my son, wouldn't they have wanted to meet him?'

'That summer was a bad one for them.' Mom had just bought her own place, Dad was not happy in his, and I was trying to straddle the chasm. Bell Valley had been an escape for me that summer, too.

Maybe Amelia was right. I had run from Jude's betrayal just as I'd run from my parents' divorce. And now I had run from New York.

I was wondering what that said about me as a person, when Amelia asked, 'Why are you here?'

Good question. Running was fine, as long as there was a point. Not wanting to say how bad my city life was, I simply said, 'I felt the need to reconnect.'

'To Vicki? To cats? To Jude? He didn't love you, you know. He loved Jenna Frye. They would have married if you hadn't come along. You were a toy, an impulse buy.'

'He went back to Jenna.'

'But not for marriage. She wouldn't have him, not after you.'

The words hurt not because they were unfair — I hadn't been able to control Jude any more than she had — but because I had grown to respect Amelia the summer I was here. She was a smart woman, the first female at the helm of the Refuge, and a good businessperson. I hated that I evoked something so mean-spirited in her.

Saddened, I said, 'Would you rather I not work here?' I wasn't offering to leave Bell Valley. After accusing me of repeatedly running from adversity, I wouldn't let her run me out of town. Only Vicki could do that.

Seeming to realize it, she made a dismissive sound and, turning away, murmured, 'Do what you want.' As she headed back inside, she took a drink from her glass. The liquid was clear. I had assumed it to be water. It struck me now that it was not.

Of course, that was wishful thinking. Blaming her hostility on liquor made the words easier to take.

* * *

You were selfish. It was all about Emily. You hung around only as long as it suited you, then you ran.

Amelia's words haunted me, because they so related to what was happening right now with my marriage and my job. As revived as I had felt

120

leaving the cats, I was suddenly filled with self-doubt.

But I did want to think of myself as brave, which was why, on my way back to town, I turned off the main road onto a nearly hidden dirt path, a rutted logging lane that had once been tamed by the wheels of Jude's pickup. In ten years' time, the forest had begun to reclaim it. As my car began the climb, it was lashed by branches and jostled by rocks, not exactly what my husband had envisioned for the BMW, but this was the easiest way of getting where I had to go. It was also the safest. These woods were farther from town and climbed higher than those behind the Red Fox. There were moose here — harmless unless confronted even inadvertently, at which point they could charge. There were fisher cats and bobcats, foxes and porcupines. And bears. *And* coyotes. Vicki still denied it, but I had heard them again Tuesday night. They were talking to me.

I jounced upward at a painstaking five miles per hour, sun low, headlights on. With aspens watching and ferns crowding in, the road seemed way too long. I was starting to wonder whether the clearing I sought had vanished — been reclaimed by a wilderness that hadn't wanted humankind here at all — when the road levelled and the foliage fell back.

As I eased my foot off the gas, the brush under my tyres brought the car to a stop. My eyes were a minute adjusting, separating the darkest of forest green from pied granite, but then I sat, hands gripping the wheel against a wave of memory.

Jude's cottage was made of stone, a one-room deal with a narrow porch, doll's house windows, and a steep-pitched roof. It remained much as I remembered, if ten years wilder. Ferns hugged the porch, keeling despite their support. Large patches of moss had spread to most of the roof. And the windows I had tried in vain to scrub clean wore a veil of birch flowers, stuck there by spring rain.

Touching the gas, I inched forward. I parked where I always had, in the spot that was barely a spot anymore, beside the pickup that was no longer there, and half expected Jude to stride through that thick wood door to greet me.

Actually, no. He had never done that. He might stand at the door and wait, a half smile on his handsome face the only sign of pleasure. Amelia had called me a toy, in which case the pleasure was amusement. Whatever, he wasn't there now. The door remained closed, its wrought iron latch dusted with pollen.

I was reaching to open my car door, when I paused. We were still hours from dark this time of year, but with the sun now on the other side of the mountain, the woods were dusky. There was something eerie about this place. I definitely felt a chill.

But time was short. I couldn't come here in the dark and I couldn't come once Jude was back. If I was to be brave, it had to be now. Besides, those doll's house windows were watching me, daring me, amused in a cocky way, as perhaps Jude had been.

Determined, I opened the door and climbed

out. The air smelled of pine, pungent and viscerally familiar. As I crossed a rough bed of needles and dirt, I heard the rustle of under-brush, but the sound was too small to be something to fear. I had barely swatted at a swarm of no-see-ums when I slapped a mosquito dead on my arm.

I had forgotten about the bugs. Spring had been moist that year, too, raising a bumper insect crop in the stream that gurgled just over the rise, and I was their favourite meal. Jude blamed my shampoo, my soap, my body cream, but I hadn't been able to give any up.

Waving a hand around my head to keep the flyers at bay, I heard the stream, the flap of a startled hawk, the snap of debris as I walked. The porch steps were intact, though littered with woodland waste. Stepping over a dead branch, I approached the oak door and raised the latch. I had to put my whole body into moving the thick wood, and a few inches was all I got, but it was enough to slip through.

The air was stale. That hit me. Then the gloom. With the two front windows giving only spotty light, the place was dark. But not *that* dark. Ignoring the scarred desk, I saw the old sofa and, behind it, the shelves stuffed full of books on foreign lands and distant ports. Photos tacked to the pine walls had curled at the edges, but there he was, hang gliding into the Grand Canyon in one and, in another, planting a flag in Antarctica.

Jude had taken pride in these shots, and thinking him a true adventurer, I had been duly impressed. Not that there was much risk in this small, contained place. What you saw was what you got — knotty wood walls, exposed rafters. Jude had cooked on a crude wood-burning stove, and had slept in the loft. His mattress was still there, bedding spilling over the side as he must have left it the day he'd packed up and driven off.

It struck me that no one had been here since, which was not surprising. The Bells had viewed this cottage as an obscene gesture, another instance of Jude thumbing his nose at what they stood for, right up there with refusing to live in the family mansion, refusing to wear khakis to church, refusing to cut his hair.

I imagined strands of that hair were up there on the pillow still. Mine might be there, too. And Jenna's.

I hadn't made it to the loft the last time I'd been here. They had been making love on that pitted desk, a sprawl of nudity hitting me the instant I walked in the door. He must have planned it. He knew I was coming. I carried groceries for a celebratory dinner; the next day, I was driving to New Haven to sublet the apartment I wouldn't need if I wasn't going to law school. I dropped the groceries, but didn't speak. I remember feeling a sudden draining of my blood, which was how I remained — blood-less and cold — for a week back in that empty apartment in New Haven before deciding that life went on. What was it Mom said, that success was the greatest revenge?

Perhaps that was why I had gone at law school

so avidly, or why I had thrown myself into James, who had seemed perfect for me at the time.

And now? I wasn't sure about law or James, but Jude's cabin looked shabby and old. Jude himself might be shabby and old. Crab fishing in the Bering Sea had to cause wear and tear, and there had been four years prior to that — of what? Hunting the great white off the South African coast? Handling boas in the Amazon? Had Jude not left here, there would have been photos of him wading through the waters of post-Katrina New Orleans, searching through the devastation of post-tsunami Indonesia, or leading an entourage through post-earthquake Haiti, all under the guise of doing Refuge business.

Was he larger than life? Maybe, maybe not. Maybe he wasn't any different from the rest of us, searching for what we wanted, not quite knowing what it was until we stumbled on it. I was stumbling — from Cape Cod, to the Berkshires, to Bell Valley — but it didn't feel as aimless as it had. Taking a last breath of this faded place, I emerged into what was left of the day and, tugging the door shut behind me, felt lighter of heart. I had faced the past without crumbling. I could face Jude.

Pleased, I crossed the narrow porch and started down the steps. I was reaching to toss away the fallen branch, when I paused. *Leave it*, Nature said, and she was right. The cottage was hers, this branch her name plate. Jude would move it. But not me.

Straightening, I stepped over it and started

toward the car, but again I stopped. Something was different now. Surely the light, which was dimmer than before. But there was more.

I was being watched. Something was out there. I wasn't alone.

My imagination kicked in, actually a good thing after several years with none. Like the taste of food, imagination was now something recovered, for better or worse. I imagined a bear. I imagined a mountain lion. I imagined *Jude*.

What I sensed, though, was something less fierce, which was why I didn't fly to the car. All was silent. There were no chipmunks, no squirrels, no bats streaking through the murk in search of bugs. Other than the distant hoot of an owl, I heard nothing but my own thudding heart.

Funny, though, I wasn't frightened. I was alone in the woods, a solid mile from the road, all of which should have freaked me out. But I was calm. Excited, actually. I scanned the perimeter of the clearing, trying to sift fauna from flora, but the light was low. More than once I imagined a breathing shape, only to realize it was a sapling or a rock.

Then my eyes skimmed a spruce, went past, and back. Still it was a moment before I homed in on the gold eyes that stared at me through the serrated fronds. In that moment of connection, I barely breathed.

The moment was broken by a howl from deeper in the woods, and my coyote was suddenly gone, evaporated into the forest with an economy of sound. I stood for a while, watching the spruce, waiting, hoping the coyote would return, but it

126

did not. Nor did I hear it howl to its mate, but now I knew. There were two.

Still watching for movement near the spruce, I approached the car. Only when I looked down for my keys did something red register. My eyes flew to the side of the clearing. The red was part of a plaid shirt, and the plaid shirt was on Jude.

This was no vision. It was the man himself, broad-shouldered as ever, standing with one booted foot on a rock, and indolent gold eyes fixed on me. And suddenly, despite my newfound strength — perhaps *because* of it — I saw red in a way that had nothing to do with his shirt.

9

'You *bastard*,' I cried, trembling with a rage that must have been simmering since that day when I had found Jude with Jenna and said nothing at all. 'What are you doing here?'

He smiled with surprising gentleness. 'I told you I was coming.'

'At the end of the month, you said — and why haven't you told your family? That would have been the decent thing to do. Okay,' I barrelled on, 'so then you'd have felt obligated to come, which is the last thing you want, but why tell *me*? All those letters — *why*? And your not writing to *them* — not one word in ten years — do you know how *selfish* that is?'

'Yes,' he said.

His lack of smugness took something from my anger. Still, there was enough left for me to say, 'You've hurt so many people, Jude. I can't tell them what to do, but if you were *my* brother, I'd have burned this place down.'

'Stone doesn't burn.'

'I'd have left it a shell with nothing inside. That's what you did to your mother.' When he didn't blink, I added, 'And your sister, and me, and Jenna. It's been a long time, and our lives are filled with other things now, so what makes you think anyone wants you back? Ahhh.' I saw. 'That's it. You were afraid if you told them ahead of time, they'd tell you not to come? You were afraid they *wouldn't* want you back.' I stared at him. 'Why are you grinning? If you're trying to look cute, don't. You're too old.'

The grin didn't slip. 'You're not. You look great, Emily. I couldn't have asked for a better homecoming gift. Missed me, did ya?'

And there it was, a bit of the old cockiness, easy to resent. 'Actually, no,' I replied calmly. 'My life has been pretty busy.'

'But you came back as soon as I wrote — '

'No,' I cut in to make it clear, 'I came back because I needed a rest. I was actually hoping to be gone before you arrived.' I studied his face, easier to see since he had cut his hair short. 'You've lost weight.' He looked gaunt without his curls, and there was a mean two-inch scar on his jaw. 'What did you walk into?'

'A fist. Tempers get short out there, and some of the guys are raw. I've learned how to fight.'

'Nice,' I mused.

'No, but it's one way to survive.'

And Jude did pride himself on surviving. 'So here you are.' He nodded. 'Unfinished business.'

'Well, you did say that in your letter, but since when does Jude Bell finish business?'

His smile faded. 'Since he turned forty. Since he saw a good friend swept into water where he didn't have a chance of makin' it out alive.' He looked genuinely upset.

I had to soften. 'I'm surprised you didn't go in after him.'

'Oh, I did. If I hadn't been tethered, I'd have drowned, too. We never recovered the body.'

I had assumed there were safeguards against

129

that kind of thing, but even more surprising to me was what actually sounded like sorrow. The Jude I had known was passionate, but not sentimental. Nor had he had many male friends. All men were rivals, as per his wildest ancestor. He was part lion, he claimed, citing his thick blond mane as proof.

The mane was now gone, but there was still an appeal. Some element of his magnetism remained, and though I found it only vaguely sexual, it was gripping. I stood there, maybe fifteen feet from him, unable to move.

'I just came from seeing his family.' He remained sombre. 'He had a wife and four kids. He was crabbing for the money to support them. So I gave them his things and what he was owed, and when they didn't invite me to stay, I left.' He brightened. 'So, yeah, here I am, seeing to unfinished business.'

'Like what?'

'My mother. The Refuge. My son.'

I recoiled. 'Son?' Vicki hadn't mentioned a son. Nor had Amelia.

He smiled, amused by that. 'They didn't tell you? Jenna had a baby after I left — and yeah, I knew she was pregnant, but she had promised me she was protected, so it wasn't really my fault. Anyway, she's married to another guy now and has three kids.'

Without those last words, I might have argued that simply by participating in the act, he was responsible. But three kids? I would give anything for one, and James would never, ever be as casual about fathering a child as Jude was.

James certainly wouldn't turn his back on one. He was as eager for them as I was.

I felt suddenly more vulnerable, but if my voice showed it, Jude was too into enjoying my shock to notice. 'Are they here in town?' I asked.

'Sure are. Jenna wouldn't have the guts to leave. She married a local boy.'

'How do you know this?'

'Google. A few clicks, and ta-da, the local paper. A few more clicks, and ta-da, your address. So. How's it going at Lane Lavine?'

'It's Lane Lavash, and it's fine.' Not a total lie. Walter was holding my job.

Jude snorted. 'Jenna didn't wait long, either. Married him before the kid was born. It would've been nice if she'd waited — y'know, to see if I'd be back.'

'*Waited?*' I asked, totally identifying with Jenna just then. 'How could she wait? *Why* would she wait? You hurt her by cheating with me, then you went back to her to hurt me, then you left. If you ask me, she did the smart thing.'

He shrugged it off. 'Well, anyway, the boy's nine. I figure I oughta meet him before he hits puberty.'

'To give him tips?' I asked cynically. 'He might do better without. Who's his dad?'

'Me.'

'No. His *dad*. The one who's been raising him.'

He shrugged again. 'Nice guy, works for the Refuge. So does Jenna, which tells you Amelia's involved, and don't bother to ask how she learned the boy's mine. He looks just like me

131

— I've seen pictures in the paper — and even if he didn't, Mother would have done the maths. I assume the whole town did.' He grew suddenly earnest. 'Don't tell them I'm here, Emily. I'll tell them myself.'

'When?' I asked, and might have wondered if he was indeed afraid of the reaction to his return if I hadn't still been hung up on the son. I couldn't imagine what it was like for Amelia, seeing Jude's face in the boy and being constantly reminded that the light of her life didn't care enough to call. Not on Thanksgiving or Christmas. Not on a birthday. If I ever missed my mother's birthday, she would be crushed.

Jude didn't answer my question. So I prompted, 'Bell Valley's a small place. Do you honestly think no one saw you coming out here?'

'Yeah, I think that. I thumbed my way east — '

'Thumbed,' I echoed, thinking that he had been away too long if he didn't know the danger of that. Naturally, for Jude, the danger would add to the appeal. Like the scar. Like the battered green duffel at his feet, which I had taken to be part of the woods. Ten years in one bag? It was totally macho.

'Nice guy, that last driver,' he was saying. 'He let me off before we hit town, so I could hike up here.' He glanced at the cottage, so visibly neglected. 'They haven't been inside. I'm safe.'

'You're staying here?' I asked, wanting to know where he'd be. Seeing him wasn't as bad as it would have been if I'd thrown myself at him. Still, he smelled of danger.

Melodramatic of me? Sure. But ten years later,

Jude remained virile. It wasn't any one feature, but the whole package. Like endless legs, with jeans faded. At the fly.

He was studying the cottage, looking dubious. 'I dunno, it must be ripe in there. I think I've had it with ripe for a while. I want a good bed and clean sheets and a hot shower. I want a cook and AC. I want to be pampered.'

That was a change, but familiar enough to make me smile.

'What?' he asked, amused by my smile.

'I came here for the same things.'

'You really didn't come for me?' he asked, and for an instant, those gold eyes held everything they had ten years before — wanting, caring, desire.

I felt it. But not. 'No,' I insisted, 'I really didn't come for you.'

'Will you leave now that I'm here?'

'That depends on my husband — '

His head went back, gold eyes brighter. 'Ah. The husband. I forgot. James Aulenbach, Esquire. So where is the good lawyer?'

'New York. He couldn't get away.'

Jude smirked. 'Too bad — for him, not for me.'

I wasn't sure whether it was the crooked smile, the shining eyes, or the sheer physicality of him — or the fact that he seemed to be slipping in and out of the old persona, making me wonder which was real. But I wasn't comfortable here. It was time to leave.

'Dream on,' I said as I opened the car door and slid inside.

I didn't say anything else, didn't even glance at

Jude as I backed around. As I drove down the rutted road, gaining speed on the descent, I held tight to the wheel. The faster I went, the more violently the car jounced, though my insides played a little part there. They were shaking on their own, a delayed reaction to seeing him, and it didn't improve even when the car emerged and oblique rays of sun fractured the road.

Leave Bell Valley, a little voice cried. *He is dangerous, and you have too much on your plate without that.* But where to go? Nothing had changed in New York. I didn't want to go home to Mom and couldn't deal with Dad yet. I had been hoping for a few weeks here before Jude arrived. I needed safe time. Now that was lost.

Still, leaving felt like failure.

Go get 'em, Emily, beard the lion in his den! Dad used to say that each time my high school volleyball team, with its perpetually losing record, played top teams on their home courts.

Beard the lion? Jude would be amused.

If asked, I would have sworn that he had been out of mind during the last ten years of my life. But seeing him now, I felt something. Desire? Not exactly. But something, and until I knew what it was, I couldn't leave town.

Feeling vaguely manipulated by Jude, I grew annoyed, which was probably why I reacted so strongly when I saw the charcoal SUV parked on the far side of the green, now with a clear line of sight to the driveway of the Red Fox. I might have thought it was Jude in that car, taunting me, if I hadn't just seen him back at the cabin, on foot.

134

With the sun slanting in a way that pierced the tinted windows, I saw the man inside look up, then back down. Texting my whereabouts? But to whom? And why only here — unless there had been a second spy at the Refuge — in which case this might be Amelia's doing, though I couldn't fathom her motive. But who else? I couldn't imagine James doing this, and Dad's man would be way more subtle.

I might not be able to control Jude Bell. But this was still my escape, and I didn't need a tail. Leaving my car in the lot, I worked myself into a snit as I strode towards the inn.

10

With tea under way in the parlour and me in no mood to be polite to guests, I entered the kitchen. The baker, Lee, was taking cookies from the oven. Vicki had just returned from the front with a plate to refill. At my stormy entrance, both looked back.

'Someone is following me,' I announced in a belligerent voice. 'I have seen the same car sitting out front since the day I arrived. I don't know who sent him, but someone is watching everything I do.'

Vicki didn't seem surprised. 'The grey SUV?'

'*Yeah*, but I don't recognize the guy inside. Who is *watching* me?'

'Not watching you,' said Lee, drawing my eye. She was wearing oven mitts and a crestfallen face. 'Watching *me*.'

Startled, I looked back at Vicki, only then realizing what I had missed in my own self-absorption. From the start, there was something she had wanted me to know about Lee.

'I think I need to be with my guests,' she said now, and slipped through the door.

Lee took a second cookie sheet from the oven and put in two new ones before looking at me again. I'm not sure if she thought I'd be at the table reading the newspaper, disinterested now that I knew *I* wasn't the one in the crosshairs.

136

But I was standing right there, waiting.

Did you hear about the lawyer hurt in a crash? An ambulance stopped suddenly.

I was no ambulance chaser, but for the first time I understood what drove some lawyers to it. *Money,* you're thinking, and for some that might be true. For others, it was a morbid fascination with wrongdoing, coupled with too much legal know-how, and for still others, just the adrenaline rush.

For me, right now, it was pure escapism. I leaned a hip against the counter, settling in.

'He's watching me,' she repeated in a small voice. A swathe of brown hair covered one eye, but the other held mine.

'Why?'

'Protection.'

'He's *protecting* you. From what?'

'My husband's family.'

Married? I wouldn't have guessed that. She had struck me as being solitary to the extreme, and she wasn't wearing a ring. 'Why is his family after you?'

'They say I stole money from them. I did not,' she vowed with such a hard look that I believed her.

'What does your husband say?'

The hard look wavered. Her face came close to crumbling before she grabbed a spatula. 'Nothing. He's dead.'

'Dead. Oh, Lee, I'm sorry. When?'

'Three years ago.'

'Foul play?' I asked, because Lee didn't look to be more than forty, and given accusations that necessitated a bodyguard, it sounded like his family was trouble. I imagined organized crime.

'He had a massive heart attack.'

Not something he had bought into. 'I'm *so* sorry. How old was he?'

'Sixteen years older than me, but he loved me. They keep trying to say he didn't and that I was just using him for the money, but I didn't want money. All those things he gave me? I didn't ask for any of it. He was the first person who ever loved me for me.'

She went at the cookies on the first of two sheets, lifting each with a spatula and slipping it onto a plate. They were oatmeal raisin cookies, and the smell was incredible, though I felt guilty even thinking that, given the subject at hand.

'Why do they say you stole money?'

She made a dismissive sound, seeming not to want to say more. I didn't know whether it was the lawyer in me begging release, the woman in me feeling compassion, or the wife in me not wanting to think about Jude, but I said softly, 'I may be able to help.'

'That's what Vicki said, but I don't know if anyone can.'

'Try me.'

Having emptied the first cookie sheet, she handed me the plate. 'Would you bring these out front?'

I half worried that in the minute it took, she would run off. But she was at work on the second cookie sheet when I returned. Clearly upset, she wasn't as efficient with these. Several broken cookies lay discarded by the rim of the sheet. This batch held chocolate macadamia nut ones, and those broken pieces were a serious temptation. It was all I could do not to grab one, they smelled so good. Or was it simply that my sense of smell, having been gone for so long, was more vivid?

The spatula skittered again. A dark sound came from Lee's throat, then a bewildered, 'I don't know where to begin.'

I did. Talking with my husband might be a challenge, but talking with plaintiffs? I was good at this. With a fleeting thought of Layla, the young woman I had been trying to help last Friday morning in New York, I asked Lee, 'How long were you and your husband married?'

'Six years.'

'Any kids?'

'No. And there weren't any others. He had never been married before.'

'How did you meet?'

She broke the rhythm of her work to meet my gaze, daring me before she said a word. 'I worked in a bar. He sat at one of my booths. He was lonely and wanted to talk. He kept coming back for that.' Looking down again, she scooped off the last cookie and murmured, 'Poor waitress dupes rich customer.'

'Was he rich?' I asked.

She seemed to consider how much to tell me. Finally, quietly, she said, 'His family is. They make junk food. You'd know the name if I said it.'

'I take it they weren't happy with the wedding.'

She rolled her eyes in response, and handed me the second plate of cookies. She was about to push the baking sheets into the soapy sink, when I said a helpless 'Whoa,' and caught the edge of one. 'You cannot throw these down the drain, Lee. I'm sorry' — I gathered up the cookie scraps — 'I truly am focusing on your story, but it would break my heart to let these go to waste.' Once I had them in hand, I set them on the counter safely distant from the suds. I took the plate of perfect cookies into the dining room and hurried back, using the time to order my thoughts.

Taking up position beside the sink with a dish towel in my left hand and a shard of warm cookie in my right, I went on. 'You say that he loved you. Did his family not believe that?'

She was scrubbing the first pan, putting anger into it. 'They believed *his* feelings all right, just not mine. You can imagine the names they called me.'

I could. They would be classic. 'And then he died.'

'Yes.' She lost her steam, suggesting what came next.

'No prenup.'

'No prenup. Just his will, leaving everything to me. That set them off.'

'How much is everything?' I asked, because wealth was relative, and Lee appeared to have none. Jeans, flannel shirt, sneakers — all were old and worn. Her hair was a mud brown that looked home-done; same with its chin-length cut. She wore neither make-up nor jewellery, and if she had a car, it was hidden from sight.

When she didn't reply, I realized how intrusive my question was. The lawyer in me had kicked in. It must have threatened her. 'You don't have to answer that.'

'Vicki trusts you,' she said. She didn't look like she fully agreed, but I sensed she was desperate. Still, it wasn't until she handed me the first pan and started scrubbing the second that she said, 'There was his share of the family money. I still don't know how much that comes to. Ourselves, we had two houses, one in Manchester-by-the-Sea — in Massachusetts — and one in Florida. I sold the Florida one after he died. It was too big, and I never felt comfortable with his friends there. The Manchester house was big, too, but Jack had loved it, so it had emotional value, and I had to live somewhere. But it's old and on the water. It cost a load to keep up, and the mortgage was huge. Jack had always said there was enough money in the family trust fund to support both homes, and then I just had the one, which should have made it easier, but the cheques I got from the trust kept shrinking until I couldn't pay the bills. When I asked the family lawyer about it, I got excuses like poor investments and a down market, and I believed it at first. Jack's friends were all talking about investment scams, and I knew the market was bad.'

She passed me the second pan and, taking one of the mitts, removed the two last sheets from the oven. Chocolate chip here. The smell was too good to be true.

Nibbling on what I already had, I waited patiently.

141

'Then it got harder to contact the lawyer,' she finally said. 'He was never in, and he wouldn't return my calls. After a while, I'd have to be really stupid to buy it. So I called the trustee.' Her eyes met mine, pleading. 'I was so careful not to accuse anyone of anything. I kept saying that I didn't understand, and that I wasn't sure what to do. I thought of selling the house, only nothing was selling, and something inside me felt like the money was there. Jack's brothers weren't selling their houses. I mean, it was pretty obvious. They were just trying to cut me out.'

'Did you say that to the trustee?'

'Oh yeah,' she said with regret. 'Right after that, I got a call from the lawyer. He said that it looked to him like I was skimming money from the trust fund, and that I'd better hire a lawyer of my own, because I was in deep trouble.'

'Did you deny it?'

'Omigod, yes. It's pretty funny he would even think I could pull that off. I don't know how trust funds work, and I wouldn't have a clue about how to skim money from one.'

'Did you tell him that?'

'Yes.' Her voice dropped, but not her eyes, which held mine, daring again. 'He asked me whether a judge would believe the word of a convicted felon over that of a well-known, reputable family.' She looked like she was swallowing something big and bad.

'You have a record,' I said.

She nodded.

'Dated when?'

'Twenty years ago,' she said in a trembling

voice and, taking the spatula, went to work plating the newly baked cookies. 'I was working as a cook for a family like Jack's. The wife was always losing her jewellery. She just left it around, and then, when no one could find it, she filed a claim with her insurance company. It was kind of a running joke in her family. This time it was a diamond bracelet. She dropped it near the toaster, a little snaky thing that tempted me just like those cookies tempted you. I left it there for the longest time. Usually she'd come looking. This time she didn't.'

'Did you tell her about it?'

'No,' Lee said, scooping up another cookie, sliding it onto the plate.

'Why not?'

'I wanted to see how long she'd leave it there. Finally, I just took it. I didn't have the guts to sell it, so they found it there in my room. Then they claimed I had taken other things that had gone missing. Since they only had me on the bracelet, I got fourteen months. The rap sheet lasts forever.'

I connected the dots. 'Your husband's family saw it.'

'But Jack knew. I told him when we first met. He didn't care.'

'She's been with me for eighteen months,' Vicki said, joining us, 'and I've never once had cause for doubt.'

I wasn't surprised. The way Lee talked, the way she looked at me or didn't, even the way she carried herself held a lack of guile. I was a fairly good judge of character.

Of course, I'd bombed when it came to Jude, and the jury was out on James.

Still. 'How did you come to be working here?' I asked.

Seeming unsure how much to say, Lee looked to Vicki, who said, 'Mom brought her. They're cousins.'

I smiled, intrigued. 'Really?' Here was a new side of Amelia the Queen. 'Did I see you at Vicki's wedding?'

Lee shook her head. 'I'm not the kind of relative you'd want to have around.'

'The problem was more Mom than Lee,' Vicki put in. 'Do you know where she came from?'

'No.'

'Uh-huh. She never talks about that. She wants you to believe she was born into high society, but her family is very . . . plain.'

'Vicki is being kind,' Lee said sadly. 'I'm not the only felon in the family. We don't kill or do drugs, we're just thieves. Mama was the worst. She got away with a lot before she was caught. In my family, you break the mould when you go straight, but some of us try.' Her face hardened in support of innocence. 'I made one mistake and paid for it, but I did not steal money from any trust fund.'

'Amelia must believe that, or she wouldn't have brought you here,' I said, and connected a few more dots. 'She was the one who hired the guard outside.'

Vicki confirmed it. 'He's a member of the local police force, and he's recovering from a broken leg, so this gives him something to do

144

other than shuffling papers at a desk. As far as the town knows, he's just keeping an eye on the green.'

'What's the danger?' I asked Lee, wanting to hear the rest of her story.

But Vicki was into it now, vehement in Lee's defence. 'They've sent thugs after her. They put ugly little notes in her mail slot and dog poop on her front step, and they show up watching her at odd times, just standing at the edge of her backyard staring at the house. Sometimes they have a camera, like they're cataloguing a crime.'

'Are you sure it isn't a local pervert?'

'The guys vary, no one knows them, and they're always gone before the police arrive.'

'Two weeks ago,' Lee said, 'two of them pulled up in a car with papers saying I had to go to the DA's office to give a deposition.'

'The papers were bogus,' Vicki held. 'Mom checked it out.'

'How'd they find you?'

Close to tears now, Lee shrugged.

'She keeps to herself,' Vicki argued, 'never says her last name, never calls her family, even though we gave her a phone. She doesn't mix with people in town, so it's not like she's flaunting herself. We figure whoever it is tracked her through Amelia.'

I thought of Jude. There he was on the Bering Sea and — ta-da — got whatever he needed on the Web. Lee's connection to Amelia wouldn't stay hidden for long. 'But why would they go to the effort?'

'Our guess,' Vicki mused, 'is that someone

really is draining that trust fund, likely the brothers themselves — putting the money in an account that Lee can't touch — so they're looking for a patsy. Lee's it. They may not be able to pin anything on her, because they sure won't find the money, but they're taking pleasure in the chase. It's all about intimidation. They smell vulnerability.'

'Because of the record?'

'Because I ran,' Lee said, pleading again. 'Maybe I shouldn't have, but I didn't know what else to do. I sold the jewellery Jack gave me so I could pay bills, but I couldn't keep up with them, and the cheque from the trust fund barely paid the heat. I'd have taken in a renter, but the zoning laws don't allow it, and if I do something under the table, I'll be caught for sure. I talked with three realtors about selling the house. All of them told me not to. And then there were people knocking on my door, asking about my bank account — '

'Also imposters,' Vicki charged.

'But what could I do?' Lee cried. 'I talked with a local lawyer, but I didn't have money for the retainer, and, anyway, he was small-time and would have had to butt heads with the biggest in town — '

'What town?' I asked. I was familiar with New York law, but each state was different.

'The brothers live in Connecticut,' Vicki injected, 'but their father lived in Boston. The trust fund is with a firm there.'

Lee looked devastated. 'They have lawyers all over the place, and money to spend. Me, I have no money and a criminal record. I couldn't win. So I ran.'

Like me. But not.

I thought of the incredible breakfast breads I'd been eating. 'Where did you learn to bake?'

'Growing up. It was one of the few things I did right.' She teared up. 'That was our dream. Jack had been tagging along in the family business all his life, but he loved to bake. We used to do it together — like, instead of going to a movie, picking a recipe and making something really good. We dreamed of owning a bakery in a nice area where people would come mornings and weekends. It wasn't going to be big, more like a hobby for him, but he was excited about it. I mean, when you have that much money, you get bored. When your family is one big corporation, there's not much to do every day. His brothers play tennis and golf. They cruise on the family boat, but even then, like, there's a full crew, so what do you do? You invite every friend you know to come for a ride, only they wouldn't be friends if you didn't have the ride —' She caught herself. 'At least, that's what Jack always said. I was his escape, he said, and I believed it. He did well with me. He lost weight, and his blood pressure went down. He said we'd start that bakery and live a long life together.'

She brushed at her tears, in the process pushing aside that swathe of hair, leaving her face open and vulnerable. For the first time, I took in broad pecan brows, high cheekbones, and hazel eyes filled with gentleness and longing, any one of which might have attracted a lonely

147

middle-aged bachelor.

'Only it didn't work out that way,' Vicki concluded, and cut to the chase. 'So what can we do to help her?'

The 'we' was really me. I was the lawyer. Yes, Vicki wanted me to hear of a woman running away under more dire circumstances than mine — and yes, it was sobering. But she also wanted legal advice.

Funny thing about that. Lawyer jokes to the contrary, we did serve a practical purpose.

'A restraining order is the obvious thing,' I ventured, 'but without evidence linking someone to what's happened to Lee here in town, there's no case. We'll need a detective to identify whoever's lurking around up here and link him to the brothers. We could also get an accountant to examine the trust fund. That would definitely shake up the brothers.'

Vicki's eyes lit with glee. 'I like it.'

Lee wasn't so sure. 'They'll retaliate.'

'Meaning that we set a trap and they take the bait, so we'll *really* get them,' Vicki promised, and turned to me. 'Go for it, Emmie.'

'Uhh, I can't.' I wasn't practising law right now.

'Sure you can. I know you. You make things happen.'

While I loved her for the vote of confidence, it wasn't entirely justified. Yes, I could make things happen. But would they be the right things? I didn't have a great history of that right now — and that was *before* Jude had shown up to mess with my mind even more.

'For starters,' I hedged, 'there's a problem with jurisdiction. I can't practise law in Massachusetts.'

'Can't you work with someone who does?'

'I don't know anyone who does probate work.' A thought came. I smiled. 'But James does. One of his college friends is with the kind of firm you need.'

'Can James call him?'

I kept the smile on my face. 'I don't know. Let me ask.'

★　★　★

I didn't ask that night. Calling James with a favour when I wouldn't do him one — like leaving my BlackBerry on — was pushing it.

So I felt guilty about not helping Lee, and guilty about not telling Vicki that Jude was back, and when she suggested that we have dinner at The Grill, I wanted to go hide somewhere all by myself instead.

But Vicki was my angel in Bell Valley. And The Grill had great zucchini sticks. So I went.

11

I didn't realize what I was in for. The heart of Bell Valley ate at The Grill, and much as I'd been sitting in clear view on the green, this was truly my public debut. The place was wood and comfortably dark — walls, ceilings, and booths — yet a steady stream of locals stopped at our table to say hello. Some remembered me as Jude's girl from ten years ago. Some only knew I looked familiar and, since I was with Vicki, were drawn by curiosity.

Not all were warm and fuzzy, our server being a case in point. We immediately recognized each other. Though he was an old friend of Jude's, he was Jenna Frye's cousin, so he and I had never hit it off. Now, other than a brief glance to take my order, he didn't look at me again.

That made me uncomfortable — not so much his relation to Jenna, but his friendship with Jude. Knowing that I knew Jude was back and he didn't, seemed wrong. Of course, not telling Vicki was even worse.

Then came Amelia — talk about feeling like a snake. I should have known she would be here. Amelia was *always* here, because she didn't cook. She and I had that in common, at least, though it was little comfort now. I cringed when she appeared, and when she slid into the booth on Vicki's side, I thought I'd die.

She must have known my feelings, because she

hit me with a bright smile and said, 'This is nice,' settling in as though she'd had a date with us all along. In a single glance, she had the server over. 'The special?' he asked, to which she gave him a nod and a thumbs-up.

Vicki said nothing, which was the only way I knew she was no happier than me. Not that Amelia gave her a chance to talk. She controlled the conversation, asking about my work in New York and what I might do for Lee, and though I bought time, saying that it might take James a while to contact his friend, the guilt I felt about that was nothing compared to the guilt I felt about Jude.

Amelia showed no sign of being affected by whatever she had been drinking earlier, and when her Cosmo arrived, she drank appropriately. Then, mid-sentence, she shot up an arm and waved her hand. 'Bob! Here!' she called in an authoritative voice.

A couple approached. They looked several years older than Amelia, whom I would have guessed to be sixty-two. She barely acknowledged the female half of the pair.

'Bob, I want you to meet Vicki's friend, Emily Aulenbach. Emily, Bob Bixby. Bob heads the legal department at the Refuge. Emily is a lawyer, too,' she told Bob, who smiled at me then.

'Where do you practise?' he asked.

'New York,' Amelia said before I could.

'Corporate?' he asked next, and since he was looking straight at me, I immediately liked him better.

'Corporate litigation, actually.' It was its own field, separate from the other.

'What firm?'

'Lane Lavash.'

He frowned, considering. 'I don't know that one. I did criminal work in Hartford before I moved here.'

It occurred to me that Amelia could have consulted Bob about Lee. Criminal work would encompass harassment. But Amelia wouldn't have wanted Bob to know that she had a relative with a criminal record.

'Emily's been working with the cats,' Amelia told Bob, 'so you know where to find her if you need help.'

'We always need help,' Bob warned, but the words were barely out when Amelia made a shooing motion.

'Here's our food,' she said. 'I'm starved. Go order, you two. Enjoy your dinner.'

I was glad to see her include the wife at the end, but the instant they were gone, even as the waiter was setting down our plates, she muttered, 'I have *nothing* to say to that woman.'

'Why not?' I asked.

'Bo-ring,' she sang, turning a brilliant smile on the server. 'This looks wonderful, Jake. As always.'

The special was baked haddock. Vicki and I had ordered hamburgers with our zucchini sticks — would likely have had the zucchini sticks alone as an appetizer if Amelia hadn't been there. But the server knew that she liked everything served at once, and since she would be the one leaving the tip, pleasing Amelia was what counted.

As we ate, Amelia told me more about Bob and about other recent hires whom she considered to be finds. At one point she glanced at Vicki. 'You're awfully quiet.'

'When would you have me speak?' Vicki asked politely enough. 'Between drinks?'

'Ouch,' Amelia said. She was on her second Cosmo, but perfectly articulate. Undaunted, she looked at me. 'Mothers and daughters do have issues. What about you, Emily? Are you and your mother best friends?'

I was trying to think how to answer when something changed in the restaurant. Conversation didn't exactly end, but was broken by a vibrating hush.

I had the briefest glimpse of Jude heading towards us, fending off hugs and backslapping, waving an indulgent hand to return people to their talk, before reaching our booth.

'Hello, Mother,' he said, bending to kiss her cheek before sliding in beside me. 'Hey, Vick, how's life?'

In other circumstances, I might have enjoyed Amelia's shock. But I was shocked myself — that he had chosen this public place to tell her he was back, that he had slid in near me like I'd known he was coming, like he and I were a pair.

He made things worse by looking back and forth between his mother and his sister before murmuring in an aside to me, 'I do love a surprise.'

Vicki was suddenly glaring at me. I blew out a

153

puff, held up a hand saying that I knew nothing (which, when it came to his showing up *here*, was the truth), and scooched away from Jude and into the corner.

He had showered — more likely, knowing Jude, had stood in all his naked glory in the stream — and wore clean jeans and a T-shirt advertising CRAB FISHING IN DUTCH HARBOR. Indoors, his blond hair was sprinkled with a grey that I hadn't noticed outside.

'What did you do to your *face*?' Vicki cried.

Jude touched the scar. 'I didn't do it. A buddy of mine did.'

'You look old,' Vicki said, but added a more gentle 'older'.

'And you motherly,' Jude replied, lazily stretching his arms over the table.

'Jude, my man!' came the cry of a friend who extended a hand in an exuberant shake. He was no sooner gone when a woman approached, another I knew to be a former lover. Jude hugged her and talked for a minute before sending her off.

Looking confused in ways that liquor hadn't made her, Amelia stared for another minute. When she finally spoke, her voice was less bold, less loud, but deep with feeling. 'Ten years and not a word, then just showing up here like this? Where have you been? Why haven't you called? Do you know how much I've worried? There were times I wondered if you were still *alive*.' She glanced at me. 'You knew about this, didn't you? You came here for him.'

Before I could deny it, another friend of Jude's

came to the table. When Jude slid out to hug him, I grabbed my chance at escape, pausing only to whisper to Amelia, 'I'm here independent of him, and call me a coward if you want, but he'll suck me into this if I stay. What you have here is a family reunion, and I'm not family.' I slid the rest of the way out of the booth and left before she could respond.

★ ★ ★

Vicki must have called Rob to say she'd be late, because though The Grill closed at ten, it was well after midnight when she cracked open my door and whispered, 'Are you sleeping?'

'Fat chance,' I whispered back as she approached the bed fully clothed. I pushed up against the pillows, but didn't bother with the lamp. I could see her well enough, and what I couldn't see, I felt, so I knew she was upset. 'How could he do that, Vicki Bell? To your mother? To you? And with me there? He must have been watching — must have wanted me there to soften the blow to Amelia. So is that where you've been — Amelia's?'

'Oh yeah. Not a happy scene.'

'Why not? Isn't she glad that he's back?'

'Totally. It's revolting.' She sank down on the duvet. 'Was she really the one who was angry back there at The Grill for his not calling, not writing, not letting her know he was alive? *Well*' — Vicki breathed voluminously — 'all that was easily forgiven. She fawned all over him.' Her voice went lower to simulate Amelia's. ''What

155

can I get you, Jude? Oh dear, I *don't* have Red Bull, but Vicki can run out for some. No? Are you sure? It'll be so nice having you sleep here in the house again. Why yes, Emma Ruth is still cooking. Roast beef hash for breakfast? With *beets*? I'm impressed, Jude. She will *definitely* make that for you. Yes, she'll wash your clothes. Of *course*, I don't mind the holes. The holes are *you*.''

She made a gagging sound. I turned on my side, letting her vent.

'I should be happy he's back,' she said. 'Right? Well, part of me isn't. He's my brother, and I love him, but it's not like he was a good guy ten years ago. He lived to annoy Mom, but there she is now, acting like he's a hero. For what? For staying alive in the Bering Sea? I work fourteen-hour days doing laundry, making beds, cleaning toilets, and she walks in with barely a hello and tells me that I'm inconsistent when it comes to disciplining Charlotte, or that the Red Fox should offer a menued breakfast, because, after all, how can I expect people to automatically like what *I* choose to serve, *especially* when some are on special diets, and if we want this place to succeed, we have to be *aware* of these things. Like I'm stupid?'

'You're not stupid.'

'And here's another thing,' Vicki spat out. 'Noah.'

'Noah?'

'His *son*. I mean, can you believe that name? He was named after Jenna's father, but talk about biblical? Mom is counting on him heading

156

the Refuge someday. But what about Charlotte? My child is *legitimate*, but has Amelia ever suggested that *she* head the Refuge? No! So ... so ... is it a *male* thing?' Vicki asked, sounding bewildered.

'It's a Jude thing.'

'She loves him more than she loves me?'

'No. It's Jude. He has a weird power.'

'And *before* he was a crab fisherman,' Vicki went on, 'know what he was doing? Dune racing in Egypt. He did it for money — like, people would bet on him and he'd get a percentage of the take. Then he led glacier tours in New Zealand. I didn't even know there were glaciers in New Zealand. But his stories are wonderful. I'll bet he has a great one for the scar. He goes on and on, and you hang on every word. He dares to do things most of us do not. He's a total free spirit. And Amelia thinks he'll stay in Bell Valley?' She blew a raspberry. 'When pigs fly.'

I was thinking of Jude's daring. The rest of us lived vicariously through him. Was that part of his appeal then?

Vicki focused on me. 'You're too quiet. You felt something for him, didn't you?'

'You don't *not* feel something for Jude Bell,' I remarked. 'You love him or hate him. There's no in between.'

'Which end are you at?'

'Both,' I said, bewildered myself. 'I hate him for the way he steps on people's feelings. But you gotta love him for that free spirit.'

'Do you find him appealing?'

'I'd have to be dead not to,' I said, trying to

157

make light of it. 'That's one of the things I was thinking of after I left The Grill. Jude's like a celebrity. He may be older now, but there's still something riveting about him.'

'It's called virility.'

'Or ruggedness. You can't look at him and not want to look again.'

She was quiet for a minute. 'He said he saw you this afternoon. Did it all come back?'

'Yup, including the betrayal.'

'The sexual attraction, too?'

'No.' I tried to explain to myself as well as to her. 'It was more a mind thing. This sounds crazy, Vicki, but right before I saw him, I saw the coyote. When Jude appeared, the coyote was gone. It's like that coyote is *him*. It is totally untamed, and it fascinates me. And it's been haunting my dreams, so maybe Jude is something I need to work through.'

'Work through how?' She sounded worried.

'I have to figure out what parts of him I want to . . . capture.'

'Like what?'

'Defying convention. Daring to be different.'

'You've done those things just by leaving New York.'

'But what to do with them now? How to make some of it stick? What parts I *want* to make stick? It's confusing.'

Vicki exhaled. 'So there's another reason I resent his showing up again. He's complicating your escape.' Her voice dropped. 'You won't leave just because he's here, will you?'

'And desert you in your time of need?'

'I'm serious, Emmie.'

'So am I. Where else would I go?'

'Anywhere else might be more peaceful.'

'But it wouldn't have you.'

She touched her forehead to mine. 'That's very sweet. Okay, so what's another thing you've been thinking about since you left The Grill?'

I was a minute returning to that part of our discussion. Then I smiled. It might be wishful thinking — and not entirely smart, if Jude was something I needed to work through — but right now, today, certainly until after I talked with James, it worked.

'Jude Bell is not my business,' I vowed.

*   *   *

Not my business. Amelia could have him. I had my own issues, the most immediate of which was Colleen Parker.

Why was I thinking of Colleen when I woke up Thursday morning? Because of Vicki. Because of how we'd helped each other last night. Because of the ease, the trust, the interest we shared.

I waited until after breakfast, then, sitting in my car, gave Colly a call. She was not happy with me — first, because I hadn't responded to emails from the other bridesmaids, and then because of what I had to say.

'You can't back out now!' she cried in horror. 'The dresses are already here!'

'I'll pay for mine anyway,' I offered.

'No, no, you don't understand. I've done the

choreography, with the music and all, and we matched it perfectly, bridesmaids to groomsmen. Now I'll have one less.'

Gently I said, 'Ask another friend, and I'll give her my dress for free.'

In another tone, to another woman, my remark might have been rude. But I knew my audience, and that audience was angry. Not sorry. Not concerned. Just angry. I tried to empathize with the pressure she felt, but it was hard. My own wedding had been small — immediate family and a handful of friends — so I had no personal experience in staging an extravaganza.

'I asked you to be in my wedding party,' Colly said, 'and you accepted. You can't back out now.'

'I can't be there.'

'Why *not*, Emily? Okay, so you're taking time off, but what could possibly be so important that you can't come back for one day? Just one day. I mean, like, are you in rehab or something?'

'No. No rehab.' Not in the traditional sense, but I wasn't explaining that. And yes, I could come back for a day. I might well *be* back, since Walter's month would expire long before the wedding. Given the size of New York and the fact that our lives never overlapped outside book group, which I could easily miss, Colly would never know if I was back or not.

For the sake of this wedding, I wanted to be away. If I showed up as a guest rather than a bridesmaid, there would be questions to answer, and the fact was, I didn't want to be at Colly's wedding at all. Her half of this phone conversation reinforced the conviction.

'This isn't right,' she said.

But for me it was. Colly collected friends like bangle bracelets, and I couldn't be one of those. It would be a betrayal of what I was starting to learn about myself — namely, that I wanted quality, not quantity.

'I'm sorry, Colly,' I said quietly. 'I'll be thinking of you, though.'

I'll be thinking of you, too, she might have said. *I'm sorry you're going through a rough time. Let me know how you are. Stay in touch.* Instead, she sighed. 'Okay. I'll make some calls. I have a cousin who might take your place.'

I repeated my apology, but ended the call feeling no regret at all.

★　★　★

I did feel regret when it came to Lee. I knew I should call James. Lee was a perfect excuse, right?

But I couldn't get myself to do it. Turning off the BlackBerry, I dropped it on the passenger's seat of the car and left the Red Fox. The charcoal SUV was on the far side of the green, protecting Lee as I was not. So that was good but not great.

At least I wasn't looking in my rearview mirror as I drove out of town, and once I turned into the Refuge road and entered the parking lot in my dead-giveaway BMW, I was being watched by someone else.

Jenna Frye.

A wisp of a woman with long blond hair and

161

ragged-hem jeans, she looked far more the part of Jude's consort than I ever had. And she had to know that Jude was back. I wondered if her husband knew and, if so, how he felt. Jude was not the kind of man that other men took lightly.

I climbed from the car, watching Jenna watch me as she crossed the porch of the big Colonial. She looked stricken. Thinking I was here for Jude? For one crazy moment I imagined that she and I might have a lot to say to each other.

I ducked back in my car to put my sunglasses on the dashboard, but by the time I straightened, she was inside.

* * *

They needed help today in the laundry room, so I spent the morning doing load after load of towels, pet beds, and scrubs. I half wondered if Amelia had requested that I be sent here as punishment for not telling her Jude was back. But the assignment could have been worse. Had she really been in a mood, she might have had me mucking out horse stalls.

But I wasn't complaining. Volunteers came here knowing they would be asked to do whatever needed to be done, and I was just another volunteer. Jude wasn't here; he rarely came, and he had made it clear to Vicki that he planned to do nothing but sleep, eat Emma Ruth's roast beef hash with beets, and watch the NFL channel. So it was just me, the regular staff, and a handful of other visitors.

My reward, of course, was spending the

162

afternoon with the cats. The wobbly kitten knew me; I was sure of it. She was sitting in a corner apart from the others when I entered the room, and within seconds was teetering my way. There were two other volunteers there, but she made a determined little beeline for me. I wanted to think she'd been waiting.

Lifting her, I put my face to hers before settling her in the cup of my legs. She was so light, so fragile, that I feared she wasn't eating, so I broke the rule and hand-fed her until other cats crowded in. Several new ones had arrived since I'd come, including a mangy Maine Coon with a stumpy hind leg and a scowl, and though he was nowhere near as cute as my Precious, I felt for him. Grumpy and pompous, he reminded me of Amelia. He was parked unhappily in a crate that, earlier that week, had been the home of a Siamese mix recovering from surgery. I didn't see that one here now, which meant either it had been moved to another room, had been adopted, or had died.

I hadn't known the Siamese, yet the thought of it dying — the thought of the helpless little tabby in my lap dying — brought tears to my eyes. But yes, cats here did die. Same with dogs, horses, and any manner of other pets that were too injured or old to recover from whatever had brought them to the Refuge. Cremated, their ashes were buried in small tins in a cemetery bordering the cornfield. It was simultaneously the most beautiful and heart-breaking spot. Thinking of it, I bowed low over the little kitty, putting my head to hers.

'Emily?'

I looked up into the face of the man I had met last night at The Grill.

'Bob Bixby?' he prompted.

I smiled. 'I remember. The lawyer.' I would have said the word facetiously, lawyer to lawyer, if this man had been younger or more natty. His polo shirt was perfect. But his too-short jeans gave him a vulnerable look.

He settled on a low stool nearby and was quickly approached by a handful of cats, which told me that he had been here before. 'I wasn't kidding last night,' he said as he stroked their heads with a knowing hand. 'I could use your help.'

'Ohhh, I dunno,' I demurred. He seemed like a nice guy, and I didn't want to offend him, but I wasn't here as a lawyer.

'It's pretty light stuff,' he coaxed, 'a few contracts and other things I'd love second opinions on.'

'You have no associates?'

'A clerical-type person, general gofer, but when it comes to law, it's just me. What'ya say? Give an old man a hand?'

'You're not an old man,' I said quickly, because age was as age did, my dad always said, and Amelia wouldn't have hired Bob Bixby if he couldn't do the job — but that put the bug in my ear. 'Amelia would probably rather I scoop litter.'

'Not true. She told me to draft you. She said that anyone who can make it in a New York law firm can lend a hand here.'

A compliment? If so, it brought no pleasure. I

164

hadn't exactly 'made it' in a New York law firm. My continued relationship with said firm was simply because one man there liked me. Or liked my looks.

That said, I had no idea how I could help Bob Bixby. 'My specialty is litigation,' I said.

It was a mistake.

'So is mine,' Bob countered enthusiastically. 'Then I retired from it, came up here, and found I could do what needed to be done. We're talking employment issues, risk management, trademark coverage. I studied these things in law school. So did you, and much more recently than me. If I can handle it, you can.'

★   ★   ★

'Can I?' I asked Vicki that night. We were slouched side by side on a bench behind the Red Fox, the soles of our feet to the woods. The moon was high, the forest dark but for the occasional lightning bug, silent but for the crickets. The humidity was low, crisping the scene.

'You sure can. You can do anything you want, Emily.'

'Should I, then? When I'm with the cats, I'm lying low. This'd be different.'

'You mean, you might see Jude.' She gave a quick headshake, blond ends quivering. 'He won't be there tomorrow. Amelia's taking him to lunch with a group of Refuge donors in Concord. She bought him new clothes.'

'Will he wear them?' I asked.

Vicki snorted. 'I doubt it. He's forty, and she's

165

buying him clothes? How pathetic is that? She's already said he can wear them or not. My mother is a hypocrite, have I told you?'

'Vaguely.'

'God forbid Charlotte wears jeans to a little girls' tea party at The Bookstore. Not. Appropriate. Says the Queen. But Jude? Whatever he does is fine. Maybe the reason he's such an impossible human being is that he was spoiled. She created the monster.'

Pulling my sweater around me, I studied the woods. Monsters? Not here. These woods were distant from Jude's. They were more tame.

I sighed. 'This setting is unreal. Just beautiful. Peaceful.'

'Like New York.'

I chuckled. 'Right.'

'Will you go back?'

'That depends on James. I can't be in New York without him.'

Vicki turned her head against the wood slat. 'Of course you can. You're a strong woman. Leaving last week took guts.'

I still wasn't sure I agreed, but hearing her say it felt good. 'I'll rephrase that, then. I don't *want* to be in New York without him.'

'Do you want to be in New York at all?'

'Bingo.'

'Where else?'

I gazed out into the dark. This place was more mine than Jude's, and the pull remained. 'Those woods.'

'I mean, for your future.'

'Those woods,' I repeated. 'They are the

ultimate hideout.' My eyes crept the length of the tree line, left to right, from the parking lot to the gardener's shed. I felt Vicki look at me and follow my gaze at the end.

'The shed has charm,' she granted, 'but it's awful close to the woods. Some people are freaked out by that.'

'Like a bear would break down the walls?' I asked, though the question was rhetorical. The shed was small, not much bigger than my city kitchen, but even the most untrained eye could see how solid it was. Massive logs framed the base, while thick planks dovetailed up the sides. The door was oak, the windows small with decorative grates rising halfway. The grates were the work of a local forge, and while, yes, they would prevent a bear from launching itself inside, that wasn't why they were there. They were there to showcase wisteria and the work of the smithy, who was a Beaudry relative.

'Want it?' Vicki asked.

I smiled. 'That'd be a hard choice — the gardener's shed or heaven.'

'I'll make it easier,' she said, apologetic now. 'I need your room. I have a couple arriving here on Monday. This will be their fourth summer, and each year they stay in the attic. They reserved it three months ago. I'm sorry, sweetie. I can't tell them that a friend came at the last minute and wanted it, when I have other rooms that are open. You could have any one of those.'

I continued to look at the shed. I had spent part of a summer living there, and that when it truly was a gardener's shed. A time or two I had

167

imagined that the hose coiled in the corner was a snake, but even then I hadn't freaked out.

So what did worry me? The same something that kept me from walking into those woods on my own, though I wasn't sure what it was. Wild animals? Coyotes? *Me?* Was I afraid I would go in and never want to come out?

But hadn't I gone to Jude's cabin and come out again?

The more I thought about it, the more I realized that the gardener's shed might work. I couldn't stay in the clouds forever. Moving from the dreamy euphoria of that attic room to the down-to-earth reality of the shed might be small and symbolic, but it was something.

Besides, part of me did want to be close to the woods.

★   ★   ★

I dreamed of James that night, dreamed he was lying with me, holding me close. I felt the brush of the hair on his legs as they moved against mine, heard the sough of his breathing as he slept, smelled the male something that was his alone.

I didn't dream of sex; my dream was erotic enough without. We always used to sleep like this, so close that we woke up aching for sex. Lately, it seemed we woke up aching only for more sleep.

When I woke up this night, it was to coyote sounds and a vision of Jude. Bolting up, I scrubbed my eyes, and the Jude on the far side of the room disappeared. The coyote sounds went on.

Falling back, I let my heartbeat steady as I listened, and in time, the sounds, too, were gone.

12

I didn't want to work with Bob Bixby. I told myself that repeatedly as I drove to the Refuge Friday morning. I was steering clear of law for a while — steering clear of all strenuous thought.

Unfortunately, in the absence of strenuous thought, I was obsessing about my phone call with James — or about Jude's face appearing in my room — or about my relationship with that coyote. But I couldn't get the loose ends to align.

So I returned to considering Bob and the charitable mission of the Refuge and decided that an hour or two wouldn't hurt. Besides, there was something to be said for Amelia encouraging this. She had issued a challenge and, like facing Jude's cabin, I couldn't turn away.

It wasn't until I reached the second floor of the Admin Building and turned in at the Legal Department that I realized what Amelia was about. Bob's clerical-type gofer was Jenna Frye.

Amelia must have hoped that would upset me, but as had been the case in the parking lot the day before, Jenna was the one more upset. That relaxed me a little.

'Hey,' I said a bit breathlessly and managed a smile. 'How're you doing, Jenna?'

'I'm okay.' She seemed frightened, though I didn't know why. She was the one who had given birth to the heir — not that I had ever aspired to that. My dreams with Jude hadn't reached the point of kids. We had been about the here and now — and it wasn't all him, it was me, too. I had been so focused all my life that living in the moment that summer had been the escape.

In a flicker of thought, I imagined that Jenna Frye had saved me from something that might have ended far worse than it had. I wanted children, but not with a dad who was still chasing dreams around the world.

Confident in that, I leaned over to look at the small family photos on her desk. All three of Jenna's children had her blond hair, but Noah stood out — not because he was the tallest, but because he did look like Jude.

Flickers of thought notwithstanding, I still should have felt betrayed. Hadn't this child been conceived within minutes of my waltzing in with groceries?

Suddenly, though, it was just a little soap opera about a boy with the same blond curls, the same gold eyes, the same self-assured grin as Jude.

I chuckled. 'This is uncanny.'

She seemed to know what I meant. 'Yeah.'

'You have three beautiful children,' I remarked, and gestured at the shot that included her husband. 'He's very good-looking. I don't think I've ever met him.'

'No. He's quiet.'

'Mine, too. A change from Jude.' I suddenly felt a need to say more. 'Jenna, if I hurt you ten years ago, I'm sorry. I didn't know how serious you were about him.'

'I wasn't.'

'Amelia said — '

'I wasn't. He said you weren't either.'

He lied, I thought. But it didn't seem to matter. I sighed. 'It could be both of us found better men.'

I was saved from having to say more by Bob, who appeared with a grateful look and ushered me inside. He showed me the kinds of things that needed to be done, and he was right. There was nothing heavy-duty here. I could easily read the profile of a woman about to be hired to work in the stables and tailor her contract to her personal situation. Likewise, the severance agreement for a retiring buildings worker. These were boilerplate documents written by a specialist in Concord and requiring nothing but tinkering. Editing the prototype for an employee relations manual was actually fun. Likewise, reviewing the witness deposition taken in a case of animal cruelty and generating questions for rebuttal.

Okay, the deposition was right down my alley, but the rest came back with surprising ease. Would I want to work on contracts for a living? No. A contract was a piece of paper. An employee manual didn't purr. And as for sitting in the same room interviewing someone who abused animals, I had no interest.

Even the most heinous criminal has civil rights, my father said. But I could pick and choose the kind of criminals I worked with, couldn't I? If I returned to law — not when but if, because as reluctant as I'd been to work here, I had felt a connection — I had to be more discriminating. I was coming to realize the importance of that. Life was about prioritizing.

That said, I did whatever Bob asked of me there, leaving little time to think about James, so I was a bit unsettled leaving the Refuge and realizing we would be talking in less than three hours.

I imagined every negative twist. He would demand to know about my unspoken past and accuse me of fraud. He would tell me that his partnership was being fast-tracked, so there was *no way* he could cut back now. He would ask for a divorce.

By the time I reached town, I was on edge.

And there was Jude on a bench on the green, rising when my car appeared and following it into the parking lot of the Red Fox. All six-four straight, he was looking annoyed by the time I opened the door.

'It's about time you got here,' he griped, like we had a date.

Not in the best mood myself, I was short. 'Weren't you in Concord?'

'Oh yeah. Same old people, same old pitch. Some things never change.'

'Thank goodness for that,' I declared, because those 'same old people' were the ones who kept the Refuge in the black.

But Jude had his own agenda. 'I need to talk with you. Where can we go?'

'Here's fine.' I didn't want to spend a long time with him.

'This is personal. I need your advice.'

'Here's fine,' I repeated, to which he paused

173

and tipped his head.

'Afraid to be alone with me? Afraid of the old wild passion?'

'Actually not,' I said. Of the many things I still felt for Jude, that old wild passion wasn't one. Or, if it was, it was buried under all my thoughts of James. 'This may surprise you, Jude,' I said, 'but I have known passion since you.'

'As good?' he asked, teasing but not.

'Better. My husband is a great lover.'

Seeming not to want to go *there*, he looked at my car. 'If you'd been with me, you'd never have driven anything foreign.'

'This from the guy who's been pocketing foreign money for years?'

He held up his hands in a truce. 'Okay, but you're still my conscience, and I have a serious issue here. I need to know what to do about the boy.'

'His name is Noah,' and I didn't want to talk about him or any other of Jude's serious issues, not right now. But the word 'conscience' gave me power. 'I saw Jenna at the Refuge.'

'That must have been interesting.'

'Very.' I felt a passion rise in spite of myself. 'She said *you* told her I wasn't seriously interested in you. You lie, Jude. You use people.'

'Well, I'm trying not to' — he actually looked remorseful — 'so help me out here. My mother thinks I should go for custody of Noah. What do you think?'

I didn't have to give it much thought. 'I think it's a bad idea.'

'Why?'

'Have you met him yet?' I asked on a hunch.

'No.'

'That's why. If you'd wanted to be a father, you'd have already been in touch. But fathering isn't your thing. Your own father was a wimp — your words, many times — so what role model do you have? Besides, you're a narcissist. Your world is about you. There's no room for a little boy who may have needs of his own.'

Jude sputtered. 'You don't pull punches.'

No. Not with Jude. Anyone else, and I'd have been more diplomatic, but Jude evoked drama.

That said, I felt a little bad. So more gently I asked, 'Should I? What good is your conscience if it doesn't tell you what you don't want to hear? Only you do want to hear this, Jude. Be honest for once. Custody must have been Amelia's idea. You don't want it. You don't want to be tied down.'

'I want what's best for the boy.'

'Your jumping in and out of his life is not it.'

'Even if I can add things?'

'Like what?'

'The Refuge.'

I levelled him a stare. 'Hello. Amelia is already grooming him for that. She doesn't need you to have custody. She just wants what *she* wants, which is for you to stay here. But you won't.'

'How do you know?'

'Just a guess.'

He looked at me for a long moment. 'Are you always this tough on people?'

I actually smiled. 'No. Just you.'

'Ahh. Payback time.'

175

I couldn't totally deny it. 'Maybe.'

His eyes sparked. 'Good.' He held out both hands, fingers beckoning. 'Bring it on, Emily. Gimme me what you got. I can handle it.'

But I couldn't. Not now.

Still smiling, I shook my head. 'Sorry, but I have more important things on my mind.'

His arms were slow to fall, his eyes to settle. I wasn't sure if he seriously felt I'd insulted his manhood, but he finally shrugged.

'Cool. I have a date anyway.'

'Anyone I know?' I asked.

'Why? Would you warn her if you did? Sorry, honey, but she lives in Hanover and I'm looking forward to an uninterrupted night. So think of me when you're alone in your bed. I'm outta here.'

He strolled off, leaving me watching, much as I had left him yesterday in the woods. But I felt I was the one who'd scored points.

Not that it was a game.

Unless it was. If the challenge was to compare James and Jude, Jude was falling behind. Take passion, which he had raised himself just now. There had been chemistry between James and me from the start. It might have suffered a little in the battle to conceive, but it was still hot. So maybe I was just remembering the best — missing James, even feeling recharged now that I'd had sleep, food, and quiet — but the best was really good. James had definitely made me forget Jude.

He was doing it now, too, because rather than imagining Jude in Hanover, I was focused on the

176

details of James, wondering whether he was wearing slacks or a suit, whether his BlackBerry was on his desk or in his pocket, whether his coffee was hot or cold. All week I had avoided seeing him in living colour, fearing that I would either wallow in guilt for having run off or, worse, succumb to nostalgia. Oh, yes, absence made the heart grow fonder, but that kind of fondness didn't last. It wouldn't help me move forward.

Right now, though, with our date looming, how could I *not* think of James? I wondered if he was at work, worrying his forehead with his fingers as he always did when he was sorting through a case. If he was as nervous as me, he might be home gearing up for my call. Or he could be catching a quick bite with Naida.

He had denied having an affair, and I believed him at the time, but suspicion died hard.

So here was another negative twist that could pop up in our talk. He could tell me he loved her.

★   ★   ★

Seven crept closer. I wasn't able to eat much dinner, though Vicki plied me with grilled chicken in the kitchen with Charlotte and Rob. Wasting time, I showered away the day's sweat, then negated the effort with a vigorous arm-swinging, leg-lengthening walk through town. In place of the grey SUV was a dark blue car, but knowing that the guy inside wasn't after me made me bolder. Or maybe it was pure escapism. The faster I walked and the deeper I breathed, the less I focused on James.

By seven I was behind the Red Fox on what I was coming to think of as 'my' bench facing the woods. I turned on my BlackBerry, got a signal, hit James's speed dial. His phone rang once, twice, three times. Unsettled, I clicked off before voice mail could kick in.

Thinking that my speed dial had gotten messed up while the phone was off for so long — an improbable thought, but James wouldn't have stood me up — I dialled his cell by hand.

The phone rang and rang. This time I did let it go to voice mail, thinking that if I heard a stranger's message, I would know that the glitch was with the network.

But there was his throaty baritone apologizing for not being able to talk just then and promising a callback ASAP.

Puzzled, I pressed END.

I sat for a minute, sorting through possibilities. There still might be something wrong with his line, but he knew I'd be calling at seven, so if his cell was down, wouldn't he call me from a line that worked? Unless he was meeting with a senior partner. Or on a conference call. In which case he would text.

I quickly checked, but there was no text from James. In fact there were few texts, period. Amazing what one week could do — amazing how quickly a person could fall off the radar screens of so-called friends. I didn't care about most, but I did care about James, which was why my stomach had begun to knot.

Clutching the BlackBerry, I sat for several minutes, waiting. This evening was warmer and more humid than the last few had been; the mosquito that hummed around me seemed drugged. I was already wearing cut-offs but, feeling hot, pulled off my sweater. Even in a tee alone, I was clammy — nerves, for sure.

The BlackBerry remained silent. *Be careful what you wish for*, I thought with a brief spurt of hysteria as I hit the buttons again. There were plenty of possible explanations for why James wasn't picking up, like he was passing through a dead zone or even in the bathroom. The explanation that haunted me, of course, was that he was ignoring the phone, knowing it was me and not wanting to talk.

One ring, two, three. Again, I pressed END, but the knots in my stomach had tightened. I knew James. His PDA was his right hand. If he wasn't answering, it was by choice.

Hurt would come. First, though, because I was his wife and we'd had a date, I was furious.

Maybe I deserved this, an eye for an eye, since I had been the one to walk out on him. Only I hadn't walked out for the fun of it. I hadn't left town on a lark. I was having a personal crisis, and if my husband couldn't see that, couldn't find it in his heart to work through it with me, we were sunk.

As the minutes passed and my phone didn't ring, that was the thought that lingered. It appeared that James was either too angry at me to be fair, or had decided I wasn't worth the grief. Either way, our future together looked bleak.

The finality of it paralysed me. Seven-thirty came and went, along with a pair of guests from the Red Fox, and still I didn't leave the bench. Empty inside, I sat holding my cruelly radiant BlackBerry, which had nothing to mark but the time and nothing to say that I didn't already know, and all the while, in front of me were the woods, growing more shadowed and murky and *alluring* by the minute.

With the pull came the old fear — like the woods were an addiction I couldn't control.

I had always equated the larger forest with Jude. But he preferred the great falls to the north, where the scrambling required all fours and a willingness to get wet. This stretch behind the inn had always been mine. I used to come here without him, feeling a totally separate attraction for it.

Was this proof, then, of a wildness in *me*? If so, it was as eerie as the purple of dusk. The lower the sun sank and the deeper those purples, the more reckless I felt. And the darkness only enhanced it. In the silence from James, I felt unwanted and unloved. If these woods were opaque, maybe even dangerous, so what? I had nothing to lose.

Defying dusk, I crossed the grass to the old wood gate behind the gardener's shed. Climbing over a rotted post, I waded through ferns and started up. Anything more than this gentle incline might have challenged my flip-flops, and I did feel the brush of ground cover on my open feet, but it wasn't hurtful, simply . . . real. There were no blazes on trees to mark the way, only a low stone wall, but what I couldn't see in the waning light, I remembered — a grandfather oak here, the arch of a boulder there.

A pair of mosquitoes buzzed. I was waving my arms to shoo them off when I heard a sound behind me and stopped. Cautious, I turned and, holding my breath, studied the woods for a creature that might be watching, but I saw nothing.

Telling myself not to be spooked, I started forward again, but I hadn't taken two steps when, with a heavy thrum of wings, something large crossed my path. Instinctively, I ducked.

But it was an owl. Just an owl.

I walked on. When I passed birch or beech, the path was strewn with leaves compressed by winter snows; when I passed pine or spruce, it was slick with needles. My footing was less sure here. Sneakers would have been better, but I wasn't going back.

At another sound, I stopped, but even before I could look back, I spotted a deer through the limbless lower trunks of the trees. Wearing a pelt that was a rich cinnamon in the dusk, it held me in its frozen gaze for several long moments before resuming its graceful flight.

The tree trunks were darker in the last of the light, and the stone wall was harder to see, covered as it was with growth, even broken down at spots. Every minute or two, I had to climb over a fallen tree, stepping through branches that overspread the path. Here was nature's pruning, the weak giving way for the strong to survive.

Desperate to be strong, wanting to survive, too, I ignored the eeriness of the encroaching dark and kept going. The smells grew stronger, a pervasive earthiness made more intense by the

181

humid air that tamped it down. There was no direct sun now, only a pale ochre glow beyond the trees to the west.

I tripped once, making a noise that echoed with the scurry of small creatures unseen. The humidity should have absorbed the sounds, but in these deserted woods it did not. Rather, they were amplified — the snap of a stick underfoot, the whisper of a fern as I passed.

At another rustle I stopped again, turned again. Uneasy, I searched the woods behind me, but if a threat was there, the shadows hid it well. I told myself that I was imagining things. But Jude wasn't the only predator around. There were hikers, perverts, *bears*.

I had the uncanny feeling that something was out there. Following me? I didn't know.

But I couldn't go back. If there was evil here, I was feeling reckless enough to tempt it. Or maybe I was just starved for comfort, because these woods did offer that. The pull. Absolutely. I was headed for a magical spot, and I desperately needed it now.

The stone wall was suddenly gone, stopped where an ancient squatter had ended his claim to the land. But I didn't need visuals. From here, I could proceed by sound alone. I've heard the brook rush after a storm or make barely a sound in the dry days of August, but this being June, after a damp spring, the water bubbled gently over its bed of stones, a chorus of tidy bells guiding me there.

Twilight had turned the water to aubergine and soot, while saplings morphed with their elders on its banks. The air was thick with pine resin, but something else as well. I stood still, listening, smelling, knowing I was being smelled, too.

I had always felt magic here. Now I felt relief when I found my favourite pine. Night had stolen its texture, but its width couldn't be missed. I leaned against it, feeling better with something at my back, and looked across the brook. The coyotes used to hang out here ten years ago, and the howls I'd heard this week came from this direction. Though I couldn't see them now, I smelled the feral musk that hung in the humid air. They were definitely around.

At the sound of a footfall I froze, held my breath, listened, but heard nothing more than my own heart. Inching around, I glanced back at the path, but if there was someone there — some*thing* there — I couldn't see. The trees weren't dense, but the darkness was, and the unease I had felt before returned, though only until I faced forward again and saw it, still as stone and oddly luminescent in the night. It sat on lean legs on the far bank, all pointy ears and muzzle, staring at me.

It was female, smaller than her mate would be but regal. This was no ghost of Jude; I had been wrong to ever think that. This creature, with her russet-and-grey coat, her lighter, cream-coloured face, and gentle eyes that easily bridged the night, was here for me.

I should have been afraid, but was not. My past, my dreams — I had a connection to this wild she-dog. Maybe I had been afraid to come here because of that, as if she were the rock

183

bottom of my life, the primal source of whatever I was now supposed to rise to be. The coyote's story was one of survival. I could identify with that.

Soundlessly she watched, perhaps as curious of me as I was of her, but there was nothing threatening in her stare. Rather, I felt a profound peace. I wasn't sure if it was the gurgle of the water, the womb-warmth of the night, the smell of pine and earth, or the company of this creature that had haunted my dreams. But here, now, this moment was the perfect antidote to the life I had left a week before.

Suddenly the peace was shattered by the thud of footsteps, for real this time and closing in. Whirling, I saw a tall form, as dark as the coyote was light, as human as the coyote was dog. I gave a frightened cry and would have run if he hadn't caught my arm.

'It's *me*, Emily, *me*!'

James? But James was in New York. James didn't know where I was. James never had this much stubble on his face or let his hair get this messed. James never wore torn T-shirts or smelled of sweat, though this man did both. James never looked *wild*.

But even as I saw, smelled, felt all that in the darkness — even with that shot of irritation raising his voice a notch, its huskiness was too familiar to mistake.

'I called you!' I screamed, irrationally furious perhaps, but he had left me bereft back in town and had *terrified* me now. 'I called, and you weren't there! We had a date, James. You — stood

— me — up,' I cried, whamming my free arm against his side with each word.

He grunted, but was otherwise unfazed. Pressing me back against the tree, where he could immobilize my body with his, he held my face with his hand and kissed me hard. *Fight, fight, fight*, a part of me wailed, and for a second, I couldn't breathe. But the taste was James, and the way his mouth moved said his hunger was huge.

Truth was, Jude lost by *miles* in this game. My attraction to James had flared the first time we met, strangers sitting beside each other two rows from the back in Constitutional Law. We slept together that very first night. I had never done that with Jude or anyone else. But something clicked with James — something as elemental and, yes, primitive as what I felt in these woods. I had known it would work.

Did I now?

I couldn't begin to think, not with him kissing me like he hadn't kissed me in months. We had been making love on the clock, putting ovulation before passion, but the clock wasn't ticking here. My heart was still pounding from fright — and shock that this was *James* — and then there was desire, which went from zero to one-twenty in the blink of an eye. My mouth had missed this. So had my body, to judge from the frantic way I pulled at his clothes. His hands found my breasts, my belly, the spot between my legs that weeped for him. When he thrust into me, I was totally ready, pulling him in deeply and holding him there until he withdrew and thrust again.

I cried his name, convincing myself that he was really here — and he was wild — punishing me, perhaps, but what initial anger there might have been gave way to raw need. He knotted a fist in my hair to hold my mouth for his taking, but beyond that it was about friction — hands and hips grasping, rubbing, building heat. His sweat mixed with mine now, producing a muskiness as feral as anything else. Our nakedness worked in the heat, and though the pine bark scraped my back as he pounded in, the pain was erotic.

Our passion might have been driven by the fact that we had been miles and minds apart, but reason was irrelevant. James was staking his claim in the most elemental way, and though I knew this didn't solve anything, I wanted it. Making love was the diametric opposite of the emptiness I had felt.

We climaxed within seconds of each other, me whispering his name in fragments now. I might have slid down the tree, just melted in a pool on the ground, if James hadn't held me up. His breath was rough by my ear, his arms and legs trembling but strong. James had always had a plan, and if the plan tonight was to fill my senses with him, he succeeded.

We made love again, this time on the ground with his back to the dirt and his hands on my breasts. The ascent was slower but the peak no less mind-blowing. Our bodies were drenched when it was done.

I couldn't speak. Even if I *could* think, which I couldn't, there were too many questions, any one of which would fracture the night, and I clung to these last silent moments when we were totally in sync.

My coyote was gone, of course. I'm guessing she left as soon as James appeared, spooked by his less-than-subtle approach and the cries we made. I might have asked if he'd even seen her, if I hadn't not wanted to talk.

In time, we knelt in the stream to cool ourselves and, eventually, pulled on our clothes. Wordless still, I led him back through the woods to the Red Fox, but we didn't make love up in that attic room. James had barely crawled into bed when, with an arm over my thigh as I sat, he was asleep.

I watched him, stunned again by how different he looked. Always heavy-bearded, he had a growth suggesting he had skipped several days, which made no sense if he was working. And though my own fingers had messed his hair, clutching handfuls when we made love, it had been messed at the start. Uncombed, it looked thicker than it did back home. And his body? I saw him naked all the time, but not smelling of sweat and lust and not sprawled on the sheets in the soft light of a place that was new and fresh. Unclothed here, he looked rugged.

How had he found me? Of all the questions I wanted to ask, that was the first. But I wasn't doing any asking with him dead to the world, and when he finally stirred, I had been sleeping myself, and it was dark. I remember murmuring a groggy *We have to talk*, but nothing after that, and when I woke up, he was gone.

13

Bolting up, I whipped around, searching, but he had left nothing to show he'd been here. I might have doubted it myself, if it hadn't been for the ache between my legs.

My BlackBerry said it was nine. Appalled that I'd slept so late — that I'd apparently slept right through his leaving — I tried his phone.

He picked up after one ring, his 'Hey' husky and deep.

My toes curled. Sitting on the bed, I tucked them under me. 'Tell me you're downstairs having coffee.'

There was a pause, then a guilty 'I'm not.'

'You're on the highway.'

'Since four. I'm almost at the Tappan Zee Bridge. I have to work.' No guilt here. Just fact. Which brought my problem home again.

'It's Saturday.' I *hated* this about our lives. 'Don't you deserve a break?'

'I took a break. Two days to chase after my wayward wife.'

If he wanted *me* to feel guilty, I refused. 'You didn't spend two days driving here.'

'Not directly. I tried other places first.'

'What places?

'Where you had a history.'

Lake George? Acadia? Both had been the site of childhood vacations in the days when my family was innocent and intact. James had heard many stories of those trips; we Scotts clung to happy memories. 'But how did you end up here? I've never talked about Bell Valley.'

'No,' he said, considering. 'That was telling.'

'But how did you even know the *name* of this place?'

He was slow to answer, then reluctant, as though confessing to something that did not make him proud. 'You have dreams, babe. You talk in your sleep.'

I caught a breath. 'About what?'

'Coyotes. And a guy named Jude.'

My silence was incriminating. Finally, I said, 'You never asked me about that.'

'I figured that what you didn't tell me, I didn't want to know. That's why I didn't head there — there first. We all delude ourselves sometimes. We tell ourselves everything is great when it really isn't.'

Here was my insightful James, apparently still alive under the raucous treadmill of our lives. That gave me hope.

'You have nothing to fear from Bell Valley,' I assured him softly.

'Not Jude?'

'Not Jude.'

I hated cell phones. If I'd been able to see his darkening face, I might have been prepared for his anger. Instead, his lower, sharper voice hit me flat out.

'I found letters, Emily. They were under the bed, where I wouldn't have looked unless I was desperate. I'd already searched your drawers, feeling like a total scumbag, thank you. JBB.'

189

Jude's typical sign-off. 'He must have been pretty important if you kept his letters. But the postmarks weren't old. Like the dreams.'

'If you read the letters, you know he was in Alaska,' I reasoned. The only mention of his return had been in the letter I'd taken with me. 'I did not come here for him.'

'So what was he to you?'

'He's the brother of my college roommate. I've mentioned Vicki Bell.'

'You never mentioned a brother.'

'Because it ended badly. Jude cheated on me, so I left. End of story.'

'Not end of story if you're dreaming about him.'

'It's not him, it's the *coyote*. Jude was just the one who introduced me to it.'

'My rival is a coyote? Come on, Em.'

'The coyote isn't about you. It's a she, and she's about me — about being wild and free. I mean,' I tried to soften it, 'think about last night. Was that incredible or what?'

He wasn't being sidetracked. 'You still don't want to talk about Jude.'

'He doesn't *matter*, James. What I had with him was over before you and I met.'

'Like, days before? How many — two? Three? You were on the rebound.'

'Excuse me. Did you ever sense anything — even the slightest instant in those first days after we met when I wasn't obsessed with *you*?'

'On the rebound,' he repeated. 'I've known you almost ten years — been married to you for seven — and still here's a big part of you that you never shared.'

'When do we *talk*?' I cried.

'We used to. You had opportunity. Hell, Emily, I knew you weren't a virgin. Neither was I. Sure, there was a guy before me, but it wouldn't have mattered if I hadn't learned about it this way.' He swore, annoyed. 'I sat there yesterday in my car, waiting to see you with him. I followed you into the woods, thinking you were meeting him there.'

I was chastened, but only to a point. Something was missing. Come to think of it, it was a pretty important piece. I didn't dream about Jude. Coyotes, yes. But not Jude, and I don't recall Jude's name or the name of Bell Valley appearing in any of those letters.

'Did you hire a detective?' I asked. Though the guy in the charcoal SUV was legit, he might have distracted me from seeing someone else.

'No.' His anger faded then, the spine in his voice dissolved. 'Christ, Em,' he said with a frustrated sigh, 'I'm too tired to argue. It doesn't matter how — how I found you, only that I did. Did you not enjoy last night?'

'I *loved* last night, but it was only half right. We didn't talk.'

'We connected.'

'We didn't *talk*. We need to talk, James.'

'No phone date,' he warned, but when he went on, his husky voice held an element of pleading. 'Come back. I need you here.'

The pleading nearly did it. I remembered his mussed hair and stubbled face. I pictured him driving those two days, searching, worrying, imagining me with a man I had never told him

191

about, and feeling alone. And now, exhausted, he was heading back to work.

I cared what he felt — cared more than I wanted to. But I couldn't live my life for James. I couldn't return because he wanted me to. I had to want it myself, and I didn't. Not yet.

My silence must have told him that, because he said a defeated 'Well, at least I know where you are. Take care, sweetie,' and ended the call.

At the 'sweetie,' my pulse skittered. Without breathing, I pressed redial.

He didn't pick up. Which was probably a good thing. Because I might have given in. Which would have been bad. Despite what Vicki had said about my being the bolder of us two, I had spent ten years following the party line. If there had been any point to my rebellion, it would be mocked if I returned now.

★   ★   ★

'He was *here*?' Vicki asked, startled. She was in the kitchen, finishing a breakfast muffin.

I joined her at the table, close as could be, and looked her in the eye. 'Briefly. Did you tell him where I was, Vicki Bell?'

She recoiled. 'Me? No way. Your marriage is *your* business. I wouldn't interfere. When did he get here?'

I knew Vicki. If she was lying, she would fidget or blink. But she looked curious, perhaps excited for me, but nothing more — all exculpatory evidence.

'Sometime yesterday.' *I sat there in my car,*

waiting. 'Omigod,' I suddenly realized, 'that must have been the blue car I saw. I thought it was Lee's guard.' I didn't see her now. 'Is she off for the weekend?'

'No. She works right through. She's having her hair trimmed. She'll be along.'

'I don't have any news,' I apologized. 'James and I didn't have much time to talk.'

Vicki snickered.

'What?'

'You have whisker burns on your face.'

Too much sun, I might have said. My breasts were red, too. Not that she could see those. But denial seemed pointless. James was my husband. What did she think we'd be doing after a week apart?

'Are you blushing?' Vicki asked sweetly, resting her chin on her hand.

With a snort, I helped myself to coffee, taking my time, knowing she would wait. Women loved talking about sex when the opportunity presented itself, and I did trust my friend Vicki.

'Isn't he usually clean-shaven?' she asked when I was sitting again.

Hidden by steam that rose from the mug, I sipped my coffee for a minute, before lowering the mug. 'He hadn't shaved in the two days it took him to track me here. He was' — I groped for the right words — 'a different James, and not only the scruff on his face. He hadn't shaved, hadn't showered — '

Vicki crinkled her nose.

'No. It was amazing, actually. Raw. *Real.*' I described my walk in the woods, which was part of it, too. 'I kept hearing noises behind me, but I couldn't see him, and lots of things make noise in the woods. So I just sat there watching my coyote — '

'Your *coyote?*' Vicki cried in alarm.

I hadn't meant to tell her. About James, yes, but not the coyote. She was mine. I felt protective. 'She ran off. I'm not even sure if James saw her, or if he waited just long enough to know I wasn't meeting a man. I didn't even believe it was him at first. He was *wild.*' My voice said that this hadn't been a bad thing.

'He was jealous,' Vicki decided. 'Skipped two days of work for you, ravaged you in the woods, carried you back, then got up in the middle of the night to drive six hours to work. That's totally romantic.'

'It's slightly crazy,' I corrected, though I ignored the 'carried you back' part, which was overly dramatic but did sound good.

In an abrupt turnaround, Vicki scowled. 'I hope you put up a fight.'

'Fight James? Why?'

'Because you had good reason for leaving, and a strong woman wouldn't cave.'

'I wasn't exactly submissive,' I said, knowing I was blushing again, but how to remember our lovemaking and not blush?

'What did you tell him about Jude?'

'I assured him Jude and I are done.'

'He'll still be nervous, y'know, knowing Jude's here.'

I started to speak, but stopped.

'Oh boy. You didn't tell him that part? How

could you not, Emmie? That's major important.'

'Not in terms of who I love.'

'But you still feel something for Jude. You told me yourself.'

'It isn't romantic. It isn't *sexual*. It's spiritual.'

Vicki sat back. 'You need to tell James.'

'I can't,' I argued. 'He wants me back in New York, and I'm not ready to go. If he knows Jude is here, he'll insist.'

'He'll find out anyway.'

'Like he found out Jude is from Bell Valley?' I puzzled. 'How did he *know*?'

★   ★   ★

James hadn't answered that. As I helped Vicki clean rooms a short time later, with the vacuum preventing talk, I brooded about it. I was still convinced that I hadn't mentioned Jude in my sleep. He wasn't the reason I loved James, and as for law school, I had been accepted there long before Jude and I were a thing. I don't recall thinking of him when I said 'I do' to James, signed on with Lane Lavash, or bought my fourth BlackBerry in succession, each a newer generation than the one before. I couldn't blame Jude for any of that. I had gone overboard all by myself.

One thing I did know as the minutes passed was that I felt better this morning. Was it the sex? A reaffirmation of what James and I had done and could do again? Or was it simply the fact that he had cared enough to come?

Whatever, I still wondered how he had known

195

about Jude. It had to be one of three people. But I wasn't about to start making calls to the suspects, because that would get me into other discussions, and I wanted to focus on James.

So I drove to the Refuge. Since the weekend volunteers were everywhere, I was able to slip past the main desk, and once I was in Rehab, my shaky kitty quickly found me. Needing to nurture, I hand-fed her, though she ate little and seemed more frail than ever. I told myself I was imagining it, that *any* kitten would be tiny compared to the massive Maine Coon that had plopped down by my thigh, minus a leg but sturdy. Still, I was worried. Had the regulars been around, I'd have asked, but they were off for the weekend, leaving the routine care to those weekend warriors. Some came for the day, making regular pilgrimages from places like Concord and Portsmouth. Others were headed elsewhere and simply stopped along the way.

There were enough of them to pick up the slack when I slid back to the wall with Precious on my lap, pulled out my BlackBerry, and tried calling James. I had four bars, so I knew my call went through. He just wasn't picking up.

I had no right to be hurt. But I was. I knew he was working. But I wanted him to be thinking of me, too.

No phone, I had told him when I first left. My rule. So this was payback.

Or he had gotten what he wanted last night and was satisfied. Or he was so exhausted that he just couldn't talk. Or he was *sleeping*, dead to the world with his head on his desk.

Most likely, I decided, resigned, he was just working, buried in it to make up for the billable hours he'd lost chasing me. I wondered if he was enjoying the actual work. I hadn't asked him that in a while. Our usual conversation ran more along the lines of complaints — an associate who wasn't doing his share, a partner pointing fingers at the wrong people, a client whose sense of entitlement was as big as the money he shelled out. I hadn't associated work with enjoyment in years.

I didn't miss Lane Lavash. But I did miss law. After sitting with the kitten a while longer, stroking her head while she slept, I set her carefully in a little fleece bed and returned to the Red Fox. Using Vicki's personal computer, in an out-of-the-way office that was piled with colouring books, littered with Legos, and smelling of a Play-dough worm that lay near the mouse, I accessed my email and sent one to James. In the subject line I typed *Legal Question*, hoping he wouldn't be able to resist.

Hey, I began. *How are you? I've wanted to talk, but you're not answering your phone. I don't blame you, James. I've rocked the boat big-time. Trust me, it's hard for me, too.* I stopped. Self-pity was wrong. Deleting the last sentence, I wrote, *I know I've hurt you. I'm sorry for that. I would have told you in person if you hadn't run off so fast.* Oops. I couldn't be critical. Deleting again, I typed, *I would have told you in person if we'd had more time, and I loved what we did do with that time, but I really need to talk. My mind is clearing. I'm starting to*

197

understand me more, but it doesn't mean much if I can't share it with you.

My fingers paused, suspended over the keyboard. *Legal Question.* That was all I'd planned to write to him about, not matters of the heart. Hadn't I sworn off machines as a means of personal communication? Wasn't I rebelling against a life of relationship-by-remote?

But technology wasn't going away. It would only get faster, easier, more common. And here was a fact: Right now, for me and James, it was email or nothing.

Besides, was sending my husband personal thoughts in an email any different from my grandmother's handwriting a love letter and sending it to my grandfather when he was fighting in Korea? Face-to-face might be ideal, but it wasn't always possible.

My using a computer now was a concession to practicality — or so I reasoned as I left these personal thoughts on the screen.

But I needed to get to the point. James's patience with me might be limited, and I wanted something to give Lee.

So I typed, *There's a situation here where I could use your advice. It involves an employee at the inn. She's a sweet person who bakes amazing cookies, but to her dead husband's family, she's a nobody, and because of that, she's being screwed. The immediate problem involves a physical threat, but the larger case is interesting.*

I stopped. I knew what James would be thinking. *Don't worry,* I wrote. *I'm not setting up shop here. My job at Lane Lavash is waiting.*

I didn't say if I wanted it. That would only stir him up.

But the James I'd fallen in love with had a soft spot for nobodies, and even if that James was diminished, the one that remained was a sucker for a good case. Last year, he had worked with warring branches of a family corporation, and though they had settled prior to trial, he had been energized. In comparison, Lee's case was tiny, but not entirely different.

She was hiding out here, I typed, *so maybe that's why I feel for her, but she's been found out, and not in a good way.* I typed a summary of her situation — felony barmaid turned heiress, dwindling trust fund, threats — and followed it up with the possibilities I had tossed out in the kitchen with Vicki and Lee. *Money isn't an issue,* I concluded. *She has a relative who will pay, but the problem is jurisdiction. You know more than I do about Massachusetts law, and you have a contact there. Do you think Sean Alexander could handle this? Or someone else in his firm?*

I paused to consider how to close, then typed, *I know I'm asking a lot, James. You may still be angry enough at me to not want any part of this. But we used to talk about helping the underdog, and you were way better at it than I was.* I was thinking of law school again, comparing the promise of James versus how he'd turned out and wondering whether, like me, the turned-out side was simply what we saw because of our jobs. I wanted to believe the other was there, hidden but alive. *I keep thinking back to moot court.*

Why is it that I feel some of my best work was done then? Resting the heel of my hands on the edge of the desk, I sighed. Then, as I anticipated his reading these words, I typed, *I can see you pressing your forehead, thinking that you need to get back to work and don't have time for my rambling. But maybe something will come to you that will help my friend. If you think of anything, will you pass it on?*

My hands hovered. I wanted to sign off with *I love you,* but feared he would think I was saying it only because I wanted something from him. Instead, as a greater act of contrition, I wrote, *I'll leave my BlackBerry on.*

★ ★ ★

The problem with that was twofold. First, when James didn't instantly reply, I was discouraged. I told myself that he would be two days behind in work and couldn't drop everything for this, and that there was no legal action to be taken on the weekend anyway. I reminded myself that Sean might be gone from the office, gone from his firm, or simply not answering his cell. I assured myself that it was *fine* if James sent me his thoughts later today or tomorrow.

Second, though, in leaving my BlackBerry on, I saw other emails. My mom wrote saying that she wanted to talk, and my dad wrote saying I was being irresponsible and was upsetting Mom. On the plus side, my sister sent a surprisingly sympathetic note of envy, while Tessa, my cubicle-mate, said she missed me.

And then there was Walter.

Here's the good news, Emily. You were betrayed by one of your fellow associates, who was so pissed at my giving you a four-week leave that he crabbed about it to the managing partner, who complained to enough of the equity partners that I'm now in deep shit. I've played the corporate compassion card, but they're not buying. Tell me you're in therapy. Tell me you're thinking clearly and will be at your desk Monday morning. Tell me something. You promised to stay in touch, but I haven't heard a word. Break your promise, and I may break mine.

I was sorry I'd read it. My hands were suddenly tense, my ears ringing with the old hums and dings. In that instant, Walter Burbridge embodied everything I hated about my work. I tried to turn it off, but no matter how loudly I reminded myself that I had three more weeks of leave, I kept hearing Walter's words. *Break your promise, and I may break mine.* The threat was a thundercloud marring the clarity of my blue summer sky.

Desperate to get it out of my head, I took a walk in the woods. There was no fear now. I hadn't been eaten by a squirrel or attacked by a moose. I hadn't been ravished by Jude, but by James, who was warm-blooded and real. Knowing that he had walked this path, that we had walked it together, gave it a new feel. Besides, it struck me that if what I had so feared before was the power of the lure, I was already hooked. It was done.

Besides, it was broad daylight. I waded through the ferns and along the old stone wall that was my GPS. And there was a snake. Lying on top in a patch of sun. I hated snakes. In utter revulsion, I stopped.

It was a garter snake. How did I know? Jude. Each time we had come upon one, he had dangled it in front of my face, his manner of teasing — or teaching, which was the interpretation he chose. What I had learned first was not to gag.

I had also learned that garter snakes are harmless, which was why I walked past now, leaving the snake to its rock and my feet to the dirt. Picking up the trickle of the brook, I followed it in. The air was less humid than it had been, hence that clear blue sky, but I had built up a sweat by the time I reached my coyote — or rather, the spot where I'd seen her last night.

She wasn't there now. I didn't have to search the other bank to know. I didn't sense her, didn't smell her. As I stood on a small rock, inches from the shallow water, minnows darted by, flashes of silver heading downstream. I knelt to let my hand trail in the cool water, remembering how James and I had bathed here. My eye slid to the tree against which he had propped me that first time, then to the bed of dirt beneath. The pine needles looked rumpled, as a bed sheet might have been. I blushed, smiled as the memory played in my mind, rocked back on my heels.

Then I went still, listening. I wasn't sure I'd heard anything. She would have moved silently through the woods, any whisper of sounds masked by the gurgling brook. I did smell her now, though, a tiny wild something intermingling with pine. My eyes rose.

She wasn't at the water's edge, but a dozen feet in, watching me from atop a boulder. Sitting erect in the dappled sunlight, she was stunning. Her pelt was grey and white, her forelegs as creamy as the pointed muzzle I had spotted last night. Now I saw apricot as well, touching the top of her head, her ear tufts, the upper part of her ruff.

I used to think coyotes were nocturnal, since their howls came at night. Not so, Jude had said. They were around during the day but knew the danger of being seen, so they took care. Darkness was the only time they dared speak aloud without drawing unwanted attention. Flying under the radar was how they survived.

Yet there she was, watching me in full view, trusting that I wouldn't raise a rifle and shoot. That said, she wasn't lolling on her back in the sun, but sat with her inordinately large ears pricked. Had I stood, her eyes would have still been higher than mine. But I didn't stand. She was alert, her nose twitching almost imperceptibly as she sniffed the air.

For a split second, I had the fanciful notion that James had come again. Only James didn't walk on silent coyote paws. Today I heard no thrashing through the woods behind me.

Before me, though, I caught movement at the base of the boulder on which she sat. I looked down when she did, expecting to see her lunch scamper by. But the creature in action was as roly-poly as my sister's bichon, if pale grey, and there was not only one but a second then a third and a fourth.

Her pups. I had wanted to think she had brought them to show me, but I guessed that her den was nearby.

Backing up to the fat pine to give them space, I watched the pups tossing something around. Belatedly I realized that I'd been half right. They were playing with a chipmunk, though whether they planned to eat it for lunch, I didn't know.

The chipmunk escaped, which surprised me. I'd have thought that if the pups didn't want it, the mom would. But she continued to watch me watch them, her gold eyes filled with pride.

It occurred to me that a coyote was too wild to communicate pride — that I was reading fantasy thoughts into those anchored eyes, that narrow muzzle, those pointy ears, simply because I needed a connection to these woods — that the tears in my eyes were my relating to her and wanting a baby so badly myself. The yearning. Isn't that what my dream left me with?

In the next breath, I realized that her stare might be a warning. *Take one step toward my pups,* she was saying, *and I'll attack.*

Moreover, if I *needed* a connection to these woods, I had no idea why. *Wanting* is something else. Wildness in animals is a curious thing to us humans. Isn't that why people watch Animal Planet?

Escape. Maybe that's why we watch. Animal behaviour is elemental. It takes us back to a simpler time.

So maybe escape is why I'm hooked on these woods, which are the total opposite of where I've been, and I don't only mean New York. Ten years ago, it was New Haven, nowhere near as large as New York, but congested for me, with students milling everywhere, standing room only in some of my classes, and three roommates crammed into a small apartment, and though I spent most of my nights at James's place, the city locked us in.

These woods are primal. They are as they were hundreds of years ago and, in that, stable and calm. There is a peace here that I don't feel elsewhere. I can think clearly here. I can breathe.

I stayed by the tree for a time, watching the coyote pups tumble over each other. Occasionally one spotted me, drawn perhaps by my scent, and held my gaze for a minute before resuming its play — and it did occur to me that, in letting me stand unchallenged, their mother might be teaching them the wrong lesson. Humans were to be feared.

But not me. I swear she knew I wouldn't hurt her pups. She sensed the protectiveness I felt, perhaps even sensed my envy. I saw four pups. The average female coyote birthed six, though — according to Jude — a single litter could produce eighteen.

Ouch.

I smiled. Four was fine. I'd settle for one. Thinking about that, I felt an ache deep inside.

I didn't ache for law in quite the same way. I missed the intellectual challenge. I missed the emotional satisfaction of helping someone who

205

couldn't help himself. But it wasn't like wanting a baby. And it wasn't like missing James.

* * *

Hey, Walter, I typed when I returned to the inn. *I'm sorry. Next week is out. I'm healing, but it's a process. Thanks for your patience.*

I sent the email and walked away from Vicki's computer.

14

James emailed me late Saturday night.

You're right, he wrote. *My first thought was that you're thinking of practising up there, but if you say you're not, I'll take you for your word. Sounds like your friend has a mess of a life. Hah. Sounds familiar. You're right about investigators. She needs to ID the tail so that you can find out who hired him. Yes re: the forensic accountant. Yes re: her need for Boston counsel. Conflict of interest could be a problem. She can't use anyone remotely connected to the firm that handles the trust fund. Give me her name and the name of the family corporation, and I'll run it by Sean. If his firm clears, he may be willing to help. What kind of cookies does she bake?*

★ ★ ★

When I asked Lee early Sunday morning, she said her last name was Baker.

A baker named Baker? I knew an alias when I heard one.

I explained about lawyer-client confidentiality and assured her of James's sensitivity to the danger she faced, but having felt powerless for so long, she was skittish. She had run away to hide, and yes, she'd been found out. But with each additional person who knew, the greater her chance of being carted away. Having been in prison once, she went pale at the thought of it happening again — and, honestly, I couldn't guarantee that once her husband's family realized that she planned to fight, they wouldn't go on the offensive. Would they want the publicity, knowing the charges were trumped up? If they were arrogant enough they would. The best I could do was promise she wouldn't be alone.

It took some convincing, but she finally gave in. Lee Cray. Husband Jack, and brothers-in-law Raymond and Duane. All beneficiaries of the Cray Family Trust.

Pleased with this little win, I shot the information she gave me back to James, ending with *Oatmeal raisin and chocolate chip, but the chocolate macadamia nut ones are the best.*

Chocolate macadamia nut cookies were his favourite.

★   ★   ★

Amelia came for brunch dragging Jude, who looked like he had just rolled out of bed. He hadn't shaved, hadn't combed his hair.

He looked amazing.

Like Brett Favre looked amazing.

But I didn't want to sleep with Brett Favre any more than I wanted to sleep with Jude Bell, though he kept staring at me like I should — like I had to remember what it was like waking up with him sexy and hard, like I should be jealous of his woman in Hanover and needed to restake my claim.

I did not. Having just heard from James, I was immune.

Lee sat with us. Her muddy hair still slanted over her forehead, but with the sides and back now shaped to complement her face, I realized that she was an attractive woman.

Amelia's first line of defence, and rightly so, was protecting Lee. In addition to the car on the green, she'd had new locks installed on Lee's windows and doors, she explained with some pride.

'That's good,' I said encouragingly. 'Now we need to build a case. Do the police have anything — pictures, fingerprints, footprints?'

'They have the notes that were put in her mail slot, and they do have pictures of the matter left on her stoop.'

'It's called dog shit,' Jude said with a smirk.

Amelia smiled. 'Not at breakfast it isn't.'

'Have they done anything with them?' I asked, ignoring Jude, who continued to stare at me.

'There's not much they can do other than keep them on file,' Amelia reasoned, but she was a take-charge sort and moved right on. 'What do we need?'

'Pictures catching someone in the act. Lee should have a camera to use anytime she sees strangers around, but we also need a motion-activated video cam on the roof of the house. It may get pictures of deer or moose, but one shot of a man doing something unwanted and we're in luck.'

'I'll have them mounted today, front and back,' Amelia promised. 'I understand your husband was here?'

'Yes. Just a quick visit.'

'I'd like to meet him next time.'

'So would I,' remarked Jude.

I'll bet you would, I thought. I could see him clapping James on the back and talking man-to-man about sex with me. Vicki was right. I did need to tell James myself that Jude was back — had to explain my feelings, past and present. It would be a pre-emptory move, because somehow, somewhere, he would learn about Jude, and it would be best coming from me.

'But I can't do it in an email,' I said the minute Vicki and I were alone.

'On the phone, then?'

'Not good.'

'But you have to do it soon. I saw how Jude was looking at you. He is spoiling for a fight.'

'Why with *me*?'

'Because you're not falling all over him. What if *he* phones James? It's almost worth a trip back to New York to tell him.'

'I can't.'

'Not even a quick one? Like his visit here?'

★ ★ ★

It sounded simple — drive in, tell James about Jude, make love to show him that *he* was the one I loved, drive out.

And I did consider it as I helped Vicki clear the buffet in the parlour. But I was afraid that if I went back I wouldn't be able to leave — that

James wouldn't *let* me leave once he knew about Jude, that I would be numbed again by my life there and unable to think until the next perfect storm made me crack. It also occurred to me that the lovemaking could bomb if it was manipulative, in which case I would have risked the most elemental connection James and I had.

★   ★   ★

I might have agonized more if I hadn't been given something else to consider. Lee took off, and Vicki and I were wiping down the kitchen counters when she left for the front hall in response to the ding of the bell. I heard an excited sound, but the dishwasher was running, muting exact words. I did get each one, though, when she returned and said in a voice that was a little too bright, 'Look who just arrived!'

Behind her were my parents.

My *parents*.

My first thought, absurdly, was relief. Thirty minutes sooner and they'd have run into Amelia and Jude. *Five* minutes sooner and they'd have run into Lee.

My second thought was guilt. Claire and Roger Scott, divorced but joined in this rescue mission, had driven the two hours from Portland to haul me back home, or so my little-girl's mind said in a moment's regression.

My final thought was dismay. I wasn't ready for them.

I opened my mouth, but no words came out. Caught between pleasure and dread, I could

211

only dry my hands on the dish towel. My parents were an attractive couple — Mom with crinkles by her eyes and long auburn hair held behind an ear with a thin yellow ribbon that would have been recycled from a gift, Dad with little hair but remarkably smooth skin. Both carried ten pounds more than their doctors wanted, but they looked L.L.Bean outdoorsy in jeans and shirts. So familiar. So dear. So unnerving.

I swallowed. 'Mom. Dad. How did you know where I was?'

I knew Mom had suspected, but I was surprised when she said, 'James called. He said you were all right, but I wanted to see for myself, and then your father said he wasn't being left out, so here we are.'

'James called *you*?'

'He loves you, Emily,' Dad stated. 'He called your mother more than once.'

Ahh. '*You* were the one who told him about Bell Valley.'

'Well, how could I not?' Claire asked. 'I sent him other places first, because I wasn't *entirely* sure where you were, and I do blame him for what's happened.'

'It's not his fault,' Dad said. 'He's the responsible one.'

'I thought we agreed to disagree on this, Roger.'

'You and I agreed, but not Emily and I.'

'Then James called again,' Mom went on, tuning Dad out, 'and he sounded so tired and worried that I felt guilty. I knew how much you loved this place that summer, and when we talked the other day, I did hit a nerve.' Stopped just short of mentioning Jude, she smiled at Vicki. 'You look *wonderful*. Motherhood must be agreeing with you. Is your daughter around?'

'How do you know she has a daughter?' I asked. Like with my dreaming of Jude, I was sure I hadn't mentioned Charlotte.

Mom glanced at a picture on the corkboard by the phone. 'Because that little girl has Vicki Bell written all over her.'

Brows arched in question, she returned to Vicki, who said, 'Her dad took her to the Refuge. She loves the cats.'

I had a sudden inspiration. 'Want one?' I asked Vicki. 'There's a special-care kitty with a neurological problem. She needs small places, like a little girl's bedroom. I think you should take her.'

But Vicki was shaking her head even before I finished. 'I'd do it in a heartbeat. Charlotte would adore it, but not all my guests are Refuge people. For the one who may have an allergy, the Red Fox has to be pet-free.'

'Is that another baby I see growing?' Mom asked Vicki. Amazing, because there was barely a bump, but Mom did have a sixth sense when it came to maternal things. She never asked me if I was pregnant. She would know.

'Sure is,' Vicki said, 'but hey, you guys need to talk. Want the den?' she asked me.

'Oh no,' Mom replied as she looked around the kitchen. 'This room is calling me. Very country farmhouse. Are the cabinets oak?'

'They are,' Vicki confirmed. 'They're original.'

Trust Mom to appreciate something I had taken for granted. She was a detail person. I used to think I was, too, until my life filled with so many that I couldn't see any one.

'That stove is no original,' Mom was saying.

'No. It's state of the art, or at least it was four years ago.'

'Well, it's a winner. And this table.' She ran a hand over the distressed wood. 'So warm.' She pulled out a chair and, beaming, sat down. 'I would love a cup of coffee. Actually, I can make it.' She started to rise again, but I pressed her back down.

'I'll do it.'

'And maybe something to munch on? Your dad's hungry.'

'Your mom's hungry,' Dad countered, but sounded indulgent in this.

I was grateful for something to do. While Vicki went to handle Sunday checkouts, I made brunch from what we had just put in the fridge.

'I'm impressed,' Mom remarked when I served them quiche with sides of sausage, asparagus, and corn fritters.

'Reheating is my specialty.'

'I thought your specialty was corporate litigation,' Dad said. 'Are you planning to just dump it for this . . . whatever that guy is?'

I stared at him for a minute, before rolling my eyes. 'You are so far off base that I'm stunned. His name is Jude, Dad, and what's going on with me has nothing to do with him.'

Still holding his fork and knife, Dad planted the heels of his hands on the edge of the table.

'Please, sweetheart. I know how these things work. You get married, everything's great, then the routine sets in and you start romanticizing the past.'

'I didn't do that,' Mom pointed out.

'I'm not talking to you, Claire. I'm talking to Emily.'

'I didn't do it, either,' I told him. 'I OD'd on what I had in New York and needed a break.'

'Um-hm,' Dad murmured and took several bites while Mom and I exchanged looks. I wasn't entirely sure she was my ally, what with her dubious opinion of James. But I did feel better with her here.

Dad put down his fork. 'You claimed you loved Jude, but you never wanted us to meet him. You knew I'd hate him, didn't you, because he wasn't going anywhere.'

'How do you know that?'

'He was here. There's nothing here.'

I was offended. 'Have you never heard of the Bell Valley Animal Refuge? Jude is in line to head the whole thing. He goes all over the world on Refuge business.' It was theoretical, of course, since Jude typically travelled for Jude. But Dad had no right to dismiss a town he knew nothing about. 'As for this town, it has a history of offering sanctuary to people who don't follow the mainstream, which, quite honestly, describes me right now.'

'The mainstream being James.'

'The mainstream being *you*,' I cried.

'Actually, it's James,' he maintained. 'You left him. That's a mistake, Emily. James is the best

215

thing you have. He keeps you on track.'

'Like I can't do that myself?'

'No, you can't right now. *Look* at you.'

I did — looked down at the sundress I'd worn for brunch, then at my hands, which were rock steady and relaxed — then back at Dad. 'I look better than I have in months.'

'She does, Roger.'

'Well, of course, you'll take her side, Claire. You never wanted to work, either.'

'That's so wrong, Dad. Mom worked her butt off as a mother. Well, maybe I want to do the same thing. Maybe I want to have kids and stay home with them.'

'But you have a *career*,' he argued. 'What *purpose* would you serve giving it up?'

'The purpose,' I said with purpose, 'is to give me something to do before kids and then something to do when they go to school.'

He snorted. 'Mommy-trackers take a hit. Is that what you want?'

'Yes.'

'And waste your potential?'

'Potential for what?' I asked. 'Being a lawyer? What about my potential for being a mother? A friend? A human *being*?'

He pointed his fork at me. 'You left out wife.' The fork stabbed a corn fritter, which quickly disappeared into his mouth.

Mom was glowering. 'You are so backward, Roger.'

He shrugged. 'That's how it is in my world.'

'Which is why I am no longer in it,' she said, and, standing up, left the room.

216

We sat in silence for a while, Dad eating slowly. I poured each of us refills of coffee. Finally, he set down his fork. He looked to be trying to decide what to say when Mom returned and said, 'I think we should take a walk. I need air.'

Dad was happy to comply. I sent them outside while I cleaned the kitchen, and found them a short time later in the General Store. Mom was still browsing, though the wicker basket on her arm was already filled with small kitchen items, candles, and cheese. I browsed with her for a few minutes, then left her to pay while I looked for Dad. I found him on a bench just outside the front door and sat beside him.

'Well, it is peaceful here,' he offered, looking out over the green.

'Whatever is going on now,' I said to reassure him, 'I am not leaving James.'

'Well, you're still wearing his ring.'

'We love each other.'

'So do your mother and I, but we can't live together. It makes me sad to think you've learned that from us. I wanted something better for you.'

'I know.'

'I had dreams for you.'

'*Your* dreams.'

'Yours, too, I thought.' His eyes met mine. 'When did that change?'

'A week ago Friday, when I realized that the dream didn't work for me anymore.'

'You were tired. You didn't mean it.'

'I'm not tired now, and I do mean it. This is

my life, Dad. *My* life. Not yours, and not Mom's. I get to choose.'

His eyes returned to the green. He let out a breath, slowly shook his head. 'Well, you do. But you want my blessing, and I can't give it.'

Mom joined us then, looking at her watch. She had a fund-raiser at the hospital that night, which meant they needed to head home. I hugged them both, waving when Mom turned to look at me, waving herself until the car was gone. Dad didn't turn or wave.

He was right. I did want his blessing.

But I was right. This was *my* life, so I got to choose.

How to have both — my way and his blessing?

And how not to brood about that?

★   ★   ★

Distraction was key.

On Monday, I moved into the gardener's shed. The room was smaller than heaven, and done up in the greens of the forest rather than the blues and whites of the sky. After unpacking, I sat for a time on the bench bolted to its forest side, but when the lure of the woods grew too great, I wandered in. The scamperings around me were innocent, the smells crisp as the sun striped through the trees. I meandered at first, breathing in pine resin and fertile soil, absorbing the peace. Inevitably, I made my way up along the stone wall. Thankfully, there were no snakes today, and I did keep a close watch. Seeing nothing more than a pair of red squirrels, a hawk, and several swirls of gnats, I continued on to the brook.

James was in New York. No word from him yet.

And the coyote? Not here either.

Alone with my thoughts, I kept remembering our tryst. Perhaps I was clinging to that memory as proof that my husband and I still had some kind of connection.

But . . . what if sex was all we had? What if we had deluded ourselves into thinking there was more? What if Dad was right, that you could love someone and not live with him? What if my running away had stripped it all down to this? We were physically attracted to each other. Period.

★ ★ ★

The possibility haunted me as Monday passed with no word. I had been hoping that Lee's case would be common ground. After all, James and I had met over law. We'd had that from the start.

I texted on Tuesday. *Are you okay?*

Working, he texted back, which told me nothing and pointed out one of the worst things about electronic communication. Lacking facial expression, tone of voice, or context, words could be taken any number of ways. With only one cryptic word now, I was discouraged.

Conversely, though, electronic communication was great when you weren't up for a whole discussion. So I texted Mom to thank her for coming. She texted back that she loved me.

I texted Dad to thank him for coming. He didn't text back. Actually, he didn't text, period, but I had been hoping that would change. My dream, apparently. Not his.

★ ★ ★

I kept busy.

Actually, that sells the effort short. After having had zero time to play in the last ten years, I was rediscovering the pleasure of having time to fill. And there was no shortage of things to do. When I was at the Refuge, if I wasn't in Rehab coaxing my kitten to eat, I was bathing dogs or grooming horses, and if I wasn't with the animals, I was with Bob Bixby. If I wasn't at the Refuge, I was helping Vicki at the inn or browsing in The Bookstore or getting — surprise, surprise — a massage at The Spa, formerly The Hair Shop, now broadened to include body care as well.

James didn't call, email, or text.

So I babysat Charlotte, which helped in ways totally aside from distraction. Since Vicki refused to charge me for my room, and since her pregnancy gave her the occasional migraine, I could cover during those late afternoon hours. Charlotte was reticent until she realized I would read *Pinkalicious* over and over again, which, apparently, her mother was not willing to do. After that came *My Mama Says There Aren't Any Zombies, Ghosts, Vampires, Demons, Monsters, Fiends, Goblins, or Things*, which I read until both of us knew the words by heart.

I'd had dinner Monday night with Vicki and Rob, barbecued baby back ribs that Rob proudly declared to be his best recipe and Vicki affectionately declared to be his *only* one. I had dinner Tuesday night at The Grill with Lee, who was in something of a holding pattern, waiting for the camera on her roof to be tripped. And Wednesday night? Not dinner, but an evening cappuccino with the owner of The Bookstore.

Actually, it wasn't just her. Apparently, Wednesday nights were something of a ritual here, an impromptu after-hours gathering of anyone who wanted to talk books. I had come out of curiosity, to see how the group worked compared with mine at home, and since I was sleeping later each morning, I didn't need cappuccino to keep me awake.

The group had been billed as a fluid one, open to anyone in town, and I was prepared for a literary discussion, which was apparently what took place when men attended. Tonight there were only women, seven of us ranging in age from thirty to sixty. I had met a few of them ten years before, though hadn't known them well, but that didn't seem to matter. I was instantly drawn into the conversation, which began with my being a lawyer and moved to a legal thriller one of the women had read, then to a paranormal thriller another had read, then to a nonfiction book on the appeal of these kinds of books.

It seemed that it had to do with why we read thrillers, why we were here tonight.

The store was closed, and though we started out in a small sitting area, we began wandering the aisles looking for one book or another to

221

make a point. We were in Biography with the likes of Thomas Jefferson, Admiral Robert Peary, and Coco Chanel, sitting on the floor with our coffee, when the front door dinged.

Our leader looked back, then at us again. Eyes wide, she put a finger to her lips. 'We aren't here.'

'Hello?' called a male voice, as deep as it was familiar.

15

I was on my feet in a second and at the door in two. Throwing my arms around him, I held on for several more, before easing back. His jaw wore only a five o'clock shadow this time, but his work slacks were wrinkled from the drive, his sleeves haphazardly rolled. Despite its perfect styling, his hair was a mess, and his eyes were tired. I searched for pleasure in them, but couldn't see past the fatigue. He did have his arms around my waist. That was a good sign. But they were heavy and, once there, didn't move.

'Hey,' I whispered. 'How'd you know we were here?'

'Who's we?' he whispered back.

I might have called them book friends and left it at that, but something inside me wanted him to see — actually, wanted *them* to see. Later I would realize that the publicity of his being here was good. Now, though, all I could think was that, even tired, he looked gorgeous, and he was mine.

Taking his hand, I led him to the others. 'Hey, guys, this is my husband. James, meet Monica, Shelly, Jill, Angela, and Jane — and Vickie, the Book V, who owns the store.'

He smiled politely at each, but quickly murmured to me, 'I'm half asleep. Got a bed?'

I'm sure I left a grin or two behind, but my eyes stayed on James. Raising my free hand in a backwards wave, I led him back to the door. The night was warm under a blanket of clouds, but I wasn't interested in stars or the moon. I was worried; James really did look beat. I was delighted; he had driven all this way *again*. I was curious.

'Did Vicki send you over?' I asked, and slipped an arm through his to keep him close as I steered him toward the inn.

'Yeah.' His hand found mine, fingers lacing, locking. I wanted to think he needed the closeness as much as I did. But his fingers were tense, reminding me of my own body when I had first left New York.

'You drove straight from work?'

'Left at four,' he said in a voice that was lower than ever, as if it, too, was bone-weary. 'Dumb move, rush — rush hour and all.'

'Has work been rough?'

'You could say.'

I didn't ask more. *Wouldn't* ask more. Work was the enemy here, or one of them.

And another? At the sound of a low vibration, James dug in his pocket and pulled out a phone. His step didn't falter as he studied the screen, typed something with his thumb, re-pocketed the phone.

'Is that a new one?' I asked.

'The firm got a deal. It's the latest.'

The latest. That was swell. I didn't say it, because I knew my sarcasm would come through, and I didn't want his visit to start with that. Besides, he looked too tired for words.

We walked the last little way in silence. When I

guided him up the driveway, he said, 'Back door?'

'Actually, a separate one,' I replied, going past the inn to the gardener's shed. I felt him balk when I reached for the knob.

He scratched the back of his head in a familiar, open-palm, vaguely facetious gesture, and said in a voice that was deep enough, *raspy* enough to be sexy as hell, 'Uh, babe, I think I need a bed this time.'

'It's here.'

I let him precede me. The place was small enough — okay, *tiny* enough — for him to take it in at a glance, but the bed was a voluminous queen, and though it took most of the space, Vicki had managed to squeeze in a wardrobe and bench. The bathroom, which had been added at the time of the conversion, was spacious and posh enough to make up for what the bedroom lacked.

Shutting out the world, I leaned against the door and waited for James to take me in his arms. Glimpses of Friday night rippled from mind to body. Watching him, all long legs, broad back, and ruffled hair, I was ready.

He had his shirt off in no time, then dropped onto the bench and removed his belt, shoes, and socks. He paused with his pants only to dig out the phone, which must have hummed against his thigh, because he held it, read the screen, and typed in a response. It remained in his right hand while his left drew back the covers. He put the phone on the tiny lamp table on his way down, made a sound that might have been relief, and was quickly asleep.

No. Apparently we weren't only about sex.

But I knew what he felt. I had been where he was, so tired that I couldn't talk. I sat on the bed for a while, thinking that a second trip here had to mean something. And that sound he had made right before falling asleep? Relief to be with me? Relief to be prone? Relief to be lying on clean, fresh sheets?

Or was it the woods that had lulled him to sleep? He had to have smelled pine and earth; they permeated the room. Then again, it had taken me a while to be able to smell again. My first night here, I was on overload to the point of numbness.

Recalling how Vicki had pampered me, I slipped back to the main house while James slept, and raided the fridge. I returned with cold drinks and a sandwich, and had barely — ever so stealthily — opened the door when I saw James sitting on the edge of the bed.

'Where'd you go?' he asked, sounding hoarse and unnerved.

I held up the food. 'Hungry?'

He barely moved. 'Tell me that guy was in the kitchen.'

Having been consumed by *this* guy for the last little while, I was slow to follow. 'Jude? Why are you thinking about Jude?'

'Was he?'

'No.' I was guarded. 'How do you know he's in town?'

'Didn't know. Guessed. Don't care. Com'ere.'

Setting the food on the bench, I approached

the bed, kicking off my sneakers and, as he watched, the rest of my clothes. He was reaching for me before the last were barely gone, pulling me under him and kissing me hard.

What happened then was even wilder than it had been in the woods, and not just on his part. Filled with his scent and the familiar texture of his body, I couldn't get enough. I took and demanded more. I figured that simply for not calling me back, he owed me this.

He was gasping loudly when it was done. Tucking me under his arm, he held me close. 'What was *that*?'

It was a minute before I could speak. Finally, with my cheek to his shoulder, I managed a weak 'Fresh air. Absence. Heightened senses.'

'You missed me?' he asked with an audible smile.

'I did.'

He released a lengthening breath. 'So. Tell me about him.'

I snuggled closer. 'Not now.'

'I need to know. How long's he been back?'

I might have gone off on a *Jude doesn't matter* tangent. Except that Jude did matter to James, and he would jump to the wrong conclusion if I didn't explain.

'A week,' I said.

His body didn't change — didn't tense up or pull back — didn't even *freeze*, just stayed eerily still. 'That's coincidental.'

'Yes. When I left, I had no plans to come here.'

'Did you know he'd be here?'

I came up over him then, wanting his eyes to

227

see mine. 'The truth, James? He wrote saying he'd be back at the end of the month. I thought I could get here and be gone before he arrived. He didn't know I was coming. He just showed up earlier.'

'And you didn't leave once you saw him here?'

'Why would I? I told you. I didn't come for him.'

'Right. The old college roommate. The sister.' He looked sceptical.

'It was more than that,' I said, because the James with me now was . . . *with* me. He was listening and thinking. 'That summer was different. I was out of college and into law school. I wasn't worried about my résumé. I was free here. There were no limits, no expectations. I did what I wanted when I wanted, and my parents let me, because I was with Vicki. I had no responsibility. No cares. No demands. *That* was what I came back for. To *breathe*.'

He considered, and said a tentative 'Okay. And the dreams weren't of Jude?'

'What I remember of them was the coyote. Did I actually say Jude's name?'

'No,' he admitted. 'Your mom mentioned him. After that, I kept hearing his name. Imagining it.'

I touched his face. 'You do not need to worry. Trust me. Please?'

Raising a hand to the back of my head, he brought my face close, but the kiss was tender, gentle as the breath that followed. 'It was never like this before.'

'It was,' I mused, laying my head on his chest. His heartbeat was steady, steady. 'At the start.'

228

He was silent for a minute, then wry. 'Go on. I'm not sure I'll like it, but you have a theory.'

'I was stunted in the city. Here I'm alive.'

He was quiet again before murmuring, 'Nope, not what I want to hear.' Without looking, he stretched out an arm. When he brought it back up, his hand held the phone. After reading the screen, he pressed several buttons. I wanted to think he was turning it off, but the screen remained lit. He dropped it on the bed by his hip.

'I can't leave New York, Em. It's everything I've always wanted.'

'Everything how?'

'The practice. The money.'

'I don't care about money. Money doesn't matter.'

'It does if we want to live in New York.'

'Were we enjoying the money? Were we doing things with it that mattered? No. We didn't have time. You're a runner, but you haven't run in months, and okay, let's talk about your practice. Are you really, honestly, handling the kinds of cases you dreamed of? Because I'm not.' I came up on an elbow, again needing to look him in the eye. 'Yes, I know, we have jobs and other lawyers don't — and yes, I know that we have a mortgage and loans, and need the money — and yes, we're paying our dues. But look at Walter. He's an equity partner. Total job security there, no loans and a *huge* monthly draw, but he's leading the same crazy lifestyle we are.'

James made a dismissive sound. 'That's Walter.'

'It's every high-level lawyer I know,' I insisted, to which he pulled me over so that I lay on him, and cupped my face in his hands. His eyes went from my eyes to my lips. When he kissed me this time, his mouth was eloquent.

I knew when I was being silenced. But he was also making me feel loved, and I was so hungry for that — gratified, reassured, *lightheaded* — that I didn't protest. By the time we had made love again, I was back to thinking about whether sex was the one thing we could agree on. By then he was snoring softly.

I slept, too, though nowhere near as soundly as he did. The slightest movement he made had me awake, fearful that he was slinking out again in the dark when we still had to talk.

In the end, though, the only talking done in the dark that night was in the woods. The gardener's shed was front row centre in this particular concert hall, and my coyotes the marquee event. I heard barks and yips backing up a duet of howls. During one particular stretch, I opened the window, half hoping that the sounds would wake James, but they didn't.

What woke him was the phone.

What woke me was his swearing as he fished through the bedsheets to locate the ring. I looked over my shoulder and watched him answer.

'Good morning.' Sounding groggy, he squinted at his watch and swore again, this time under his breath. 'Nine. I see it, Mark. I'm sorry. I must have slept through the alarm,' he lied, and, bowing his head, rubbed the back of his neck. 'I know. At eight. How did it go?' As he listened, he rubbed

230

his eyes with thumb and forefinger. 'Okay. I can do that, but not today. I can't hold my — my head up. Yeah, must be. A lot of that going around.' He was quiet. 'No. Nothing's going on. No, Emily's great. Yeah. I understand. I'll be there tomorrow.'

When he ended the call and sank back on the bed, I turned over to face him. He stared at the rafters for a minute, before turning his head on the pillow. His blue eyes were tired. 'I missed an eight o'clock meeting.'

I refused to say I was sorry. 'Were you planning on being there?'

'I was going to conference in.' He dropped an arm over his eyes. 'It's been a lousy week that way, thank you, Emily. I can't sleep. The condo's a sty. When I'm at work, I'm only — only half there.' He exhaled. 'Mark's an intuitive guy. He knows something's up. I'd tell him — tell him what it is, if I knew.' Without moving his arm, he said, 'They caught a coyote in Central Park last week.'

I gasped. 'They didn't kill it, did they?'

'No. Tranquilized it and relocated it. Who knows, maybe to somewhere near here. They figured it got lost and wandered into the city and didn't know how to get out.'

Drawing on what Jude had taught me, I picked up the story. 'So they dropped it off in a wooded place where it could get the food it needed to survive, only it couldn't stay there. Coyotes are territorial, and this territory was full. So it moved on until it found space.' Amazing, the analogy. 'I've seen my coyote here, James — I mean

231

literally, I've seen her. She lets me watch her pups play.'

He got the message. Letting his arm fall away, he looked at me. 'I can't do small town, Emily. I came from one. I can't go back.'

'I'm not asking you to. I don't want to live here.'

'But something pulled you back.'

I tried to explain. 'Think refuge, small 'r'. That's what Bell Valley means to me. I was escaping that summer, too. LSATs, interviews, papers, exams — it had all just bunched together. When I first got here, I slept for three days straight.'

'Then or now?' he asked tiredly.

'Both. Well, not actually three days, but you know what I mean.'

'I sure do. There's nothing else to do in places like this.'

'But there is,' I argued softly, more patient with James than with my dad on this score. 'There are books and bikes and paths in the woods. There's a farmers' market every Saturday in July and August. And, yes, there's the Refuge, which always needs help. And friends. I had *good* friends here.'

'And Jude.'

I let out a breath. 'And Jude. He was my first serious guy. Like everything else that summer, he was different. Ask him about his career path, and he'd laugh in your face. Everything about him was irreverent. That fascinated me. I've never been irreverent in my life.'

'Until now,' James said, eyes sad, voice fading.

'I just don't know what to do with this, Em. And I'm so — so friggin' tired.'

I leaned over and kissed him lightly, then watched him sleep until my stomach rumbled. Aching for coffee, I got dressed and slipped out. The kitchen was crowded. Vicki and Charlotte were doing stickers at the table, Rob stood on a ladder fiddling with a strip of molding, Lee was at the stove.

All eyes turned my way, curious and expectant, but much as there was solace in knowing they cared, I didn't want to talk.

'He looked exhausted,' Vicki said when I touched her shoulder in passing.

'He's burning the candle at both ends,' I agreed, and went on into the dining room. Taking a tray from the stack designed for those sleeping in, I loaded it with coffee, juice, hard-boiled eggs, fruit, cherry-chocolate muffins, sticky buns, and maple oat scones.

'Woo-hoo,' Rob teased as I passed back through the kitchen, 'breakfast in bed?'

'When he wakes up,' I sang, and slipped outside.

⋆   ⋆   ⋆

He woke up at noon and ate everything that I hadn't eaten myself, even drank cold coffee — all without leaving the bed. The Red Fox wasn't the White Elephant, where we had stayed while honeymooning in Nantucket, but breakfast in bed was breakfast in bed.

'She made all this,' he surmised.

I nodded.

He slid down and stretched out. 'She's good. She could make a bundle if she had her own place.'

'That was her dream. She was going to do it with her husband.'

He folded his hands on his belly, but they were tight. 'So were we. And now here you are with Jude.'

'James,' I protested, but gently. 'I chose *you*. And y'know what, you show up here looking half dead, and I *still* choose you. I have not once regretted marrying you.'

'You walked out on me.'

'On our life. I can't take the time clock, the traffic, the shallowness, the *noise*. I love you, but I never see you. I'm not rejecting law, just the way I practise it. I'm not rejecting you, just the way our lives force us to be.'

Sliding down beside him, I pressed my face to his shoulder. He drew me closer. Reassured by the gesture, I waited for him to respond, but his breathing levelled.

'Must be a sedative in the air,' he murmured, and fell back to sleep.

★ ★ ★

I didn't sleep, simply closed my eyes. I didn't have to see to appreciate the warmth of his skin and the texture of his body, but what I felt just then was less arousal than a pleasant familiarity. It was gratitude that he had come and cared enough to listen, and even respect, yes, respect a

234

work ethic that made him feel guilty for missing a meeting. It was also hope. He *had* missed that meeting, and he hadn't balked at telling Mark that he wouldn't be working today.

Bottom line? If James made me choose between returning to New York and divorce, I'd return to New York. What we had was too good to give up.

That said, I didn't like the choice. There had to be a better one.

⋆ ⋆ ⋆

I was no closer to finding it when James woke again. It was nearly two. While he showered, I sat on the bench under the window, dreading the moment when he would climb in his rental car and head south. I was thinking that he hadn't fawned over the BMW, and that that was a good sign, when another sign came.

He wore a clean pair of jeans low on his hips and was bare-chested and barefooted, scrubbing his hair with a towel when he said, 'I might as well meet your friend Lee while I'm here. I want to hear the facts myself before I call Sean.'

⋆ ⋆ ⋆

The facts didn't change. Lee told him the story much as she had told me. Naturally reticent, she didn't ramble on, but responded to one question at a time, in the order he asked. And he was wonderful with her, patient and focused, as I'd known he would be. Interacting with people, be it clients, witnesses, or juries, was his strength. Even the depth of his voice lent something genuine to the meeting. Watching, listening, I was more convinced than ever that his current work — *our* work — was wrong.

At one point, when she was tense talking of her record, he relaxed her by saying, 'You didn't learn to cook in prison. Those scones were amazing. Most are like lead, but not yours. What makes them so light?'

'Buttermilk,' she said shyly. 'I tinker. It's about getting the proportions right.'

'Well, Sean loves to eat, so bring muffins and he'll be your slave forever. He's a good guy. One of his high school pals spent a year behind bars on a negligent homicide conviction, so he gets the personal side of that. He does the trial work for a firm that handles major estates, and he's already checked, there's no conflict of interest.' He slid me a glance before telling Lee in an even gentler voice, 'He'll need a retainer. It's the policy of the firm. Is there someone who can pay?'

'I can,' Amelia said from the door. I didn't know how long she had been there, but assumed that if she was willing to take my husband's recommendation, it had been a while. She would have seen his professionalism and sensed his skill.

James stood. After introducing himself, he said, 'His name is Sean Alexander, and he's with Henkel and Ames. Do you know the firm?'

'No,' Amelia said baldly.

'It's a small, all-purpose firm with extensive

resources and an impressive client list. You can check it out online.'

'We'll do that,' she said in a tone that said she wasn't about to take *his* word, which annoyed the hell out of me. Of *course* she would check it out; a shrewd businessman wouldn't do any different, but she didn't have to be abrasive about it.

James, bless him, remained unfazed. Mindful of who would be paying the bill, he didn't quite turn his back on Amelia. But he was focused on Lee again, now with his phone out, accessing his contacts. He jotted down Sean's number, then his own, and as he passed Lee the paper, ran through some of the things she should discuss with Sean. 'He's expecting your call,' he finally said. 'If there's a problem, let me know.'

'Tinkering,' I said a short time later, when we reached his car. 'That's it, y'know.' When he looked lost, I said, 'Lee's scones. She tinkers with the recipe until she gets the proportions right. That's what I want to do, James. It's not about dumping my life but adjusting the ingredients. And you're right,' I said, seeing it clearly then but, more importantly, feeling confident enough about James to confess it. 'Jude mattered to me once. Everything I've been since I left here is what he was *not*. He was an extreme. But so are we. I want something in the middle.'

Opening the door, James tossed his duffel in the passenger's seat. Then, bracing his hands on the door frame, he hung his head.

'You liked Lee,' I argued. 'I know you did. I

saw something different back there in the kitchen. A calmness. A brief, deep satisfaction.'

'What you saw' — he angled his head to meet my gaze — 'was me not repeating myself, because I've had enough sleep for a change.'

'Maybe, but not all.'

'She's had a raw deal,' he rasped. 'I'd have to be a piece of ice not to react to that.'

'A brief, deep satisfaction,' I repeated. 'Funny how helping people brings that out in you. Do you get the same feeling at work?'

With a concessionary sigh, he straightened. 'Come back, and we'll find middle ground.'

I hugged myself. 'If I go back, I'll be swallowed up again. I shake just thinking about it.'

'Well, I can't leave,' he insisted. 'I could change my job — maybe — and we could sell the condo and buy something small in Brooklyn with a yard for the kids — but there aren't any kids yet — have you thought about that?'

I felt a sharp little pang. 'I've been escaping that, too.'

'What we were doing wasn't working.'

'I know.' The next step involved medication whose possible side effects included headaches, nausea, cramps, even hot flushes, according to the websites I'd seen — and yes, I know, those are only *possible* side effects. Most women have no side effects at all. But how not to worry once you've read all that?

Getting pregnant was supposed to have been easy. It was what a woman's body was *made* for. I had always *dreamed* of this.

Physically, though, I was now here and James there. 'Things happen for a reason,' I thought, not realizing that I'd said it aloud until he shot back a response.

'What's the reason here? We're not supposed to be parents? We work too hard? We don't have *time* for kids? That's a crock of bull, and you know it, Emily.'

The force of his response was actually reassuring. He wanted kids as much as I did. But how to make it happen? I hugged myself tighter.

He stared at me, stared at the woods, stared at the car that wasn't his. Then, with a grunt, he dug out his phone and his keys. 'I gotta go. I'll work while I drive.' He was halfway into the car when he climbed out again. His eyes were level. 'I've come here twice. I've offered to start looking for a different job. It's your turn now. What are you willing to give?'

I didn't know. Idealism, friends, husband, law, time, taste, fun — I felt as though I had already given it all up back there. What of that life to keep? What to ditch? If life was about getting the recipe right, I had to figure out the ingredients before I could tinker with proportions. The problem, of course, was that I couldn't do a test batch in the kitchen one afternoon.

'Think about it, Emily.' When he entered the car this time, it was for real. A minute later, the car was skirting the green. I watched until it turned a corner and was out of sight.

That was when Amelia approached.

16

Feeling as vulnerable as I did, I would have given anything to avoid a confrontation with Amelia. But I couldn't just turn and walk away. Forget cowardly; it would have been *rude*. It also would have been imprudent. Amelia had been respectful to James, and she was paying Lee's bills.

She looked totally together in her plaid shirt and khakis. When younger, she'd had the same pure blond hair as Vicki and Jude, and though hers was now mixed with white, it remained thick. For as long as I'd known her, she'd kept it short, brushed back behind her ears in a clipped, CEO-appropriate style. Gentleness wasn't a priority for her. Even today, under a cloud cover that softened the afternoon light, she looked flinty.

She also looked smug. 'Trouble in paradise?' she asked in her ballsy alto.

'Actually, no,' I replied without lying. New York was no paradise, not by a long shot.

'He didn't look happy with you,' she pressed. 'No kiss? No hug?'

'You weren't with us last night.'

'No,' she conceded. 'I suppose it was kind of him to come.'

Kind? What about loving or devoted or worried? Even *horny*? Amelia had chosen the blandest word, so I tossed it right back.

'James is that way. He cares about people.

He's the kindest person I know.'

Kindness was the last word anyone would ever use to describe Jude, who had to be behind this somehow. My presence stirred up things in Amelia; she had made that clear at our last one-on-one.

'Does it upset your parents?'

'His kindness?'

'Your separation.' There was a gleam in her eye. I didn't want to think it was malice, but I couldn't blame it on booze. She had been with Charlotte prior to our meeting, meaning she wasn't drinking then, and she didn't have a glass with her now.

I gave her a puzzled smile. 'There's no separation. He's busy at work, and I need a rest.'

'A trial separation, then?'

'Not in the sense you mean.' I thought to leave — make up an excuse, say I didn't feel well — but if Amelia had a point to make, she would make it either now or later. Better now, while we were alone.

'Jude says you're avoiding him,' she began.

I smiled, curious. 'Is that what he says? No. I'm not. We just don't have much to say to each other.'

'I'm sorry for that. I was hoping it would be different.'

'I'm married, Amelia.'

'But not happily,' she said, raising a hand to forestall my reply.

'Say what you will, but I sense problems. And that's all right. Every marriage has its tests. You would have had those if you'd been married to Jude, too.'

Amazed, I laughed. 'Jude and I couldn't pass the *admissions* test.'

'I'm sorry for that, too. I used to hope you were the one.'

I was flattered, but not surprised. She had liked me that summer. The dislike had come when I left and she had needed a scapegoat. 'He's probably better with someone else.'

'Who?' she asked, less composed. 'He messes up every time. Why *do* children let parents down?'

I didn't have to think about that one. 'Maybe because their expectations are too high.'

'Shoot low and you get low.' She moved to the space where James's rental had been, now an empty spot beside Vicki's van. After scuffing the gravel for a minute, she studied the van, running a hand over its logo before turning to lean against it.

Pensive, she stared at the woods. 'It's hard with kids. You raise them to be one thing and they turn out to be another. You do your best, but there are no guarantees. Vicki was easy. My son? A challenge from the start. He knew just which buttons to push.'

Thinking of some of the outlandish things Jude had done — like bet with his buddies on football, with the loser having to run naked around the town green, which I only heard about but would have loved to see, since Jude had lost and been quite pleased about it, Vicki said — I had to smile. 'At some level, it's endearing.'

'Fine for you to say. You aren't his mother.' She looked at me then. 'And you aren't his wife.

Tell me, where's James from?'

'Maryland.'

'What do his parents do?'

'They work for the government.'

'Career bureaucrats?'

'Not bureaucrats. They're civil servants. Administrations come and go, but they stay.'

'Do they own a home?'

'A small one. Why the questions?'

'I'm trying to get a fix on why you chose him over Jude.'

'Amelia,' I reminded her with an astonished laugh, 'Jude ditched me. He chose Jenna.'

'Well, I know that,' she granted, 'but for you to choose someone so different — I'm just trying to understand. What was the appeal?'

'James isn't different. He's everything I'd grown up planning to have and to do. Jude was the anomaly. James coming along when he did was a reminder, a *sign* of where I was meant to be.'

'I don't believe in signs,' Amelia stated.

Not wanting to mention cars that stalled or coyotes that howled, I remained silent.

'Things just happen,' she went on, 'and not always the way we plan.' She shot an aggrieved look towards the green. 'I didn't plan to be in *this* town, that's for sure.'

Resentment? 'But you love it here,' I protested.

'Really? I'm here because I married Wentworth Bell. I did not plan on his dying at the age of forty-eight, any more than I planned on heading the Refuge, but when there's no one else to do it, and you have to sleep at night with the echoes of those Bells saying that the Refuge has to stay in the family, you can't walk away. My taking over when Wentworth died was the only responsible thing to do.'

'But you *love* it,' I insisted. To me, that had always been her strength. She was possessive of the place, involved in every aspect of its operation. The Refuge had grown on her watch. 'And you're *good* at it.'

She sighed. 'Well, it's what I have, and there's no point in doing something unless you do it well, but it isn't what I'd grown up planning to do.'

'What was?'

'You've talked with Lee. Can't you guess?' She folded her arms. 'She and I didn't grow up together. She's much younger — her mother was my mother's baby sister. And my side of the family wasn't in trouble with the law. We were just poor. I was working from the time I was ten. My dream was not having to work.'

'A woman of leisure? I have trouble picturing that.'

'We grow into our lives. You see me as I am today. But I wasn't always the one giving orders. When I was in high school, I worked in a nursing home, and I did whatever I was told. The pay wasn't great, but it was something.'

'Where did you meet Wentworth?'

'Oberlin. I was on scholarship. Needless to say, his family wasn't pleased with his choice.' Her mouth twitched. 'Sound like Lee?'

It did, though having thought of Amelia one way for so long, it was still an adjustment.

244

'Bretton is an aristocratic name.'

'Isn't it though. Amelia Bretton Bell. I'd have chosen something else, if it hadn't had a certain ring to it.'

She was staring at me, her gaze defiant but vaguely . . . diluted. It struck me that her fawn eyes were faded, their gold flecks less noticeable than I remembered them being. Of course, gold eyes were a Bell trait, and she was a Bretton. In that, just then, she seemed more human.

'Why am I telling you all this,' she said, a question but not.

Me, I was still waiting for the other shoe to fall.

'Maybe because I want you to know that I do occasionally have reason to be sour. Vicki thinks I drink too much, but I don't. I'm careful. I grew up with sots. I know the pitfalls. Not that I don't imbibe now and again. Drink can lighten the mood when you think you're doing the right thing but get it thrown back in your face.'

Absurd, since we weren't really friends, but I felt like she was confiding in me — like she was trying to share something and not succeeding terribly well. I waited.

With another sigh, she pushed away from the van, and for a minute, I thought the conversation would end there. Then her step faltered, and I felt that small window of humanness open wider.

'Jude thought I was awful. He made fun of my house, my car, my jewellery. Did he not see how hurtful that was? Fine, if he didn't want to live in a house like ours, I could live with that, but in a filthy cabin? Do you know how a parent feels when an adult child rejects her like that?'

'He just wanted to do things his way,' I tried gently, though I'm not sure she heard. The tidy ball that was Amelia had begun to unravel. She was speaking again barely before I was done.

'But how was I supposed to deal with that? A parent cares. Her children think she's immune, because she is officious, because her life has *demanded* that of her, but she has feelings. Every mother does. You have no idea what it's like to see your child doing one destructive thing after another, when there are better options. But he won't listen. You point out facts. He sneers. You try to talk sense into him, but he is deaf. You raise your voice and get emotional for once, and what does he do? He walks away!'

'He's here now,' I said softly, but I felt bad for this different Amelia. Her eyes were haunted. I had never seen them like that.

'He'll leave again. He isn't comfortable with me.'

'I thought things were going well.'

'For him, maybe,' she said, and sputtered. 'What's not to go well? He takes what he wants and ignores everything else. But I see it coming. He'll leave again unless someone like you gets involved.' There it was, the other shoe. Her eyes drilled mine. 'You could save him, Emily. Are you sure there's no hope for the two of you?'

The only reason I felt even remotely bad was the pleading I heard, which was odd — sad — coming from as regal a woman as Amelia. But this other shoe didn't fit me.

'I can't,' I said, pleading right back that she

not ask this. 'The time for Jude and me is done. But not your time with him. If he doesn't want to head the Refuge, he can do other things.'

'Like what?'

I tried to think what might work. 'Create a title for him. Make him a roving ambassador — VP at Large, or something.'

'Isn't that what he used to be?'

'Not formally, and not with a promise he wouldn't end up back here as CEO. That's what terrifies him.'

'It terrifies me, too,' she argued, her voice rising. 'What happens when I die? Who'll take over? Noah? Oh, lovely. He's nine. And if he inherits his mother's brains, I'm sunk.'

'What about Charlotte?'

'She's *three*.'

'There are cousins — '

'It was supposed to be Jude!' Lowering her voice, she tried again. 'He loves you, you know.'

I might have reminded her that she had denied that barely a week before. But suddenly there seemed another point to make. 'Jude loves what he can't have.'

'He came back for you.'

'No. He didn't know I'd be here. He came back for *you*. He wants ... ' I stopped, considering.

'What? Tell me. I'd give him almost anything.'

I was suddenly on that bench outside the General Store with my dad. 'My parents would say the same thing. The only thing I want is to be loved as a grown person with the right to her own dreams.'

'Don't I love Jude that way?' Amelia argued. 'I let him live where he wants, even if I think it's a hovel, and dress how he wants, even if he looks like . . . like someone I grew up with and spent my life trying to escape. I *let* him do this.'

Just as my father 'let' me stay here. 'But he feels your disapproval.'

'Because what he's doing is *wrong*,' she insisted.

'For you, maybe, but he can't live for you.'

'Help me, Emily. If you care anything for Vicki, you'll do this, because I'm her mother. I love my son. I want a relationship with him. I went ten years without. I can't do that again.'

'Oh, Amelia,' I said, regretful not about Jude but about Amelia's inability to accept the truth. 'I can't control Jude. My life is elsewhere, and it's everything he hates. I don't have any pull with him.'

'You do. You are the best woman who ever entered his life. He calls you his conscience.'

Well, I did know that. The fact that Amelia did, too, suggested Jude might have put her up to this.

'Talk to him,' she pressed. 'Reason with him. Tell him that he *should* get custody of Noah. Tell him that he could revolutionize the Refuge — that he could leave his mark — that he could make it a one-of-a-kind place for his son to inherit.' She took a quick breath. 'Help me in this, Emily. Would that be *so hard* for you to do?'

I didn't answer, and she left me soon after. A week and a half earlier, when my head had been filled with static and my energy depleted, I would have packed my bags and driven off. I had problems enough of my own without taking on hers. But the similarities between the two couldn't be missed. I was to my father what Jude was to Amelia — a child rejecting a parent's dream. If in helping them I helped myself, we might both benefit.

At least, that was my rationale for not leaving Bell Valley that day.

★ ★ ★

And then something happened that clinched it. Lee woke up Friday to find four flat tyres on the truck she had been driving to and from work. The truck was old, the tyres new, and the deed was done in a way that wouldn't be captured on film. Someone had fired a gun from cover of the trees, likely using a silencer to avoid waking Lee.

We met with the police in the kitchen of the Red Fox — three of Bell Valley's finest munching on apricot scones while Amelia insisted they had a murderer to catch, which did nothing for Lee's peace of mind. The police promised to watch the house, but beyond cataloguing the kind of bullet used, there was little else they could do.

Lee was freaked out, and I couldn't blame her. But while she used this as an example of why she shouldn't rock the boat, I used it as an example of why she should. It took a while — and Amelia's insistence — to convince her. Leaving Amelia to tell the police what we would need from their files, I led Lee to Vicki's small office to make the call in private.

'Monday at ten?' she echoed Sean, looking at me. When I nodded, she said, 'Yes. Thank you. Yes. Ten. I'll see you.'

Still looking at me, she hung up the phone. With a shaky hand, she pushed that swathe of hair back from the eye it hid, revealing double the fear. 'I can't go then,' she cried meekly. 'I'd miss all of breakfast, because I'd have to leave at *seven* to get there at ten, traffic will suck, and I don't even know where to *park*.'

I held her arms. 'You'll get everything ready the night before, so that Vicki can just pop it all in the oven. This is important, Lee. If someone has gone to the extent of thwarting cameras by using a gun on your car, he's enjoying himself, which means it won't stop. And you're not signing your life away. If you don't like Sean, you'll walk out and it ends there. I don't know where to park either, but we'll find out. I'll drive. And if traffic slows us down, we'll call Sean, and he'll wait.'

I was arguing for more than Lee or Amelia or Sean. I was arguing for James and me. Helping Lee was common ground for us, which meant that the stakes were high.

★ ★ ★

James must have sensed it, too, because we had barely settled in the lawyer's office in Boston Monday morning when he called Sean, who looked increasingly pleased — smiling, jotting notes — as the minutes passed. I was starting to wonder what James was saying when Sean put

250

the call on hold and gestured me toward the conference table at the end of the room.

'Want to talk with him while I get background information from Lee?'

I did. Pulling out a chair there, I picked up. 'How are you?' I asked softly enough not to disturb the others.

'*Great*, babe,' he said, sounding more energized with those two words than I'd heard him in months. 'Wait'll you hear this. One of our associates is from a prominent family in Boston. I don't usually work with him, but just for the hell of it, I dropped the name of the executor of Lee's trust, Albert Meeme. Instant reaction. His family had used Meeme until weird stuff started showing up on their trust reports — dozens of charges, little things that added up. Meeme cried innocent, but when they started asking around, they learned he had a history of fraud.'

'Proven?' I asked excitedly. This would make Lee's case.

'No, just bar infractions that stopped short of prosecution. Dubious record-keeping, funds mysteriously moving around, evasive manoeuvres.'

'Tax evasion.'

'Right. But — and this is right down Lee's alley — there have also been claims that estates were fiddled with to favour one or another of the beneficiaries, with Meeme getting a kickback. No one has been able to prove it, and the firm covers it up, so only insiders know. Sean has heard rumours, but disgruntled clients start rumours all the time. Lee is something else. She

251

isn't disgruntled. She's an innocent victim, and Meeme's history gives juice to her claim. Plus, it adds incentive for Sean. If he can finally pin something on the guy, it'll be a feather in his cap. But that's not all, Em. I got an amazing case this morning.'

'Did you?' I asked, still delighted for Lee.

'It's pro bono, but it could be an interesting case. The client is a woman — Denise Bryant — who is serving time for vehicular homicide for hitting a kid on a bike. She had no record, but forensics showed she was over the speed limit when she tried to pass another car. It was a passing zone, but the weather was bad. The boy was fifteen. He and his friends were riding their bikes off a ramp into the street. She's suing the boy's family for letting him ride without wearing a helmet. Do you love it?'

'Interesting,' I said, because the philosophical issue certainly was. But while I was pleased for James, I was not so pleased for me. If I was holding our work to be the enemy, a good case wouldn't help.

He heard my hesitance. 'I know, Em. It's a gesture. Mark knows I've been frustrated with the cases I'm on. Derek Moore is the partner of record, but he's so busy that it's basically my case. I'll be at Bedford Hills interviewing the client. I'll be in court. I'll be working with the corrections department, the judge, and the ADA — all personal interaction. I'll be able to build my name doing something meaningful. A case like this can go a long way in tiding me over until things get better.'

That worried me, in part because I didn't trust Mark's motivation. I feared that James was being patronized, or that piling on work was a test of his stamina. Mark knew that a pro bono case would be hard for James to refuse. Heck, it would be hard for me to refuse. Helping someone who was being punished, when the victim shared at least a bit of responsibility? I could happily build a practice of cases like that. Unfortunately, they wouldn't pay the bills, a fact of which Mark had to be acutely aware.

'Do you have time for it?' was all I asked.

'I'll make time. How's it going with Sean?'

'Okay, I think. He's talking with Lee now.'

'How was the drive?'

'Fine.'

'No claustrophobia?' he asked with just enough dryness to make his point. I had run from one city. Was this one any different?

'Honestly, I was so focused on making the right turns and getting into the parking garage that I didn't see much else,' I said. 'I'll let you know on the way back. Thanks for that information, James. You did good.'

I hung up the phone telling myself that he had a right to wonder about my frame of mind, but that his interest in Lee's case was positive, that his pro bono case might not pan out, and that, in any event, I was glad he had asked to talk to me. We used to call each other often about new cases, old cases, cases where a co-worker wasn't doing his share. It was a reminder that we had *us* above and beyond the rest.

'Just finishing up on history,' Sean explained

when I rejoined them. A pleasant-looking guy with short red hair and wire-rimmed glasses, he asked a steady stream of questions, pausing to reword only when Lee looked blank. I figured that his usual client was more savvy, certainly more wealthy.

Listening to the last of it, I asked Lee a question or two myself when I felt she had left something out. She gave him the police file documenting the harassment, as well as trust statements showing the dramatic decline in value from before her husband had died to after. Reading those, Sean's cheeks grew more ruddy. 'One bad lawyer makes the rest of us stink,' he said, clearly irritated. 'Pinning something concrete on Albert Meeme would be a community service.' To Lee, he said, 'We have a big probate department here. I handle the trial end, so I've done this before. First thing, we petition the court for an accounting of the trust.'

'What does that entail?' I asked.

'Submitting a brief, these files, maybe an affidavit containing Lee's statement. We could take that now. I'd submit the petition as an emergency, vis-à-vis the harassment.'

'Will this stop it?' Lee asked timidly.

'It should,' he said, though tentatively. 'If someone knows they're being watched, it'd certainly up the ante to continue with it.'

'I wouldn't have to be there, would I? In court?'

'Yes. You're a compelling witness.'

'I'm *not*. I don't know what to *say*.'

'That's what makes you a compelling witness,'

254

he said, and included me again. 'I've had petitions granted with less cause, so I'm not worried, and I know the clerk at the Probate Court, which means a quick hearing. Once it's granted, the court has the right to appoint an accountant, but if I suggest a name they know, they'll use it. I know the best person. She's quick and she's smart.'

'What happens then?' Lee asked.

'She examines the books.'

'Where?' I asked.

'The easiest thing would be doing it at Meeme's firm.'

'But then Jack's brothers will know,' Lee said.

'They'll know anyway. They'll be notified by the court about the petition hearing. They'll send someone to try to get it denied. Whoever it is won't have much luck. Like I say, there's precedence with less cause than this. And Lee will be a good witness.' He eyed Lee. 'Now's the time to decide. Do you want to move ahead with this?'

She wasn't happy, and for a split second, I felt as bad as I had talking with Layla in New York. Going forward would be frightening, but doing nothing was worse.

I didn't have to say it. Slowly, her reluctance became resignation. To Sean, she said a quiet 'Yes.'

★ ★ ★

I paid attention as we left Boston. Yes, there was traffic. And yes, I hated it. Yes, there was construction. And yes, I hated it.

Was it claustrophobic to me? By the time I went back and forth making comparisons to New York, we were crossing over the Charles River. There was still traffic on the other side, still construction, still noise. But I knew it would end and that once we moved farther along I-93, the cityscape would flatten.

What did that mean?

It meant that Boston was less offensive as cities went, but that I wasn't any wilder to rush back to it than Lee. I'd do it, as would she, because the Probate Court was there. And it would be bearable as long as I knew I could leave.

What did *that* mean?

It meant James and I still had a long way to go if we were hoping for a meeting of minds.

17

Lee had done well in Boston, but what I felt best about was James's involvement. So I called on the way home to give him an update. He picked up right away, both then and when I called again that night at ten, though in the latter instance he sounded groggy. I had woken him up.

'Oh, hey, I'm sorry. Go back to sleep.'

He made a stretching sound. 'Nah. Gotta work.'

'Are you at the office?'

'Home. Kitchen. I must have dozed off.'

'With your head on the counter.' And his laptop pushed aside, his arms on the granite, and his neck crimped. He'd done that before. 'Oh, James. You need a bed.'

'I need you,' he said, and yawned. 'I need — need a longer day.' He swore. 'Yeah, I'm goin' to bed. I'll call you in the morning.'

★   ★   ★

But I was the one who called Tuesday, right after I heard from Sean. 'We have a hearing Friday afternoon.'

'Will Lee testify?' James asked.

'Yes. We'll prepare her by phone, but he doesn't want to overdo it. He wants her lack of guile — his words — to come through. She's terrified, but she did agree.'

257

'Have there been any new incidents?'

'No. They're making her wait. Suspense is part of the terror. How's it going there?'

'Unh. Okay.' He didn't sound as enthused as yesterday. 'Something's up. I was at Bedford Hills this morning interviewing Denise Bryant, and got back to have Mark all over me about getting three different briefs done. He — he keeps telling me I'm behind because I've been skippin' out, and — and I keep telling him I'm behind because I don't have the help I need, and he keeps insisting I'd be able to do it myself if I — if I kept my focus on work, which means he's not talking about Denise Bryant but about *us*. What do I say to that?'

I had an answer, but it was crude.

'I think someone's all over him, too,' James mused. 'I'm guessing the figures coming in for the month aren't good, but — but worse than the first quarter? If firm management is freaking out, things are bad.'

'How bad?' If James was laid off, we were in trouble. Or not, according to the silver-lining theory.

'Good question. The associates are the last to know. It's about suspense here, too. Keep us on edge. Like Lee.'

'I'm sorry, James,' I said quietly.

'Well. That's the game. It's why I need this partnership. The vote's in October. I can hang on until then.'

★   ★   ★

258

I texted him an hour after that to let him know I was thinking of him, and I did it again in the middle of the afternoon. We went back and forth each time. It was nice, though I imagined him texting under the edge of his desk, where Mark couldn't see.

Vicki saw. I was helping set up for tea, after insisting that she sit. She looked tired. Like James, she needed more help, but the economics of the Red Fox didn't allow for it, so I was glad to fill in. I kept my BlackBerry in my pocket, texting between runs from kitchen to parlour.

'What happened to the woman who swore off electronics?' she asked as I typed another reply.

'This is palatable,' I said, returning the BlackBerry to my pocket, 'because I'm mixing it with arranging tea bags, washing pans, and eating cookies. James would be jealous.'

'Would he?'

She was right. 'Maybe not. He's so into work right now. But the channel of communication is open, and I don't want to close it again. My day is better when I'm in touch with him.'

'That sounds like dependence.'

'No. It's choice.' And very clear to me now. For this alone, my escape had been productive. 'I like hearing his voice. I like sharing things. Maybe I feel guilty being here, while he's going through a hard time at work. But if he needs to vent, I want to listen.'

'You want him dependent on *you*,' she teased.

Better me than Naida, I thought, but said, 'What I really want is the hope. Our talking means we're alive — *us* — as a couple. It means

259

there's something else besides work, something that no one can take away. We used to have this. I like that it's back.'

'Does that mean you can take New York again?'

I considered. 'It means I love my husband. It means I want to be with him.'

'What about New York?'

'I don't know.' I did feel the weight of decision. 'I should be thinking about it every minute, right? I should be doing things to help me decide. But maybe that what's changed. I've always had a clear image of where I was headed. I never just went with the flow. But I feel like I have to do that now. I can't force the issue. It'll come to me.' When my cell rang, I pulled it out, fully expecting it to be James. I was surprised to see the local area code. Jude? Amelia?

'Hello?'

'Emily? It's Katherine from the Refuge.'

'Katherine,' I said. I wouldn't have recognized her voice. It was taut. 'Everything okay?'

'Your kitten isn't doing well.'

'Not doing well.' I felt instant dread.

'Could you take a ride over?'

'Now? Of course.'

After two more minutes of setup, I ran out of the Red Fox. I hit sixty on the straightaway, not a wise thing, but I felt the urgency that Katherine hadn't quite expressed. Threatening clouds filled the sky, mirroring my fears. With the receptionist gone for the day, I ran right in.

My kitten wasn't in Rehab. I didn't see her anywhere. I was still looking frantically around

260

when Katherine arrived and led me to a small room, where a young man, clearly a vet, stood. Precious lay on her side on the examining table. Her little eyes were open but didn't look to be registering much.

'Did she fall?' I asked, wanting to believe the most innocent problem. I could nurse her back to health. Katherine must have known I would, which was why she had called. I could keep her with me. There was nothing of danger in the gardener's shed.

But Katherine looked stricken. It was the vet who said, 'She isn't eating or drinking. Her systems are shutting down.'

'She was okay yesterday,' I protested.

'But weaker and weaker. You saw it.'

'Still,' I resisted, 'shutting down? Can't you do something? Give her fluids, maybe?'

'They'll just run through her,' he said apologetically.

I didn't like what was not being said. Frightened, I looked at Katherine.

'At best, we'd buy a week or two,' she said, 'but I'd hate to have her suffer.'

I looked around, frantic for a solution, but all I saw were two syringes. My eyes filled with tears.

'She won't feel pain,' the vet promised. 'The first shot will sedate her. It'll be quick. She's halfway there now.'

My throat grew thicker, but even if I'd been able to argue, what he said made sense. Yes, I'd been told Precious could live a long life, but deep inside I had worried from the start.

'Can I hold her?' I asked, knowing that was

why I'd been called.

As soon as we were alone, I put my face to her tiny one, feeling the soft fur, the fading warmth. Ignoring the antiseptic smell of the table, I focused on the smell that I knew. 'I'm here, baby,' I whispered, touching her head. Her eyes closed, opened, found mine. That was all the encouragement I needed. Lifting her gently, I cradled her and sat in the only chair in the room. It was metal, with a padded seat and back, but I would have sat on burning coals for this poor thing that had never really had a chance.

Bending over her, I murmured soft words of love as I rocked back and forth. She stretched out a paw, moved her head against mine, then grew still. And I knew. She had been waiting for me. Rising up only enough, I touched the velvet of the ears she had never grown into. As I watched, the pink drained, little veins no longer pumping blood. I held her close, preserving her fading warmth until Katherine and the vet returned.

His stethoscope confirmed it.

None of us spoke. I held her a moment longer, before burying my face in her fur and silently telling her I would always remember. Then I watched the vet carry her down the hall.

Katherine looked drawn. 'Thanks for coming.'

Unable to speak, I nodded, raised a hand in goodbye, and headed back outside. The clouds had let loose a deluge. Though I ran, I was soaked by the time I reached the car, and once inside, I burst into tears. I wasn't sure why I was so emotional — whether it was dredging up other losses, like the deaths of my dogs — whether, like my taste buds, my emotions were suddenly roaring back to life — or whether it was just wanting so desperately to have something living to love.

But I sat in my bucket seat and cried with my hands over my face. Five minutes passed, maybe ten before the passenger door opened. I barely had time to react — and then only to shift my fingers to see — when Jude scrambled in and slammed the door.

'Wow,' he said, leaning forward to peer up through the windshield. 'I haven't seen rain like this since Seattle. Not used to driving in the wet, city girl?' he asked, gently teasing. When I didn't answer, he looked at me. My hands still covered my nose and mouth, but my eyes were free.

'Are you crying?' he asked, unsettled.

'My kitten died,' I said. Even muffled by my hands and the rain on the roof, my voice was nasal.

'You mean, a kitten here?' When I nodded, he reached out and cupped the back of my neck. His gold eyes were understanding. 'It's the way of nature, Emmie.'

'I know. The strong survive. But she *could* have been strong. Why didn't she have that *chance*?'

His eyes remained gentle, fingers kneading my neck. 'Some don't. I've always admired the people here who live through that every day. It's hard to watch.'

'Is it ever.'

'She's in a better place,' he offered.

My throat was tight. I could only nod.

'You'll see her someday,' he added.

'You're just saying that to make me feel better. You don't believe in heaven.'

He smiled sheepishly. After a minute, he said, 'Want to take a ride? Get away from it all?'

I gave a shrill laugh. 'I thought I was doing that!'

'No. A fifteen-minute drive.'

I thought of my kitten. I did like the idea of seeing her in another life, but I couldn't see her now. The poor little thing was alone. Me, I didn't want to be.

We sprinted from my car to his, a Range Rover that Amelia had recently bought and for which, despite having mocked my BMW, Jude made no apologies. With the wipers working double time, he backed around and sped off. We didn't say much. I was recovering from crying, and he — well, I had no idea what he was thinking and didn't have the wherewithal to ask. We headed away from town through unabating rain.

Ten minutes out, he turned onto a logging road that I would never even have seen. The SUV handled the bumps better than my BMW, though I still held the hand bar for dear life as we bounced up the mountain. Time and again we skidded on mud or wet leaves, but Jude recovered easily. Having a good time, he stopped only when boulders blocked the way. Then he ran around the car and opened my door.

'I'd offer an umbrella,' he said, grabbing my hand, 'but this is a trip down memory lane, and we didn't have umbrellas back then.'

I was trying to see through the rain. 'Memory

lane? I don't think so. I haven't been here before.'

'You have. Wait.'

I had to scramble to keep up, but less than a minute later slithered to a stop beside him on the far side of a granite wall. And there they were — Jude's falls — a wild cascade of water tumbling over a ledge ten feet above and hitting the brook with a raucous spray before pulsing downstream.

If it hadn't been raining, I'd have heard the falls sooner. But my disbelief now had a different cause. 'Excuse me.' I yanked my hand free. 'We *drove* here?'

'Yeah.'

'You knew there was a *road*?'

'Yeah.'

'So last time — and those other times — why were we scrambling for three hours up vertical rocks to get here?'

Rain dripped over his smirk. 'Because that's the side of the mountain that's fun. I had to drive today, because I promised you fifteen minutes.'

'That's not the *point*.' I remembered scratched hands and knees, and legs that were sore for days. 'It was dangerous. I risked my *life*. You never said there was a road.'

'You never asked. Did you not get a sense of accomplishment hiking up?'

'It was *hard*.'

'Most good things are,' he drawled with a brief, telling look, but before I could think up a fitting reply, he had his shirt over his head. 'I'm going under.'

I'd have argued if his jeans had followed the

265

shirt, but he left them on — they were soaked anyway — and felt his way carefully over the slick rocks until he could stand under the falls. Despite the sheer volume of water, he held his head high. The skies remained dark but his face was lit with pure joy.

How to sustain anger? This was Jude at his best — in his element and a pleasure to watch. He might be insensitive to the extreme, but he was the epitome of rugged.

In time, he opened his eyes and backed out of the torrent to a narrow alcove. Balancing carefully, one stone to the next, I joined him there. Once I was safely settled, I closed my eyes. The smells were clean, the sounds loud but natural. There was something primitive here, something exciting that had nothing to do with coyotes.

We were sitting wet thigh to wet thigh with our backs to the rock, when he said, 'Remember?'

'I do.'

'You wouldn't stand under the falls then either. What are you afraid of?'

'Drowning. I can't bear so much water pounding on my head.' I did like sitting on this ledge, though. I was drenched but sheltered. And Jude was all daredevil beside me, perfectly able to keep me safe.

'What else?' he asked.

'Snakes.'

'Still?' His eyes were mellow, conducive to talk.

'Always.'

'What else?'

I didn't have to think long. 'Losing my job. Losing my husband. Losing my future.'

'How could you lose your future?'

'By losing James.'

'He's that good?'

'For me, he is.'

'Is that a message for me?'

'No. Just a statement of fact.'

Jude studied me for a minute before putting his arms on his knees and his chin on his arms and looking out through the sheeting water at the forest. He was silent for a time, and then his voice barely made it past the roar of the falls. 'I'm afraid of failure.'

Startling, hearing such a confession from Jude. I looked at him, but he kept his eyes ahead. Gently, I said, 'We all are.'

'It's worse for me. When you set yourself up to be invincible, you have a problem.'

'That's insightful.'

He turned his head. 'Are you being sarcastic?'

'No. I completely understand. You like being seen a certain way. What are you most afraid of failing at?'

'Family. I'm bad at it.'

'And that bothers you?'

'Definitely sarcasm there.'

'Maybe, but it never bothered you before.'

He looked out again. 'I've always done what I'm best at — physical things — things other people can't do. I'd be a *great* captain of a fishing boat. I'd be *great* climbing Everest. If they ever offered it, I'd be first in line to walk on the moon.'

I didn't doubt that. And he would be great at that, too.

'Relationships are something else,' he went on.

'I can't muscle my way through.' He shot me a self-effacing glance. 'No one understands why I haven't seen Noah yet.'

What could I say? I didn't understand it either.

'I'm trying to consider the boy,' he explained. 'Should I be coming into his life if I'm just gonna leave it again?'

It sounded like he was looking for an excuse not to try, which was a switch. 'Last time we talked, you were considering custody.'

'I still am. I guess. But I can't do it alone. Help me, Emmie.'

I drew back, startled by the panic in his eyes. 'Uh, with what?'

'I'm meeting him tomorrow. I don't know what to do. It'd be easier if you were there.'

I doubted that. Besides, I had no desire to mix with Jude, Jenna, and the child they had conceived together. 'Why me?'

'Moral support. You're my talisman.'

'Last time, you said I was your conscience. All I am is a piece of your past. I can't be your future, Jude,' I fairly sang.

'I'm talking present.'

'Uh-huh. You always are.'

'Okay. I deserved that. What I mean, though, is *your* present. There's a reason why you needed to leave New York now. Don't you think it's awful coincidental that after ten years away, we both end up here at the same time? You're here as a gift to me.'

'That is totally egotistical.'

He shook his head. 'There was a greater purpose.'

'And that is?'

'Helping me. Look, I know you're married. I get it. You're married, and you love the guy, and he's probably better for you than I am, though there's still the question of why you're here and he's there. But what kind of guy is he if he'd mind your helping an old friend?'

'Forget James,' I argued. 'This is about me and your son. I won't be part of his future either. So why should I be there?'

'Because he'll *like* you,' Jude said with feeling.

Fear wasn't something I associated with Jude, not even when he used the word. But it was in his voice now. He was afraid of Noah.

'Just give me a start,' he begged. 'That's all I ask. You don't have to say anything. Just be there for moral support.'

'Oh, Jude.' I felt pulled in opposite directions, not wanting to be sucked into his life but not wanting to be responsible for having a little boy not know his dad.

And then he had the audacity to say, 'You should have been the one having my baby, y'know. If you'd gotten pregnant that summer, my life would have been different.'

Same with mine, though not for the better. 'Don't go there,' I warned softly.

When he took my hand and fingered my wedding band, I repeated the warning. 'Unless you're going to tell me how beautiful this is, don't say a word.'

His fingers stilled. After holding my hand for a minute, he set it down with deliberate care. It was a watershed moment. Just as Jude accepted what he couldn't change, I accepted what I didn't *want* to change. The Jude I saw here held no power over me. Rather, the power was in the life that teemed around us. Such was the rare beauty of this place.

★   ★   ★

By the time we left the alcove, the rain had let up. The falls continued to rush, but the sound was muted once we reached the other side of the granite wall, and further past the Range Rover, a break in the trees showed a dramatic layering of gun-metal grey and flame.

'The coyotes are gone,' Jude remarked as we stood admiring it. 'Haven't been here since I left.'

I might have told him otherwise if I hadn't been thinking just then of my kitten, a bright little spark in that fire, winging its way to a place where it wouldn't wobble.

And that night, when the coyotes again serenaded me with their howls, barks, and yips, Jude was off somewhere and none of my affair.

★   ★   ★

That said, I did go to Noah's game the next day, though I was doing it less for Jude's sake than for Amelia's. I couldn't be with Jude the way she wanted, but this was something. And who was I to predict Jude's behavior? He might just be mercurial enough to take one look at the boy and be the best dad in the world.

None of the local towns had enough children

270

to field a team, so the draw was regional, with games played at a park just south of Bell Valley. Since Jude was in Concord again, hence coming from the opposite direction, I drove myself there.

The teams were warming up when I arrived. My eye immediately found Jenna. Blond hair nearly white in the sun, she stood apart from the other parents, wispy against a waist-high chain fence near third base. She was clearly startled to see me.

'Jude asked me to come,' I explained, joining her. 'He didn't tell you?'

Of course he hadn't. He would still be thinking that Jenna and I were rivals, though I no longer felt it at all. 'I'm just a spectator,' I assured her. 'He wanted the moral support.'

'Wonder why,' she muttered. She didn't look happy, though I sensed it had less to do with my showing up than with her son meeting Jude. When a man appeared at her side with Dunkin' cups, she introduced him. 'This is my husband, Bobby Horn. Here for moral support.'

'And to see my kid play,' Bobby added, quietly possessive.

I looked out at the boys on the field. 'Which one is he?' They wore uniforms and ball caps, one identical to the next.

'Number fourteen,' Bobby said, pointing at a group near the coach. Once directed, I'd have picked him out even without the number. Seeing Jude's face in miniature, I felt the same tiny jolt I had seeing his picture on Jenna's desk at the Refuge.

The warm-up ended. The teams gathered at

271

their benches. I glanced back at the cars, looking for Jude, but he hadn't arrived. Pulling on my ball cap to get my hair off my neck in the warm, humid air, I must have looked like just another one of the moms, because when Noah grinned at his parents, he took no notice of me.

'Does he know Jude is coming?' I asked Jenna.

'No.'

'Does he know Jude's his dad?'

'Yes.'

'Are your other children here?'

'No.'

Noah played shortstop, and it was uncanny. He was built like Jude and, even at nine, never having seen the man, he had the same moves. When he was key to getting yet another out, I said, 'He's a good athlete.'

Jenna didn't answer. She was looking back toward the cars.

'Traffic,' I suggested.

But she wasn't buying that, and rightly so. Maybe, just maybe, there was a tie-up leaving Concord, but Jude wouldn't have hit traffic after that.

The first inning became the second, then the third. Noah struck out once with a powerful swing typical of Jude, but when he connected — which he did in the bottom of the third — it was a home run. On the other side of Jenna, Bobby hooted his support and returned the fist-pump Noah shot him right after he slid home.

Jude had missed it. I checked my phone for a message. I tried calling him. Nothing.

'Good thing I didn't tell Noah,' Jenna said flatly.

'He'll be here,' I replied, though I was starting to wonder. The fourth inning came and went, then the fifth. By then I was apologizing. 'I'm sorry, Jenna. He said he wanted to come. He should have been here by now.'

Her eyes stayed on the field. 'It's okay. I don't want him in Noah's life anyway. I only agreed to this because Amelia helps us out. He's my child,' she reasoned. 'I want him to have everything he can.'

I searched the parking lot, thinking that Jude might be watching from there, too nervous to approach, but there was no Range Rover, no tall spectator, no blond-haired biological dad.

When the game ended with Noah's team up by six runs, the boy ran to his mother. 'Did you see that last play?' he asked excitedly, and imitated it with his glove scooping the dirt.

Jenna hugged him. 'You were *great*.' But he was already heading back to his teammates.

'He's a fine boy,' I said.

The pride on her face clouded over. 'I worry. Y'know, that he inherits things.'

'Like?'

'Well, his body is like Jude's. He's tall for his age, and he's a good athlete. But he can be cocky. He's into being cool. There was a . . . thing with bullying at his school. I don't think he was involved, and we talk with him about being kind to kids who can't do what he does. But it's scary.'

'Maybe it's just the age.'

She shot me a wary glance. 'I don't want him to be like that. Amelia can give us money, but I

273

won't let her raise him. Look at Jude. He's totally irresponsible. Look where he's been for the last ten years. Look what he did today. Noah thinks his father just lives off somewhere else. Can you imagine if he'd been waiting today? I mean, I knew this would happen. I don't trust Jude any more'n I can throw him.'

It was the most she'd said to me at a stretch, and she was clearly emotional. I searched the parking lot again, though part of me felt it would be worse for Jude to show up now than not at all.

'He didn't have the guts,' Jenna said with scorn. 'We're better off without him, right?'

I would have agreed if she'd stayed long enough to hear, but the words were barely out when she went off to join Bobby and Noah. I returned to my car. This time when I called Jude, I left a message.

'Either you have a great excuse, or you were right about bombing as a dad. Where were you, Jude? I was there, Jenna was there, Bobby was there. Noah played a great game, only the guest of honour didn't show. And you wonder why I told you not to seek custody?'

★   ★   ★

Jude didn't return my call. This time he was in Burlington, on what Amelia claimed was *not* Refuge business. Much as I had felt bad for her before, so I did now. She had no control over him, and he continued to disappoint. I could argue that she had been wrong to push a meeting with Noah — but what man wouldn't want to

274

meet his own child?

Defective. That was the only word I could use to describe Jude's character, though I didn't have to say it aloud. Vicki did it for me, arguing tenaciously when Amelia came over that evening. *Where are his brains? Where is his* heart — *does he even have one? Am I actually related to this man?* More noticeably pregnant, she was emotional to match her baby bump. I understood that, but Amelia wasn't as forgiving. She fired countercharges back at Vicki — *Did you ever try to help him?* — until they both stormed out, leaving me alone in the kitchen with the remnants of their ill will.

The ill will lingered through the next day, with Vicki grumpy, Amelia annoyed, Jude back as though nothing had changed, and Lee scurrying around with one eye out for a shooter.

★   ★   ★

There was no shooter. This time it was an arsonist, and the target wasn't Lee's bungalow in Bell Valley, but the unoccupied mansion in Massachusetts. The call came Thursday night, early enough for Lee to panic, but too late for any formal declaration of arson prior to the court hearing the next day.

18

Vicki woke me with the news Friday morning. Within minutes, I was in the kitchen with Amelia and Lee, and once I had the basics, the only thing I could think was that I wanted feedback from James.

Someone tried to burn Lee's house in MA, I texted. *Call when you can.*

The BlackBerry was still in my hand when it chimed. Barely a minute had passed.

'Hi,' I said, and stepped out of the kitchen onto the back porch of the Red Fox.

'What happened?'

'There was a fire last night. The house was alarmed, so the fire department got there before the whole thing was engulfed, but there was still a lot of damage. Lee is traumatized.'

'How did she find out? I thought the bank repossessed.'

'Not the bank,' I said, telling him what I had just learned. 'The mortgage was taken over by a company called East Sea Properties.'

'Owned by the brothers?' James asked.

I smiled. 'My first thought, too. The brothers would have wanted the insurance money. But no. East Sea Properties is actually quite large. Some of its holdings date way back, and they aren't all on the coast. They cut a swathe inland, all the way to Bell Valley.'

'Amelia,' he deduced as I knew he would.

'It's not that she actually thought Lee would ever want to live there again, but she says it has emotional value and that Lee, not those brothers, should be the one to decide what she does with the house. Amelia's pretty belligerent about it. It's the principle of the thing, she says. I'm not sure Lee agrees. She isn't into belligerence. But there's no way Amelia would want that house damaged. She's kept it maintained so that it would be ready for Lee if she wants to return.'

'A kind thing to do, but a tip-off. The brothers must have followed the trail. Otherwise, there'd have been no motive. Are the police sure it was arson?'

'Not yet, but the way the fire spread is suspicious. They're putting a team on it today. They want to talk with Amelia and Lee, but I want to talk with that team. It's a small town. Think they can handle this?'

'I'm looking at the website,' James said, sounding distracted as he read. 'The police department has more than twenty officers. So they have the numbers, but I doubt they see much arson. You may want to ask.'

'I will. I take it we can't use this in court today.'

'No. Arson, vandalism, threatening letters — they're a whole other case. Today's only about the trust fund. Sean may be able to slip in something about a pattern of intimidation. The other side will object, but the judge will still hear it, and if Lee is as sympathetic a witness as I'm guessing, it could register. I'd give him a call.'

'Right now. Anything else?' I had my own list

of questions, mostly for Amelia and having to do with her insurer helping with the arson investigation. But James was good at this.

He considered it. Finally, he said, 'Yeah. Meet me there?'

'Where?'

'At the house in Massachusetts. I want to see it. I also want to stop in at the police station to meet whoever's doing the investigation. Actually, I have a better idea. I don't know how early I can get out of here, but if the hearing's at three, I could catch a shuttle and be at the courthouse by five. We could drive there together.' He smiled then — I could hear it when he said, 'I'd do the driving. I miss my car.'

I wasn't offended. I liked his plan. I might have said he would miss precious work time, or that Mark wouldn't be pleased, or that he would be dead on his feet moonlighting this way. But I didn't. I might be occasionally impulsive, marginally irresponsible, or borderline cowardly, but I wasn't dumb. Arson in Manchester-by-the-Sea was a gift.

★   ★   ★

Leaving Bell Valley later that morning, we took two cars. I had been planning on driving Lee anyway, but Amelia insisted on coming, and then Jude, at which point I told them I was meeting James afterwards, and while that might have been fine if it had been Lee alone, the thought of Amelia and Jude in the BMW with us wasn't my idea of fun.

So Jude drove the Range Rover. I had no idea why he was coming — whether he hoped his presence would redeem him on the responsibility front, or whether he just wanted to be in on the action. I did know that he wanted to meet James.

That said, I was hoping he would get lost along the way, but there he was, standing with us in the courthouse lobby at two-thirty. Lee, who was looking nervously at the people nearby, made an involuntary sound when a new group arrived.

'Which one is Albert Meeme?' I whispered.

'Round one, bald head,' she whispered back.

I couldn't miss him. He was looking directly at us. Likewise, the three men with him.

'Do you know the others?'

'The one in the dark suit is the lawyer for the family. The one in the navy blazer is Jack's brother Duane. I don't know the third.'

Sean did. Joining us, he said, 'The tall guy is a former county sheriff, currently a private investigator. They've brought him along as a statement that they have the law on their side.'

'But if he's not currently the law . . . ,' I began.

'It's all about image. They're the dream team. Big local names. All of them.'

'Will the judge be swayed by that?'

'He shouldn't be. But the old boys' club still exists.'

I was thinking that Sean looked uneasy, and was hoping that Lee didn't notice, when Jude said, 'I know that guy.'

'Which one?' I asked.

'The investigator. He was on my boat once.'

'Uh, Jude . . . '

'Seriously. Take a few tourists for a week at sea, film it, and what they pay for the privilege covers operational expenses for the trip, so it's pure profit for us. Every guy is up for playing Deadliest Catch, and that one was really into it.' To Sean, he said, 'His name is Billy DeSimone, right? Can't forget the name. He uses it in the third person all the time.'

'Same guy,' Sean confirmed.

'He was a good poker player. He won't recognize me cleaned up, but I stared at that face a lot. We used to go at it for hours. Say the word, and I'll distract him.'

Amelia looked appalled but was saved from responding by Sean, who warned, 'Do that and they'll turn it into an attempt to influence the witness. Right now, Lee is the victim. There's a purity to that.'

Jude looked annoyed, but Lee distracted us.

'Duane is staring at me,' she said, frightened. 'He made a play for me when Jack died and didn't like when I said no. I don't see why they have to be here.'

'It's their legal right,' Sean explained. 'They have something at stake, too.'

'Yeah,' Jude groused, 'a reputation for getting off the hook. Billy DeSimone knows how to use the system. Give him a couple of beers, and he'll tell you all about it. He'll make mincemeat of your case, Sean. You have no evidence linking Lee's husband's family with what's happening to her now.'

'That's not the point of this hearing,' Sean

said, and suddenly glanced toward the elevator. Following his gaze, I saw James striding towards us. He looked confident, handsome, and utterly professional in his blue suit and sage tie. Eyes excited, he was looking at me.

If I hadn't already loved him, I would have fallen head over heels again. Only after he kissed me did he greet the others.

I'm sure he knew exactly who Jude was, but, incredibly, their meeting was a nonevent. They had barely shaken hands when James introduced us to an older man who accompanied him. His name was Lyle Kagan. 'I work with Lyle's son in New York,' James explained, 'but Lyle lives here in Boston, and he has experience with Albert Meeme. He's agreed to testify.'

★ ★ ★

Lyle Kagan was a powerful witness. A respected real estate developer, he packed nearly as much star power as Billy DeSimone. Where Lee was appropriately meek, testifying simply to the facts of dwindling cheques and non-answers to questions, Lyle described a pattern of irregularities with his own trust that he had never been able to prove. It might have taken a while for Lyle to have his day in court, but it struck me, with pleasure, that Albert Meeme had messed with the wrong guy.

Affidavits were entered into evidence, along with Lee's files. The other lawyer argued — condescendingly, as though Lee were either a gold digger or pathetically naive — that Lee

281

simply expected more than a fluctuating stock market could produce. But when the judge looked over the provided trust statement and found it inadequate, the lawyer couldn't answer to the specifics of disbursements.

The petition was granted. Sean even got his requested accountant to examine the trust fund. It would have been a total victory, had not Lee's brother-in-law whispered to Lee once we were in the lobby again, 'Dye your hair all you want, but we know where you are. My offer's still good. Say the word, and I'll be your protector.'

Full voice, for our benefit, she repeated the threat verbatim, to which Duane made a face and said, 'Where did you come up with that? All I did was ask how you're doing.' With an elaborate annoyance, he left.

Lee was trembling. 'I shouldn't be doing this. It'll get worse.'

'But now we're on the record,' Sean assured her. 'If they try anything more, it'll backfire. First, we establish trust fund fraud. By then we'll have a report that arson was committed. Each piece of the puzzle will fit it.'

'With me as the bait,' Lee guessed.

But Amelia was one step ahead. 'That man will not protect you. We will.' She homed in on Jude. '*You* will. You can keep her safe, Jude. This is right up your alley.'

Jude looked cornered.

'No. Jude.' Amelia was firm. 'I need you for this. No one else can do it like you can.'

★ ★ ★

We left soon after — Amelia and Lee with Jude, James and I alone. The plan was for Jude to lead us to Manchester-by-the-Sea, but, with typical machismo, he wove through traffic in a way that was impossible to follow. After a halfhearted attempt, James caught my eye and, with a satisfied smile, turned on the GPS.

I wasn't as interested in where we were headed as, there and then, with what my husband had done. Ebullient, I took his hand. 'You made our case. You were amazing.'

'Nah,' he said in the deep voice I loved, 'I just lucked out with Lyle.'

'But he didn't go after Meeme when it was his own trust fund. Why now?'

'Time has passed. Lyle's name is bigger now than it was then. And he felt for Lee. I've been talking with him since Tuesday, but he didn't commit to testifying until this morning. That's when I decided to catch an earlier plane.'

An earlier plane raised an interesting point. 'Any trouble getting out of the office?'

His chin rose a fraction. 'I don't know. I didn't ask, I just left. I was up half the night finishing a brief for Mark. I'd put in my time.'

'You don't look exhausted.'

'Funny how you forget exhaustion when you score big in court. Besides, I have to look good to hold my own beside you. You look amazing, honey. Where'd you get the skirt and blouse?' The blouse was white, the skirt red and short. My sandals were black and high-heeled.

'Vicki's closet. A change from a blue blouse and black slacks, don't you think?'

He gave the outfit another admiring glance. 'You could wear that to work.'

'I could not.'

'Well, you should. Or maybe not. You look too good.' After squeezing my hand, he returned his to the wheel. Rush-hour traffic was heavy, but he didn't seem to mind the starts and stops. Gripping the wheel at ten and two, he gave a deep, satisfied sigh. 'Boy, does it feel good to drive.'

A man and his car, I thought. But it could have been any car, I realized. He had been so busy that he hadn't driven other than to come to Bell Valley.

'Freedom!' I said.

He echoed the word with enthusiasm, only afterwards realizing the admission and adding a quick, 'There's just no reason for me to drive in New York.'

'But you do love driving. And you do love your car.'

He did a thing with his eyes that said it was true.

'And you love your work,' I added.

He snorted. 'You know I don't. I love the Bryant case, but the rest of it stinks. I'm just counting down, doing what I have to, to get that partnership in October. Once I have it, I can pick and choose.'

'But you said something's up at the firm. What if it folds?'

'It won't fold.'

'But what if it did? What would you do?'

'Look for another job.'

284

'Would you ever consider leaving New York?'

'You're being transparent, babe.'

'Would you?' I wanted to know if this was still a total roadblock.

Rather than answering, James switched to the one topic he knew I wouldn't ignore. 'Your Jude is a real piece of work. What do you see in him?'

'Talk about transparent,' I said, but allowed the change of subject. All things considered, James had been remarkably civil to Jude. 'Nothing now. Ten years ago? Lots. I was young and inexperienced. He was worldly.'

'Neanderthal worldly.'

'He's not that bad,' I said, though James wasn't entirely wrong. 'He says he's grown. But he still doesn't understand the concept of responsibility.' I told him about Noah and the baseball game. 'Jude knows what he should be doing, but he can't quite do it. There's a disconnect.'

'He still loves you.'

'Not my problem,' I said.

'As long as you're up there, it is. I know the type. He'll keep trying.'

'He can try all he wants. I'm not available.'

'What if we were separated?'

My heart stopped. 'Do you want that?'

'Hell no, but if we were, would you be with him again?'

'Why would I? I don't feel anything for him.' I'd certainly had opportunity, though telling my husband that would only invite jealousy. 'Ten years is a long time. He hasn't changed. I have.'

It must have been the right answer, because

James reached for my hand again and held it as we headed north on I-93. We talked a little, but the silence between was sweet. Every so often, he fingered my wedding band, not unlike what Jude had done but with a greater sense of rightness. When a buzzing came from his pocket, he ignored it. He answered a second one, but let a third go.

The town was an easy twenty miles north of Boston, but it was well after five when we reached Lee's house. Though surprisingly close to the road, it was low and sprawling, definitely a good thing, given what had happened. A fire would have spread upward more quickly, causing greater damage. Instead, the destruction was limited to the bedroom wing of the house, which was broken and charred.

The front door opened to living areas that I guessed to be exactly as Lee had left them. Decorated fittingly for an oceanside home, it was done in beige and glass. With large windows covering every ocean-facing wall, artwork was sparse but spectacular, a collection of large nature pieces encased in weathered wood. As amazing as they were, though, I was riveted to the small framed pictures of a light-haired, happier Lee with her husband, who, while not traditionally handsome, exuded kindness.

Though the entire house smelled of smoke, it was more concentrated in those parts that had burned. The master bedroom was the worst. Someone had known where to start for the greatest impact. Built-in units, his and her chaise-longues, a king-size bed once dressed in fine linens — all were unsalvageable. What damage hadn't been done by the fire had been done by the firefighters in their effort to control the blaze. Adding insult to injury, the moist salt air poured through gaping holes where huge windows had been.

I felt sick to my stomach, but Lee looked worse. When she went back outside, I followed. The others weren't far behind. Amelia had seen enough and wanted to get on the road; I suspected that though she regretted her lot in life, she found Bell Valley as comforting as anyone else. Jude, looking irritated as he toed ashes outside, joined her at the car, but Lee was the first in, angling away from the house she had loved.

Once they were gone, James and I walked along the bluff. Below us, the tide was out, exposing wet sand, snarled seaweed, black rocks. For a time, we sat shoulder to shoulder with the sun at our backs, enjoying the cool breeze off the Atlantic. Our fingers were linked. It was a special moment; I felt closer to him than I could remember.

'I've missed this,' I said, burrowing even closer.

'It was your choice to leave,' he breathed against my forehead.

'I mean the big picture. This has been gone for years.' I turned my cheek on his shoulder to look at him. Everything appealed, from his wind-blown hair to his blue eyes to the shadow on his jaw. 'Don't you miss it at all?'

'Hell yes, I miss it,' he said. 'I miss this, miss

drinking with my college buds, miss playing pickup basketball — but things change.'

'Not things like this,' I argued. 'What we have here, now, is a personal relationship. It may not be as easy to come by as it was when we were in law school, but we have to make time for it.'

'What about responsibility? Your Jude doesn't have it, you said. Well, I do.'

'Too much. There has to be a happy medium. I've said it before — I don't want to be an extreme. I can't *live* as an extreme. Why did I have to walk away from my life to see that?'

He didn't answer, but I knew he wasn't convinced. Either that, or he was just more stubborn than I was. Or more blind.

We didn't stay much longer. James had a plane to catch. We did stop at the police station on our way out of town, and though only a skeletal staff was working, the fire was big news. They had nothing to add to what we already knew, but James was able to introduce himself and leave his card. He also made an impression, something I never ceased to appreciate — and the dispatcher wasn't even female. He was a guy wearing a Red Sox hat, and though James had little time to watch games, he could talk baseball. Me, I'd have been all business, but James had a way of doing business and making a friend in the process, guaranteeing that the guy in the Red Sox cap would call the instant there was news. The fellow also recommended a fabulous eatery right next door and even made a call to guarantee us a quick in and out.

'You're so good at that,' I commented while

we waited for our lobster rolls. 'He's your best bud now.'

James was looking around the restaurant. 'It's easy to be nice to nice people. You're the same way.' His eyes found mine again. He seemed wary. 'Could you live in a town like this?'

'In a heartbeat.' We were an easy drive from a city; there was no traffic to speak of; our server seemed to know everyone in the place.

'I couldn't. I'd feel choked.'

'Like I feel in New York?' I didn't want to rock the boat of our earlier goodwill, but that had been my big mistake. I had to learn to express myself. Urgently, I leaned forward. 'Don't you see, James? This is the best — of us, of *life*. My mom used to argue that tombstones don't list jobs. They list relationships — daughter, wife, mother. Forget everything else right now; I need to recoup the *wife* part.' Straightening, I wagged a finger between us. 'You, me, woods, beach, lunch together — I want *this*. Can I get it in New York?'

'Yes,' he said without a blink. 'I'll show you. Come back with me, Emily. We'll have this weekend. We'll relax, we'll play, we'll talk.'

'What about work?' I asked, because, for us, Manhattan was synonymous with that. 'It'll still be in your face.'

'I'll do it between what we want to do.'

Sitting back, I studied him. He was open, vulnerable.

Funny, I had been worried that he would sway me with words. But it was the look that did it now. I could have returned to Bell Valley to

289

consider. I could have walked through the woods and communed with my coyote. I could have fully analysed the pros and cons.

But three weeks had passed without Manhattan stress, and if I was to decide which road to take next, I had to test my strength.

'Okay,' I said.

He did blink then and straightened. 'Yes?' He seemed to be holding his breath. 'Just like that?'

'For a visit,' I cautioned, but James seemed relieved enough to not fault the word.

'What about your stuff in Bell Valley?'

'I can do without it. There's something to be said for spontaneity.'

'Hah,' he barked, but teasingly. 'Try insurance.'

I smiled. 'Like I'll have to go back for them? Maybe I'll just want to go back. I still have another week before Walter expects me at work.'

★ ★ ★

I wasn't thinking of Walter during the drive south. As the sun sank, headlights went on, and traffic picked up, I was thinking about what I'd told James. *Tombstones don't list jobs; they list relationships — daughter, wife, mother.* Even as I addressed the wife part, the daughter surfaced. I had to call my dad and let him know I was trying, but I wanted more privacy than the car allowed.

Besides, another call was more urgent, or Vicki would worry. Not only was she my best girlfriend, but she was my direct link to Bell Valley news. Her report this night was that Jude was camping out at Lee's, not so much to protect her as to escape Amelia after a harrowing drive home.

★ ★ ★

Had the timing been different, I might have been more nervous about my return. But since it was the start of the Fourth of July weekend, more people were leaving New York than coming. It was after midnight when we entered the city. Traffic was light in our part of town, pedestrians were few, and the dark hid a wealth of things I didn't want to see.

And then there was James, plastering me to his side when we left the car at the garage, backing me against a streetlight for a kiss and then some foreplay that had us running the last block. Dropping clothes wherever, we made love in the front hall and again on the bed. It was two in the morning by then, but he was up at four-thirty working — or so he confessed when I woke up at nine. When I started to say, *See, nothing's changed*, he showed me it had.

We went out for brunch. We walked around Gramercy Park and up Park Avenue. We shopped. When I complained about the heat, James reminded me of the furnace in Bell Valley that first day in the woods. *Not as hot as this*, I argued, to which he laughed and dragged me into the nearest ice-cream shop, and when I argued that between Bell Valley and this, I was eating too much, he said I looked better than ever.

He tried. Really he did. He reminded me how

much fun we could have in New York. But there were still those times when the sounds of the city penetrated closed windows or the ding of his BlackBerry tripped a reflex and my stomach tightened up. There was no one I wanted to call. I didn't know anyone on the street. I felt lonely.

Moreover, by Sunday morning, I was starting to worry about James. He worked whenever we were home, furtive when I was around, open about it when I was reading, sleeping, or showering. It was utterly sweet and positively insane. He couldn't sustain this kind of schedule. He put up a good front, but with Friday's excitement fading, his speech was suffering from exhaustion once more.

Using this as proof that we had to make changes in our lives, I put off calling my father. He would only argue that we had jobs most lawyers would die for, and he was likely right. With the Sunday *Times* spread on the kitchen table, I studied the help-wanteds. Seeing nothing remotely interesting, I surfed the Web for legal positions in Stamford, Newark, even Philadelphia. Granted, a headhunter would know of better openings, but what I saw here was discouraging.

Humbled, I emailed Walter. How could I not, with guilt nagging as I watched James work?

Just wanted to check in, I typed. *I'm doing better, but I'll need the last week you've given me. I'll email before next weekend to let you know about Monday.*

LET ME KNOW? Walter typed back quickly and briefly. *It's next Monday or nothing.*

Just thinking about it, I felt a roiling inside. I

called Vicki, who let me vent in ways James might not have, and though I felt better, nothing was solved. I stood at my closet for a long while, looking at those black slacks and blue blouses, not wanting to wear any of them, but knowing that I would if I returned to Lane Lavash.

I dreamed of my coyote that night, and she wasn't alone. She was with her pups and several other adults, no less than eight pairs of coyote eyes watching me with an odd expectancy. Too soon, they dissolved into the forest. I went after them this time, only to slip on a granite ledge and awaken abruptly.

James didn't know about the dream. My arm felt cold sheets on his side of the bed, and when I found him working in the kitchen, talk of a dream seemed silly. Humouring me, he came to bed and was quickly asleep, but I lay awake worrying for a time. By sunup Monday, I was feeling queasy — knowing how hard James was trying and wanting to please him, but feeling the old life lurking, waiting to pounce.

So I baked corn bread. Had I ever done that before? No. Did I know what I was doing? No. But on one of those Bell Valley mornings, I had loved eating Lee's corn bread, and I couldn't think of a better diversion. I found a recipe online, ran to a convenience store for the ingredients, and while James typed nearby in a pool of papers, I played cook. Two loaves were in the oven, and I was opening the door every few minutes, waiting for their tops to brown, when my cell rang.

Seeing the New Hampshire area code, I felt a twinge. Last time it had been my kitten. Now I

293

feared it was Lee or, if not Lee, Jude. But the problem was Vicki. 'She's in the hospital,' Amelia reported. 'She started having contractions last night. They've let up, but she's being held for observation. The problem is, the doctors may recommend bed rest for the next four months, and Vicki is panicking, which makes the problem worse. She won't listen to her husband, and she won't listen to me, but she may listen to you.'

I immediately called Vicki, and Amelia hadn't exaggerated. Panic was the only possible cause for her frantic rush of words. I promised her I would be back by nightfall.

'Nnnno,' James wailed, slumping when I told him.

'I have to. She was there for me, and now the tables are turned. This is what it's about, James. It's what I've been saying.'

'But you just got here. Today's the holiday.'

'And you need to work.' I kissed him, but his mouth didn't yield. 'I'm not moving there permanently. I just want to help her figure out what to do. I know you're not happy, but this is important. It's who I want to be.'

'The runaway wife.'

'The trusted friend. What if this was us? What if *I* was pregnant and there was a problem and we needed someone to help us sort it out?'

'We'd do it ourselves.'

I sighed. 'Then I guess women are the ones who need the village, and for me right now, Vicki is it. I want to be there for her. Can you love me for that?'

He snorted. 'Do I have a choice?'

294

I smiled and kissed him again. 'No.'

Moments later, I was in the bedroom. Technically, I didn't need to pack anything, since my bag was still in Bell Valley. But, for the sake of variety, I took a few things. And my laptop this time. And my diamond studs.

Always needing hair clasps, I was rummaging through a cabinet in the bathroom when I spotted a box of tampons. I picked it up, thinking to take it, because I'd had my period before leaving New York last time and had to be due again.

Actually, if I hadn't had it since then, I was late.

I was never late.

Granted, a drastic change in lifestyle could affect a woman's body.

But I was *never* late.

My heart began to pound. Cautious, I set the tampons down and took a different box. Like any woman who was trying to get pregnant, I had a supply of these, but I was conditioned to expect disappointment. When the first strip showed positive, I threw it out and tried again. When the second read the same, my hand began to shake.

'James,' I called in a tremulous voice. Fixing my clothes, I left the bathroom. I was shaking all over by then. 'James!'

Eyes distant, he looked up from his screen. I held out the second strip. He stared at it, disoriented, before realizing what it was.

'Positive,' I whispered, afraid to say it aloud in case it wasn't true.

But it was. James saw the results, too. I was *pregnant*.

19

James was as stunned as I was. We had absolutely *not* been trying. I'd been gone!

His expression went from startled to amused to positively giddy. Sweeping me off the floor with an arm under my knees, he held me with such ferocity that I would have cried out in protest if he hadn't quickly gentled. He let my legs slide to the floor, leaving possessive arms around me.

'When?' he asked excitedly.

'That night in the woods, maybe?' *That* had been something. 'Or afterwards, in my room?'

'You didn't suspect?'

'I've refused to *think* about it. That was part of my escape.'

'I knew you looked different,' he crowed, and who was I to say that a woman didn't look different after only two weeks. I wouldn't have thought I would feel nausea this early either, but other explanations? I had never been the queasy type.

'Omigod.' I put a hand on my belly. 'I didn't expect this.' His eyes were electric. 'It changes everything.'

'Does it *ever*.'

'I don't want you going back to Lane Lavash. There's too much pressure.'

'I wouldn't go back even if I *weren't* pregnant,' I declared, victorious.

'Pregnant.' He tested the word. 'Are you sure?'

I was suddenly *very* sure. Everything about this felt right, starting with the idea that my baby hadn't been conceived on the clock. 'I did two tests. Both read the same. And the symptoms are spot on.'

'If you conceived two weeks ago, when would you be due?'

I tried to do the maths, but with so many other thoughts in my head, he beat me to it.

'March. *Perfect* timing. I'm named partner in October — my pay goes up in January — you won't have to work *at all*.'

'I do want to work, just not at Lane Lavash,' I cautioned, because, in that split second of imagining my legal career over, I had felt a tiny loss. I did love law.

'Will you see the doctor this week?'

'Not necessary. She can't tell us anything right now, and I already have the vitamins.'

He shot a triumphant look skyward and, looking back at me, grinned out a huff of air. 'We'll celebrate — dinner tonight at Cipriani?'

'As soon as I get back.'

'Get back?' He seemed suddenly mystified. 'You can't go now.'

'Why not?'

'You're pregnant.'

I might not have been able to calculate when I was due, but regarding the why of it — why I was pregnant now and not before — it was suddenly clear. '*Exactly*,' I said as it all came together. 'Don't you see? My getting pregnant in Bell Valley is the ultimate sign that I was meant to go there. There was no way I was going to get pregnant here, because our lives wouldn't allow it.'

His arms still circled me, though more laxly now, and his voice was quiet. 'I want you here.'

'I'll be back right after I help Vicki.'

'I'm the father of this baby. Don't I get a say about where the baby goes?'

I tugged on his shirt, teasing. 'James. It's not like I'm taking it white-water rafting, and it's not like I'll be five hours from civilization. Bell Valley is soothing and safe.'

He was silent for another beat. Then his voice came low and vehement. 'There is no way in hell that I'll live in that town.'

Another time, I might have been patient, but I was wanting to be happy, not rehash an old point. 'Me *neither*, so maybe we need to discuss where we *will* live. If I'm pregnant, we have to make a decision. New York doesn't work for me,' I declared. 'I can't live here. I can't work here. Okay, you are not living in Bell Valley, but I am not living here. So where *will* we live?'

He looked startled by my outburst. So was I, actually. I had always thought he would be the one to issue the ultimatum. But I wasn't sorry I'd done it. We had been dancing around the decision for days now.

'Do we have to decide this today?' James asked.

'You raised it,' I pointed out, then relented. 'Oh, James. Bell Valley isn't us. It just happens that I have a good friend there who needs help.'

'Can't she wait a little?'

298

'She's in crisis now.'

'I want you here.'

'You want me to choose,' I said. We stared at each other in the silence that ensued. Finally, I said, 'I'm just going to visit for a few days.'

'Last time it was three weeks.'

I threw up a hand. 'And if it is this time, too, what else would I be doing? You've told me not to go back to Lane Lavash, and since I don't know where we'll be, but I do know I'm pregnant, I can't in good faith look for something else, and *you'll* be working all the time, and it's not like I can walk a microscopic baby in the park.'

'You could miscarry.'

'I won't.'

'You can't know that.'

'I do. I feel it. This pregnancy is *solid*.'

★ ★ ★

James wasn't convinced. I suppose that his worrying about me — worrying about the baby — was a good sign. But he was upset enough to retreat into work even before I left the room to finish packing. Hating the distance at this time when we should be feeling especially close, I went to him when I was done and put an arm around his shoulders.

'We'll work this out,' I said.

Fingers typing, he grunted.

'I'll call from the road. Will you pick up?'

'Of course I'll pick up.'

'I love you, James.'

'I know.'

When he didn't say more, I kissed his cheek and left.

★   ★   ★

Alone in the car, I tried to process the fact of being pregnant. In spite of my being so sure, it still seemed unreal. I had run another test before leaving, and it was positive, but I had two more strips in my bag. I wanted to see that little + again. And again. I also wanted to tell someone — was *bursting* with it — but my best friend was in the hospital with baby problems of her own, and not a single other friend came to mind. If I called my mother, she would only ask a raft of other questions. Same with my dad. And if I told Kelly, she would call them.

So I stifled the urge. This microscopic something belonged to James and me. It was our little secret, better kept that way until we had a grip on what was happening.

An hour out, I called him. 'Are you okay?'

'Yeah.' But he sounded annoyed.

'I want you excited.'

'I might be if you were here,' he said, and let loose with every dark thought. 'But you left like a shot, like you couldn't get away fast enough. So I'm alone with these problems. Hell, Emily, I don't know what to do with this. It's like you changed the rules in the middle of the game. I wasn't the only one who wanted to live — live here. You did, too. Okay, so if you need an escape, we can buy a weekend place somewhere,

300

but if we want money for that, I can't change jobs. I won't get as much money anywhere else.' He grabbed another breath. 'And that's the bottom line. I'm supposed to be the breadwinner, but how can I do that if — if we move? I'll be starting all over again. I've spent seven years making contacts here. If we move, it's back to square one, and — and that's assuming I can get waived out of taking a whole other bar exam. Have you thought about that, Emily?'

I hadn't. I had been dealing with generalities, selfishly perhaps. But I couldn't back down. I was fighting for two now.

'It's about priorities,' I argued. 'When we were in law school, the priority was getting the best grades so that we could get into top firms. And we did. And maybe it worked for a while, but I'm tired of hearing lawyer jokes in my head. Your job is as bad as mine. You aren't happy, and I don't care what you say, it won't magically change once you make partner.'

'At least I'll be in a better position to decide what to do. Where do you want to live? Tell me.'

I thought for a minute. Specifics eluded me, but the priority was clear. 'Somewhere personal. I want a life filled with humans. I don't want my dearest friend to be a machine.'

'And you think you're unique?' he shot back. 'Don't you think at least *some* of the eight million people in this city want that, too? Don't you think some of them *have* it?'

'It isn't about New York. It's about lifestyle.'

'We can live differently here.'

But I didn't believe it for a minute. Lifestyle

was addictive. Hadn't I felt it this weekend — a tension creeping in the minute I let down my guard? Our staying there was like asking an alcoholic to work in a bar.

He sighed, weary. 'This is why you need to be here. We have important things to discuss and we shouldn't be doing it while you drive. Please focus on the road. You're not in the left lane, are you?'

'I'm in the middle lane going sixty. I am being passed on both sides.'

'Is that safe?'

I had to smile. In the midst of the other, his worry was actually sweet. 'Yes, James, it's safe. I'm going against traffic. Everyone else is heading back to the city.'

'Okay. Fine, well, hang up and don't call anyone else. Why don't we have Bluetooth?'

'I don't know. It's your car. Why don't we?'

'Because it's an old model. We need to get something newer, maybe a van.'

'For one baby? I don't think so.'

'I'm hanging up now,' he advised. 'Keep your eyes on the road.'

★ ★ ★

He called an hour later to ask how I was feeling. I didn't tell him that despite thickening clouds and occasional sprinkles, I was increasingly relaxed.

'Eating corn bread,' I said with a full mouth, and swallowed.

'Corn bread isn't nutritious.'

302

'Mine is. I used organic eggs and milk. James, about the other, I keep thinking about Lee, and about Denise Bryant. You love working on these cases because they involve personal interaction, your words. Personal interaction says it all. I had to leave New York to realize it, because I was too consumed by our lives to see. But I have perspective now. And I think you're exactly the same as me. You want to be a good lawyer, but you've always talked about what you want to do as a father. How can you be both, living the way we do?' My mind was filled with little insights, more and more the farther I drove. 'Take Jude,' I said. 'He wants whatever he can't have. If it's forbidden, that's the appeal. But you're not like that. You *can* have what you want. You just have to realize you want it.' Helping him do that was my new mission.

But he was silent for too long.

'James?' I tested cautiously.

'I'm here. Did you know that eating junk food in the early months of pregnancy can increase the risk of miscarriage? I just read that. You won't eat junk food, will you?'

Changing the subject? Okay. I couldn't ask for immediate surrender. But I wasn't giving up. 'Do I ever?'

'You drink wine.'

'Socially.'

'And caffeine.'

'I'll limit it.'

'Thank you.'

Ending the call, I wondered if James was simply being evasive about things he didn't want to discuss, or if he was turning neurotic on me. Another little insight, though, as I drove on? He was doing the only thing I had allowed him to, and while I liked being in control, I understood. Men felt helpless at times like this.

★ ★ ★

Knowing that visiting hours would be ending soon and that I had to see Vicki before they did, I went straight to the hospital. Hooked up to an IV, she was as pale as the sheets, and while my arrival didn't change that, her relief was instant.

'Ahhhhh,' she breathed, and reached for my hand. 'I wasn't sure you'd come.'

'Oh-ho,' I teased. 'I learned my lesson about *that.*'

'So now I feel guilty, because you were finally with your husband, but I don't know what happened here, Emmie. It's not like I was lifting mattresses or changing tyres on the truck, I was doing what I always do, and I didn't have any trouble last time. I'm starting to dilate — at sixteen weeks! That is so bad! They're using drugs to slow things down, but they'll probably put me on bed rest, and I can't do bed rest — not with a three-year-old child and a bed-and-breakfast to run.'

Sitting beside her on the bed, I cradled her hand. 'You have Rob. He knows what to do.'

'Oh, pooh. Men can only do one thing at a time. Rob can handle Charlotte or the Red Fox, but not both, and if this is happening now, chances are it'll happen in another pregnancy, so

304

can I risk another one?'

'I thought you only wanted two children.'

'But what if I decide I want three? Or four? Hah! Three or four? It looks like I can't even do *two*. What did I do wrong?'

'You didn't — '

'My mother didn't have trouble, *her* mother didn't have trouble, so it's not like there's a family history of this, and they did more physical work than me. Every test shows the baby is fine, it's just *me* that's mucking it up.'

'Shhhhhh — '

'I saw it, Emmie. They did a sonogram before, and the baby was moving all over the place, arms and legs, everything. This is a *real person* I'm putting at risk.' Blond hair spilled every which way on the pillow, but the hands framing her belly were precise. 'I need to hold it in here for at least another twelve weeks, or it'll start life in the NICU and have lung problems and liver and sleep and digestive problems.'

I might have interrupted to say that doctors knew how to deal with these things, but hearing about all this, I felt sick myself — wondering if James was right, if I was minimizing the fragility of pregnancy, if I should be back home with my feet up, googling the first weeks of pregnancy.

'And bed rest creates its own problems, like weakness, dizziness, and blood clots,' Vicki was saying. 'And even if I don't get a blood clot, I'll be in lousy shape when the baby finally comes. So if I'm weak and dealing with a baby with problems, *plus* Charlotte, *plus* the Red Fox — how am I gonna do this?'

305

I ignored my unsettled stomach. Vicki needed me to be calm. 'Are you done?'

Her eyes held mine. She was silent for a minute, before murmuring a helpless 'Yes.'

'Take a breath.'

She took a breath.

'First,' I said gently, 'you're assuming the worst, when there are all sorts of better scenarios, and you do have a right to be scared. This came out of nowhere, but that's how life is, and you, Vicki Bell, are level-headed enough to get through *anything*. You'll love this baby, you'll recover from bed rest if bed rest is what it takes, you'll learn to delegate at the Red Fox, and as for Charlotte, she feeds herself, is toilet trained, and talks. If the best you can do for the next four months is read her *Green Eggs and Ham*, you'll be way ahead of a lot of other moms.'

'But she's only three,' Vicki pleaded. 'Amelia helps, Rob helps, but I'm the one who makes the arrangements and supervises play-dates and stays with her at birthday parties. Three is a crucial age. She needs to be with other children, and, okay, someone else can take her, but what happens when she wants me and I can't do it?' She was close to tears. 'She will hate this baby even before it's born!'

'She will not. She'll just love you more for the attention you do give her.'

'Oh, Emmie' — tears began to fall — 'you make it sound easy, but you don't *know* the reality of having a child.'

'I will soon,' I blurted out. I probably should have waited, but she needed a distraction, and

306

despite the business about this being James and my secret, I was *dying* to share the news.

Staring at me, she began to cry in earnest. 'Are you telling me something?'

I nodded. 'I'm like, two weeks, and I wouldn't have said anything except — '

'It happened up here?' she asked, sniffling, but I could see she was pleased.

I nodded again.

She held out her arms and, hugging me, laughed through her tears. 'That's *the* best thing you could have told me.'

'No one else knows, just you and James.'

She drew back, eyes wide. 'And he let you come here?'

'Not happily.'

'I'll call him. I'll tell him that I won't let anything happen to you or your baby. You are *such* a good friend.'

'She is,' Jude said from the door. I had no idea how long he'd been standing there, but from the mischief in those gold eyes, feared it was longer than I wanted. Vicki looked irate, not a good thing.

'Rest,' I ordered, forcing her eyes back to mine. 'Think about this baby. Think about Charlotte. Think about *us*.' It was as close as I could come, with Jude right there, to saying that our children would be close, the idea of which I loved. Without waiting for her to answer, I went out into the hall, facing Jude only after the door closed.

'You are a good friend, racing back here so soon,' he said. 'A baby, huh?'

307

'You weren't supposed to hear that. I'd appreciate it if you keep it to yourself.'

'Why?'

In no mood to be witty, I said, 'Because I'm asking you to.'

He snorted. 'That's a lousy answer. Did you tell it to Vicki just to make her feel better? Is it even true?'

I smiled sadly. 'Only you would ask that.'

'Cynical me.'

'Why, Jude? You used to be upbeat. Why cynical now?'

He leaned against the wall and watched a nurse walk by. 'Things haven't gone my way.'

'Excuse me? You've had every advantage in the world!' I cried, because his self-pity was unacceptable when, all over this hospital, people were dealing with life and death. 'Have you seen Noah yet?'

'From a distance. We haven't met. I don't see the point. Noah doesn't need me. And I need action. I'm not good with this, Emily. I'm hanging out at Lee's, but if something doesn't happen soon, I may die of boredom before the bad guy arrives. Do you honestly think someone would be dumb enough to try to hurt Lee now that she's gone to court? Anything happens to her, and they'll *know* who did it.'

'Not without evidence,' I argued. 'She's the plaintiff, Jude. If she's gone, the case disappears. And yes, I think someone would be dumb enough, if whoever it is is greedy enough.'

★ ★ ★

308

I might have been more worried if the full narcotic of Bell Valley hadn't kicked in as soon as I passed through the covered bridge and the town green appeared. The sprinkles I had encountered during the drive were now full-fledged rain. It was nearly ten, and given the day that it had been, I should have gone to bed.

Instead, though, I sat on the bench on the forest side of the gardener's shed. The night was warm, the air positively saturated, drugging me more. Folding up my legs, I held the large umbrella that had been stored in the closet for guests. But the beat of rain on nylon was easily eclipsed by the more gentle, oddly resonant patter of rain in the woods.

And then, barely five minutes into it, came the coyote. One howl followed another, the second closer, the third closer still. I watched, listened, wondered how close they would come, but the wet forest floor muted the sound of movement, and visibility was nil. In the absence of stars and moon, the woods were opaque, with only a glitter coming now and then from the reflection off raindrops in the light on the shed.

Was I frightened? Absolutely not. James might have called this severe risk-taking, but I knew these coyotes. They wouldn't attack. And I wanted to share my news.

So I thought the words — *pregnant, pregnant, pregnant* — over and over again. I smiled when the yips and barks came, and studied the darkness, but the coyotes didn't move closer. They didn't have to. We had a meeting of minds.

For the longest time, there was silence. I knew

they were there, but they didn't move. Though the rain went on, the air was warm, I was dry under my umbrella, and everything about the forest world soothed. In time, coyote voices rose again, melodious, if receding now. But I still felt a warmth inside at the thought that my baby had heard its first lullaby.

★   ★   ★

Communing with the coyotes was one of the things I wanted. There was another, but it wouldn't happen until noon the next day, and in the meanwhile, I had a bed-and-breakfast to run.

20

I was in the parlour setting up for breakfast when Lee arrived. She, too, was early. *Just covering for Vicki*, she explained, though from the way she kept glancing out the window when she thought I wasn't looking, I suspected she felt safest here.

Between the two of us, we handled things surprisingly well, though it certainly helped that Tuesdays were always quiet. After brief instruction from Rob, I was able to process the checkouts, and when it came to housekeeping, the girl who normally helped Vicki brought a friend to work with her. All I had to do was tell them which guests were staying and which were leaving.

'You're having fun,' Amelia said, observing me while Rob finished dressing Charlotte.

I was at the computer in the front hall, checking for guests who were due to arrive. The program was amazingly easy — and smart. Type in a name and you had a guest's history at the Red Fox, including anything else Vicki or Rob had picked up in conversation. For instance, a woman arriving tomorrow had adopted two cats during her last visit; asking how the cats were doing would blow her away.

'And you're good at this. I'm offering you a job.'

I laughed, then realized she was serious. 'Omigosh no, Amelia. I'm just visiting. I can't

311

stay. Besides, Vicki's going to be fine.'

'Is she? They're sending her home today, but I just talked with the doctor. They don't want her on her feet more than thirty minutes at a stretch. She's going to need help.'

'Let Lee do more,' I suggested. 'If she were busier, she wouldn't worry so much.'

'I'm busier, and still I worry. Lee's a sitting duck, what with her complaints public now, an arsonist at large, and two brothers and a team of lawyers out to get her.'

With a glance at the kitchen, I put a silencing finger to my mouth.

Amelia snorted. 'I'm not saying anything she doesn't already know.'

'But your saying it confirms it,' I whispered.

'And that right there is why the Red Fox needs you. Not only are you having fun working here, not only can you use a computer, but you are sensitive to people's feelings.'

'Not selfish anymore?' I couldn't resist.

She waved a hand. 'Ach, I was upset when I said that. You brought back thoughts of Jude, who, by the way, is in Hanover again. Honestly, I don't know what the appeal is there, because the idea that anyone at Dartmouth would be interested in my academically challenged son is laughable.'

'Sex appeal is universal.'

'No. He's there because I want him here. *You* won't let me down that way.'

The woman was nothing if not wily, but I wasn't being sucked in. 'I'll stay for a day or two,' I offered, 'but Vicki needs long-term help,

312

and I can't be an innkeeper. I'm a lawyer.'

'Who hasn't worked in three weeks.'

'I'm a lawyer,' I insisted.

★ ★ ★

The conversation stayed with me, particularly my insistence that I was a lawyer. A knee-jerk reaction? Possibly. Being a lawyer had been my sole identity for the last ten years. It had taken precedence over being a wife, a daughter, a friend. When you were trying to build a career in a highly competitive field, single-mindedness was a plus.

My needs had changed, though. On the ladder of important things in my life, being a lawyer had dropped several rungs. Personal matters were higher now, which was why, as soon as Vicki was settled back home, I left the Red Fox and drove to the Refuge.

Burials always took place on Tuesdays, typically at noon when the sun was highest and most hopeful. Last night's rain had cleared, and though smoky clouds lingered around the highest of the mountains, the cemetery was bright. My kitten's ashes weren't the only ones being buried, but they were the ones that had drawn me here. Each little canister had a name. While the groundsman buried two others, I held the one that read *Precious* to my heart. When it was time, he let me place it in the ground myself.

This was therapeutic. There were no tears today, just a pervasive sense of peace.

I remained after the men left, sitting on the

ground studying the freshly turned earth, and it struck me that every life needed a turning now and then. Part of it was burying the bad, like a cerebellum that was too small and an oppressive job. Part was bringing up the good, like a kitten's spirit and my own need for life.

Sitting at my kitten's grave, I forgave myself for the last ten years. Wrong turns? No. I had acted in good faith, doing what I thought was right. But what was right, now, was seeing that my needs had changed.

One of those new needs had just surfaced. I wanted a pet. I didn't care what kind; James could choose. Or not. He would argue against it, but when I thought of my baby and the world I wanted it to have, this was a must. A home was different when it had a pet. It wasn't as clean and tidy, and, like balsam at Christmas, the scent was distinct. I had known this growing up, but had lost the thought. Only now, sitting in the peace of the cemetery, did it come again. A pet was a living, breathing thing with very basic needs and an unlimited capacity to love.

As analogies went, turning the earth to bring up fresh soil was a good one. Same with reordering the rungs on a ladder. A third came to me now, though. It was the idea of painting the canvas of a new life, one brush stroke at a time. Sitting here remembering a little kitten that had wobbled to me each time I'd come to visit, I added a furry stroke.

I didn't tell James about it when he called that night. He'd had a bad day at work. This wasn't the time to argue about a pet. And though his voice remained tired when he called Wednesday, he did have other news.

'We have a suspect.'

My eyes flew to Lee. We were all in the kitchen — Lee, Vicki, Amelia, and I, even Charlotte, who had refused to nap in her room, lest her mother disappear again, and had fallen asleep on Amelia's lap. It was nearly as improbable a sight as Vicki with her feet up, but, stubborn as her daughter, she too refused to be in her room. Rather, she had been instructing me on the proper way to cut fresh roses — diagonally, under lukewarm water — when my cell rang.

We have a suspect. We. Manchester-by-the-Sea. Arson.

Excited, I repeated the news aloud as I dried my hands. Grasping the phone more firmly, I asked, 'In custody?'

'Yeah.' I was nodding to the others as he went on. 'One good thing about a small town — people notice who comes and goes. Add buzz about arson, and they start calling the police. They were all mentioning seeing a white van on the day of the fire. No one had ever seen it before. The driver actually sat in the coffee shop for a while, either really hungry or just trying to look nonchalant, like he was on a local job and — and taking a break.'

'Letting people get a fix on his *face?*' I asked in amazement.

'Oh yeah. Talking with the server, buying cigarettes at the drugstore. It's a new approach.'

Giving a thumbs-up to the others, I asked James, 'Can anyone place him on Lee's street?'

'A neighbour can. He was coming back from dinner Thursday night and saw the van in her driveway. He didn't think anything of it at first. A house like that needs maintenance, so he sees trucks there all the time. He took a second look, though, because the van was from a window company, and he needs window work done himself. He wrote down the information.'

'Don't tell me,' I said. I was beginning to enjoy myself. 'The neighbour tried to call, and it was a bogus company.'

'Oh, the company was real. But the van was stolen from the factory, which is in . . . ' He paused for a silent drum roll.

'Connecticut,' I put in, smiling.

'Yup. Home of Lee's brothers-in-law. It was the Connecticut tags on the van that raised red flags.'

'One of the brothers hired him, then?'

'That's to be determined. Turns out, the window company knew who'd stolen the van. His name is Rocco Fleming, and he's done it before, but the owners never had the heart to go to the police. Fleming used to work for them. His uncle still does. Besides, he always returns the van. This time it had an empty tank and enough extra mileage on it to account for a trip to Manchester and back. They're holding him in Hartford.'

I repeated that for the others. Lee was pressing her chest, looking like she was afraid to believe.

'Can they keep him in jail?' Amelia asked.

'At least until they return him to Massachusetts and a judge rules on it.' Into the phone, I said, 'Extradition?'

316

'He's fighting it. But at least he's locked up now.'

I repeated the last.

'Am I safe, then?' Lee asked.

Amelia, never tactful, declared, 'Assuming he's the only one involved.'

'I doubt he was,' James said. 'I can't picture either Albert Meeme or those brothers being dumb enough to use only one not-so-bright guy. Whoever was in Bell Valley covered his tracks pretty well. Besides, Bell Valley is as tight-knit as Manchester. Someone would have noticed a window company van with Connecticut plates.'

I didn't repeat this. Lee looked frightened enough.

'It's a first step,' I tried to reassure her. 'They'll question him about where he's been, what he's done, who he's worked with. And they'll get a photo to the Bell Valley police, who'll show it around town to see if anyone here recognizes his face.'

'But what if there *is* a second person?' she asked. 'What if he tries to burn me out here?'

'Anyone creeping around will set off cameras and lights.'

'I'm going to be afraid to fall asleep.'

Amelia said, 'Jude will keep watch.'

Vicki must have believed that about as much as I did, because she said, 'You can sleep here. We always have room.'

That would do double service, I was thinking — hide Lee and give Vicki a live-in helper.

'But I like my place,' Lee insisted.

'We can move things faster if Amelia's willing

317

to pay for an investigator,' James suggested. 'My firm has a good one. He'll get answers sooner than the police.'

'The firm won't appreciate that,' I warned. Large firms — like James's and Lane Lavash — kept the best investigators on retainer for their use alone. Competition was fierce, with the most highly sought bidding themselves up.

'It'll be fine,' he said with such curtness that what I heard was *I don't care if the firm likes it or not,* which gave me pause.

'Everything okay?' I asked.

There was too long a silence, then a reluctant 'Nah. I'm off the Bryant case.'

'*What?*' When everyone in the kitchen grew alert, I waved a dismissive hand and headed for the front hall. 'Why?'

'Mark says the firm can't afford it. They want me working on — on cases where — where I'm billing full price. So they'll give the pro bono case to a new associate whose hourly is lower, and I — and I lose the most interesting case I've had this year.'

I had been ambivalent about that case — doubting Mark's motives, wanting James to hate *everything* about his firm. But I couldn't not feel his pain now.

'I'm sorry,' I said, letting the screen door slam behind me as I crossed the porch. 'When did you hear?'

'This morning. Barely had a foot in the door, when Mark was in my office.'

'You should have called me then.'

'You'd have only said I told you so. But you're

318

wrong, Emily. This was — was an economic decision. Mark had no choice.'

Startled that he could still defend the firm, I said, 'Of course he did. A lower associate may charge less per hour, but he won't be as efficient as you. He'll either do a lousy job or spend twice as long at it, leaving the firm short on resources. Besides, Mark knew how much you wanted this. He could have lobbied for you.'

'It's about the bottom line. Hey, I'm not the only one in this boat.'

'That doesn't make it right.'

His pause wasn't as long this time. 'Why did I know you'd say that?'

'Because it's the truth.'

There was another pause, then a caustic, 'Where are you now?'

'On the front steps of the inn.'

'What do you see?'

'The town green. Trees, benches.'

'My view is different. I see the tops of dozens of buildings, each of them filled with companies doing the exact same belt-tightening as my firm.'

'That doesn't make it right,' I repeated.

'So what should I do?' he asked in a frustrated voice. 'Go door to door complaining to every partner? Organize a grassroots protest among associates? You tell me, babe. What should I do?'

21

I couldn't answer his questions, neither then nor later that night when I called to see how he was. The conversation was short. He was still at the office. And I was discouraged. Baby or no baby, the rift between us had widened again. I was starting to wonder whether I ought to give in, go back to New York for good, and just let him do what he wanted. My escape wouldn't be wasted. I would do things differently if I returned. In that sense, I was safe.

The baby changed things. I couldn't stay apart from James now. And I did love him.

But I couldn't force him to change. If he was to get to the place where I was, he had to do it himself.

There was one glimmer of hope. He continued to be interested in Lee's case. I didn't know whether he was just angry enough to defy his firm, or whether he simply needed a small victory of his own, but he pushed his investigator hard.

And the man was good. By Thursday morning, he had linked Rocco Fleming to Duane Cray, the younger brother of Lee's late husband. There were no incriminating phone calls between them; that would have been too obvious. But the cell Rocco had been carrying at the time of his arrest was registered to a small construction company owned by Duane. Conclusive evidence? No. Rocco might have stolen the phone. But it was a mighty strange coincidence.

Passing the information to the Manchester police, James felt a deep satisfaction. It gave resonance to his voice when he called me afterwards, and I savoured the sound, particularly when a very different one came the next day.

★　★　★

Friday afternoon. Two-forty. I had just processed a check-in and was refolding a map of the town for a pair of newbies, when my cell vibrated in the pocket of my jeans. As the guests walked off, I pulled it out.

The first things I heard were honking horns and James swearing.

Then he muttered, 'Sorry. People are so friggin' impatient. They can honk all they want, but if I can't move and the car in front of me can't move, what in the hell do they want us to do?'

'Where are you going?' I asked. *Out to lunch* was something neither of us ever did unless the lunch was work-related, which I assumed this was.

I heard another volley of horns.

'What is going on there, James?'

He exhaled loudly. 'Know something? I'm too irritated to explain. I'm sending an email.'

He clicked off before I could do much more than process his irritation, leaving me to wonder whether it was me he was angry at or the traffic, the city, even his cabbie.

321

His email was the forward of one he had received two hours earlier, sent from the management of his law firm. I read it twice. Staggered, I called him. 'A freeze on naming new partners? But this is *your year.*' Any lawyer would understand the relevance of that.

'Tell it to the judge,' James muttered.

'They named *twelve* partners last year. How can they not name a single one now?'

'You saw the email. They say they can't afford it. What they're not saying is that they could afford it if they put a freeze on their own incomes, but of course they won't do that, the selfish bastards.'

I was livid. 'Does Mark agree with this?'

'Mark? Oh, listen. This — this is rich. I get the email, and the first thing I do is go to his office, and he's gone. For. The. Weekend. Same with Rhine, Hutchins, and McAdams,' three other senior partners with whom James worked. 'So I try Mark's cell. Of course, he doesn't pick up. I keep calling every two minutes until he does, and I go through all the arguments about how I've been promised this — I've worked my *tail* off for it. I even said my wife was pregnant. Know what he said? He didn't say a damn thing about the pregnancy — no congratulations, no *Great news, James.* He said that if I kept up my hours, I'd be a shoo-in for partner next year. Another fuckin' year of this pressure?'

There were three sharp honks that punctuated his words too perfectly to have been made by a cabbie. 'Are *you* driving?' I asked, suddenly seeing that.

'You bet I am.' His tone was rash now. 'I'm outta here. I need a break.'

Déjà vu, I thought, but for James this time. 'Where are you going?' I asked with a taste of the alarm he must have felt when he had received my note four weeks before.

'I'm going to see my wife. By the way,' he added, 'they had Rocco Fleming in court an hour ago. He waived extradition. They'll transfer him Monday morning.'

★ ★ ★

Traffic was bad, which didn't improve James's mood. He called me every few minutes to vent, and I was totally sympathetic. I didn't talk about it being the start of a weekend at the height of summer, and when he spent an hour at a standstill, waiting for an accident to be cleared from the Hutchinson, I didn't raise the issue of who might have been hurt. He knew all these things. His upset about the partnership was colouring everything else. I understood that.

By the time he reached Bell Valley, it was nearly ten. I was sitting in the dark on the front steps of the Red Fox, looking in the direction of the covered bridge. When headlights finally appeared, I rose. I was in the parking lot, at his door, when the car came to a stop.

I couldn't make out his expression, but when he climbed out, he held me for a long time. Drawing back, he touched my belly. We didn't talk. I imagined that if he had tried, he would have repeated too many words. Shouldering his

323

bag, he slung his other arm around me as we walked to the gardener's shed.

We didn't make love. He was quickly asleep. I lay awake watching him for a time, thinking that he had taken a page from my book and wondering what this latest twist would mean. Then I fell asleep as well.

I swear, the coyotes knew what was going on. They let us sleep for several hours, just enough to take the edge off, before starting to howl. James bolted up.

'Coyotes,' I whispered in explanation.

His eyes shot to the window. 'Where?'

'Up the trail a little.'

Dropping back to the pillow, he listened. They didn't go on very long, only long enough to make sure we were awake enough to make love, and it was exquisitely sweet, even extraordinarily romantic to pleasure each other to the sound of the coyotes' serenade. There was no fierce physicality now. James kept things slow and controlled, though whether because of the baby or his need to stop the world, I didn't know.

The final yips were fading into the distance when, in the last throes of passion, we sank back to the bed. We didn't talk then, either. James simply pulled me close and held me until we were both asleep again.

★　★　★

I would have given anything to sleep in. I wasn't feeling great, and James was reassuringly solid beside me. But I needed toast to settle my stomach, and besides, Vicki wasn't magically better simply because James had arrived. The inn was full for the weekend. She needed my help. And James would sleep for a while.

So I ran over to the kitchen and nibbled toast while I set up for breakfast. Since no one would be checking out on a Saturday, I stayed to replenish the buffet and visit with guests. By the time I returned to the room with breakfast, it was nearly eleven. James was sitting up in bed, studying his BlackBerry.

If I'd had a camera, I'd have snapped a shot, though it could never have done him justice. The sheet was carelessly bunched at his hips, which I knew to be bare beneath. Dark hair fell on his brow and brushed the tops of his ears, and hair swirled on his chest. His shoulders weren't heavily muscled, though they had a natural breadth. Strong hands, long fingers, memories of where they had touched me hours before — my breath caught.

'Hey,' he said, looking up.

I smiled. Putting the tray on a flat portion of sheet, I poured him a cup of coffee. Then, careful not to tip the tray, I sat beside him. Our arms touched, skin to skin. From this vantage point, I could see a full BlackBerry screen. 'Anything interesting?'

'Tony is threatening to sue. Samantha wants to leave.' Both, like James, had expected partnerships in October. 'Tom McKenna wants to know where I am. He's a mid-level partner. They just put me on one of his cases.'

'Did you answer him?'

'Yup. I said I was away for the weekend. There's also a plea for help from the associate they put on the Bryant case. She doesn't know what in the hell she's doing. I told her I'm not on the case anymore and that she should talk with Derek Moore.'

I leaned into him. 'Good for you.'

'Not if they tell me to screw myself,' he said on a grim note. 'Your walking out was different from mine. We can deal with one of us not working, but two?'

'We can get other jobs if we want.'

'None of the firms are hiring.'

'Not in New York, but maybe elsewhere, and maybe not in a firm. Maybe we have to open our mind to other possibilities.'

'With you pregnant?' The BlackBerry dinged. He thumbed to his in-box and smiled. 'Your dad.'

'*My* dad?' I asked in alarm.

'Yeah. We've been going back and forth. The poor guy's been worried about you. Wait'll he hears about me.'

'Don't tell him! He'll have a coronary!'

James snorted. 'He isn't the only one. My parents have never rebelled against anything in their lives. But hell, it's not like I'm leaving the firm. I'm just taking the weekend off.'

He looked at me. I might have argued that a weekend wasn't long enough, not for the kind of thinking we needed to do, that nothing would change if he was back at his desk Monday morning.

But I was silent. Right here, right now, we

were a couple again. I wasn't risking another rift, wasn't wasting this precious time.

★ ★ ★

So we played. Since he had already seen the town centre, I showed him the scenic outskirts — a ravine filled with blue lupines, a woodsy path that rose to a breathtaking outcropping of rocks. Solicitous, he helped me over slippery stretches, taking his cue from me that the baby was fine. In time, we found ourselves in a six-table café at a crossroads just south of Bell Valley, desperate for iced drinks after hiking to a lookout several miles down the road.

'The truth,' James said once the worst of our thirst had been slaked. 'Last time, you were here with Jude.'

'Sure was.' I grinned, refusing to be put on the defensive where Jude was concerned. 'Aren't you glad? Most people don't know about this place — or about the lookout or the ravine. He was a great guide. Now you and I have our own mark on them.'

'Just for the weekend,' he cautioned quietly.

I nodded. 'That's all.'

'We can't both be unemployed.'

'I know.'

'I do have to go back — '

I pressed my hand to his mouth. 'Our escape — just a little longer?'

★ ★ ★

327

He used his BlackBerry twice that day. The first was in an exchange with Sean, who forwarded a note from his accountant. Having followed the trail of trust disbursements to an investment firm in Panama, she had hit a wall. Sean told her to keep at it, but she warned that it would take time.

James wasn't patient, hence his second exchange, this one with his own man, who had ways of getting information under the table.

What had happened at the firm made him feel powerless. This was one way of countering it, but his frustration remained. A little line between his brows came and went, came and went. I saw it, but didn't comment. I did want this to be our escape.

★　★　★

We heard the coyotes again that night. Their howls lulled us to sleep, but I was awake again at dawn, thinking of the sound. Coyotes also made yips and barks, but howls, Jude said, were a gathering call. I might be crazy, but I couldn't shake the sense that they were calling for us — and as escapes went, what could be better?

It was a beautiful Sunday morning — dry, clear, cool — and James had been sleeping since nine the night before. So I woke him, pulled a sweatshirt over his head while he pulled on sweatpants, and led him past the old wood gate, over the rotted post, and through the ferns. We followed the old stone wall, passed the grandfather oak and the granite arch.

Between our passage and the slow spread of daylight, the woods were starting to waken. Tiny bodies scurried out from the undergrowth; birds flew off to look for seeds. Catching a small movement, I stopped, but it was a minute before I spotted a doe and two fawns, carefully camouflaged as they munched on a wild shrub. Silent, I pointed them out to James. They stared at us for a breathtaking second longer before bounding off.

By the time we heard the brook, sunlight was gilding the tops of the trees. I dropped my head back and inhaled. Of all the rich and earthy scents, the strongest was serenity. I didn't look back to see if James felt it. His hold of my hand was relaxed, his fingers warm in a way that went beyond the physical.

The water flowed downstream in reflections of blues, golds, and browns. Settling on the bank, watching the far side, we listened for sounds above the gurgle. In time, as though they had been waiting for us, they appeared.

'How did you know they'd come?' James whispered.

'They know when I'm here. We have a meeting of minds.'

He shot me an amused look that I felt more than saw, since I was keeping my eye on the far side of the stream. 'Look,' I said softly. 'The pups. They're bigger each time I see them. The den must be nearby.'

'Is this safe?'

'Our being here? Absolutely.'

'They won't attack?'

'No. They know me. You're with me, so you get a pass.'

'I'm serious.'

'So am I. They know my scent. Besides, coyotes don't eat people. They don't even eat housecats when they can get things like mice, squirrels, and rabbits. Where do you think all those ageing rodents go? It's about the food chain.'

'What about ageing coyotes?'

'Bear.'

'If they aren't shot first by sheep farmers.'

'Coyotes only eat sheep when they have nothing else. They also eat insects and fruit.'

'And garbage. That's what the ones in Manhattan get into.'

'Not their favourite meal. But they adapt. They do what they have to do to survive.'

'See, that's what we need to do,' he said, 'find a way to survive in New York.'

'Or relocate to a place more suited to our needs.'

He paused. 'Is this the pitch?'

'No,' I said. 'But I do identify with the coyote.'

'A coyote is a wild animal. We're domesticated. We think.'

'Maybe too much.' I glanced back at the fat pine against which our child might well have been conceived. 'A little wildness is good.'

I wanted to think a part of him agreed, but he looked troubled as he continued to watch the coyotes.

'What,' I coaxed. I felt safe here, buffered from reality.

'Look at them, just tumbling around. Their lives are simple. I envy that.'

'Why do ours have to be complex?'

'Because we're human. Because our food chain is complex.'

'Ours isn't about survival,' I said. 'It's about ego.'

Another coyote appeared. Slightly larger than the mom, it sat by the trunk of a tree, watching us. I guessed it to be the dad.

'The whole family, out havin' fun,' James quipped.

'Like us,' I said, and kissed his jaw.

'About the ego thing, babe — are you saying that's what drives me?'

'I'm asking it, and it's not only you, James. I'm just as bad.'

'But ego has to do with self-esteem, which is good.'

'Do you get self-esteem from your work? I don't. Do you get it from the friendships you have in New York?' His silence said it. 'Some people get self-esteem from technology,' I continued, 'like if they master it, they've mastered the world. Not me. If there's one thing I've learned about myself in this last month, it's that I do *not* get happiness from all that. I love you, James. Love *you*. But the rest of what I was doing is . . . is like spinning. I sit in a room of thirty people I don't know, and I pedal faster and faster to keep pace, but when I'm done, I haven't moved an inch. Okay, I can check off exercise as done, but do I walk home smiling in satisfaction? No.' I took a quick breath and softened, pleading. 'I do smile when I help Vicki. I get satisfaction helping Lee. And the Refuge. I feel good there. I want you to see that, too, sometime.'

* * *

I left it open. If he was heading back today, I wanted him to choose what to do before he left. It was enough that I had dragged him into the woods to see my coyotes.

The Refuge was my priority. Sleep was his. He got several more hours while I helped set up for brunch at the Red Fox. When I returned to the shed late in the morning with a tray, he was just getting out of the shower. I half expected he would be wearing slacks, readying for the drive straight back to the office. But no. A T-shirt and jeans. That was a good sign. Likewise, when he carried the tray outside so that we could eat on the bench facing the woods.

He was the one who suggested going to the Refuge — perhaps appeasing me in advance of his leaving, but he actually seemed curious about the place. I could see his surprise at its size and spread, could see him lift his head to sniff horse and hay when we got out of the car.

'Who are all these people?' he asked, studying the sign-in sheet when I added our names.

'Volunteers. They pretty much run the place on weekends. Some are up for the day from Concord and Portsmouth. Others just stop off on their way elsewhere. Guests at the Red Fox stay longer.'

He stopped out back to read the weather vane of lopsided signs, looked around in alarm when a loud bray came sudden and close, but I led him to the cats first. I wanted him to see where I spent so much of my time, but I also felt a need to see my friends, and I swear, the cats did know me. They came without pause, hungry for scratches and rubs, though there were other volunteers around. Talk about ego. Mine soared. When I shot James a satisfied grin, he actually laughed.

'You are such a bleeding heart,' he said in a good-natured way that would never, *never* have happened two weeks before. And it was the same when I took him to Rehab. 'How much time have you spent here?' he teased when the cats crowded in.

'Not that much,' I assured him, stroking the massive Maine Coon that had plopped down by my thigh, minus a leg but so much sturdier than my kitten had been. I told him about her, how she had wobbled to me, how she had died in my arms, and though he couldn't possibly feel my emotion, he stroked my arm when I was through.

Sensing my affinity for these particular cats, he gave me time, wandering out while I stayed to freshen water. He didn't keep poking his head back in to see if I was ready to leave. He wasn't even waiting right outside the door. I had to go looking for him, one bungalow to the next, asking about a tall, dark-haired guy wearing a blue Gold's Gym tee.

I finally found him behind one of the dog

huts, leaning against the wire mesh of a large, open-air pen. Curling my fingers by his on the mesh, I watched beside him.

'I never had a pet growing up,' he finally said.

'Did you want one?'

'Every kid wants one. The house was too small, my parents said. We had no yard. They both worked. It sounded right. I didn't learn the truth until I was home for college vacation and out on the front walk, talking with neighbours who had just moved in next door. They had a spaniel puppy. It was small and jumpy. Mom backed away and hurried into the house.'

'Scared of dogs?' I asked in surprise.

'Terrified. She told me that when she was little, she'd been chased by a dalmatian. Sad to base a phobia on one experience. I mean, look at these dogs.' Several had approached us. He lowered his hand so that they could nose it. 'They aren't wild. They're homeless. How can you not feel for them?'

I leaned into him.

'Oh no,' he warned. 'We don't know where in the hell we'll be living in six months. Now is not the time to get a dog.'

'I know,' I said, though with regret. 'And these dogs will find homes. The Refuge places hundreds every year.'

'Look at that one.'

I followed his gaze to a distant corner of the pen, where a dog sat alone. It was midsize and heavily furred, with a black body and white markings on its chest and face.

'It's an Australian shepherd,' James said. 'I had

334

a friend who had one. They need a ton of exercise, but I've been here for fifteen minutes and that dog hasn't moved. He's frightened. Look, see his eyes?' They grew especially fearful when a man emerged from the hut. 'He's been abused.' When the man approached, the dog shied away, then bolted off. 'What'll happen to a dog like that?'

'They'll work with him,' I said. 'He'll stay here as long as it takes, but they'll find him a home.'

'They have their work cut out for them with that one.'

'Mm. But totally rewarding when they break through.'

★ ★ ★

James wasn't about to suddenly crave a dog. But something about breakthroughs, satisfaction, or self-esteem must have been in play, because he didn't pack up and head to New York Sunday night — though he did set his BlackBerry to ding at four Monday morning, so that he could do it then. When the alarm rang, though, he turned it off, pulled me close, and went back to sleep.

I left him sleeping while I worked at the inn, but I was back with him at nine. He had just emailed Mark that he wouldn't be in. At least, not in the office in New York. Rocco Fleming was due in Manchester-by-the-Sea by noon and would be interviewed at the police station. We wanted to be there.

22

We drove to the house first. In the ten days since we'd seen it last, holes had been boarded up, and though police tape still stretched around much of the bedroom wing, I suspected that whatever evidence there was had already been bagged.

The police station was humming. Fleming hadn't yet arrived, which gave James a chance to talk with the detective in charge. Selfishly, we weren't as concerned about the arson investigation as with anything Rocco might know about further harm aimed at Lee. And though we knew we wouldn't be allowed in the room while he was questioned, the detective noted our questions.

Rocco had a buzz cut and an overhanging gut, but his eyes were what compelled. They were half-lidded and mean. Seeming unduly sure of himself, he didn't blink when three separate townsfolk picked him out of a lineup. After being Mirandized, he waived his right to an attorney and was closed in with the detective and the chief. He admitted to being in Manchester that day, insisting that he had been sent there on a job. He claimed that what they were calling an 'accelerant' found in his truck was a fluid used in the installation of windows.

He had a point. We had googled that. But there was still the fact of the window company, which, apparently frightened by the extent of his crime this time, denied both sending him on a job and authorizing his use of the van. Still, he was defiant. He denied having been hired to torch the house and challenged the police to find any money he might have been paid. He claimed he had never heard of Duane Cray or his company, that he had found the cell phone in the van, and that whoever had put it there must be the bad guy trying to put the blame on him. He even agreed to take a lie-detector test — though hearing this via intercom in an adjacent room, James was sceptical.

'Guys who spend their lives lying come to believe their lies so completely that they don't react,' he remarked. I agreed. I had read what he had.

Rocco continued to stonewall. When the detective asked if he had ever heard of Lee Cray, he said he had not. When the police chief asked if he had ever heard of Bell Valley, he said he had not. They explained the sentencing guidelines for arson and suggested that a judge might go more easily on him if he shared what he knew. He insisted that he knew nothing and was being framed.

His attorney arrived then, a white-hair named Sam Civetti, and the interview ended, just like that.

James immediately texted the lawyer's name to his man in New York. We were barely back on the road when we learned that Civetti worked out of a one-man office in the same building as Albert Meeme. Granted, the building was a high-rise whose thirty-two floors held dozens of law firms. Anyone who wanted legal representation could find it there. And there was no long paper trail showing Meeme feeding cases to Civetti. But there was a short one.

I called Lee and Amelia to update them, then called Vicki.

'Okay, Vicki Bell,' I said, vaguely teasing, 'it's test time. I've talked with your mother and Lee, and they're on top of things there. I need to know if you'll behave while I'm gone and let them do their thing. Rocco Fleming won't be formally charged in court until tomorrow morning. We thought we'd hang around here until then.'

'James isn't rushing back to New York?'

'Not yet.' He hadn't told the firm. But he was the one who had suggested another night, and he wasn't thinking of Manchester. His plan was to hang around Boston.

★　★　★

It was the vacation we wouldn't have allowed ourselves if James hadn't learned about the partnership freeze. We hadn't brought clothes for an overnight stay, so after checking into the Four Seasons, we shopped. Yes, we spent more money than we should have. No, I did not need the bangle bracelets that James bought me. Did I like the bracelets? Yes. Did we both like our new clothes? Yes. Likewise dinner at the Bristol, though I suspected that the Kobe beef was amazing because of the time, the setting, the company.

I didn't drink wine. But the dress I bought was

338

fitted, which made it a particular splurge. While the fabric had a little bit of give, I wouldn't be able to wear it in another two months.

We were living for the moment.

★ ★ ★

James wore a tie Tuesday morning, and my skirt was blue and my own this time, as were my three-inch sandals, additional products of our spree. If only in appearance, we were a power couple. My dad would have been pleased.

Rocco Fleming couldn't have cared less. He was arraigned in Essex Superior Court in Salem and, as expected, entered a plea of Not Guilty. He was granted bail, which was arranged through a bondsman, but we never got to asking who had secured the bond, because more immediate news arrived first.

James's detective, pulling international strings, had linked Duane Cray to the Panamanian investment firm into which trust disbursements had vanished.

He had also found email communication between Duane Cray and Albert Meeme. The two had every right to email each other, since Meeme was the executor of Duane's family trust, but the latest exchange stood out. It was a discussion of the damage Lee could do and the possibilities of dissuading her from pursuing her case, but it was largely in code. Lee was referred to as 'the wife.' Money was mentioned — *she wants a bakery* — with Duane saying he'd gag before coughing up dough, pathetic as puns went. He said he knew where she lived. He said he knew who her protector was. Meeme's only response was *Stay cool.* If there was a threat, it was veiled.

Sitting in the car outside the courthouse, we made the detective read us the email exchange several times. When we finally let him go, James was guarded. He pulled at his tie, unbuttoned his collar.

'Can't be sure,' he finally said.

'Because they don't mention names?' I was perfectly happy playing bad cop to his good one. 'That exchange is too coincidental. The scenario fits Lee. Duane Cray hired Rocco Fleming. And he won't stop there.'

My husband shot me an amused look.

'What?'

'You're sure about that?' he asked.

'I am.'

He thought for a minute. 'Then I think we'd better tell Lee. But in person. She'll be frightened.'

★   ★   ★

We returned to Manchester-by-the-Sea to share what we'd learned with the police, and once we were on the highway again, I called Lee. Promising an update on what had happened in court, I told her we'd meet her at the inn at six.

I had one other call to make.

'Hiya, Emmie,' Jude said, picking up with a familiarity I was glad James couldn't hear. He knew I had nothing going on with Jude, but he

340

also knew the history. That put a different twist on familiarity.

'Where are you?'

'Actually, I am . . . in . . . Schenectady.' He sounded like he'd had to check a signpost to be sure.

'What are you doing there?' I asked, but immediately changed the thought. It didn't matter what he was doing there. Amelia had said he would watch Lee's house, and he couldn't do it from Schenectady. 'How soon can you be back in Bell Valley?'

'Tomorrow. I'm spending the night here.'

'Lee needs protecting.'

'Lee always needs protecting, but nothing happens.'

'That may change, Jude. We're closing in on the bad guys. We now have incriminating emails. Once they realize that, the ante goes up.' Albert Meeme, Duane Cray, and his brother — they'd soon know we'd been snooping, just as they had to already know that Rocco Fleming would rat on them to save his own skin. 'Lee is the linchpin. All she has to do is to say that she was wrong, that she misunderstood what her husband promised her, that the trust fund is legit. If she drops her case, they're safe. They'll do anything to make that happen.'

'You're watching too much TV.'

The remark annoyed me. 'Actually, I don't watch *any* TV, but I do know criminal law.' Jude did not, and his complacency was insulting. 'Those murderers who claim insanity? It isn't insanity. It's jealousy and rage and fear. Do you

341

want to expose Lee to that?'

'I can't be her bodyguard,' he shot back, disgruntled. 'Amelia needs to hire someone else. She can't *pay* me enough to do this job. Sitting around is not my thing.'

I gentled. 'Right now, you're all we have. Please? We're meeting at the Red Fox at six. Can you be there?'

'Hell, *no*. Come on, Emily. I have done nothing good in Bell Valley.'

I'd have to have been deaf not to hear his defeat. Coaxing, pleading, I said, 'Here's your chance to change that, Jude. Six at the inn. See you then.'

In the ensuing silence, James rolled back his sleeves. 'Will he be there?' he finally asked.

I kept my eyes on the road. 'That's anyone's guess. He's struggling to figure out who he is.'

'You can't do it for him.'

'No, but I can help.' I turned my head on the seat. His profile was hard — eyes unblinking, chin out a little too far. 'He has potential, James, really he does. He just . . . *sucks* at doing Bell Valley. He has too many emotional issues there.'

'You being one.'

'No. His issues started long before he ever met me. I am not the problem.' I pushed a hand into my hair, lifting it away from my scalp. I had worn it down that day, but now it felt heavy. 'I don't want to argue about this, not with you. Jude is not an issue for us. He's an issue for Amelia and, right now, for Lee. It'd be great if he came through for them, but he's not terribly reliable.' I smiled. 'You, on the other hand, are.'

James was a minute softening. 'That was smooth.'

'Easy to do, when it's true.' I took his hand. 'Have I told you how much I value that? Reliability, patience, smart — you have it all, James. Thank you for being here.'

He didn't speak. After a minute, quietly, he said, 'I'm driving back tonight.'

'I know.'

'There's just too much work to do right now.'

'I understand.'

'I may tell them I'm taking two weeks in August. I can't keep killing myself for the firm. For all I know, they'll freeze partnerships next year, too.'

I didn't say anything.

'Any word from Walter?'

'Oh yeah.' I had called him Monday, but he was on vacation, so I'd left a message. 'Here.' I thumbed through my in-box, bypassing notes from my parents, my sister, my yoga teacher. 'No 'Dear Emily,'' I said, and read Walter's email aloud. ' 'I knew where this was going, so your cubicle is already filled. We boxed and mailed your personal stuff. Too bad. You're a smart lawyer, you have a future somewhere, but not here. That's the best I'll be able to write in a recommendation.' ' I lowered the BlackBerry and looked at James. 'I guess I burned that bridge.'

'It's okay,' he finally said. 'You're doing something more important.'

I wanted to think he meant that.

★ ★ ★

343

We reached Bell Valley at five to find Rob in a frenzy. Lee hadn't shown up for tea and couldn't be reached on the phone, so Vicki was on her feet doing the work. Rob was distracted, trying to take over everything Vicki started, and Vicki was talking a mile a minute about Lee being upset that Rocco was out on bail, which Amelia had learned from Sean and had tactlessly shared. Vicki was convinced Lee had run away to hide somewhere new.

I didn't think so. When I talked with her, she had sounded fine. She couldn't have lied so convincingly if she was already planning to leave, and besides, she had family here. She had friends here. I wanted to think I was one and that she would have trusted me enough to have called me if Amelia had scared her that much.

'Where is your mother?' I asked, pulling Vicki away from the dishwasher and steering her to a chair.

'At a board meeting at the Refuge, so she's no help. But the real question is where's Jude, because he was supposed to be guarding Lee and — I can load dishes, Emmie. Thirty minutes, the doctor said.'

'She times it,' Rob murmured as he stuffed wet coffee grounds into the trash. 'Thirty minutes standing, fifteen sitting.'

'Where's Charlotte?'

'At day care,' Vicki said, propping bare feet against the edge of the table. 'Rob needs to pick her up.'

I shooed him out. 'Tea is almost done. I can handle stragglers.' Looking hugely grateful, he took off.

Other than consolidating fruit and cookies, there was little in the parlour to do. Back in the kitchen, I tried Lee's cell as I finished loading the dishwasher, but there was no answer. I tried three minutes later, then three minutes after that.

'She does not sleep during the day,' Vicki announced, 'and if she's been in the shower all this time, she must be a prune by now. She has never not shown up like this, not like my brother, who *never* shows up when you need him. Does he not have an ounce of responsibility in that gorgeous body of his? I mean, what if she's sick? *Really* sick? What if she had a stroke or something?'

'Why don't I go to her house,' James offered. He had actually been drinking a cup of coffee, trying to stay out of the way. 'Tell me how to get there.'

But Vicki rubbed the air as if to calm it. 'No. Ignore me. I'm being emotional, because the timing of this is lousy, so I'm jumping to conclusions. Lee is healthy, and she's tough. She can take care of herself.'

I eyed James. He didn't look convinced.

I autodialled her number at increasingly shorter intervals, and was about to quit when she actually picked up. 'Hello?' she said in a small voice.

'Lee! Omigod, we've been trying you forever. Are you okay?'

'I'm fine,' she said, but her voice was strange, numb. She never said much, but what little she did say usually had more feeling.

345

'Are you sick? Sleeping? It's not like you to miss tea. We were supposed to meet you here at six.'

She cleared her throat. 'Oh wow. I'm sorry. I think I have to skip the movie. I'm not really up for it. I kind of have a headache.'

I caught James's eye. 'A headache. Can I bring you anything? Maybe leftovers of some of the lentil soup you made yesterday.'

Vicki drew in her chin. There was no lentil soup.

'It was too salty,' Lee said. 'I just want to sleep. Will you tell Vick that?'

'I will. Okay, Lee. Feel better.' I clicked out of the call and looked at the others. 'Someone's there. Someone must have been listening in.'

'Does she have a boyfriend?' James asked.

Vicki shook her head.

'Maybe a brother?' I asked. Lee came from a large family that, by her own admission, was shady. If someone from that old life had shown up — wanting to visit, wanting to *hide* — she might be upset enough to talk nonsense.

Vicki was on my wavelength. 'There are several brothers, but she never told them where she was. Maybe they found out. Maybe they're hitting her up for money.' But she didn't really think that. I could see she was worried.

So was I.

When James made for the door, I was right behind, standing aside only to let in Rob, who held Charlotte.

'*Where is Jude?*' Vicki hollered after us.

In Schenectady? On the road? Unless he was just about to reach Lee's, it didn't matter.

23

Lee lived five minutes from the Red Fox. Her house was at the end of a narrow road. Shy and unimposing, it was little more than a box with a roof. More modest than the others we passed, it was very Lee with its taupe siding and brown shutters, as if it wanted to fade into the woods. She was easily several acres from her nearest neighbour, and with much of that land treed, she had privacy. The downside, of course, was that neighbours couldn't see who came to her door.

Her truck was alone in the dirt driveway. If someone was with her, he had either been dropped off by another person or had parked elsewhere and come on foot through the woods. We intentionally parked in front to announce our arrival, but even then James wanted me to stay in the car.

I refused. I said we had no proof that Lee was in danger, and that I would be better able to read her face and her voice than he would, since I was the one who knew her. I wasn't being left out of this. She was my friend.

As we walked to the front door, we watched for signs of movement inside, but though the windows were open, they were shielded by blinds. We saw no light through the slats, heard no talk, no music. The early evening air was warm and still, the only sounds those of spring

347

peepers in the woods.

I rang the doorbell. When Lee didn't answer, James knocked. We called her name. Nothing.

The cameras were still in place, looking like part of the drain pipe at the eaves, but since they didn't relay images in real time, they wouldn't help now. That said, there was no sign of violence or struggle — no overturned chair on the porch, no broken window, no shattered lock. The only thing that might be remotely telling was the laundry basket in the backyard. It held a single pillowcase, wet and wrinkled, though the rest of the sheets had been neatly hung.

'She might have been surprised here,' James whispered.

'Or her headache got so bad she couldn't see straight.' Or think or talk straight.

Clinging to that last little bit of hope, I called her cell. She picked up after a single ring.

'Lee. It's Emily. We're out back. We just want to make sure you're okay. Can you open the door?'

'Uh . . . ' There was a lengthy pause. 'Uh, okay. Wait a minute.'

That was exactly how long it took. When she finally opened the door, her inky hair was messed and she wore a robe, but she didn't look sick. She didn't squint, as she might have with a migraine. Her hazel eyes were wide, too wide, and her hair didn't hide either one.

'I'm okay,' she said. 'I just need sleep. I'll see you tomorrow.' She tried to close the door, but James's foot was in the way.

'Is someone here?' he asked softly.

'No. I'm alone.' She didn't blink. 'Thanks for coming.'

He let her shut the door and, taking my elbow, led me back to the car. As soon as we were inside, he started the engine. 'Call the cops.'

'He's still there, right?' I asked, pulling out my BlackBerry as he turned around in the driveway.

Nodding, he drove down the street. 'How'd she seem to you?'

'Scared.'

'Right. Call the cops.'

'Lee is fastidious,' I said. 'She wouldn't leave a wet pillowcase in the laundry basket. Besides, Lee isn't bold. She'd have to be pretty frightened to look you in the eye that way for that long.'

'Or hopped-up on something.'

'No way.' I was furious at him for even suggesting it. 'She never did drugs. She wouldn't.' But someone else might, someone who was forcing her into something she didn't want. It would be a different form of abuse.

'Make the call,' James ordered. Having reached the main road, he turned the corner and pulled over. I had barely conveyed the message, when he took the phone from me. 'Have them park out of sight,' he told the dispatcher. 'We don't want anyone spooked by a cruiser.' He ended the call, gave me back the phone, and opened his door.

'Where are you going?' I asked in alarm. I had assumed we would wait there until the police arrived.

'I'll circle around and see what I can find.' He stared at me. 'Drive back to the Red Fox, Emily. I want you there.'

'To do what?'

'Be safe. I don't want you taking chances.'

'What about you?' I cried. 'You're taking chances.'

'I'm not pregnant.'

'What's he going to do — shoot at *me*? You need someone to watch your back.'

'Not you.' He climbed out of the car.

'Then the police,' I called, leaning over the console. 'Wait 'til they get here, James. You're not trained for this.'

'And the Bell Valley cops are?' he said as he bent back down to see me. 'I'll bet I've talked with more criminals than they have.'

I probably had, too, but I kept picturing the mean eyes of Rocco Fleming, who probably didn't know right from wrong. And whoever had hired him? Not much better.

'What if he's an ex-con? What if he's armed? How're you going to protect yourself?'

'I have common sense and, by your own claim, a way with people.' His tone turned soothing. 'Emily, I am not doing anything rash. I'll be perfectly safe, but if you're at the inn, I'll have one less worry.'

Still I argued. 'We had every reason to be at her house just now, but if you go again, it's suspicious. I think you should wait for backup.'

He was suddenly impatient. 'Would you have Jude wait?'

'Don't mention Jude. Jude is a stuntman. Jude can't *live* without danger.'

'And you think I can't handle it?'

'What I think,' I said, struggling to speak

clearly with my heart in my mouth, 'is that you can handle it just fine, but that you are much, much, much more precious to me, and if anything were to happen to you, I'd be crushed.'

He stared at me for a second, then leaned farther in to give me a single fierce kiss. 'I love you, too, Em,' he whispered against my lips and backed away. 'Go. I'll see you at the Red Fox.'

I didn't try to stop him as he loped off. Nor, though, did I start the car. My stomach was churning. I hadn't eaten in a while, but I wasn't going back to the inn for a cracker when James was out there. Besides, I had a granola bar in my purse. So I sat with an arm around my middle and nibbled while I scanned the road in the direction James had gone.

The nausea persisted. I opened my door and sat with my feet on the ground, trying to get a handle on it, but the only thing exposure to the air did was to alert me sooner to the arrival of the police. Not that I wouldn't have heard even with the doors closed and the windows rolled. There were two cruisers, sirens blaring.

They did kill the noise when they sped past me, but they didn't stop. With the squeal of tyres, they turned the corner. Not about to be left behind, I closed my door, scrambled over the centre console, and followed. They parked right in front of Lee's house. I was pulling up behind, frantically searching for James, when he darted from behind the house into the woods and came through the trees to the street.

Emerging twenty feet from us, he shot me a punishing look, but he wasn't any more pleased

351

with the police. 'So much for stealth,' he said, and, hands on his hips, gave them a slightly breathless sum-up of our concern. 'She could be alone in there or not, but something's not right,' he was concluding when my phone rang.

Lee started talking the instant I clicked into the call. 'Why are the police here? I . . . I . . . I didn't ask you to come, I don't want the police, this is a . . . a private thing, and you all need to . . . to respect me and leave.'

Someone was feeding her words. I heard it each time she paused.

'Do you know him?' I asked.

'Please leave.'

'Is he threatening you?'

'I want to be alone.'

'Okay,' I said, playing along. 'But you call if I can help.'

I heard a click and she was gone. I raised my eyes to James. 'He's threatening her.'

'You're sure?'

'Yes.'

Two other cars had pulled up. One was the charcoal SUV that had sat for so long on the green. The other belonged to the chief of police.

We were gathered on the street, with the cruisers between us and the house, which, I suspected, was one of the reasons James didn't mention my returning to the Red Fox. The other was his own focus.

'I'm going in,' he announced when the two men reached us. 'My guess is that someone came here just to scare her, but it's gotten out of hand — and that's our fault. He knows we're here,' he said. 'We can't just walk away. He knows we'll be watching. He knows we'll follow him when he leaves. I can talk with him. Make a deal.'

'Shouldn't I be doing that?' asked the police chief.

'This is my strength, sir. I've spent hours in prisons talking with guys like this. I know how their minds work. He may be less threatened by me than he would by you.' James was also younger and civilian, perhaps less threatening than the chief in his khakis and badge.

'What kind of deal?'

'I won't know that until we start to talk, but trust me,' he added dryly, 'I'm an expert at plea-bargaining.'

'I won't just let him walk away,' the chief warned. 'I protect the people who live in my town.'

'I understand. But Lee's safety comes first. We need to get him out of that house.'

'Who the hell *are* you? I haven't ever seen you before.'

James tipped his head at me. 'You know her. I'm her husband. I'm a lawyer working on Lee's case. I'm with a firm in New York.'

The New York part did it. I could see the way the chief's eyes changed as soon as James said it. He might think lawyers caused more trouble than they were worth, but New York was New York — and I might resent that, but it was fact.

His voice carried new respect. 'Okay. Go give it a try.'

I had a sudden flash of fear. Plea-bargaining in a prison meeting room with a guard in view was different from this. James was right; the presence of the police had upped the ante. I didn't want him going anywhere *near* that house.

But he shot me a look as he turned. His eyes were blue and avid, filled with determination — filled with *excitement* — and I caught it. How could I not? Here was rain after a drought.

Besides, how could I stop him, when what he said made sense? If anyone could defuse the situation, James could.

He started up the front path with a hand in his pocket, but halfway there took it out and held both away to show whoever that he was unarmed. Watching him go, my stomach turned. The baby didn't like this any more than I did.

My BlackBerry vibrated as he knocked on the door. Thinking it might be Vicki, I pulled it out. *James*. Immediately understanding what he'd done, I clicked in. When he knocked again, the sound echoed in my phone. Putting the connection on speaker, I held it so that we could all hear. I might hate my BlackBerry as much as I resented New York, but it was coming through for me now.

We watched, listened.

'It's me, Lee,' James said, head down, deep voice muted by the phone. 'Open up. I can keep the cops at bay if you do.' He paused. 'Open up, Lee.'

After another minute, the door cracked open. The robe was gone, leaving the sweatshirt and shorts she must have been wearing beneath. Through the phone, her voice was distant.

'Go home. I'm okay.'

James stood with his head up, back straight. 'I want to come in to make sure.'

'He's . . . he's someone I know. We're . . . we're . . . you know.'

Having sex? I didn't think so.

James wasn't falling for it either, because he said, 'I want to meet him, Lee. If I can convince everyone out here that you're okay, we'll leave. But no one's moving until I meet the guy. Let's just clear this up and move on.'

She didn't turn away. I saw fewer details as the sun inched lower, but I pictured her holding his gaze for dear life. After an agonizingly long moment, the door opened wider, but only enough to let him in. I heard the thunk as it closed, then, through the phone, a coarse 'Who the fuck are you?'

James said his name, adding, 'I'm a friend.'

'Not of mine. She already told you to leave, but you came back with a crowd. What part'a no don't you get?'

'It's a small town —' James began in what I assumed was an explanation for the concern of the police, but his words were lost to the roar of a car. I looked up as the black Range Rover careered around to park head-on at the nose of the first cruiser.

The cavalry had arrived.

Dismayed, I struggled to hear James. ' . . . care about her,' he was saying. 'What's with the gun?'

'I got a permit. Live free or die, and all.'

'You don't need a gun. I don't have one. Want to put it away?'

Jude was at my shoulder, staring at the phone.

'What's goin' on, babe?'

I shushed him with a hand, but it was too late.

'What the hell?' the man inside cried, having clearly heard a voice in James's pocket. 'Hands up!' Seconds later, he muttered, 'You *shit*,' then yelled directly into the phone, 'What, you all have nothing better to do than stand around in the street playin' Hawaii Five-O? You are embarrassing this woman. I have every right to be here. She invited me in.'

The phone went dead, all sound gone. *Connection terminated*, my screen read.

I glared at Jude, who seemed more alarmed by my reaction than by what he'd done.

'How was I supposed to know?' he asked. 'No one told me it was bad. All Amelia said was that you were at Lee's.'

I didn't know where to begin. Throwing a hand in the air, I pocketed the BlackBerry and faced the house, leaving the police to brief him. One of their own, he was a giant in their eyes for the places he'd been.

He was contrite when he joined me. 'They don't think he's local. No accent.'

'He knew the state motto.' *Live free or die.*

'It's on the licence plates.' Jude looked around. 'No car? I'm gonna look.'

'Jude — 'But he was off, sprinting back down the street and into the woods. He would go through to the next road, where either a car or an accomplice might be. I couldn't blame him for wanting to try. Helplessness didn't suit Jude.

It didn't suit me either. I was dying standing there, just waiting with James in that house.

Five minutes passed, then ten, and the only one who showed up was Amelia. More discreet than her son, she parked at the end of the line of cars. Vicki was with her, both of them out by the time I reached them.

'Jude called,' Vicki explained. 'Anything happening?'

I shook my head and led her back to the cruiser. Side by side, we watched the house. Two of the patrolmen had gone through the trees to keep an eye on the back, but they reported seeing nothing. Jude did find an abandoned car on the far side of the woods. He gave the plate number to the chief.

Another fifteen minutes passed. I could only imagine what James was doing or saying — or worse, what was being done or said to him.

Vicki wrapped an arm around me. 'He'll be fine.'

'We take things for granted. Who'd a thought it, here in Bell Valley?'

The police chief must have agreed. Never having experienced anything like this, he called in the state police.

'SWAT team' was what he murmured when he joined us again.

'SWAT team?' Jude asked in affront. 'I can handle this. It's only one guy.'

'He has a gun,' I argued. 'And my husband. And Lee.' I didn't like the idea of a SWAT team either, but mostly because it said that the situation was as dangerous as I feared.

'I can *handle* it,' Jude insisted.

The chief held him off. 'Wait. It's only been an hour.'

Another thirty minutes passed. The state police arrived, two unmarked cars, followed by a SWAT van. Then the media. Then the neighbours.

It was after eight by then, and the light was fading fast. I made Vicki sit in the cruiser. After a few minutes, I climbed in behind.

'How do you feel?' she asked softly.

'Lousy.'

'You look green.'

'I feel it.'

'We need food here.'

'We need this *over*,' I remarked.

Jude caught that. Bending in with a hand on the door frame, he said, 'I can make it happen.'

Oh yes, he would storm the house in a heartbeat if given the word. But at what price?

'Not yet,' I was saying when I saw movement at the door. Nudging Jude aside, I scrambled out of the car and watched James come toward us. Sombre but unhurt, he was holding his phone up, letting us know that the man inside was listening.

It wasn't a bad thing. It simply meant that we had to watch what we said.

Cameras clicked and whirred. The local police moved bystanders back, but the media held their recorders high to catch every word as the state police closed in around James. I was slim enough — determined enough — to snake my way through to the front.

'Do we have a hostage situation here?' the state captain asked.

'We do,' James said with a glance at the men in SWAT gear, 'but he isn't irrational. He isn't making wild threats. He's just nervous.' He spoke in the same low, keep-it-calm tone that I imagined he had used inside. 'Lee is fine. He says he won't hurt her if we play our cards right.'

'Who is he?'

'A friend of her late husband,' James said, shooting me a look that said he doubted it. 'I don't know his name.'

'John Laughlin,' Bell Valley's chief offered, wanting the hostage-taker to know that we did have resources. 'The car's a rental from Nashua. He gave a Durham address.' He shook his head to indicate that the name and address were likely phoney.

'What's his gun power?' the state captain asked James.

'He has one handgun. I don't see anything else.'

Silent now, the captain pointed at duffel bags near the SWAT team members.

James shook his head. No duffel bags with extra guns. 'He's not holding the gun to her head. I don't think he plans on harming her. Right now he's more pissed at me — us — everyone here.'

'How big is he?' Jude asked — looking in that instant, I swear, like a cat at the Refuge, puffed up and ready for a fight.

James was debating how the question would be perceived inside. Finally, judging as I did that it was strictly factual, he said, 'Six foot, maybe six-one, two hundred pounds.'

'What are his demands?' the state captain asked.

'He wants you all to clear out. He says he

won't even talk until that's done.' He looked at the cruisers, the Range Rover, our BMW. His eyes touched me before returning to the captain. 'I said I could make that happen.'

His credibility rested on it. That went unsaid. Lowering the phone, he backed away and, to the snap of cameras, returned to the house.

The police talked briefly, then pointed us all to our cars. I followed the others, driving only far enough down the street to suggest we were leaving. Two local cruisers kept the noise going by continuing on. They would park on the back street and return through the woods.

I had a fleeting thought that if John Laughlin, or whoever he was, was really into hostage-taking, he might take Lee or James back there with a gun to their heads and be infuriated when his car wasn't alone.

But the police guarding the back would be discreet. I kept telling myself that as I followed the rest on foot. We stopped at a spot where the trees were dense, though twilight alone would have kept us hidden. The SWAT team was gearing up — masks, vests, guns. The prospect of violence made my stomach churn.

Lights had gone on in the house, a vague tracing around each window. The state police had binoculars, but couldn't see through the blinds.

'You holding up okay?' Jude asked softly, coming to my side.

I nodded. 'Your mom took Vicki home. She doesn't need the tension.'

'Neither do you.'

'He's my husband. Where else would I be?'

'Does he know about the baby?'

'Of course.'

'And he's risking his life in there? That's a dumb thing to do.'

My eyes flew to his. 'I don't think it's dumb. He's good at this.'

He stared at me, at the house, at the SWAT team. He was walking off when my BlackBerry vibrated.

'Emily,' James said. 'We're having a little problem here. He's watching TV and knows you're all out there. So here's Plan B. First, put me on speaker.' I did. 'Is the captain there?'

'Right here,' the man said.

'He feels this has gotten out of hand. He doesn't want anyone hurt. He just wants to be allowed to leave.'

'All he has to do is come out with his hands up.'

'He's preparing a statement. He says that as long as the press is there, he wants the world to hear it.'

A murmur slid through the media.

'Fine,' the captain said. 'We can read it.'

The call ended. Another ten minutes passed. The cruisers had returned to the front of the house. I was leaning against one, arms around my middle as I watched the door, when Jude came over and said, 'What do you think he's doing in there?'

I had asked myself that dozens of times in the last five minutes. 'Probably helping write the statement.'

'Why would he help the guy do anything?'

I sighed wearily. 'Jude, we want this done. If the man needs help writing a statement that will end it, let's help him. For all we know, he's illiterate.'

'How long does it take? It's almost nine, and nothing's happening.' Slapping a hand on the top of the cruiser, he walked off.

I was as frustrated as he was. The wait seemed endless. When my BlackBerry rang again, I jumped a mile. Heart pounding, I put the phone to my ear.

'Okay, here's the thing,' James said, not bothering with speakerphone. 'He just got a call from someone who's been watching this all play out on TV and is now forbidding him to make a statement.'

'Who — '

'So I've talked him into coming out with me and turning himself over. I've guaranteed him safety, but he's skittish. I want you to tell the Staties — ' There was a crash in the background and an alarmed 'What the — Jude, *wait* — Don't — ' His voice gave way to sounds of a struggle, then the crack of a gun, then a cry that was raspy enough to have come from James, though I wasn't sure, since I had never, ever heard him make any sound like it before.

24

The phone connection held. As we raced towards the house, we heard coarse swearing and sounds of a struggle, then Jude yelling, 'The front, the front, open the front.'

Driven by raw fear, I barged through with the first wave. My periphery took in Lee frozen in shock and Jude sprawled over the gunman, but my attention was on James. Still clutching the phone, he was sprawled on his side on the floor. He was covered in blood — his shirt front and back, shot straight through — and the blood continued to spread.

I touched his face. He opened his eyes. Frantic, I pressed his side, front and back, not so much to stop the blood as to push it back inside.

'Ambulance is on the way,' said a trooper, coming down beside me and replacing my hands with pads that he held tightly, while a second trooper cut away the shirt.

Wiping my hands on my skirt, I moved up to his head and cupped his face. His eyes held mine for a second before they closed.

'Pulse is low, but his airways are clear,' a second trooper reported.

Vaguely aware of Lee beside me now, I put my mouth to James's ear and whispered, 'Hold on, babe, help is coming, you did so good.' When he didn't respond, I shot a frantic look at the troopers. 'He's breathing, isn't he?'

'Yes.'

'Why is he unconscious?'

'Shock. Loss of blood.'

Hands framing his face, I stayed by his ear. 'You will be fine, you will be fine, I need you, we need you.' I repeated it over and over until the ambulance arrived, pausing only while they shifted him to a stretcher and carried him out, and even then I held his hand. Though I gave the paramedics room, I wasn't letting go. James needed to know I was there.

Once the ambulance was wailing through the night, there were questions about allergies, medications, last food that he'd eaten. Though I answered them, I felt totally helpless. They hooked up an IV and oxygen, and continued to compress the wound, but he was too pale, too quiet. Through an endless ride, my eyes swung from his face to theirs and back, watching for change in any of them that would suggest he was doing worse.

Later, I would be told that we had reached the hospital in record time and that a full team of trauma doctors had been waiting. At the time, all I saw was James being whisked away. Agonizing in the waiting room while he was in surgery, I imagined every possibility — his being fine, his being maimed or permanently in pain, his dying — and I felt totally at fault. I kept thinking that this wouldn't have happened if he'd been in New York, that a second-best life was better than no life at all and that I would give anything, *anything* to have that old life back if it meant that James would be well.

Lee was quiet beside me, possibly feeling more guilty than me. Amelia arrived with Vicki, who had threatened to drive herself if left behind. A member of the Bell Valley force showed up to report that by all accounts the gun had accidentally fired during the scuffle between the suspect and Jude, and while that sounded innocent enough, my husband remained in surgery.

Someone brought coffee, but I couldn't drink. Vicki talked softly, and when I couldn't answer, simply held my hands to warm them up.

'I'm sorry,' Amelia said as the minutes stretched on. She sounded defeated. 'I kept hoping he would change — you know, that he would see that there were good things he could do here. He's never been able to follow direction.'

I couldn't console her, not when my husband's blood remained on my skirt. The standoff had been about to end when Jude had barged into that house. If maybe, just maybe, he had been more rational and less impulsive for once — if he had put his own need for heroics behind our need for caution, James would be well and intact.

But Jude had needed to prove himself. To me? Amelia? The town?

I didn't know and, just then, didn't care. 'If onlys' were no good. I couldn't turn back the clock.

And that clock crept. It wasn't until two in the morning when a doctor finally showed up at the waiting room door and gestured me to join him in the hall. Heart pounding, I was on my feet in a flash.

'He's a lucky man. The bullet grazed a rib but

didn't hit anything vital. We had some cleanup to do, but he'll be fine. He's in the recovery room. Do you want to sit with him there?'

I didn't have to be asked twice, though I didn't expect to promptly pass out. Something about seeing him attached to needles and tubes and totally out of it — something about the reality of what had happened, the fear of what might have been and the relief of what *was*, must have done it. I had no sooner taken his hand when I heard a buzz and saw white.

There was a distant 'Ooops, wait, catch her.' The next thing I knew, I was sitting on the chair with my head between my knees and a none-too-gentle hand kneading the back of my neck. A cold pack replaced the hand.

'Breathe deeply,' came another voice. It was female and pleasantly commanding.

'I'm *sorry*,' I whispered.

'Don't be. You're not the first, and you won't be the last. When loved ones are nervous — '

'I'm pregnant.'

There was a pause, then 'Well, there you go, you were nervous for two. Do you want to see a doctor? Maybe lie down?'

'This is fine.' I took a breath and, holding the cold pack, slowly straightened. I was still vaguely light-headed, but it didn't get worse, and when I looked at James, I saw that his eyes were heavy-lidded but open. Passing the ice to the nurse, I put my arms over the bed rails and held his hand.

Shortly after seven Wednesday morning, he was wheeled to his own room, and once the nurses had settled him and left, I climbed carefully onto the bed with him and fell asleep.

★ ★ ★

When I woke up, my parents were there. My mother was on her feet and beside the bed in an instant. 'Hey,' she whispered with a teary smile.

I looked quickly from James to the heart monitor to the IV. The nurses had to have been checking, but I hadn't heard a thing. Everything looked right. He continued to sleep, but his fingers were holding mine now, rather than being held. Here was my sign.

Reassured, taking care not to disturb him, I levered myself up. 'How'd you guys know to come here?'

'You're all over the news,' Mom scolded softly, 'and we were absolutely not staying away. I know you wanted your space, but this isn't a time for people who love you to give you space.' Mocking emphasis on those three words. 'Once we had a look at James, we called his folks to tell them he was okay.'

'They are not happy with this,' Dad said, coming alongside her with a very large frown.

'They were worried, your father means. That must have been one awful scary time for you.'

'For James,' I said. I sat sideways, keeping my hand in his. 'I was outside the whole time.'

'What was he doing in that house?' Dad asked. 'Why not the cops? It was their job.'

'Roger, hush.'

'I'm just trying to make sense of it, Claire.

There are too many pieces here that we just don't know. Aren't *you* concerned? Emily looks like she's been through the wringer.'

'*Roger. Please.* First things first.' Mom moved my hair back from my face. 'How are you feeling?'

I seesawed my free hand. My stomach was iffy.

'Roger, we need something to eat. There's a coffee shop downstairs. Make yourself useful.'

James's lids moved. I leaned closer. 'James?' With some effort, he opened his eyes. 'Hey,' I said softly.

His smile was lopsided.

'How do you feel?'

'Thirsty,' he croaked. I held water while he sipped from a straw, but even when he let it go, his voice was raspy. 'What happened?'

'Jude broke in — '

'After. Did they get the guy?'

'Yes.' I told him what I knew, but Dad knew more. He had made himself useful in this, at least, pulling the strings that he had as a prosecutor in Maine.

'I talked with the state police. He's being held in Concord on kidnapping charges. His real name is Anton Ellway. The gun was registered to him. Why in the hell were you two there?'

I held off the question with a hand. 'Is he talking?'

'Not yet. He's waiting for his lawyer. They said his being at Lee Cray's house is part of a larger case. What larger case?'

'Who's the lawyer?' James whispered.

'I don't know.'

'Can you get the name, Dad?' I asked. 'It's

368

important for Lee's case.'

'*What* case?'

I was suddenly too tired, too nauseous to say. Stretching out on my back beside James, I closed my eyes and focused on breathing.

I heard Mom's voice. 'They'll tell us later, Roger. Right now, I need you to go to the coffee shop. Buy us something sweet, like a coffee roll, and maybe some of those cheese-and-cracker things.' I heard corridor sounds, muted only when the door closed again. Mom's hand was light on my head. I opened my eyes to excited eyes and a smug smile.

'You. Are. Pregnant. Don't try to deny it, your face is different, and it has nothing to do with whatever happened in that house. I won't tell anyone, certainly not your father, who is driving me *crazy* with his talk of safety and responsibility and' — she imitated his growl — 'doing your own job and not someone else's.' Her voice danced again. 'How far are you?'

I glanced at James, whose smile was crooked, though possibly from the pain pump? I chose to believe not.

'March, I think. I haven't been to the doctor yet — and don't go ballistic on me for that, Mom, there's no need for me to go yet. I take this very seriously, I know what I feel, it's my body, my baby — '

'Shh. I never went to the doctor until seven or eight weeks, and you and your sister were born just fine.'

'Dad will see it as one more lapse of responsibility.'

'Dad is having trouble letting go.'

'I'm thirty-two.'

'And about to be a mother.' My mother beamed, before asking archly, 'Are *you* telling him right now? Because I certainly am not. You're right. It's your baby, your body. It's your life. If he can't see it the way I do, that's too bad for him. You'll tell him when you're ready and not a minute before.'

*　★　★*

She actually sent Dad home. He didn't much like that, especially since he hadn't gotten the answers he wanted, but she was firm in our defence, arguing that James was groggy, I was exhausted, and hospitals were her thing. Once he left, she was in her element, pampering us in ways I so welcomed that it scared me. I might be thirty-two and expecting my own child, but I loved having my mother there. She befriended the hospital staff, ensuring James attention. She brought us water, Jell-O, and toast. Taking our car, she shuttled to and from Bell Valley for my laptop so that James could skype his parents, for clothes so that I could change, and for Vicki Bell, who brought chocolates from Amelia and a huge vase of green hydrangeas from the inn.

Lee sent enough baked goods to feed every nurse on the floor, not that we needed raisin nutmeg scones or even Mom to draw attention to James. His heroism had preceded him. Add good looks and blue eyes, which were well open by Thursday, and the staff was checking in on him all the time. Once they had him up and walking, he cut back on pain meds. I could see him wince when he moved, but he wanted to be clearheaded.

That served him on two fronts, first with the police, who came by to question him about what he had seen, done, and heard in the house. I was his lawyer, prepared to filter his words, though it turned out that wasn't necessary. He was amazingly coherent, given what he'd been through.

Likewise Thursday afternoon, when we talked with Sean. I was propped on the pillows beside James, our ears sharing the phone as we listened to the news.

'I hate it when the media shows up,' Sean said. 'It's hard to get an unbiased jury when the whole world watches a crime unfold. But it worked for us here. Your gunman wanted to make a statement. You told the police, the police told the media, the media told their viewers. One of those viewers didn't want a statement made. Normally he'd work through channels, but he panicked, figuring there just wasn't enough time. So he called your guy directly.'

James smiled. 'Albert Meeme.'

'The call came from his phone. The cops are talking with him now. He'll try to shift the blame, but he's done that once too often. This time, the charges are too serious and there are too many people involved. Rocco Fleming wants to talk. Duane Cray wants to talk. And the other brother? Here's the best part. He claims not to have known his brother was working with Meeme. He's taking the trust fund to another firm, and he wants to make a settlement with Lee.'

'Yessss,' I whispered, and though Sean went on, I was too elated to hear. When my dad walked in, I jumped off the bed.

'Important call?' he asked. He knew the basics of the case by now, and though he was marginally appeased, there remained an unsettled something between us. He was so familiar to me, with his plaid shirt and bald head, that the unsettled something hurt.

But here was good news to share. Excited, I held his hand and told him what Sean had said. He was nodding by the time I was done.

'This is good.' He spoke levelly. 'I'm glad you were able to help her. It makes the deviation worthwhile.'

'Deviation,' I repeated, thinking, *There it is, so fast, the unsettled something.* 'It's a little more than that, Dad. We've actually been able to help someone. *You* know how good that feels. You do it in your work all the time, but James and I don't.'

'That's the trade-off. You're in New York. The prestige alone makes up for warm and fuzzy.'

'Uh. I don't think so.'

He ran a hand over his scalp. 'You're still on that? I thought a good rest would do it.'

'It did,' I said with determination. 'It's made me realize that I was right to leave. I'm done with Lane Lavash, Dad. I resigned.'

He stared at me, then glanced at James. 'Does he know?'

'Of course he knows.'

'He didn't tell me.'

I almost laughed. This was part of the problem, wasn't it? 'Should he have? Isn't that something between him and me? He's my husband, Dad. I've been married for seven years and have lived away from you for a lot longer. I'm not . . . just . . . your little girl. Speaking of which, I'm pregnant.'

I popped it on him just like that. It probably wasn't the best time, but what time would have been better? I knew where he stood. He had already told me what happened to female lawyers who had kids.

But his eyes lit, and for a minute he seemed to forget. For a minute, he was my father, loving this new turn, excited to become a grandfather again. 'Pregnant? That's *great* news, sweetheart!' Then his eyes rounded, and his chin rose. 'Ahh. So *that's* what all this is about. I knew there had to be something. I suppose it makes sense. You take a leave, have your baby, get your child care set, then go back. They'll see you differently, but hey, you want a family, I do get that. Like I say, it's a trade-off.'

I smiled. 'I actually think I'm getting the best part of the deal.'

'Will Lane Lavash take you back part-time?'

'I told you,' I said, my smile curious now. 'I resigned.'

He seemed startled. 'For *good*?'

'Yes.'

'Where will you work?'

'I don't know.'

'What are the possibilities?'

'I don't know.'

'Shouldn't you? These are important questions. You need a plan, Emily. Good things don't just happen by themselves. You seem lost.'

I wasn't lost. Oh, I had been. But no more. I'd found my path. I might not know the exact twists and turns it would take, but that was part of what I'd learned. Options changed. Needs changed. I could wing it a little. The important thing was seeing the overall picture. The forest.

'Your husband, though, is not lost,' Dad was saying with confidence. 'I'm sure he's thought it all out. Ah, James. Off the phone.' He went to the bed, hand extended. 'Congratulations, Daddy. Your bride just told me the news. How're you feeling?'

I suddenly wondered that, too, and I didn't mean physically. The last time James and I had talked about what to do and where to live had been before his firm's freeze on partners. I hadn't broached it since then. We'd been having too good a time together to let anything intrude.

But we couldn't avoid it forever. James's firm knew what had happened this week, but they expected him back. I hadn't wanted to push.

Dad would. Absolutely. My instinct was to hang back and listen, but this concerned me. When Dad was passionate about something, he stopped at nothing — a trait I had always admired but feared now. He wouldn't hesitate to try divide-and-conquer here.

As I approached, he was grinning, warning James about the emotions of pregnant women and things like cravings and sudden tears. Then he grew serious. 'You're looking good, son. You have your colour back. I'll bet the ribs are still sore. That'll take a while. How's your firm doing with all this?'

James was neutral. 'They're putting up with it.'

'Well, they should. What you did was remarkable, looking down the nose of a gun to negotiate with that guy. I bet you're anxious to get back.'

James opened his mouth to respond, but Dad didn't give him the chance.

'We think about crime in New York, but what about here? You could have been killed. An inch over or up and that bullet would have hit something vital. You were very lucky, son. I would not want to think about a repeat of this. Nor do your folks. They told me *that* in no uncertain terms. They'll be thrilled when you're back in New York.'

James opened his mouth again, but Dad barrelled on. 'I have to agree with them. You may complain about your practice not being relevant, but a dead lawyer isn't relevant to anything — '

'Except people who write jokes,' I cut in dryly. 'Dad — '

'That is not funny,' he scolded. 'Would you have rathered this come out another way, because it could easily have. And now it isn't only about you. It's about a baby, whose father is lying here in this bed because he was putting something that *felt* good over something that is far more important in the larger sense. I suspect you were a big influence on him in that.'

Stunned, I was searching for a comeback when he said to James, 'See what I mean about pregnant women and emotion? You'll have to put up with that for a little while, I'm afraid. But I gotta tell ya, what happened here makes you appreciate the civility of your firm. Hell, it makes you appreciate the civility of the *city*. When was the last time you personally witnessed a shoot-out there? Never. See what I mean.' Smiling, he added a man-to-man 'I'll bet you're dying to get back.'

James was silent for a minute, no doubt waiting to see if my father was actually done. I knew he was. This was when he wanted James to admit that, yes, he appreciated the civility of his firm now and was dying to get back. James didn't look at me. In hindsight, I realized he didn't have to. He knew how I felt. There was nothing to discuss.

'Are you kidding?' he asked, and still I didn't know which way he'd go. Then, sounding stronger than I'd heard him in days, he said, 'I haven't done anything as rewarding as this since I passed the bar. It was *the best*, Roger. I totally know what you mean about feeling good when you help people. I would represent one person like Lee any day over the jackasses I've been working with for the last seven years!'

Dad was the one searching for a comeback then. Not me. I didn't have to say anything. When I reached out for James, he grabbed my hand and pulled me to the bed. I lost my balance, which must have been what he wanted, because he was braced for it. He didn't wince, just covered my mouth with his.

By the time we separated, my father was gone.

25

We returned to Bell Valley Friday morning. Safe haven that it was — a tech-lite zone, so to speak — James could recuperate with relative impunity before having to deal with New York. We would go back, of course. He did have his job, and though he felt no urgency to tell the senior partners, he had decided to leave. To leave the city as well? We hadn't thought that far. All he knew was that he wanted to wake up in the morning looking forward to the day. I was totally on board.

As recuperative centres went, the gardener's shed was five-star, with breakfast from the Red Fox, lunch and dinner from The Grill, and silence enough for sleeping with the windows open and a solicitous wife, rather than a nurse, at his side. Vicki and Rob wanted us to take the one guest room with a Jacuzzi. But James liked sitting on the bench facing the woods in the mid-July warmth, wearing only his bandage and shorts. He liked challenging himself to walk four minutes up the path and back, then eight minutes, then ten. He gained strength every day, but still slept more than he liked, though it was anyone's guess as to whether this was from his injury or retroactive to years of deprivation.

I used his downtime to wrap up things in Bell Valley, which mainly meant making sure Vicki had plenty of help so that she wasn't on her feet more than the doctor allowed. When she overdid it, she contracted, not a good thing if she wanted to carry this baby anywhere near to term, and I took the risk personally now. I was four weeks pregnant. My breasts had begun to swell and I was doing no better on an empty stomach, but the baby was fine. I did have a cosmopolitan health-care mentality, meaning that, despite my mom's reassurances, I was feeling increasingly guilty not seeing a doctor. Hovering over Vicki was my rationale for the wait.

Lee was a godsend. In addition to managing the kitchen, she was overseeing the new housekeeping hires, and though she wasn't computer literate, she was willing to learn. I think she would have done anything for Vicki. And for me. She was still cooking for James every chance she got, but it wasn't until Sunday morning, when he insisted on dressing and coming to the parlour for brunch, that she caught me in the kitchen.

'I haven't said it out loud,' she murmured, 'but I need to thank you.'

'You do not,' I countered. The swathe of hair that had hidden her for so long was behind her ear, so that I could see two hazel eyes, both brimming with heart. Just knowing how much better she was doing — how less vigilant she was, how she was even starting to talk more with guests — was thanks enough for me.

'I need to thank you,' she said, gesturing toward the parlour, 'and him, but it's hard knowing where to begin. No one has ever done anything like this for me.'

'Amelia's been pretty darn good.'

'She has money. That's different from risking your life.'

I smiled. 'Well, we got something out of it, too.'

'What?'

I opened my mouth, stopped, tried again, then laughed and echoed her words. 'It's hard knowing where to begin. Let's just say we're even.'

She might have argued if the bell on the front desk hadn't dinged. I made her do the checkout this time, even left her to do it unsupervised when another couple approached. I wanted to check on James, though I needn't have worried. He was comfortable talking with guests, any one of whom was happy to bring him refills of bacon and coffee.

Watching him from the door, I was gratified. No, we were absolutely *not* settling in Bell Valley. For one thing, Lee's case notwithstanding, there was no work for litigators here. For another, long-term, we wanted a wider circle of friends and restaurants. But he hadn't been this relaxed on our honeymoon, when anticipation of the move to New York and new jobs kept us both on edge. Major change was in store now, which was good reason for nerves, but we were calm. We had grown.

★ ★ ★

I wanted to see my coyote one last time before I left. I wasn't sure if I'd be back before Vicki's baby was due, which would be winter, and who knew where she and her family would be then, or whether I'd even be able to make the climb, with the snow deep and my belly large.

It was late afternoon when I set off, past the old wood gate, over the rotted post, through the ferns. The day had been warm, but the sky had grown dappled with clouds, and the air was starting to cool. I passed swirls of gnats, but they ignored me. Likewise mosquitoes. This was a first. The baby must make me smell different, which was actually no surprise, since my surroundings smelled different to me as well.

No. Not different. Just more intense. And nothing about it upset my stomach, for which reason alone I'd have continued the hike.

This walk along the stone wall toward the bubbling brook was like a pilgrimage for me. Once there, though, I had to wait. In a whimsical Bambi moment, I imagined birds, rabbits, and mice spreading the word.

In time, the forest richened with the coyotes' approach. I sensed them, smelled them, even heard them, as the pups burst enthusiastically through the foliage. The mom approached the bank and sat. Several of her pups, suddenly sobered, sat with her. All watched me.

And that's what we did, just sat watching each other with water rushing downstream between us. I had to believe I would see them again — though whether this russet-and-grey mom with her cream-coloured face and gentle eyes would be as trusting then, I didn't know. She might be made more feral by something that would happen between now and then. She might be dead, up with my kitten that wobbled no more. She might simply have moved on.

I had a sudden urge to touch her — to wade through the water, to reach out just once and put my fingers in the tiered fur of her ruff.

But that would be crossing a line. Escapes could only go so far.

So I stayed on my bank until, losing interest, the pups wandered off. The mom was the last to go, committing me to memory as well, before turning and dissolving into the woods.

I stayed a while longer, letting the woodlands console me, but the come and go of the sun under those fast-travelling clouds suggested change. As I walked down the hill, I found myself hoping that wherever James and I landed, my coyote dreams would follow. If I yearned, I yearned for good things. The dreams would remind me of this. They would transport me back here in times of stress, and there would be those, regardless of how different our lives became.

For the first time, I could fully understand Jude's attraction to the wild. It was us, tens of thousands of years earlier, a simpler time for sure.

As if thinking his name had brought him, I emerged from the woods to find Jude leaning against the trunk of my car. This was the first time I had seen him since the shooting, but I was feeling calm enough, sentimental enough, not to be bitter. There was just the same nostalgia I had felt up by the stream.

With his hair grown long enough to curl again, he looked more like he had ten years before. His T-shirt was black, his jeans worn. There was a rough edge to him now, again, as if he had given up trying to look civilized. Add to that an aura of sadness around him, and my nostalgia increased.

He nodded toward the shed. 'Is the old man asleep?'

I smiled. 'Actually, the old man is at the Refuge. I was just going to pick him up. He's not supposed to drive, we had a small fight about that.'

The Jude of four weeks ago would have picked up on the fight part, but this one must have finally accepted that I was married, because all he did was ask, 'Why's he there?'

'He likes it there. He says it's peaceful.'

'A convert.'

I was shrugging when I noticed the battered green duffel at the edge of the grass. My eyes flew to his, which were still gold, if tarnished. 'You're leaving.'

He nodded, sniffing to make light of it.

'Amelia will be upset,' I said.

'I talked with her. She knows this is best.'

I couldn't begin to imagine what the admission had cost her. Being pregnant hadn't given me enough insight for that. 'She's giving up the dream?'

'Guess so.'

'What's yours?'

'My what?'

'Dream?'

'Haven't got a clue,' he said without smugness.

'I'll tell you when I find out.'

'Will you?' I asked. 'Will you write?'

'You don't really want that.'

'I do. You're my friend.'

'Your *loser* of a friend.'

'No, Jude. My friend who needs to find himself. My friend who helped me find me.' When he looked doubtful, I said, 'You showed me the side of life I was missing. The memory of it was here in Bell Valley, waiting for me. Now I have to go home and blend the two — right brain, left brain — rational, intuitive.'

I wasn't sure he understood, not because he didn't have the capacity, but because his reality was poles apart from mine. He took pride in the scar on his jaw, though to me it was more a sign of daring than valour. There was a difference. But I'm not sure he would get that, either.

So, like Amelia, I gave up on that dream, and opened my arms. Hugging him, I closed my eyes, and for a split second, felt the old connection, a remembered thread of the best of what we'd had. I held the feeling a minute longer, before letting it slide back into storage. It would stay there — memories of Jude, memories of coyotes, both were a part of who I was.

★   ★   ★

I half expected James to be stretched out on a bench along one of the Refuge paths. When I found him, though, he was with the dogs again, this time inside the enclosure, resting on the ground with his back to a post. He must have been there a while, because the dogs had grown tired of him and were off by themselves. The only one that remained was the Aussie, which sat ten feet away, staring at him.

'He still has a ways to go,' James said, 'but look at him. How can you not feel a tug?'

The dog was certainly beautiful, with its thick black body and those white markings on its chest and face. And while I didn't feel the same tug James did, I understood. 'It's hard,' I said, thinking of my own attraction to cats. And to coyotes.

'I told the guy to call me when he's ready to be placed.'

I looked at James. He looked at me.

Finally, blinking, he returned to the Aussie. 'He won't be ready for a while, and anyway, someone here may want him. That's probably better. A dog like this needs room to run. And we may or may not have it.' He made a clicking sound with his tongue and extended a hand. The dog didn't move. 'Those eyes. Even when the Refuge guy was here, they kept looking at me. I feel guilty leaving. I feel like he needs me. Like we have a personal connection.'

I smiled. 'I feel that way about my coyote. Different from a dog, though. Not exactly attainable.'

'A dog is.'

'You really want a dog?'

'No,' James said. 'I really want *this* dog.' Then he smiled and extended a hand for me to help pull him up. 'A guy can dream, can't he?'

Epilogue

I was wrong. We returned to Bell Valley often in the months to come. I had never before seen the town in September, when apples, beets, and corn were sold from carts on the green, or in October, when the leaves flamed crimson, orange, and gold. By November, much of local life had moved indoors, but the crafts bazaars at the church drew artisans for miles, remarkable for such a small town. And now December? What could I say? Bell Valley did define charm.

James and I wouldn't change our minds. We still knew that, long-term, we needed more than charm. But I was working part-time for a former Lane Lavash lawyer who had struck out on her own and was grateful for the help, and though James was no longer fixated on billable hours, his days remained long. Bell Valley offered a weekend escape. He came to feel the same visceral *ahhhhh* I did each time we passed under the covered bridge and were welcomed by the town.

I was not feeling as relaxed this day, though. I was holding Vicki's baby in the kitchen of the Red Fox, trying to get him to stop crying. Gentle rocking wasn't working. Snug cradling wasn't working. 'Rock-a-bye Baby' wasn't working.

'Help me, Vicki Bell,' I pleaded. 'I am not doing this right.'

'You're doing it totally right,' she assured me.

'He's hungry, is all, but I don't want to feed him for another little while.' She had Charlotte anchored between her knees and was working the child's blond curls into a French braid. Her own hair looked like a cyclone had hit it, but that was Vicki Bell. 'Try walking with him. Go on out into the parlour. And be calm. Babies sense moods. If you're tense, he's tense.'

Listen and learn, I told myself, and consciously relaxing my arms, I carefully backed through the swinging door.

The last of the guests, just putting their breakfast dishes on the tray, broke into smiles when they saw the blue bundle I held.

'Is this Vicki's baby?' one asked. Then another, 'How old is he?' And another, 'What's his name?'

'He is Vicki's indeed,' I sang softly, swaying to soothe both the baby and me. 'His name is Benjamin, and he's four weeks old.'

'He's a *little* guy.'

'You should've seen him at birth.' Vicki's water had broken a month early, at which point the doctors could no longer forestall labour. Lee had called me, and I was on the road within the hour. Though the baby arrived before I did, I held him in the NICU. *That* was scary. Long and gangly like his father, he had still been all skin and bones. By comparison, he was now positively robust.

Not that I was an expert on the size of babies. My own was still three months from birth. We had seen it on a sonogram, and it was fully formed but barely two pounds, maybe nine inches long. Did we know the sex? No. Too much of our lives had been preplanned. We wanted a few surprises.

Intrigued by the tall front windows, Benjamin seemed to have momentarily forgotten about hunger. Crossing the room, I put a knee on the window seat and, propping him on the shelf of my belly, let him look out. Bell Valley had already had a major winter storm, and though the snow was melting now in the sun, plenty remained for brilliant reflection. Benjamin would see this, though not yet any details. Me, I took in lights on the bare oak on the green, wreaths on door fronts, and store windows with snow scenes. The logo of the Red Fox wore a Santa hat, and here in the parlour, where garlands draped the fireplace, the buffet table, and the large Bell family portrait, the scent of balsam was heady.

'See?' Vicki said as she joined me, tucking the baby's blanket away from his chin. He seemed to have fallen asleep. 'The magic touch.' She gave me a little hug. 'I'm always better when you're here. I wanted to stay up last night until you arrived, but I was beat, and I knew Ben would be up way too soon to eat again. How was the drive?'

'Easy. It's nice doing it together.'

'Anything new with the condo?'

'We had a bite this week, but it didn't pan out. This isn't the best season to sell. Spring will be better.'

'With a newborn?'

'Mmm. Not ideal.' I had been around newborns with my sister's kids, but only with Vicki's Ben was I taking it seriously. He had

387

been fussing for the last hour, though now, in this peaceful moment, he was a dream with his eyes closed and his tiny mouth sucking something imagined. 'One of the jobs James is considering would buy the condo from us, so we'd have the money to turn around and buy something else.'

'Is this another Boston job?'

I nodded. Most had been. When Boston had seemed too easy a choice, James broadened his search to include Albany, Harrisburg, and Baltimore, but the offers weren't as good. Thanks to Lee's case, he had impressed Sean's firm, which needed a good litigator; Lyle Kagan, who needed in-house counsel; and the Massachusetts attorney general. There had even been a teaching offer from one of the local law schools. And an offer from a not-for-profit to do advocacy work. Amazing what a few headlines could do.

'An employer buying the condo,' Vicki mused. 'That's a no-brainer.'

'Actually, not. We don't want to make a decision based only on money. We did that before, and it wasn't pretty. This time, the job has to offer the kind of cases James wants. Now that he's tasted excitement, he can't go back.'

'What does your dad say?'

I began swaying again, more for me this time. 'The usual.'

'He has to like the idea of your living closer to him.'

'Ya think?'

'Oh dear. He's *still* obsessed with New York?'

388

I sighed. 'He'll get there. Mom's on it.' James and I were trying to distance ourselves from them when it came to deciding what to do next. This had to be *our* dream, what *we* wanted. 'How are things with Amelia?'

Allowing for the shift, probably because it so related to my issue with Dad, Vicki said, 'Interesting. She's been taking Charlotte to the Refuge instead of dropping her at day care. Remember Katherine? She's training Charlotte to work with the cats, and Charlotte loves it. So does Mom. I mean, Noah is still the star, but Charlotte is actually registering on her radar screen. It's like she has finally accepted . . . '

'That Jude is gone.'

'Yeah. She just got another postcard from him, by the way.'

'So did I. From Nepal. He's training to climb Everest.'

'Problem is,' Vicki said, 'he needs a permit, and it costs twenty-five thousand dollars. He asked Mom for the money. She was all upset — 'I am not wealthy, the Refuge is a drain, money doesn't grow on trees.' But she'll do it. She's a sucker for him.'

Looking at my friend, I chided softly, 'And you wouldn't do the same if this little guy grows up and sets his heart on doing something like that? Or Charlotte — what if she decides she loves, say, ice-skating and sets her heart on being an Olympic figure-skater? Training would cost a fortune, but you'd take out loans if you had to.'

'Fortunately, I won't have to,' Vicki said with a smug smile. 'Charlotte's going to be a vet.'

389

I laughed. 'And med school is cheap? Hel-lo. Besides, how do you know she's going to be a vet? She's barely four.'

'She loves the Refuge. And there's never been a vet in the Bell family before. She'll be top doctor there one day.'

'Her dream or yours?' I asked.

Vicki paused, shot me a contrite look, and reached for the baby. 'Mine for now. When she's old enough, it'll be hers. Maybe.'

'And if not?' I pushed. Vicki might be the expert on infants, but I was the expert on dreams that didn't work. History should not repeat itself.

'Okay. I get it.' Ceding the fight, she found a change of subject behind me. 'Here's Lee. Go look at the space she's considering. We want to know what you think.'

★ ★ ★

Soon after, Lee and I walked down the driveway in our bulky down jackets and UGGs. The sidewalks were clear to pavement, though a foot of shovelled snow remained on the sides. The sky was a clear, deep blue and the air bracing in ways that even the coolest summer morning was not. Winter crisped things up. I drew it into my lungs, wanting the baby to feel it, smell it.

If you accepted Lee as a friend, as I had in these last few months, you accepted that she wasn't a talker. Other than her asking how I was feeling when I carefully eased the jacket zipper over my belly, we walked in silence. When we reached the end of the green and crossed to the stores, she pointed to the spot. Sandwiched between The Bookstore and The Grill, it was small.

'What was here before?' I asked, for the life of me unable to recall. The space was vacant now and might have bucked the holiday spirit if the single edge-to-edge window in front hadn't been part of a mural connecting it to its neighbours.

'A realtor,' Lee said, pulling the door open, and once we were inside, she started to point. 'I'd put display cases on this side, with baked goods in the front, and coffee and tea back there, and I'd line this whole other wall with a long bench and skinny tables and chairs.' With growing excitement, she faced the front. The colour on her cheeks was heightened, as much from that excitement as from the cold, I guessed. Her hair, too, had more oomph. No longer in hiding, she was slowly returning to the blond she'd once been. 'The window isn't big, but I can fit a counter there and maybe three stools for people who want to look out. We figure the whole place can sit, like, sixteen people, but not everyone would want to sit. Lots of them just buy and leave. Vicki wants to decorate. She's thinking charcoal, cream, and sage green. What do you think?'

I had seen charcoal and cream once too often in my city world, but they would look different here. Add splashes of sage to the scent of melty chocolate chip cookies and fresh-brewed coffee, and you had something that was smooth and warm.

Warm thinking about it, I unzipped my jacket. 'I like it — space, colour, location. Is the settlement money finally coming through?' Timing had been a minor stumbling block. Amelia had offered to stake her until it arrived, but Lee refused. She wanted to do this on her own.

'It's starting,' she confirmed. 'There was a load of paperwork moving the trust fund from one firm to another, but he's being generous.' Raymond, Lee's brother-in-law. 'There's a big settlement up front, but it'll be divided in thirds, and then I'll get some money each quarter — like, for life, which is pretty wild.'

'Jack intended that.'

She shrugged shyly. 'It's what he'd have gotten from the trust fund himself if Duane and the lawyer hadn't been stealing it. Sean says they've recovered most of the money, but getting it back to this country takes time.' She lifted only one shoulder this time. 'It's really too much. I know Ray is just trying to make sure I don't sue. They don't want publicity. It's bad for chips.'

I smiled at the reference, which wasn't entirely tongue-in-cheek. 'He's probably also feeling guilty as hell.'

Kindhearted even in this, Lee defended the man. 'He didn't know what Duane was doing.'

'No, but he knew the trust fund was shrinking, and because he had independent money' — *and because*, I thought but didn't say, *he had resented his brother's much younger wife just as Duane had* — 'he looked the other way.' I squeezed her arm. 'But it's worked out for you. I'm glad. This was your dream.'

Seeming melancholy, she was silent.

I dipped my head. 'What.'

'It's a different dream. I don't have Jack. But I'd be sad if I keep trying to think of what he would want and say and think.' Her dark eyes met mine, then skittered away. 'I feel a little guilty about that.'

'You should not. If Jack was still alive, you'd be doing this together. But he isn't here. That's a fact. You have to do this yourself now. And you have to be happy doing it. Otherwise, the whole thing's a waste.'

She took a long breath and looked around. 'Well. Anyway. But you haven't seen the best part of this place.' She led me through a door at the back. 'This was used for storage, but it'd make a neat kitchen. I mean, I don't need anything huge. It's not like I'm making dinners. But I could have more than one oven and they would be waist high, which is easier. And there's room for counters, and a big sink, and storage for pans and plates and mugs. And a pantry.' She looked at me, questioning.

'I *like* it,' I said.

'The bookstore wants more space to sell craft kits, so if I did this, she'd eliminate her coffee shop. People could get their coffee and pastries here, then go next door to browse.'

'Or browse first, then come here to read. You'd be on the main drag, Lee. This is perfect.'

'You really think so?'

'I do.' I was touching my stomach. 'So does the baby. It's turning around so that it can see everything.'

Lee smiled, but with a touch of sadness. 'You probably won't be able to come back as often once the baby's born.'

'Are you kidding? Vicki's baby and mine are going to be best buds.'

'If yours is a girl,' she said brightly, 'they could marry someday.'

'Let's get whatever it is born first,' I warned. Childbirth scared me to death. I was trying not to think about it.

Lee helped, nicely changing the subject. 'Amelia's been meeting with the realtor down in Manchester. She knows I'm not going back there, so they're getting ready to list the house. Are you sure you don't want it? She'd give you a good price.'

Lee had made the offer before. She really wanted us to have the house — and James and I had considered it, but not for long. It had too many downsides for us at this point in our lives. 'The house is gorgeous, Lee. It is so striking, there on the water. But we need something we can comfortably afford, and we need a neighbourhood with kids.'

She grew tentative. I knew what was coming well before she said, 'Then, then James is feeling okay?' It was the same awkward tone she always used when asking this.

'James is fine,' I assured her. 'His ribs have healed, and other than a scar — '

'Two scars,' she put in, lest I minimize the sacrifice he had made on her behalf.

'See, I had forgotten the second, it's fading so fast.'

'He was at breakfast, but he left. Is he still sleeping a lot?'

'If he is, it's because he works too late.' But I hadn't seen the car when we left the inn. 'He's probably driving around. He can't do that in New York. Give him a straightaway that isn't a highway, and he's in car-guy heaven.'

★ ★ ★

Did I begrudge James that? Absolutely not. I loved being in Bell Valley with him, but he would be bored watching me string beads with Charlotte or burp Ben. And though he would have liked to see the place where Lee's bakery would go, I wasn't waiting around for him to return. The sun remained bright, the breeze minimal, and I wanted to walk.

Stopping back at the Red Fox for a hat, mittens, and fur-lined galoshes from Vicki's mudroom, I slogged through the backyard snow to the old wood gate and climbed over the fallen post. There were no ferns to wade through now, just several inches of snow that no one else had walked on. There was something special about being the first human here. But my tracks weren't the only ones. As I paralleled the stone wall, I crossed the small footprints of squirrels and the larger ones of a snowshoe hare. There were spindly bird tracks and the often singular marks of deer, putting a rear foot where the front one had been. I looked for the brush strokes of a coyote dragging its tail in the snow, but saw none. I listened. The winter woods were more quiet, with none of the rustle that passage through summer's undergrowth made.

The grandfather oak still wore a few dried brown leaves, each clinging with a last tenacious thread. The boulder arch looked granite-cold, and beyond, in the play of sun on snow, lay a mirror forest of shadows.

Without the rich spread of birch or beech, the landscape was open and bleak, but I found it no less appealing. Here was another side of forest life, with chickadees sifting through hemlocks not for bugs, now, but for cones. And the brook — there it was, leading me in with the soft trickle of water around and between jagged shards of ice.

Breathless, I brushed off a rock and sat on my side of the stream. My hands cupped the baby through my pockets, though it warmed me in this frozen world, rather than the other way around. I studied the opposite bank, but the snow was undisturbed.

I had seen the coyotes in September and October, but by November, they were elsewhere, and though I continued to hope, I was a realist. With the forest pruned and lots of open space, they would have heard me well in advance — if not the crunch of my boots, then my breath, which came quicker under the weight of the baby.

With less to block its path, sound was augmented, which was why I jumped when my phone rang. I hadn't felt it vibrate — there was too much padding between it and me — and the ensuing ring echoed.

'Hey,' I said, clicking in to James's number.

'Hey, yourself' came his deep voice with an element of excitement that I was hearing more often. 'Where are you?'

'Up by the stream.'

'In the *woods*? Geez, Em. Is that safe?'

'Coyotes are gone, bears are in hibernation, and fisher cats are nocturnal.'

'I mean, hiking alone.'

'That's why I have my phone.' Oh yes, phones had their uses. 'If I'm in trouble, someone can be here in minutes.'

'Try ten. I'm on my way.'

Starting down myself, I met him in five, though I stopped well before he saw me. Still a distance away, he was distracted, alternately walking and trotting, talking softly to someone — no, to some*thing* at the end of a leash. Its fur was thick and black, its face and chest white as the snow. Its eyes, which I already knew to be blue like his, swung worriedly from James to me and back.

Pressing my hands in my pockets, I stayed where I was. When James saw me, he lit up, though his voice remained low and calm. 'Is this amazing? I can't let him off-leash, because he might get spooked and run, but look at how far he's come. He knows me. He remembers me.'

'He should,' I remarked, amused. 'You're there with him every time we come back.' When he looked ready to deny it, I said, 'I'm doing my own thing, and where else would you be? There are only so many places to go.'

'He needs a friend.' Clearly, James was it. The

dog was sitting by his side, looking up at him now, waiting for direction.

'So,' I began cautiously, 'is this a . . . trial run?'

James didn't speak.

Not a trial run, then. The real thing. Oh my.

'You don't look surprised,' he said.

How could I be? 'Like I didn't see you studying the cargo area of the SUV we were looking at last week? Like I haven't walked past your shoulder and seen Aussie info on your computer screen?'

'And you're thinking the timing is bad,' he said, 'but it may not be, Em. I've found a dog trainer who will work with us on the abuse issues, and I've talked with a dog walker in our neighbourhood who will take us on. Yeah, we'll be moving, but we already know we want a house with a yard and neighbours with kids, and neighbours with kids have dogs, which means parks and dog walkers wherever it is.'

'How will he be with the baby?'

'*Fine*. That's the best part. One of the handlers at the Refuge has been walking around in the pen wearing his newborn in a carrier on his chest, and this dog is totally gentle.' As steadily as the dog's eyes were on James, his were on me. 'We can do this, Em. I know we can.'

Testing, I walked slowly down the hill toward them. The dog was watching me now, though it had inched close enough to James so that its flank brushed his leg. I stopped an arm's length away and hunkered down.

'Hey, there,' I said softly, and held out a hand. It took him a minute, but he sniffed it. '*Good*

398

dog,' I cooed. Though he didn't look entirely comfortable, he let me scratch his head. I looked up at James. 'This dog needs a name.'

'Pal.'

'That's hokey.'

James wasn't put off. 'It's short. It's easy to say. And it's spot-on, because he will be my pal. We'll be running together.' Yes, he was running again, another priority higher now than work. His eyes were filled with hope and as blue as the sky. 'Don't you see? This dog won't let us forget to make time for things like that. We need him, he's our safeguard. Other than a microchip for ID, there is nothing high-tech about him. If we own a dog like this, there is no way we'll go robotic again.'

'But we're having a *baby*,' I tried in a last-ditch shot at reason.

James didn't blink. 'Kids need dogs. Dogs teach them responsibility.' He hunkered down by this one's side, as I continued to scratch its ruff. I would have sworn the dog was smiling at having us both nearby, just as I knew that if a strange person were to suddenly thunder up the hill, he would freak out. But James was right. He had come a long way. We could give him a good home. A stable home. A *kind* home.

'Please,' James said softly.

Resting on my heels, I wrapped my arms around my knees and studied my husband. He had given so much, had come so far himself in the last few months. I wasn't sure I could deny him this, especially not when part of me wanted it, too. Wanted it? Was *desperate* for it, now that

399

the possibility was immediate and real. Hadn't I made this a priority that day when I buried my kitten?

Getting a dog right now, particularly one with special needs, might not be wise, but wise wasn't always best. Heart had to come into play, and looking at this dog, that was where I felt the tug. My kitten hadn't made it to my home, but this dog could. He needed us. We needed him. Bringing a living, breathing creature into our family would be personal and rich. That had to count for something. Right?

The baby answered with an emphatic kick. My sign.

And so the dream grew to include Pal.

Acknowledgements

The concept for *Escape* came to me within hours of finishing the writing of *Not My Daughter*. That one had been a long haul, with lots of wonderful personal interruptions, like the wedding of my son, but I had been under tremendous work stress and was exhausted. All I wanted at that moment was to get away from my computer, turn off my BlackBerry, and . . . and escape from anything that required deep thought.

That was in June 2009. And I did chill out for much of the summer while I considered one story idea after another for my next book. But I kept coming back to the theme of our busy, tech-dominated lives and the fantasy of escape. In September, I posted a note on my Facebook page, asking readers where they would go if they were to pick up one day and just disappear — and the response was overwhelming, both in the number of notes and their enthusiasm. Apparently, I was not the only one fantasizing about running away.

That did it. How could I not write a book about this?

So I herewith acknowledge my readers, who were the single most important influence in the writing of this book. I didn't use outside people for research with *Escape*, as I've done with other of my books. This one came straight from the heart.

We do hope that you have enjoyed reading this large print book.

Did you know that all of our titles are available for purchase?

We publish a wide range of high quality large print books including:
Romances, Mysteries, Classics
General Fiction
Non Fiction and Westerns

Special interest titles available in large print are:
The Little Oxford Dictionary
Music Book
Song Book
Hymn Book
Service Book

Also available from us courtesy of Oxford University Press:
Young Readers' Dictionary
(large print edition)
Young Readers' Thesaurus
(large print edition)

For further information or a free brochure, please contact us at:
Ulverscroft Large Print Books Ltd.,
The Green, Bradgate Road, Anstey,
Leicester, LE7 7FU, England.
Tel: **(00 44) 0116 236 4325**
Fax: **(00 44) 0116 234 0205**

NOT MY DAUGHTER

Barbara Delinsky

A pregnancy pact between three teenage girls stuns their parents, shocks the town and electrifies the media. Susan Tate, one of these mothers, has struggled to do everything right. A single mother herself, she is the headmistress of the girls' high school. Soon fingers start pointing, criticising her as a role model. She is seen as unworthy of the responsibility of young students, and as a lax mother. Battling with the implications of her daughter's pregnancy, Susan knows that her job, her reputation and her dreams are all at risk. The emotional ties between mothers and daughters are stretched to breaking point. Can they all fight back against the rising tide of scandal and find their own way?

WHILE MY SISTER SLEEPS

Barbara Delinsky

World-class runner Robin Snow is at the top of her game when her heart inexplicably fails and she sinks into a coma. As hope for her recovery fades, her family is left with a terrible choice — a choice which no-one should ever have to make. Faced with a heartbreaking decision, it is quiet, younger sister Molly who finds herself stepping out of Robin's shadow and into the heart of the family's terrible dilemma. Will they have the courage to do what is right?

THE SECRET BETWEEN US

Barbara Delinsky

One lie sends a family into turmoil when Deborah Monroe's car hits and kills a man on a deserted road on a dark and rainy night. Questions of who is to blame muddy the already complicated life of a woman who is newly divorced and struggling with emotions that are rampant, in a house with two vulnerable children. Deborah's daughter, sixteen-year-old Grace, was behind the wheel but, desperate to protect her daughter, Deborah covers for her and takes responsibility for the death of the man. However, when it seems that the victim may or may not have been suicidal, issues of guilt and responsibility, truth and honesty, are all brought into sharp focus.

THE FAMILY TREE

Barbara Delinsky

Dana Clarke has it all — a husband, Hugh, whom she adores, a beautiful home and a baby on the way. But, when her daughter, Lizzie, is born, what should be the happiest day of her life turns out to be the moment that her world falls apart. As a family is divided by bitter mistrust, all their beliefs in each other, in their family background, are challenged. Will the birth of their first child destroy their marriage or can they overcome the repercussions of a secret told years ago?

THE SUMMER I DARED

Barbara Delinsky

What comes after the moment that changes your life forever? A question that haunts Julia Bechtel, Noah Prine and Kim Colella, the only survivors of a boating accident off the coast of Maine. Julia, a forty-year-old 'loyal' and 'obedient' wife and mother, realizes after her brush with death that there is more to her than she imagined. Feeling strangely connected to Noah, and to Kim, Julia explores the possibilities offered by the island of Big Sawyer . . . Resolving that she must have more from life, Julia fearlessly embraces uncertainties in a way she couldn't have imagined only a few weeks ago.

FLIRTING WITH PETE

Barbara Delinsky

Although Casey Ellis didn't really know her father, she learns on his death that he has left her his beautiful townhouse in Boston. She is of half a mind to sell it, but then she visits the house and finds it enchanting. Yet always in Casey's mind is the question of why her father chose to acknowledge her in this way. Sensing that he had an ulterior motive, she searches the house and finds the first part of a manuscript. Convinced the story is true — even more, that her father has left this manuscript as a message for her — Casey sets out to find the rest of the pages and to finally come to understand her father's past.